NYLOS IN THE CACHE

JADE KIM MONSEN

SIJA PUBLISHING

Sija Publishing

ISBN: 978-1-965078-05-1

Edited by David Candland Monsen and Jennifer Rees

Interior Design and Formatting by David Candland Monsen

Cover art and design by Rachel Sierra

Cartography by Michael Harrington

NYLOS IN THE CACHE

JADE KIM MONSEN

BOOK ONE

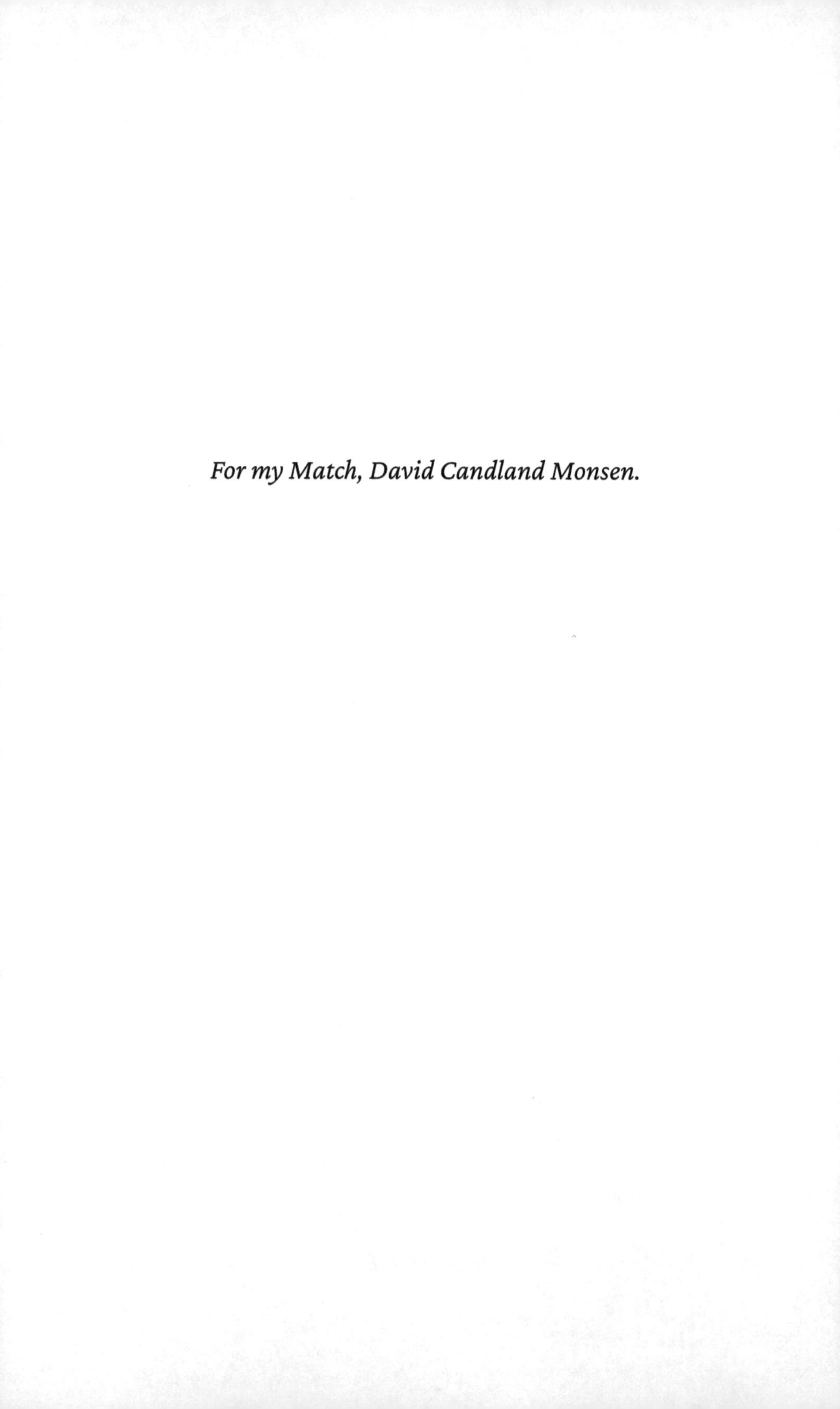

For my Match, David Candland Monsen.

CONTENT WARNING

This story includes difficult and heavy matters such as self-harm and suicide. Continue with care and take care.

CONTENTS

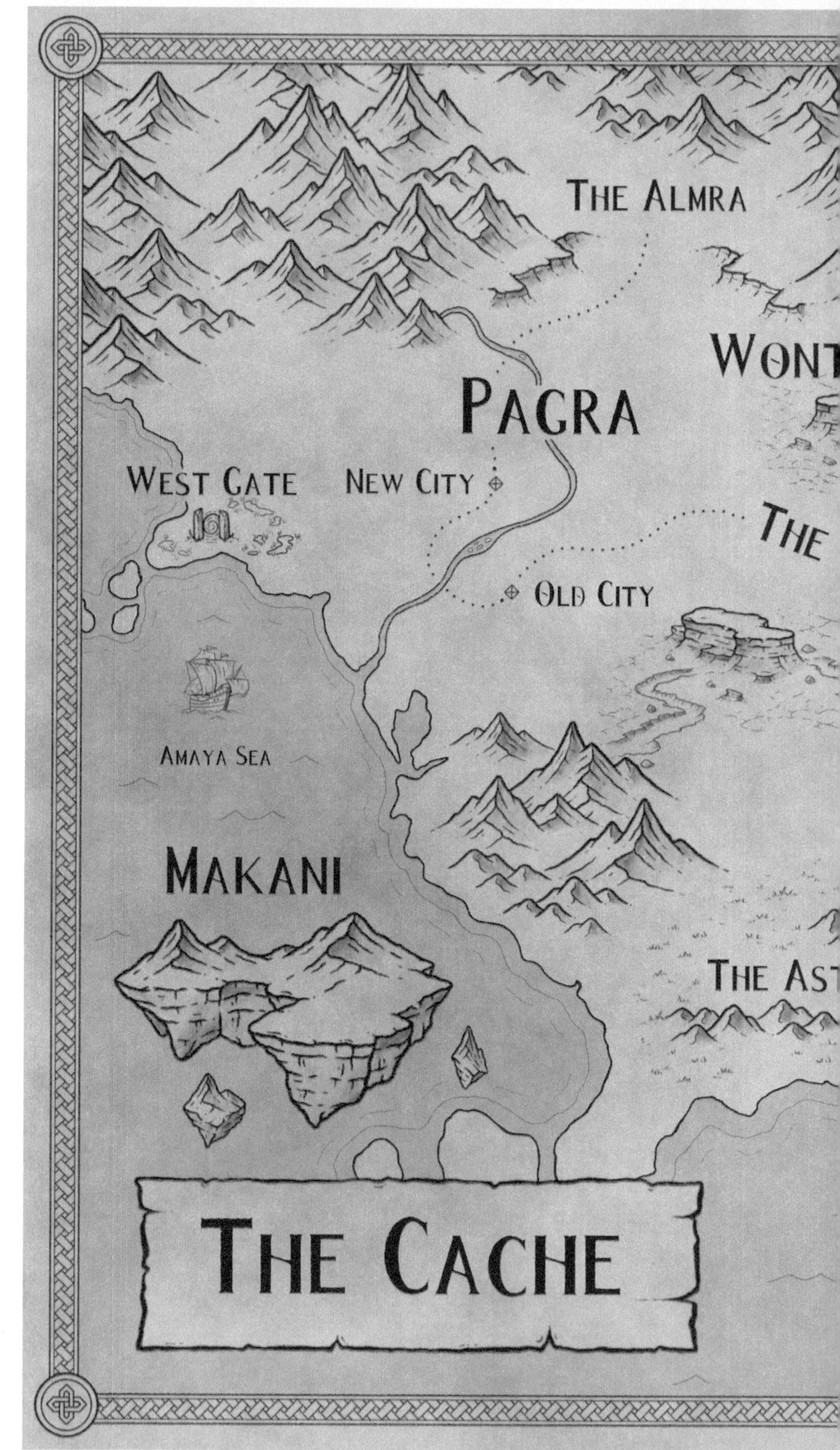

THE ALMRA
WONT
PAGRA
WEST GATE
NEW CITY
THE
OLD CITY
AMAYA SEA
MAKANI
THE AST
THE CACHE

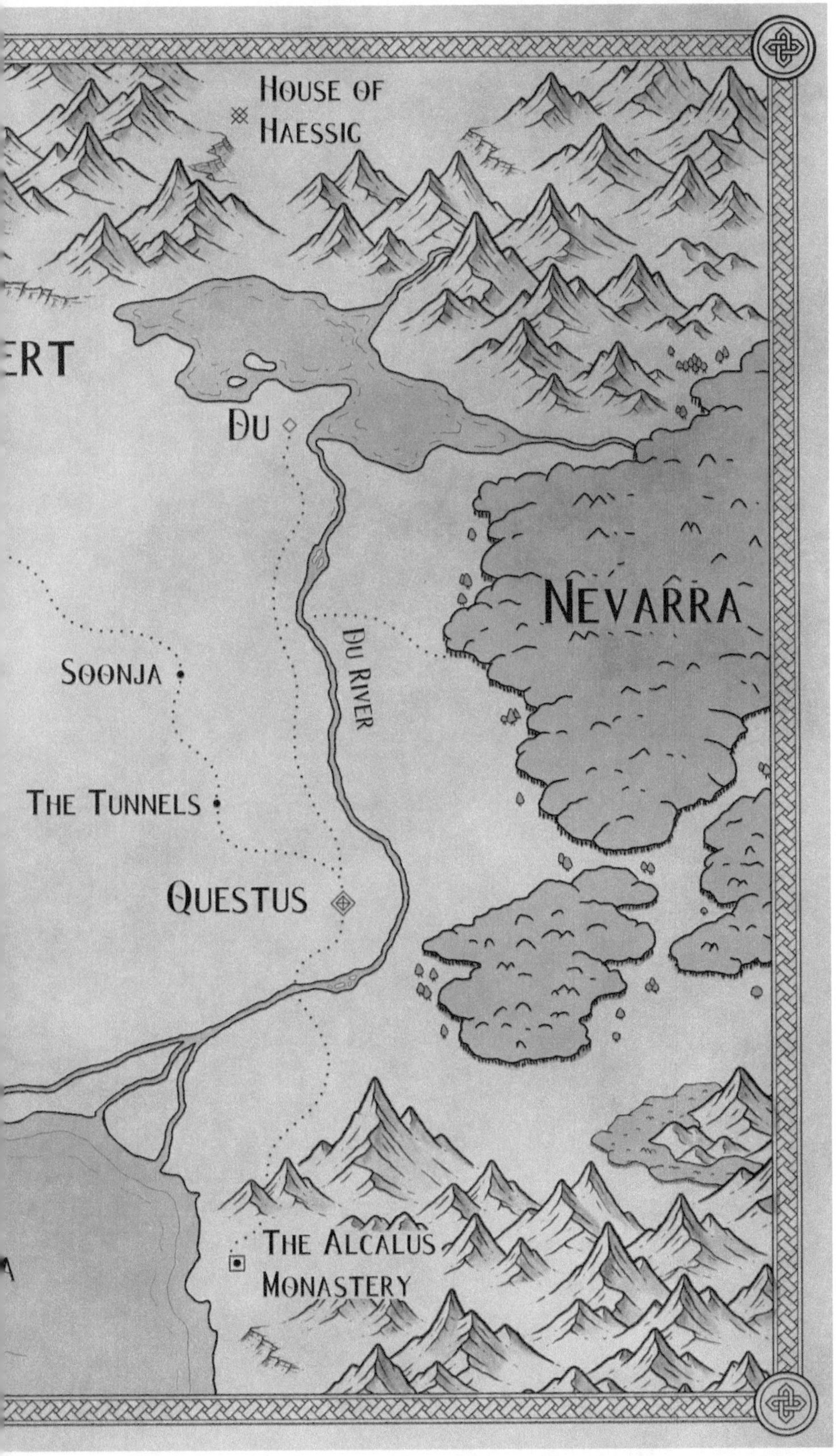

HOUSE OF HAESSIG
RT
DU
DU RIVER
NEVARRA
SOONJA
THE TUNNELS
QUESTUS
THE ALCALUS MONASTERY

PART 1

CHAPTER 1

THE EXPIRING BASTARD BRAID

AVA

Ava had spent the morning trying to find the right words to express how she felt about Gannick. What would she say to him? How should she say it? When would she tell him how she felt?

Well, it wasn't so much *when* for Ava. Her tongue was impatient and the way—not just secrets—but all of her thoughts and feelings poured through her lips, one would think that her mouth was full of holes. She knew the *when* was coming soon. Her heart had barely managed to keep how she felt from him for this long. It was just a matter of how she would tell him, and what she would say. For such a strong jaw, it lacked the control she needed for this kind of thing.

Ava's Nylo, a white axolotl, floated about as Ava cared for her plants that made the inside of her little bungalow in the Tunnels look like a mystical rainforest. The creature's limbs took lazy paddles every now and then, and his tail waved side to side as he swam through the air, sometimes dusting off a leaf or two. The stripe on his nose, the water-lion gills, and his feet and tail were all accented with a shade of green only a creature born in a rainforest could produce. Ava had Matched with Axol so many years ago that she hardly noticed the trail the creature left behind on his elevated path: fading white and jade green sparkles—as if he were shedding fairydust. It got everywhere. On her clothes, in her eyes, in her mouth… it had become a small nuisance Ava had gotten used to. But for anyone else, they might walk through the glimmering mist with awe and walk away with a mild feeling of rejuvenation.

The green Mark on Ava's right cheek appeared on her when she and Axol had Matched. Whenever a Nylo Matched with a human, they left a Mark on the human's body as a symbol of their bond. Ava's Mark was made up of intricate tracings, delicate enough to be mistaken as freckles at first. A desert flower bloomed at the center of the Mark, surrounded in a tight circle of leaves and other floral-like patterns.

"Ava, good day!" a woman called out from the open window.

"Good day, Cothia. What will it be today?"

"I would love my regular fill of klee, and maybe some leines if you have any." Cothia said as she rested her elbows on the broad window shelf.

"I have both. Planning on a trip above ground?"

"Just a week to visit family. Not looking forward to it, honestly."

Ava turned to a hanging plant. She lifted up a small branch, and Axol flew over to bite it cleanly off acting as a pair of garden pruners. The scent of fresh cut greens filled her nostrils. Ava took the branch and wrapped it in thin, brown paper. Then she picked a few purple flowers, very small blooms, and mashed them in a bowl before sprinkling them into a small pouch.

"Here you go. Two pieces and four bits or twenty jun. Whatever you have."

"I still can't believe you can grow leines in the Tunnels. You're the only one that can do it without proper sunlight," Cothia said as she handed Ava a few silver coins.

"Just have to have that touch, I guess," Ava smiled.

"It's got to be something with your..." Cothia pointed to Ava's cheek. Ava touched her Mark. It was simply a darker tone than her regular skin color, but glowed green when she was using Axol's powers. It was not glowing now. All of this to say that she had a lot to thank Axol for—mainly the magical power she channeled from him to heal herself instantly—but Ava's botanical skills weren't quite one of them. Everything she knew about flora and fauna was thanks to her mother.

Cothia went on her way, and Ava continued to give water and love to the plants, humming here and there. While the Tunnels being underground always had a humid feel and smelled of the earth, her little bungalow smelled of a dewy garden. The room (which accounted for Ava's entire home) was filled with floating gels above, glowing in a rainbow of neons for light. Gels were what many in the world of The Cache used for light thanks to their bright shimmer. These liquid filled bubbles the size of Ava's fist were created from a spell the Gatekeeper sent out from West Gate to illuminate the world. While full of magic, over the years they had become commonplace across all kingdoms in The Cache and could be found even in some of the smallest villages.

The Tunnels were forever dark—sunless in the day and starless in the night; but with the gels (and the underground city's native glowing flora and fauna), the Tunnels were also forever neon. Ava turned around so that Axol had to quickly brake in midair in order to not crash into her face. He was able to avoid collision and stopped, looking wide eyed into his Marked's brown eyes.

"Okay. You be Gannick. And I'll be me. Okay. Okay. Here we go." Ava took a breath as she finished watering a ticking lily and flicked her long brown hair behind her shoulder. "I know we're different. We're actually alarmingly different. I live here in the Tunnels, you live above ground. I'm an... orphan. You're a— that's great, Ava. Just bring up the fact that you have no parents and dampen the mood before you tell him how you feel." She rolled her eyes, lightly knocking on her head with her knuckles.

Ava started to mix soils with different bits of glittering tree bark. Her mind had already wandered off to the first time she had met Gannick. Actually, it was before they met. She had seen him before he had seen her. She was out on her nightly route, making her way through the intoxicated crowds—the best customers for her morning mix. She sold small packets of folded paper with dry botanicals, crushed into a small peppering that dissolved into any drink. It was the perfect cure for the inevitable headache most would wake up to the next day. Her concoction had become a well known favorite in the Tunnels.

While shuffling through the crowds, making a quick sale with a glance, nod, and exchange of a packet for coin, Ava stepped outside to get some air. Though her customers were all packed inside the noisy interiors of the taverns, she could only handle the noise and ocean of people for so long before she felt she needed to come up for air. She had made her way to a narrow alleyway that shared the backdoor of a handful of the watering holes she was making rounds through. That's when Gannick had stepped out of another back door directly across the alleyway. Ava stood straight, hidden in the shadows as long as she kept still.

His hands were cupped together, carrying something. Gannick crouched down, opening his palms to let a small spider creep out safely from his hold. She recalled being struck by how large his hands were and yet how gentle and slow they released the multi-legged bug. Ava knew the yellow insect well. It was a reffa. They were inert.

Meaning they weren't Nylos. They were plain, non-magical crawlers. While most in the Tunnels found the spiders to be quite disgusting, they were great companions to a handful of the plants she grew in her home. She welcomed them for their protection against nasty pests that ate without satisfaction. She had thought she was the only one that didn't smush them as soon as they were discovered given they weren't Nylos.

"See? It's better out here," Gannick had whispered to the spider. "Trust me. Now keep out of trouble, okay?"

When he leaned in as if to see if the spider had been listening, that's when Ava had first seen Gannick's face. His rather shaggy brown hair, his sharp nose and chin, flushed cheeks, deep set green eyes, timid smile. Looking at him in that moment as if he had found the spotlight in an empty alleyway had warmed Ava's neck and cheeks. Gannick had stood up slowly, taken three deep breaths, and then returned through the door he had exited.

The simple act had tugged at Ava's heart. If he had taken the time to help the reffa, an insect most humans in The Cache were repulsed by... maybe he could feel kindly toward someone like her, despite her being what everyone in The Cache despised: a green-blooded Atrox.

"Okay. Let's try again. And Axol. Less slobbering this time? Okay. Gannick?" she looked at Axol swimming above her shoulders. "I wanted to tell you how I feel about you. I know we're different, but that's just one of the things that I love about you and me together... and that's what I'd like to be more of: together—"

Ava heard a strange noise. It wasn't a carelessly loud noise that was reserved for her close neighbors or regular customers. In fact, it caught her attention because it was so intentionally quiet. It was almost so quiet that it was as if it wasn't a sound she heard, but a glitch. Like something in the world had gone terribly wrong, but only for half a second. Axol had swung towards the direction of the sound or lack of sound—so Ava knew it wasn't just her imagination. The open window. Ava reached up and took one of the floating, glowing gels in her hand and held it in front of her to chase away the dark as she slowly —inch by inch—moved towards the opening.

The front door knob turned slowly and then the door violently jolted open. Ava's body pivoted towards the door and then froze. The sight immobilized her. It wasn't a Nylo. Nor was it an inert creature. At the doorway was a monster. It had long, angular limbs—too long for the thing even as it stood at such a height. It took the shape of a man, though everything else about its nature reminded Ava more of an arachnid.

The glistening face was the most concerning though. Ava stared intently into the face, but she could not focus on any one feature. She knew there were eyes, a nose, a mouth, a smile, but she could not find them. And the harder she focused, the more of a blurring confusion its head became. And that was when she knew what it was. The mythical creature she had only ever heard of and been warned about.

There it was, dripping in front of her: a Vhyka.

It was then suddenly that she became very aware of her unique gift from Axol: the ability to heal very quickly. She then envisioned the many ways she could be torn apart before her body pulled itself back together only so the Vhyka could tear her to shreds again. All of the stories she had heard growing up had taught her that she was the Vhyka's sustenance. It wouldn't tear her apart necessarily, it would devour her. Would her powers heal her quickly enough for her to become the Vhyka's honeypot: a never-ending meal? Or would the Vhyka's appetite consume her entirely and lead to a death she thought might have been impossible?

The Vhyka stood, balancing on its long, sharp legs. Ava noticed a puddle below it. It was dripping. This made Ava step backwards; her first movement since the door had flung open. And the wetness didn't bother her as much as something else. It was something stranger, something very wrong about what was in front of her. She involuntarily scanned the monster once more to figure out what was bothering her aside from its presence alone. And that's when she realized what it was.

It wasn't breathing.

It was still. No inhale or exhale. Just a steady focus on its prey. However, Axol was breathing enough for everyone involved. He fluttered like a miniature hurricane around Ava. Ava stood still under a shower of green sparkles, wishing she was able to flit and fly like Axol. Her panic was then subdued by submission. Her instincts of survival had lost itself to the strange realization that she was likely experiencing her first moments approaching death. At first, from the Vhyka's arrival there had been fear. But now she stood two strides away from the bastard-eating beast, and the fear had been replaced by wonder.

In a daze, she began to distract herself with existential questions she never took the time to consider. Was the Light what she would find in the end like the people of Pagra believed? Or were the Questonians right and she would drown in an ocean of decay—the punishment all Marked suffered according to their religion, known as the Blood? Or maybe, hopefully the Nevarrians would be correct, and she would be incarnated into some other creature and live another thousand lives.

Her acceptance of her fate was interrupted by the Vhyka. Just as it came, it crept away into The Tunnel's ever-constant darkness. It never stepped foot inside her home. Left with strange religious and philosophical questions she had never considered before, Ava fell to her knees, green and white sprinkles raining over her vision as she hyperventilated her way back to a state where she could move properly once again.

After laying on the ground where the Vhyka had left her for an unknown amount of time, Ava sat up, the symbol of her bond with her Nylo glowing green on her right cheek, meaning the magic of Axol was healing something of Ava if even just her nerves. Though Marked weren't technically allowed on Questus territory, there was still a small population that hid in the Tunnels. Ava knew different people had different opinions about a Marking on the face. Some liked to be able to flaunt that they were Marked with power so subtly by the simple location of their Mark. Others didn't like to have their tricks and trades out in the open for everyone to see. Ava had no opinion on showing or hiding her power—only she felt that the Mark and its location were a part of her in the same way she had eyes and a nose in designated areas on her face as well. It was never something she questioned or wished was elsewhere. It was simply a part of her.

Axol, her beloved Nylo, flew to her chest as soon as he saw her rise. Their cheeks touched and her Mark lit up for a few moments before it faded away to small glowing embers of green once again. The glow didn't always mean magic was being used, sometimes it simply reacted to the strength of the bond between the Nylo and human.

Ava put her hand on her neck, her fingers tracing a thick metal tube around her neck with the circumference of her pinky finger. It was her bastard braid, and its protection was weakening.

"The Vhyka left... That means I still have a little more time before the protection has completely worn off."

Axol looked at her, his wide mouth turned slightly downward at each end. Ava stood up, unhooked her small satchel from the wall. She hesitated before heading out the door. She knew if the Vhyka could kill her, it would have. She was still safe. But it felt unsettling to walk out the same door the Vhyka had appeared in front of.

"C'mon, Axol. We have to go see Gears and get a new bastard braid."

———

Midday, when the sun was directly above The Cache, was the only window of time the Tunnels let in sunlight. The desert earth above filtered the rays so that a thin film of sunlight was cast through the ground and landed on Ava's pale, sun-deprived skin as she walked down the path from her neighborhood into the city. In the darkness, under the glow of the bright neon plants that grew relentlessly throughout the Tunnels, Ava could see quite a fair distance ahead of her. And now, in the dim of noon with the subtle shimmers from above, she felt she could see everything.

Ava looked up at what would have been the sky if the ground didn't rest between them. With the exception of the noon sun, the Tunnels allowed nothing through. A traveler above would only see the sand below them and the dunes ahead. However, from below, the Tunnels allowed its inhabitants a full view of above. Ava could see the sparse plants grow up as their roots grew down. And when a traveler passed by, she could see them too. There were no travelers above—it was, after all, midday. No one willingly traveled through the Wontine Desert under direct sunlight.

The view above always reminded her of the life she had before or at least the bits and pieces she could remember—the life where she had the warmth that can only come from things like sun rays on skin and a mother and father. Ava lowered her gaze back to the giant cave of a city. It had its own charm with its outline lit up by the rainbow lights coming from its native plants—not to mention the hidden nature of its location. It was good for her. With the exception of the newest threat from the Vhykas, it was safe.

Ava arrived at Gear's shop in the heart of the city after a brisk 20-minute walk. She was constantly spinning around, trying to spot the Vhyka should it decide to follow her. She couldn't shake the feeling something was watching her. When she reached the metal doors, she took a long deep breath. The front of the shop was mostly made of metal. There were no windows, and some of the metal had begun to rust. It looked quite beat up which gave the impression that Gears was just getting by with the business, but Ava knew better.

While Gears wasn't an actual doctor, he was the closest thing to it in the Tunnels. He had spent time in the House of Haessig, where the best healers in The Cache studied and dedicated their life to saving other lives. While he admitted to only being an apprentice who didn't finish his studies there—something about needing more space for experimentation—he still knew more healing techniques and was privy to ancient secrets that the House of Haessig kept locked away in the northernmost mountains. Ava knew that Gears was overworked and couldn't handle the amount of injuries the Tunnels threw his way. It didn't help that he had a habit of never turning away a patient.

Ava walked through the entrance that opened up to a narrow hallway rather than an actual foyer. She could reach out and touch a hand to either wall, the space was tapered so. The inside was dark and musty. Most places indoors were lit with vibrant house plants and floating gels. Here only two plants a distance ahead flickered low, moody light. As Ava's eyes adjusted, she noticed stains on the stone floor. Blood? Goo? Oil? Ooze? There were different textures that Ava decided not to try to guess.

Axol flew in and casually slapped his small tail against a rug that hung from a wall, sending puffs of dust up into the air that reflected the white glow of his skin. Surprised by the clouds of dust, the white and green salamander retreated into the comfort of Ava's core so that she held him gently against her belly where he coughed up the remaining debris he had liberated from the fabric on the walls.

A small child of 5 or so appeared at the end of the hall. Ava came forward as the young host waited silently. As Ava approached, she realized under the shadows that the child was bandaged around his head so that his eyes were completely covered. It was not unusual for Gears to take in the odd children and give them work—and Ava thought to herself—purpose. She wondered if the child's sight would return or was this as far as his medicinal skills could go?

Axol floated just to the left of Ava. She was glad to have him there as his green and white sparkling skin was the brightest thing there and lit up the hall rather well. Her little host turned and led the way forward with Axol glimmering just behind. There were no twists and turns, only a straight hall that seemed to be growing narrower. The hallway continued for some time, revealing the interior of the shop was much larger than it assumed. The lights from the plants had faded away, and now Axol was the only illumination. The corridor finally opened up into a large chamber. It was an expansive space with high ceilings and plenty of large and unusual machines.

"Ava?" she heard the familiar voice. She turned to the corner to see a boy with golden hair and eyes so blue that they always seemed to be beaming with electricity. She started walking towards him. She then saw the boy laying on the table Gears stood over. He was just finishing tying a makeshift sling for the boy's arm. In normal circumstances, Gears would be considered handsome. He had a symmetrical face, pleasing features, and again, that electricity that made him stand out. However, he wasn't normal. He was a bit eccentric. So he never was just a blonde-haired, blue-eyed boy. He always had the reminiscence of a half medical, half scientific explosion gone off in his face—Ava could never tell if it was from an experiment gone right or wrong. Today, Ava saw half of his face was covered in what looked like ash. His hair was growing every which way as if it hadn't been combed in ages, resembling more of a wheat field in a windstorm than an actual hairstyle. And he was always wearing some strange contraption somewhere around his body. Today, he had a headset on so that his left eye had several layers of eyeglasses held over his pupil, making his left eye look giant compared to the rest of his face... And rather ridiculous, Ava thought to herself.

Still, it was what she loved about her friend. Their friendship had started as a business partnership: Ava could grow some of the herbs needed for his healing needs. When Gears had learned Ava could heal on her own almost immediately thanks to the unique power granted to her by Axol, he once admitted in so many words that it was a relief to have someone that would show up on his doorstep without a cold or worse, a life threatening injury. He also was fascinated with Axol, and after years of patience, Gears finally asked if he could collect some of the scales Axol shed.

"Gears."

"You're just in time. I just purchased a welding machine. I can finally work with metal again," he grinned. Then he patted the boy gently on the back. "All done. Try not to move it. Come back before the full moon so I can check up on it, alright?"

Ava tried not to laugh as she looked at his magnified eye with that wild smile. Though Gears had said House of Haessig was not for him, Ava knew deep down, he probably wasn't for them either. His approach and methods seemed rather... messy at times, and he just didn't have the polish and virtue that the House of Haessig was always rumored to be. After all, they were living, breathing saviors who had done everything short of bringing humans back from the dead. From what she had heard, their house felt more like a sanctuary than an infirmary.

"What do you need to work with metal for?" Ava asked genuinely curious.

"There's a clean break of the bone. And then there's when bone is completely obliterated," Gears said with a fascination that Ava was sure the House of Haessig wouldn't approve of and that Gears didn't try to hide. "And sometimes when the will is weak, the bones are too and they need some... convincing. Fire and Metal can be quite persuasive in those cases."

Ava's face paled. And then she remembered why she had come. She cleared her throat before she could ask more questions about welding and healing.

"Gears. I need your help."

"My help?" he asked, surprised. "My healing friend needs my healing help?"

"Sort of. It's my necklace."

Gears looked down to the silver tube. "Your bastard braid?"

"A Vhyka came to my place this morning."

Gears swatted the magnifying glasses over his left eye away so he could look seriously at Ava.

"It just stared at me, and then it left."

"Your bastard braid is expiring!" Gears exclaimed. He rushed over to stand over a large metal workstation, and he slid a single eye glass from his head set back over his eye. "May I?"

Ava turned around and Gears took the necklace from her neck and laid it onto his metal table. He unscrewed the end. A second necklace slithered out as he held the tube sideways; thin silver threads woven delicately together with short stubby spikes scattered across the length of it.

"Vhykas only eat bastard children when they have an audience. There has to be another human present. The isolation, the fear, the loneliness, that's what they season you with before they eat you," Gears muttered as he slid a second layer of glass in front of his eye to examine the hardware with a closer eye. "Thus, being alone protects you. And then when another human is present—all it takes is one other person—a Vhyka will absorb you like any poor starving animal would."

"How did it find me?"

"No one can hide from them. It's your necklace. Its end date is near. They can sense it. It's basically like them smelling a fresh meal cooking over the fire. The visit was just to see if its meal was nearly done." Gears took the spiked silver thread in his fingers and again brought it closer to his electric blue eyes. "Most braids offer 5 years of protection from those starving beasts. This one looks like it had 10. Very expensive. Your mother cared for you."

Gear's bedside manner was always a little rough. Ava

knew he said the last words very matter of fact, but it made her heart feel slightly heavier. Her bastard braid had lasted her all of her life, and now she was having to figure out a means of getting her hands on a new one all on her own.

"Do you have another braid I can purchase?" she asked.

"I sold my last one a week ago. The rate of bastard children being born seems to only get faster and faster. There's no time to wait for the traveling merchants. And waiting for Makani to be hovering over us will take far too long as well."

The floating islands of Makani were never floating around the Tunnels when she needed them to, Ava thought. She had never set foot on the islands, but it would have been a wonderful excuse. She had heard it was beautiful up there. She pulled herself back to reality. Not seeing the islands this season was the last of her worries.

"How long do I have?"

"The next full moon. At most."

"Thirty days. That's something."

"Twenty-four days, actually, Ava. It's not long."

"Do you know where I can find one?"

"Pagra will be your closest market, which is across the desert. And they don't come cheap. You should leave today. It's not an easy journey." He frowned.

It made sense that Pagra would have them. It was the closest house to West Gate where the Gatekeeper cast her spells—one of them being the protection spell of the bastard braids.

"I can't leave the Tunnels," Ava swallowed.

"You can because you *must*," Gears said. "I can give you something... to help with those feelings that come up."

"I can't go above ground," Ava started to feel light headed already.

"You don't have a choice. Here. Take this before you travel up to the desert." Gears placed a small vial into her hand, nodding.

"I need to say goodbye to someone first..."

"Goodbye? To who? Ava, this is life and death."

"Someone." *The love of my life.*

"Is it the unicorn that's been following you?" Gears asked.

Ava raised an eyebrow. "What unicorn?"

Gears nodded into the far back corner of his makeshift laboratory. Ava turned around, not sure what she was supposed to be looking at. Slowly, something shifted. Something moved. Something came forward. A slow, white figure that looked to be a play of the light seemed to solidify in the corner. An Asting. She had never seen one before.

"I mean you no harm." The white figure said as they stepped forward. Without changing their appearance whatsoever, they had gone from somehow blending into the walls of Gear's workshop to clearly standing there in plain sight. When they announced themself, it was clear where they had been standing the entire time—as if they only needed to will her to see them. Ava took a step back, rigid not from fear but surprise.

The figure in front of her had skin so pale, hair so white, and eyes so frosty pink, they practically glowed in the dim light. A salmon colored, four point star was stamped on their forehead, extending wide past the start of their eyebrows. Their robes matched the angelic and mystically pure whiteness of their body.

"A unicorn!" Ava turned to Gears. "You didn't think to mention the unicorn until now?"

Gear shrugged, "I thought you knew."

"My name is Kavi. I am a member of the Asting."

Ava blinked slowly, remembering what she knew about unicorns that belonged to the Asting. They were all powerful beings. Like her Nylo, Axol, they were one of the only direct sources of magic that existed in The Cache. She knew they had sworn off physical intervention because they were so powerful. They would not so much as touch her if they were members of the Asting—the largest network of scholars that existed in The Cache. They were known for their dedication to broadening their knowledge on all subjects and for their peaceful nature. She had never met one before, but from what she knew, she was safe. In fact, from what she knew, it was an honor to even see a unicorn, let alone have the opportunity to speak with one.

"Wh-why are you following me?" Ava asked.

Kavi looked up at Gears, "I think you might prefer I share this reason privately."

Ava looked at Axol who also seemed curious, but not threatened, by the Asting's presence. Ava had a secret. A big one. She couldn't risk having it revealed if the unicorn somehow knew that she was an Atrox. Though she knew Gears was a good person—one of the best people she knew—the last time she was discovered to be an Atrox, it hadn't ended well. She looked at Gears sheepishly. He took it to be a questioning glance.

"They're not dangerous. I saw lots of them in Haessig. They're just... strange."

It was funny to hear Gears say someone was weird, given he was usually the strangest person in the room. Ava nodded.

"It looks like you two have some talking to do," Gears said. Ava turned to see a family show up at the opening of the chamber. More patients for him to help. Gears turned to Ava. "Drink the elixir before you go up. It's strong. Leave the Tunnels. Find a safe way to Pagra through the shift. You don't have much time."

Ava wanted to ask Gears to come with her. She didn't think the bottle Gears had given her would be enough for her to leave the Tunnels. She didn't know how she was going to get across the desert. But she knew too many people depended on Gears here like the family politely waiting behind her.

"Okay."

"Come visit me when you return," Gears said. Then

he swiftly walked past her and greeted the family and began inquiring about their visit. Ava looked at Kavi. They bowed in response. Then Ava walked back through the corridor, the unicorn politely tracing behind her.

Ava walked beside the unicorn. They both were stealing glances at one another. Kavi smiled often with their lips pressed together. The smile was so large, their eyes nearly closed at the peak of the expression. It was strange how benevolent they looked. It was a contagious mirth that made Ava enjoy her new white shadow next to her.

"So... why are you following me?" Ava asked once again as they made their way through the city. They were cheerful and serene, but she still knew so little about unicorns.

Kavi leaned forward slightly, "I know what you are."

Ava's breath hitched in her lungs. They could mean anything, she reminded herself. But most likely... Given an Asting was walking beside her, they knew.

She hesitated for a moment, her voice becoming a whisper. "What do you think I am?"

"You come from the foreign world beyond The Cache. Through the portal the Gatekeeper watches. You bleed green because you are an Atrox."

The blood in Ava's temples began to pulse so that she could feel every heart beat in her head. Her fingers tingled with anxiety. Her survival counted on her not being discovered, and here she was... discovered.

"You are the most universally hated creature in The

Cache. There is no Kingdom that allows your existence. No people that grant you asylum or safe passage. Your kind were once hunted, but the hunting has stopped because there are so few of you left. Some believe you to be extinct."

Ava rubbed her temples. The stress was rising every second, only calmed by the fact that Kavi whispered their unnecessarily long description of herself. "Okay. I get it. You know. That still doesn't explain why you're following me."

"With your permission, I would like to follow you for my studies."

"For your... unicorn school?" Ava asked.

"Not exactly. The Asting is many things. It is a wealth of ever-growing knowledge. It is a network of all unicorns who pass 73 years in The Cache. It is my home and my family," Kavi said, taking their time with their last sentence.

"...Okay. So you want to study me?"

"As you may know, as a unicorn and scholar of the Asting, each unicorn chooses their topic of study when they turn 73 years of age. The topic that I chose was... Atroxes."

"What would studying me entail?"

"I will simply observe you and ask questions. I will record my learnings and it will eventually be connected to the Asting. I cannot physically intervene. I will help when I can, but the first rule of the Asting is as follows: *The nature of The Cache is the natural course that must be taken. No action may disrupt the flow, only a unicorn's word may be spoken."*

"That's the *first* rule?"

"Because we are so powerful, it is important that the boundaries are set in order for harmonic coexistence with other species."

"So humble," Ava said, her eyes squinting towards her new observer. "So if I'm dying… you won't help, you'll just study how I die?"

"That is correct." It was the first time Kavi wasn't smiling.

"I didn't realize how brutal unicorns were."

"We are fair and just. The rules are there for a reason."

"I'll remember that," Ava said dryly.

At this point, Ava knew she would accept. It was an honor to see or speak with a unicorn. To be chosen like this was a once in a lifetime opportunity. Although they were a stranger to her, she was familiar with unicorns and their stories. She couldn't help but want for a companion to be there when she traveled to Pagra. It would be nice to not be alone. She hadn't left the Tunnels since she first arrived when she was little.

"How long will you study me?" she asked as they turned onto the path of her little underground cottage.

"As long as you are alive—unless I find a more interesting Atrox. However, your kind are very rare. And to be Marker Matched," Kavi looked at Axol, "That is something."

"That sounds like... a long time."

"Statistically speaking, my studies with Atroxes have been rather short. Not only is your kind hard to find, but they don't seem to live very long."

Ava pressed her lips together. It was clear why. Well, some of it was. Everything Kavi had said was true. Everyone hated Atroxes. She understood that. She understood that she had to hide what she was and if anyone other than a unicorn found out, she would be killed and in some terrible way. She had heard of her kind stoned to death, torn apart by angry mobs, even crucified... She never heard of a clean death.

What she didn't understand was why. She didn't know where the hatred had come from. She didn't understand why her kind was so terrible. She had heard name-calling and slurs, but no one took the time to explain what her ancestors had done that was so terrible. And she could never ask why—she was too afraid to bring attention to her kind at all. Maybe Kavi could enlighten her in the coming days.

When the three were home, Ava began to pack a small bag for her journey to Pagra. Kavi quietly observed with their closed lip smile that caused their eyes to squint. She packed light with just the essentials. It would be a long trip across the Wontine Desert, but without the bastard braid, she'd soon be eaten every night by a Vhyka as long as there was an audience. She promised herself she would have a new bastard braid well before the next full moon. She just needed to say goodbye to Gannick first.

She set the pack down and started to get ready for a night out in the Tunnels. It was the week of the Blood ceremony after all, and Gannick was coming to visit. And if there was anything as important as not getting eaten by a Vhyka for a 15-year-old bastard girl, it was to stay long enough to tell the boy of her dreams that she loved him.

CHAPTER 2

ARE YOU NERVOUS?

CANDLAND

Candland sat with his fingers interlaced, staring up at his brother who stood with his arms out as the servants placed the final additions on Keyes' uniform. Keyes' blue eyes gazed forward as if he could see his future laid out before him. It wasn't a difficult future to foretell as he was the firstborn prince of Questus. His path was clearly paved for him before he left his mother's womb. Second sons, however, had more wiggle room to branch out, or in Candland's case, hide.

There was a chattering of vague words that quickly transformed into low roaring by the volumes of people only royalty can bring filling the room. Candland looked over towards the door, his gaze searching for the source of crowds that were growing a few levels above. They were in a room underground. The kingdom of Questus had an impressive underground system, many passages used for religious practices. A few long tunnels connected them to the Blood Chambers where only royal blood could pass through, but they weren't going down any tunnels today; they were going up. Above them was the largest amphitheater in the kingdom—nearly filled to the brim with Questonians.

"Are you nervous?" Candland asked.

"I was born for this," Keyes responded, his bright eyes still surveying his future under blonde locks of hair.

Candland looked down at his own calloused hands. Keyes was the future king. He looked it, too. Even the shadow he cast was upright and regal. Candland—if he had any shape that was strong enough to be labeled a role—it was the shape of a sculptor; strong, but not much without his tools. He had once thought his primary role to be brother, but a brother to a future king was like a shadow to a sword in the middle of the day. Brother wasn't a role that his parents approved of or that Keyes cared for very much—at least not anymore. While Keyes had a look made up of brightness with brilliant eyes, golden hair, and fair skin, Candland was the opposite. He was made of colors that blended together with sandy brown hair, green eyes, and olive skin. Candland rubbed a white scar on his left palm, kneading the meat of his hand the way he might with clay. He liked to massage his hands to feel the physical sensation of his fingers digging into his skin—especially when he felt nothing on the inside.

"The cape looks good on you," Keyes said. He now looked at his younger brother, a smile peeking through one side of his mouth just long enough for Candland to see it.

"It feels... unnecessary."

"The Blood made all of this for us. From the single thread that makes up your red cape to the ability in our fingers to weave it together." The Blood. It was the one and only religion practiced in Questus. And there was no one who was more loyal to it than Keyes. A servant pinned the last brooch on Keyes' chest, and he stepped down. Candland thought about how neither he nor his brother had ever set out to attempt to weave anything with their own fingers. Candland could feel Keyes' eyes on him, demanding his attention—which wasn't uncommon.

"Thus everything is necessary, Candland." Keyes smiled and put a hand on his shoulder.

Candland stared at the many decorations that hung from his brother's shoulders, from the matching crimson cape to the golden buttons that were stationed uniformly from his neck to his waist.

"I just don't see how all of this is necessary." Candland waved his hand around the adornments of his older brother's outfit.

Keyes frowned. "Not today, Candland."

"What?"

"I don't need you bringing your rain cloud out with us when we go upstairs. The last thing I need is gloom treading behind me on my first time hosting the Pre Ceremony."

"I don't mean to be gloomy."

"Mother says you were born brooding," Keyes sighed.

Candland wanted to say that he doubted his mother remembered much about when he was born or really the first few years after that, but Candland held back. "Perhaps I was surprised to be born at all."

"Ugh. There it is. The gloom!" Keyes rolled his eyes.

"Hey. The Blood created the gloom too," Candland said. "Didn't you just say everything is necessary?"

Keyes didn't bother to respond. He only took toward the exit, walked up the steps, and headed towards the cheering crowds he was always so fond of.

The Blood's Pre Ceremony kicked off the biggest celebration in Questus. It started in the evening when the year's sacrificial name of Marked was chosen by the Blood and read on the petal of a blessed rose by the royal family. Many traditions were celebrated throughout the week, including large neighboring dinners where each individual would stand up and call out their greatly desired wish along with the weight in their life they would remove to make room for such a fortune. A night of recognitions and awards for admirable characteristics such as loyalty, faithfulness, and dedication to the Blood. And Candland's favorite—a midday parade with dancers, funny men in costumes, serious men with fire, and even elephants. The elephants were blessed by the Blood like all inert animals that were kept in the kingdom—unlike the Nylos, also known as Markers, that were infused with dark magic and, of course, not allowed to roam freely in Questus. The same restrictions applied to any human a Nylo had Matched with. These people were otherwise known as the Marked due to the Marking they received once bonded with the magical, albeit cursed, creatures. Once they were bonded, however, the humans were able to harness the magic of the Nylo they Matched with... But any magic harnessed from anywhere but the Blood was forbidden in Questus, and just like the Nylos, the Marked were considered cursed.

The main event, the Blood Ceremony, took place on the seventh and final day. It was always on this day that the individual who was chosen at the Pre Ceremony— always a Marked human, cursed by the Nylos—was sacrificed to the Blood. Like many children, Candland didn't understand many parts of the tradition and religion he was born into. He didn't know how the Blood chose who or why they chose what, but he did love the blessed elephants among other highlights of the celebration.

This year, the importance of the ceremony and sacrifice all seemed to become more tangible with his brother in the center of the open dome. In previous years, when it was his parents partaking in choosing the sacrificial individual, and Keyes was by his side, it had felt more like any other fluffy event that his parents participated in and led for royal appearances. It seemed very normal.

However, standing in the shadows alone surrounded by guards donning their red armor and seeing Keyes standing in front of their mother along with the Blood Council—the 12 trusted men and women who advised the crown and managed different branches of government—it was different. This was more than a royal charade. It was Keyes reaching the age of true manhood at 18. Candland couldn't hear the boy in Keyes when his brother addressed the crowd through his booming diaphragm. There was no boy left. Candland wondered what Keyes would be like as a man. Seeing his brother at the center of it all was impactful in a way that Candland could feel but not put into words with his 16-year-old mouth. He felt something. Something was happening. Changing maybe. But what was it? He watched in silence as the sacred rosebush—the thorny plant that had grown since before Questus was given its name—ascended from the ground to offer its petals to be plucked by the new, young host and reveal the name of the year's sacrifice.

The rumbling of the earth made him slightly queasy, mixing together Candland's existing nerves. The shaking stopped when the rose bush was fully erect. The leaves were aged so dark, they appeared more black than green, and the thorns were so matured that they competed with the actual flowers in size. It was said to be the very rose bush the first name was called from, Edimere Idoa, a native to Nevarra, a country that didn't see Nylos as cursed. In fact, Nevarra was dedicated to protecting Nylos and, thus, a natural enemy of Questus. The Nylo of Edimere was a flightless bear with wings made of antlers that Questus claimed was simply the dark magic that had infected the once inert bear. The claim was that the wings were not wings but a disease. An unintended growth. Remembering his teachings of the history of Questus over the years, Candland imagined the bush must have been thousands of years old.

Candland watched his mother gently put her hand on Keyes' shoulder, signaling it was time for him to step forward. Keyes did so and stood before the rose bush in its glorious thicket. Keyes stood still, and the audience responded by quieting so that Candland thought he could hear Keyes' breath. Candland wondered if his older brother could smell the flowers. Studying the blackened petals, Candland guessed that, while once sweet, they didn't smell like roses any longer. He looked up at the people of Questus, an audience that covered the full circumference of the dome. So many faces, so much anticipation. Who would the Marked be that would be slaughtered in a week's time? What would their Nylo be and what dark power would they wield for not much longer? They would know in only a minute more. Candland gulped. He thought about his heavy cape, the gold buttons glimmering from Keyes' uniform, and then finally, the elephants...

The Pre Ceremony was pure entertainment for the people who attended, but the sacrifice was a part of what kept the kingdom running so smoothly. The blood of the sacrificed was stored underground in a chamber only the royal family were allowed in. And it was only the direct line of Questus that could drink the blood to use the power the Marked were harnessing. They could also bless the blood for others to use as well. So the royal line blessed thousands of gallons of blood a year to power the kingdom. From blessing blood of water-wielding Marked to support in Questus' farming, or aiding to control wild-fires to blessing blood of light-wielding Marked to help illuminate the dark outer paths of the city, the blood of the Marked humans who Matched were vital to the king-dom. And it seemed the rose bush always knew which name to pick. It always knew whose magic the kingdom needed most for the year's future challenges or hardships.

Like every main host of the Pre Ceremony that had stood before the rose bush each year for hundreds of years, Keyes plucked a single petal from the largest rose. The petal was nearly a third the size of Keyes' hand. He then pricked his finger on the largest thorn of the bush. The blood flowed from his finger quicker than he had expected, and he jerked his hand back. Keyes quickly looked around at the audience, Candland guessed he was checking to see if he had broken the spell of presentation. Keyes smiled when it was clear each citizen of Questus was still holding their breath. He then held his bleeding hand up in a fist and let the blood drip onto the petal he held below. Candland heard the entire kingdom of Questus hold their breath.

The crowd was quiet, but there was still sound. An electric energy that made the hairs on Candland's limbs harden and separate. Keyes lifted the petal and held it in front of his royal blue eyes to read the name of an unlucky Marked human that would appear using his own blood to spell the name. Keyes paused. He jerked his head around and turned looking at his mother. She nodded reassuringly, looking proud. Candland leaned forward to catch any words that might escape his brother's lips, but his brother said nothing. Keyes turned to look further back, his eyes now locked onto Candland.

Don't be gloomy, Candland heard his brother's voice replay in his head from earlier. *Don't bring the cloud upstairs.* This was his brother's first time hosting the Pre Ceremony. And he was looking to him now for support. This was important. This was Keyes' moment, and this was Candland's moment to show he was there for him. Candland pressed his lips together, smiling, moving his head through half a nod of encouragement, and what Candland hoped looked like happiness. *No rain cloud here,* he assured him with his emerald eyes. Keyes spun back around facing the crowd. There had never been more quiet in the presence of so many.

"Keyes, Dear..." His mother started. It was not a caring tone. She spoke out of impatience from her purpley pink lips.

Keyes turned and ran.

His toes turned the dirt beneath into packs of dust that flung into the air. And Candland's performance for his brother on what happiness might look like if Candland had felt it ended with his own mouth flung open in the final act of confusion and an encore of bewilderment. And the crowd went wild.

The queen looked back at Candland. It was the first time she acknowledged him on that special day of the Pre Ceremony. If she was blaming him for something Keyes had not followed through on, it wouldn't be the first time. Candland only shrugged—not because he didn't care but because he was just as confused as his mother. His performance had ended seconds ago, and there was no more acting left in him to pretend to be jolly. Utter confusion filled his face. The queen started after her first son, and the crowd erupted into a whole new kind of chaos that Candland hadn't seen before in all of his public appearances. His mother, her servants, the guards, the Blood Council—all 12 of them—and more guards all left the main platform, leaving Candland to realize he was the only one left for the crowd to gaze upon. He took a step or two and bowed quickly at the booing audience before he retreated on his own. The confusion among the people had turned to a realization that their show had been cut short. How were they supposed to celebrate the next few days if they didn't know who was going to die at the week's end?

It was bizarre. From the moment Keyes had twisted his body on the royal stage to look at his family with the bloody petal in his hand and for the rest of the day. Just bizarre. The strange disappearance of his brother had left Candland wanting to be close to the family he had that was still present, but his mother was so frantic in trying to launch multiple initiatives to find her eldest son, that Candland found no solace from her. The crimson guards were sent out, the Blood Council sent out their own special forces and confidants, and even the people of Questus had made it a game to find the prince of Questus —and more importantly the petal with the name of who would be sacrificed that week that he had taken with him.

The Blood Council sat with their queen in a large chamber at a longstone table—each with their own area of expertise to make up the twelve components of government that supported the queen. Westahn, councilman of distribution which oversaw the Blood, blessings, and allotment caught Candland's eye for a moment while the queen paced back and forth near the head of the table. Candland had been sitting on a chair along the wall. He watched his mother's threat of her son's punishment when Keyes were to be found for the embarrassment he had caused their family turn into more desperate bargaining and pleas. He wanted to ask his mother if there was any news, if she knew where he might have gone. However, he knew it wasn't the right time to approach her. So instead, he sat back hoping he could glean some information when direct orders were given and official reports with no progress were received.

Finally Candland decided there was no news to be found in the room, and figured he could try his luck elsewhere. He stepped outside the strategy room and started down the hall. Westahn stepped out of a door, closing it quietly behind him.

"Prince Candland," he said.

"Westahn."

"How are you doing?"

"I feel a bit sick," Candland said honestly.

"Do you know why Keyes ran away? Did he say anything to you?" Westahn asked.

"No."

"Oh well. Now, make sure you don't go running off too far. We can't have both princes lost by nightfall."

"I won't," Candland said.

"To hold you to that, I have a little something to keep you busy while you stay put." Westahn pulled out something from his infinite sized pockets in his blood-red robe. Candland waited excitedly. Westahn was the only one from the council that talked to him or even noticed him. The rest only glared at him every now and then making him feel as if he was in the wrong room or maybe even the wrong castle. Westahn pulled out a pouch. Quickly dumping the pouch, a small glass tube that was corked at the top landed in his hand. Inside of the tube, there was a type of sand the color of slate with a more chalk-like texture to it.

"What is it?" Candland asked.

"It's a special clay from deep within The Cache's core.

Said to be where the first king of Questus hid—before he became a king. Deeper than the Tunnels. Oops, don't tell your mother I mentioned the Tunnels now, will you?"

"Where did you get this exactly?"

"Where anyone finds anything, of course. Makani. I happened to be near the east coast as it was floating by. I had forgotten the seasons, but I got lucky!" Westahn winked. "I thought you might be able to use it for your sculpting."

Candland recalled once visiting the floating island of trade with his parents and Keyes. Makani made its way around the entire Cache, buying and selling goods across the world. It seemed if there was any kind of wonder, be it a rare gem or even rare Nylo, it could be found there.

"Thank you!" Candland said, holding the glass tightly in his hand before returning it to the small pouch.

"Now run along, but not too far, alright?"

Candland nodded, and Westahn gave him a short wave goodbye. Keeping Westahn's request in mind, the prince stayed close to the inner castle but decided to visit the places he and his brother had spent time together when they were younger. There was the upper lounge with arguably the best view of Questus where he often played with his brother. It was large with open balconies equal in size looking out every direction. All of the furniture was designed with rich red and golds and built low, made for laying and relaxing. It was often used for the king and queen's intimate parties. However, there hadn't been many of those late night gatherings since Candland's father had died. And so Keyes and Candland spent more time there than anyone.

It was most memorable to Candland for when Keyes had pushed him whilst the servants had gone to be relieved by the next round of caretakers. Candland's memory of the incident was fuzzy since it had occurred only a couple of years after he had learned to walk. Candland had known it had been an accident the second he had lost his balance as a small child and tumbled down the golden spiral stairs that led up to the lounge. Still, from then on, he was extra cautious whenever Keyes was near him and a set of stairs below—just so history didn't repeat itself.

Remembering the tumble, Candland quickly glanced around the lounge. It was empty as it was vast, and Candland confirmed that Keyes was not in the lounge with a view and the golden, spiraled steps.

Candland tried his own studio. If he was being honest, he hoped he wouldn't find Keyes there. It was the only space in the entire castle—including his bedroom—that felt truly his. No one understood the tools and space and stone and clay the way he did and so no one bothered with the accessories of the room and so no one came up to the large space at all. This was the way Candland preferred it. Keyes, of course, had tried to take interest a few years ago. Again, an unfortunate accident, but Keyes had picked up one of Candland's sculptures of an elephant and dropped it so that the trunk and one of the tusks departed the body. Candland knew there was no foul play that day, and that accidents, of course, happen, but still held his breath when he heard Keyes' steps come up the stairs to his studio.

Keyes was not hiding among Candland's countless creations.

The final place Candland investigated was the small creek just past the formal edges of the royal courtyard. The water flowed through just on the other side of the dark trees. Candland and Keyes had played there as young boys in the summers under the shaded trees. This was the place Candland hoped to find Keyes. This was the place where he and his brother had rolled up their pants to stand in the cool stream and try and catch small fish in their hands. Feeling the life in the water tickle his fingers with their scales and slime had given Candland enough delight. He never curled his fingers to cage them, he only let them wiggle for a few moments as he said hello before he returned them to the water. Keyes let most of the fish go, but not all.

Here they had laughed in the grass and swung in the trees. It had been the perfect play place for two young boys. And when Candland found it empty, he realized quickly that his decision to come looking for his brother here was more wishful thinking than a true and practical investigation. They hadn't played there in years.

So where was Keyes? It was strange for him to run away. It was out of character for him to not do what he was supposed to do when in front of the crowd. He was dependable in that way. Mother was the same. Candland hoped Keyes knew it was okay that he ran away. Candland often ran away, especially when there were a lot of people about. He was flighty that way. No one in his family understood that about him. However, he thought, maybe Keyes did now. Maybe this first disappearance today would bring them closer together in the end.

CHAPTER 3

HIS SISTER'S DAY

CHINCHIN

Boris cleared his throat, and Chinchin's gray-blue eyes flickered up.

"...86?" Boris repeated.

Chinchin, also known as 86, had been zoning out again. She put her pen down. "Yes?"

"I was going to head out a bit earlier today. You see... it's my sister's day."

"How about that. Let her light shine!" Lana said. She was a scientist on Project 222 who sat across from Chinchin, a new scientist who graduated early from Pagra Academy. Everyone on that floor worked on Project 222, an experiment Chinchin had started while at the academy that had allowed her to skip the three years left of education and work as an apprentice in Pagra Labs on her own project.

Chinchin smiled. It was insincere, but given out of

kindness nonetheless. What did Boris' sister's birthday have to do with saving lives?

"She's 17. Can you believe it?" Boris asked.

Chinchin could. "Our days come, and our days go."

"They grow up fast," Lana said with a warmth that made Chinchin uncomfortable.

"See you tomorrow," Boris waved.

"See you, Boris. Happy day to your sister," Chinchin waved. Again added fluff, but she always tried to be kind to Project 222's test subjects. He had progressed well in experimentation and had proved to be their most successful examinee to date. It was important to keep them motivated.

Chinchin ran her fingers through her long caramel-colored hair, pulling gently at the dark roots because the gentle sting felt good. She was hunched over a report, consumed by the latest details that were hardly ground-breaking in any sense. But they were details and some-where in them was an answer. She had created the mutation that was supposed to allow anyone to be able to choose and Match with a Nylo. And her mutation, the key focus to Project 222, had done just that. A simple injection that turned the tables and allowed humans to choose the Nylo and not the other way around. Except, now the test subjects who had been injected with the power to choose had been dying off without an explana-tion—and all in the forms of suicide. She was supposed to give everyone a chance to live a better life by Matching with a Nylo and granting them power from that bond. Instead she had accidentally given them death.

The facility, not to mention the entire half of the city, was made out of Obsidian V—the mysterious black stone that was capable of such things that the difference between its technology in the lab and actual magic could not be distinguished by the common folk. One of those many things was that the walls saw all. Like the surface of a lidless iris, the smooth walls, floors, and ceilings never blinked. They took everything in, absorbing what happened in the city—alerting the Sovereign Minister of Pagra and her trusted advisors if anything seemed to be out of the ordinary.

All-seeing was a characteristic that was unsettling for most, but not Chinchin. For one, she was no stranger to being watched. She grew up not knowing what it was like to breathe without a pair of eyes on her. And then her restless attention to detail made the spying material more relatable for her than anything. She, too, looked at everything carefully in the Labs. At least she used to. She hadn't been able to think very clearly since her creation, the synthetic mutation, had taken a dark turn. No, she hadn't been the same since the first casualty of the project. Maya's death.

"86."

Chinchin looked up, rubbed her tired eyes, smiled. A slender boy leaned on the black door frame with his arms crossed. Under the black lab coat all of the scientists in the Labs wore, he donned a violet-colored shirt made of linen. Chauson was the only other early graduate in Pagra Labs. Like her, he too, was a scientific prodigy who accelerated through that academy based on his breakthrough with data and technology. Unlike her, he seemed to like the attention that came with being a kid genius.

She had never seen him look worried or stressed. He always seemed to be at ease. Maybe that was because his parents basically owned the place with his father running the Labs and his mother being the sovereign minister of Pagra. He was 546 to Pagra Labs, but Chinchin made it a point to address everyone by their given name. It wasn't because she wanted to be warm like Lana, it was because the names reminded her that everyone was human. Everyone in the Labs, test subject, scientist, janitor, guard. They were all human. Sometimes in a lab full of sharp black edges and reflective walls, people forgot that.

"Chauson."

"Walk with me?"

Chinchin stood up, and headed down the hall with Chauson, the youngest person to work at the Labs in history at just 16 years of age—Chinchin was only a year older. Besides Maya, he was the only person she had felt like she connected with beyond the work.

"I heard you hadn't eaten all day," he said. He handed her a black box. Chinchin took it, pressed a barely visible button, and the box revealed a sweet, breaded treat. She could see the steam rise from the box. In seven quick bites, she downed half of the pastry.

"Lights! You were hungry. Looks like I heard right," Chauson said. Chinchin could feel him studying her face. She knew she had circles under her eyes so dark they might have looked like shadows. She knew her usually plump lips were beginning to crack, a tell-tale sign that she needed to hydrate better. She licked her lips, pushing her appearance to the back of her mind. Usually, she knew, it played to her favor. Today was most likely not the case.

"I'm so close to figuring out how to stop my test subjects from killing themselves," Chinchin said. "It's hard to justify taking too many breaks right now. But thank you for—"

"The thing you just devoured? 86. If you burn yourself out, you won't be any more helpful than someone after they've soaked through the mud wall. They don't even remember their real names anymore. If you don't eat, that will be you."

Chinchin thought of the mud wall that existed in the very building they walked in now. The mud walls were also made of Obsidian V, just in a very different form. Pagra attached people to those sticky walls—enemies, criminals, anyone who wouldn't give up critical information—and the ooze of the walls sucked out the information leaving nothing left but what Chauson described. Bodies without memories. Without identities.

"I have to figure it out, Chauson. The test subjects' lives are in danger until I do, and I can't have that. Look. Thanks for the snack. I gotta get back to work." Chinchin turned back around toward the direction of her office. Chauson pivoted smoothly with her.

"Send me your files. I'll use my tech to comb through your data. See if my algorithms pick up on any patterns."

"You're not even on a project remotely related to my work. You'll have to make a formal request in order for me to send you anything without it getting flagged."

"It'll be ages until I even get to look at the data if I do that. Do you know how much red tape I'd have to get through? And we thought the academy was bad... the Labs are even worse. I could make a formal request *or* you could just send me the files tonight, and I'll cross-reference them through my entire database. We'll figure out what's happening with your test subjects, and you won't even have to skip a meal."

"For someone whose parents created all of these protocols, you certainly don't like following them."

"I'm a kid. It's my job to rebel against my parents. Even if my parents are sort of in charge. Big deal. The rules of being a kid still apply."

Sometimes Chinchin forgot how young he was. How young they both were.

"Why are you so interested in helping me?" she asked.

"Maybe my parents aren't always obvious about it, but they do care about our people. I don't want anyone else to die either, 86. Besides, this is just an opportunity to show how useful technology can be to the Old City."

"I don't think the Old City will be impressed to hear

that, because of technology, Pagra Labs has *only* killed 5 people—and that's just one of their projects."

"Their deaths won't be in vain," Chauson said with a stern tone.

"There weren't supposed to be any deaths at all," Chinchin said. "Every day. Chauson. I'm failing. And people are dying because of it. Because of my project. Because of me."

"What's done is done. I can help. Send me Project 222's files."

"Without a formal request, that's against the rules." Chinchin's looks bounced off of the many black walls to remind her friend that they were never alone. That the walls were recording everything that went on in the Labs. And if they broke a rule, it wouldn't go unnoticed.

"Break them," Chauson whispered, swiftly moving in and squeezing Chinchin's hand for half a second. She felt his breath on her ear. Without looking down, Chinchin felt him press a small rectangular slab into her hand. She knew what it was. She looked around at the solid Obsidian V walls, an uninvited but ever-present audience.

"Okay, Chauson. This is my stop," she said, careful not to agree to his plan out loud—not that she had agreed to it at all.

"Send them to me. Tonight," Chauson whispered with a confidence no 16 year old should have mastered, and then he disappeared and left Chinchin in her office where Lana was still examining samples under a microscope. Chinchin sat down at her desk. She took a quick peek at the slab Chauson had snuck into her hand. A small piece of Obsidian V, but with no reflection. In her hand, it was simply a small, rectangular matte stone. But she knew its purpose. As long as she held it in her hand, she would be invisible to the eyes of the wall. She could sneak around or access and send files without being noticed. It made sense that he would have these, given who his parents were. She quickly slipped the stone into her pocket, and then placed her hands flat on her desk.

Like all furniture, Chinchin's desk was grown and connected and ready to change into whatever shape that her lab work demanded. If she needed a taller desk, a soundproof pod, or a bed for a power nap, she only needed to request it through the surface of her desk and it would become that thing. On top of the black desk was white paper with black writing. And on top of the inked details were quick-to-dry and nonsensical loopty-loops and X's drawn over and over until all shapes were lost to the blackness. It was not like Chinchin to doodle her blank pages into a black oblivion. She didn't feel like herself. Sure, she always seemed confident on the outside for the most part, but the insides of her had changed. On the inside, Chinchin was burnt out. Details that wouldn't normally fall through the cracks were starting to escape her.

"Lights!" Chinchin stood up as she realized something very important. Her black block of a chair receded back into the ground to avoid being bumped into by Chinchin's sudden start. Chinchin headed for the door.

"Where are you going?" Lana asked.

"Send Scouts to Boris's pod immediately."

"What? 54's pod? Why?" Lana asked, startled.

"Boris doesn't have a sister!" Chinchin shouted as she rushed out of her lab room with the ends of her black lab coat fluttering as she ran.

———

Chinchin was still running when she made it down to the lab's dormitories even though she knew in her blood that she was too late. She passed by the identical black-cubed homes that were clustered together, her reflection shimmering as she continued.

She stopped at Boris' homepod as she called out his name. The door was open. Shadow Scouts, the official guards for Pagra, including its Labs, were already inside. The guards covered in black from the top of their helmet to the steel toe plates of their shoes were standing around a fixture above, using black, shiny tools to record the incident.

"Who are you?" A Shadow Scout asked.

"86."

"Did you know 54?"

"He's one of the test subjects in Project 222. I'm a scientist assigned to the project." Chinchin caught a glimpse of Boris' bare feet through the doorway. They were level with her eyes. She paused and looked up to see the poor, sisterless man hanging from the ceiling fixture —a black chandelier. *No.* She thought. *Not another one.* Another test subject lost to the mysterious suicidal tendencies her mutation was causing. Maybe the academy should have held her back instead of listening to her demands to graduate early and work on her project in the Labs.

"I need to examine the body," Chinchin said.

"Not possible."

"I'm 86. I work on labs 52, 53, and 55 for Project 222. I'm looking at the body of my test subject."

The Shadow paused. Chinchin stared fiercely into the tinted shield over the man's face, but could only see her angry eyes in the reflection staring back. She knew he was examining information on his side of the screen.

"You may proceed."

"I know," she said, brushing his shoulder coldly as she stepped inside.

Chinchin approached the body. She studied Boris' lifeless face, circling the corpse. She took his hands in hers and examined his fingertips. Only four fingernails remained of the 10 fingers. It was a strange and unexplainable side effect of her synthetic mutation. The previous five test subjects who had died had also been missing fingernails. Chinchin looked up once more at the man who died by her creation.

She remembered how excited he was to volunteer as part of Project 222. Without the injection and the mutation it caused in its subjects, Nylos were the ones choosing who was "worthy" of Matching. They singled out a human being if it suited them. And sometimes they never chose a human to bond with, which in Chinchin's opinion, was the biggest waste of magic of all. All of their power a human could leverage, but if a Nylo didn't match with them, it was just untapped power that was never used.

Like inert animals, Nylos came in many species. Some flew, some swam, some rolled. And the power they had was always related to their species—but the power a Matched human could harness was always unique to the combination of the Nylo themselves and the human they chose. So when Boris first joined the program, his one request was that his first Nylo he Matched with be from a Nylo that was deeply related to water. He had wanted to be able to wield water like he had seen others do. So Chinchin had found him an Octopus that was covered in golden scales. When Boris Matched with the Nylo, their bond was unique. And the power the Octopus had given him was the ability to essentially squirt water from his ears. It was a strange result of a Match, and Chinchin was rather disappointed in seeing the magic be used in such a pointless way... but Boris—who had loved water in all forms—was delighted with the Match.

"I'm sorry, Boris," she said. It was a sincere expression. She let go of his hand and walked out into her small neighborhood, slowly retracing her steps and returning to stare at the report in her office she had scribbled over.

She placed her hand in her lab coat pocket, fingering the small shard of Obsidian V Chauson had given her.

Six were now dead, but there was a way to save the rest of the people who were still a part of her experiment and injected with the serum that allowed them to Match with a Nylo of their choosing. She just needed a little more time to figure out what the hell was happening, to shine a light in the darkness... and reluctantly, she knew she could use all of the help she could get—even if it meant breaking the rules.

CHAPTER 4

THE PARADE

CANDLAND

The third day came without the first heir of Questus to be found, and the thought of Keyes having fled beyond Questus borders was starting to set in. Candland watched quietly from the shadows as his mother, having sent every abled set of legs that served her to search the grounds, coordinated with her inner circle on how to control the confusion. What was the story for her child? Nerves on hosting the Pre Ceremony for the first time? Keyes could hardly resist commanding a crowd when he came across one, but the story—nevermind the character—was believable. It could, the queen considered, even be seen as endearing in a way.

Candland didn't care about telling the right story. He couldn't begin to think of telling a story when the story unfolding before him made no sense. He only wanted to deal with one story at a time. Keyes had left, and he hadn't come back. And as Candland stood in his studio, getting materials ready for a new sculpture, he wondered about his brother. And as the minutes passed, he wondered about wondering about his brother. How long would he not know where his brother went and why? Would Keyes show up in the next minute at the top of the stairs? Would he come back when he was an old man, or would he never come back at all? Candland didn't know. So he began preparation for his next sculpture: the elephant.

Of course this had to be done while multitasking. His tutor stood with a straight spine that seemed incapable of bending, waiting for Candland to answer his last question.

"Isn't it funny that you have to ask the prince himself about the governing body that serves him?" He rarely brought up his title, but when he did, it was to chastise and tease his tutors. A minor form of rebellion that would be allowed with all of the aftermath of his missing brother.

"It isn't funny. It's necessary," his tutor insisted. "And I might add that the prince is stalling because perhaps he's not as familiar with the Blood Council as he pretends to be."

"The Blood Council acts as advisors to the crown, making up 12 distinct governing bodies that they oversee."

"And what are these 12 areas?" the tutor inquired further.

"For the love of Blood! My brother's missing and you want me to recite the roles of the council?"

"Today, you are the only heir that stands in the palace. Please, entertain your teacher. What is the first counselor managing again these days?"

Candland swallowed. Though he didn't like to talk, he didn't like to hear the reality of the situation with what his brother's absence meant even more. So it was time to talk. "The Blood and Spirit. They cover temples, worship, and the Blood Chambers—a sacred place where only direct family are allowed. Second, The Commerce. Economic growth, business, and labor. Third, The Crown. Royal estate management, staff, and the family lineage."

Candland lifted a hand from the stone that he had been thumbing and put his hand briefly over his chest as if he were performing.

"Fourth, The Cursed. Marker and Marked Control, this would include the The Questus Treatment Center for the Cursed. Fifth, The Defense. Soldiers, guards, the equipment they use to arm our castle with. Next, The Diplomacy. Foreign affairs, representatives, immigration. Basically the folks who ignore the fact that the Tunnels exist... Where was I? Oh, The Distribution. Blood, blessings, and allotment. Westahn manages those procedures where one of us royals blesses blood so that anyone can drink it and reap the powers it carries. Eighth, The Events. They are in charge of the community, the celebrations, but they're most pressed now, during the week of the Blood Ceremony. Ninth, The Health. Medicine, healing, and recovery. Still second rate compared to The House of Haessig is what I hear. Tenth is The Justice. Loyalty, rewards, and punishment. Eleventh is The Sustenance. Agriculture, inert animals, supplies, trade. They manage our relationship with Makani when the island is floating somewhere above us. And twelve. The Teachings. Education, theology, missionaries, and, ah. You."

"You recited them in an incorrect order than the script," his teacher said after a pause.

"I decided to go alphabetically. So teachings came last," A smile landed on Candland's lips for a shy second as he eyed his teacher, and then it disappeared and his gaze returned to his stone.

"You're clever like your brother," the tutor said.

"We both know I'm nothing like him."

"Two sides of the same stone." His teacher gestured to the rock in his student's hand. "Perhaps one side is light and the other dark. But still the same stone."

"I take it I'm the side without the sun?" Candland smiled, raising his eyebrows at his teacher.

The tutor opened his mouth and then closed it. Then he opened it again ready to speak, but was interrupted by a third voice.

"Undeniably so."

Candland turned to find Westahn walking in among his sculptures.

"Ah, The Distribution. We were just talking about

you," Candland said, his eyes already back on the stone he was running his hands along—getting to know the cool material before he began his work.

"It sounds like we were talking about you, and your… darkness. Anyways. I came to let you know that the Queen asked that the lessons be finished early today. Prince Candland's brother is missing and though education is, of course, important, she would like him to do what Keyes would most undoubtedly be doing right now: prayer."

The tutor nodded, bowed, and left Candland's sanctuary. It was clear to Candland that his tutor didn't need to be told twice to leave.

"My mother asked for me to pray?"

"Maybe. I lied."

"Why?"

"Perhaps it's *my* dark side," he smiled. "What's this next piece going to be?"

"An elephant."

"One of the greater inert animals," Westahn nodded.

"Maybe I *should* be praying," Candland said.

"It would be what your brother would be doing right now… but you're not him."

"Why are you here, Westahn?"

"Can't I come for a visit to gaze upon your art?"

Candland didn't answer.

"Your mother did send me up here actually. She wanted me to tell you that if your brother isn't found before the half moon, your own royal Blood ceremony will be expedited."

"For blessing the Blood...? But I'm only 16. I have to be at least 18 to bless or drink anything."

"These are unprecedented times. Or, they will be if we don't find your brother. You may need to step up."

"But... I'm... I'm..."

"You're the Prince of Questus. And when it comes time to be there for your people and do what's right, you'll know."

"I'm not ready."

"I'll be there too. It'll be okay."

"Keyes. He was meant for all of this. He's been waiting for this. He's actually old enough and already had his own Blood ceremony!"

"What we were meant for and what we become are two different things."

"He'll come back."

"Maybe he will. But if he doesn't. Half moon. The Distribution will need to distribute. People rely on the power from the Blood. And I'll need your help to make sure they have what they need to keep the kingdom running."

Westahn put a hand on Candland's shoulder squeezing it tight before he walked away. As Candland listened to Westahn's footsteps grow quieter, he wondered what blood tasted like. Of course he had wanted his brother to return since he had been missing, but now he wanted that more than ever. He shuddered at the idea of pressing the red liquid to his lips like he had seen Keyes do at his own ceremony on his brother's day —the day he turned 18 years old.

And that's when Candland heard something from the open terrace to his left. He turned, looking past some of his artwork, eyeing the wide banister and open sky. He saw a figure. His brother had come back. And to see him first, too.

To the left of the shadow, an owl flew in, swooping in gracefully so that the ends of its feathers from its spread wings swept the ground just before it landed on its large talons. Its eyes were yellow and circular, with eyebrows made for anger. Candland's steps quickened. It wasn't Keyes. He saw the dark figure approach. Light steps, thick leather straps around the shoulders and torso, and a smug smile below smug eyebrows.

"Rocky!" Candland exclaimed. He rushed forward and wrapped his arms around the boy who stood a few inches shorter than him. Just like he remembered, hugging Rocky was like hugging a stone. His body was light, but solid with wiry limbs. Rocky grinned widely under golden irises, showing straight white teeth. Under his bushy, black hair, he wore these ridiculous leather strapped goggles for flying. It wasn't until he saw his friend's smile that Candland realized he had missed him so much.

Candland then remembered himself and the circumstances that had made Rocky's visit to his kingdom quite risky. Rocky was a lethal Nylo Guardian from Nevarra—

an assassin who was sworn to protect all Nylos. And the general's son, no less. He looked around to see if anyone had seen Rocky fly in.

"What are you doing here?" Candland whispered.

Rocky's grin quickly disappeared. "Actually, I came to deliver some news."

"Is it about my brother?"

"No. I did hear about that on my way in. Sorry about... him," Rocky sighed. Then he walked out to the edge of the terrace and placed his hands securely on the stone railing. Candland eyed his left arm, Marked by his Nylo, a golden owl named Berns. The long winding, yellow-glowing Mark reminded Candland of a fire. "It's about my sister."

"Is she back?" Candland turned and leaned on the edge of the terrace with his hands on the railing. He was still looking about, failing to be casual. While playing with Rocky when Candland was younger, his sister would walk up with wide hips and a loud stance he couldn't ignore. He was still so young then and hadn't understood the tingling on his neck whenever she had ruffled his hair and laughed.

"She's dead," Rocky said.

Candland wanted to ask Rocky to repeat himself, but he had heard the words clearly. The news took all language away from Candland's lips.

"We're still investigating."

"Was it... a mission?" His sister was a Nylo Guardian as well. He knew they went out on missions all the time.

He ached for her laugh, for her smile, for the attention she showed him as his best friend's older sister. His mouth suddenly felt dry.

"...Yeah. We were on a mission. All that was left to do was escape. We were all clear, and then she just stopped and turned and walked into a river. She... had a bomb. I saw her activate it. Her skin and bones disappeared in front of me. Just fire," Rocky's eyes were dry, but his lips quivered slightly before he bit down on them.

"She did it on purpose?"

"Something was wrong with her. It all looks like suicide to everyone. But it's not. You knew Maya. That's not her. Something went wrong."

"What do you mean?" Candland was remembering her more clearly now. She was... powerful. Ambitious. Willing to risk her life to save the Nylos.

"She didn't kill herself," Rocky's eyes stretched under his furrowed eyebrows to make his point. "I know what it sounds like. But I was there. I could show you if you want." Rocky lifted his Marked hand to touch Candland's head. Candland watched the Mark on Rocky's hand begin to glow gold, and Rocky's eyes also glowed with the same color. Rocky's Nylo gave him the unique power that allowed him to share his memories or read memories just by a touch. Not everyone who had Matched with that species of owl had the same power—it all was a product of the Nylo and the individual. Every power was unique in its own way.

"That's okay." Candland took a step back. He didn't

want to see it. He only wanted the memories of Maya he had cherished over the years, and nothing more. "Will there be a funeral?"

Rocky's eyes returned to normal and his Mark went dormant as well. "My father's preparing for the ceremony. It'll be in Nevarra for the next eight-star line night. I know it's during your celebrations, but you're welcome to the funeral. My father knows I'm here."

Candland didn't say anything. Leaving for Nevarra of all places when his brother was missing just wasn't possible.

"I know how you felt about her," Rocky said.

"I'll be there," Candland said quickly. He'd figure out the logistics later. "Rocky. I'm sorry."

"It's part of being an NG," Rocky bit down on his bottom lip again and looked away. "That's just how it is. Now, what about your brother? He ran away?"

"He ran away."

"Why?"

"I don't know. We were in the Pre Ceremony. It was his first time hosting—he's 18 this year. He took the petal and... he just ran away."

"You don't know where he went?"

"I'm just now beginning to realize he really left."

"Your mother?"

"Trying to pretend like it's not a big deal... and then find him before the news gets too far past the kingdom walls."

"Everyone else?"

"Well, no sacrifice has been announced."

Rocky turned around and leaned his hip on the railing. "Must be sooo tough not knowing which Marked will be drained by the neck."

"You should come in and sit inside. Someone might see you," Candland said, ignoring Rocky's comment.

"I'll fly away if they do," Rocky shrugged. Rocky lit a smoke. Candland could smell the foreign spices. He leaned in to get a whiff of the sweet aroma with a bitter note at the end of his inhale.

"I can't fly away. And I'll get in trouble too."

"What? You can't hang out with your ol' Nevarrian buddy?" Rocky held out the roll to his friend who happened to live in enemy territory.

"It's frowned upon," Candland smiled and took it. He took a deep inhale and held the smoke in his lungs. He loved the bitter ending of each breath as much as he did the sweetness in the beginning. He looked out. He was in the far corner of the castle, tucked up and away, but was granted the height to see out past the outer wall. It was his favorite place in the world, though he had never gone far beyond Questus. Rocky's owl, Berns, flew to the railing and Candland gently stroked his feathery head. He felt he could be himself around Rocky, but there was always the thought of his mother's disapproval of his friend that loomed over him.

"So my sister's dead and your brother's missing," Rocky said. "Well. It's all just going to shit. Isn't it?"

"Total shit," Candland agreed. He handed the friendly token back to Rocky after another deep inhale.

"I want to go back and find out what happened to Maya. What really happened."

"How?"

"I'll go back to Pagra. She was really close with one of the scientists at their lab. Some prodigy that made a breakthrough with the Nylos. I think she knows something. The only problem is I can't get too close. They know my face."

"Then sneak in like you always do, *NG*."

"Questus is a lot easier to snoop around in. It's not just the people you have to hide from in Pagra. Even their stones have eyes... But... they don't know your face."

"That's because I've never been... because, oh yeah, last time I checked, my family's their sworn enemy."

"You could come with me and we could find out what really happened to Maya together. No one knows your face. You could be my guy. My in."

It was true. His parents were easily identifiable. Keyes was recognizable. Candland... wasn't. Rocky had had this question tucked away all along.

"C'mon," Rocky said. "I know how you felt about her. Don't you want to know what really happened?"

"I'm sorry, Rocky. I'm not a Nylo Guardian like you. I'd be caught and executed within 15 minutes of being inside their borders. And I can't leave with my brother missing."

"You're just afraid."

"Um... Yeah."

"You're working in your studio. What are you making? Some non-Nylo lump of a creature?"

"It's an elephant," Candland said sharply.

"Ditch the inert animal. Come with me. No one would even know you were gone."

Also true. It still hurt though.

"I'd know. As the only prince in Questus right now, I need to stay." Candland hardened, and so did Rocky. Candland thought of the conversation he had had with Westahn and the duty he may need to perform in order to keep the distribution of blood going while Keyes was away. Without someone with royal blood to bless the newly collected blood, no one in the kingdom could drink it and use the power of the Blood. Their guards wouldn't have the blood to drink to strengthen their defenses. And even the civilians who used the Blood's many different powers to maintain their way of life from farming and irrigation to construction and medicine wouldn't be able to do so. It hurt to think of what kept their kingdom going, and it was impossible to bring up with Rocky. It was Marked blood Candland would have to drink to be able to bless the rest of the Blood. It was Marked blood that he would bless and the power of the Marked that was pulled from the blood that would be used for the kingdom. Sometimes Candland forgot that Rocky was Marked. Othertimes, Candland wondered how Rocky could ever have let a friendship with someone like him come about.

"I came here because we're friends. I thought you'd help me," Rocky said. His stance was straight, arms crossed.

"We are friends, but I can't go to Pagra. It would be a sui—," Candland didn't stop himself in time and so he let the last words go quietly. "Suicide mission."

"Okay. I see how it is. I'll go myself," Rocky pushed through his hands and leapt up so he stood on the railing. He balanced effortlessly and fearlessly on the edge of what Candland could only guess was hundreds of feet. Even though he knew Rocky was an assassin, Candland worried he might slip.

"Rocky... Don't go. Stay here and we can go to the funeral together."

"How can I honor her death until I know what happened? Look... Nevermind. I'll see you at the funeral," Rocky looked at Candland with what could only be recognized as disappointment. Then he casually stepped off the ledge, coming into a freefall. Berns skimmed Candland's head so that his feathers pricked Candland's ear. Then the magical oversized owl dipped down towards his Marked. Candland watched over the railing as the large bird's claws aggressively snatched Rocky's leather straps wrapped around his shoulders, and his best friend flew through the air like the shadow of an angel.

It had been two long weeks since Candland had visited the Tunnels. He had promised he would return that day, but needed a night to himself after Rocky flew from his balcony. He had hidden himself away in his bedroom where he took a break from chiseling stone and instead massaged wet clay in his hands for hours upon hours. He kept out of his mother's way, and he did not hear from her since he had made his way up to his studio earlier that morning.

The seclusion of his art space was his sanctuary, but even a lone wolf can't survive without other creatures. He had to get out. Like he always did before he headed for the Tunnels, Candland removed his loud ornaments and patches that could garner too much attention and give his identity away while he was underground. His cloak was the exception. It was black on the outside and Questonian red on the inside, and the family emblem was small and uniform at his throat. It wasn't uncommon for the average folk—even in the Tunnels— to wear a jewel that dawned the Questus emblem, a rose with a single long, curved thorn. After all, many of those who called the Tunnels home had belonged to Questus once upon a time.

He rode horseback towards the Tunnels. Rocky wasn't fond of inert animals, but Candland liked them all very much, magic or no magic. Especially when he compared them to people. He rode through the outskirts of Questus, west towards Soonja—the last village in Questus territory before the Wontine Desert. In the beginning of his trip, Candland was surrounded by trees fit for a charming forest, complete with the sounds of woodland creatures and their pleasant song. And then the forest thicket abruptly became sand. This is where the desert began just as suddenly as the forest ended. Behind Candland were rolling fields, meadows, and trees; and in front of him was a desolate desert with only rocks and spiked, bulbed plants for deviation. This meant Soonja was only a couple hours' ride away, and the Tunnels even less.

He knew little about the village of Soonja, come to think of it. Questonians were generally blue-eyed, blonde-haired, and pale, but not in Soonja. As the last village to be conquered by Questus, they were known to be a different and stubborn people. They were one of the few territories Questus had, for the most part, left alone. Soonjis kept their language. They kept their culture. All under the agreement that they would be the official look out for Questus—being the first village a Pagra invasion would meet from across the desert.

Finally, the second prince of Questus arrived at the Tunnels. A traveler or stranger to this area wouldn't know it. All they would see was a vast desert. Since riding on the treeless land, Candland had felt the air turn dry. He noticed the soft ground had turned hard, cracked, and barren under the hooves of his horse. The sudden change comforted Candland. He was a shadow getting closer to the darkness.

He loved the change in environments and how immediate and unexplainable the change was. Candland had heard the Tunnels were cursed, and the abruptness of the forest ending was to show for it. But what did being cursed really mean to him when he was so drawn to the places and people his guardians had always said were marked with evil? Perhaps that's why he and his brother were never able to be as close as he was with Rocky. Candland was drawn too much to temptation when Keyes despised it.

"The Tunnels belong to the demons as does everyone who visits," his brother had once said. (His mother never spoke about it because she simply did not acknowledge these evils in case that would make them more real.) What did belonging to the demons really mean? Some days, Candland thought it meant isolation and loneliness, but from his experience, it meant freedom. All of the above didn't sound so terrible to him.

Though so close to Questus that some may even consider it a part of the kingdom, the Tunnels was a whole other world. It existed underground, with the only way in and out through quicksand. It was the perfect hiding place for some... and escape for others.

Candland's horse stepped nonchalantly onto what looked like more sand in a vast desert. This patch of sand, if one looked closely, swirled. Constantly sinking, it swallowed, first the horse whole, then Candland. They landed softly on the other side of the world onto a pile of sand with more sand still trickling down onto their heads as if they had just passed through the center of an hourglass.

Candland shook his head side to side, and his horse followed. Candland dusted off a clump of sand that had latched onto his horse's mane, then dusted off his own shoulders as they walked away from the sand portal above.

They walked down a trail in the bold darkness that was custom for the Tunnels. The sun was not directly above them, so no light shone down through the desert ground. But with the darkness came an oceanic-like world that was full of shrub and weed made of bright neon colors that no plant above ground could compare to. The plants along the path shone brightly, some even blinked with strobe-like petals in bold pinks, yellows, greens, and blues. So bright was the wildlife that the Tunnels felt more awake than the bright sunlit desert above. The surrounding darkness, just near enough to escape and hide if needed, comforted Candland in a way he could not replicate above ground.

As the two made it down towards the center of the Tunnels together, the path became more crowded. The blonde hair and white skin that was common at Questus was painted over with different dyes in every color imaginable. Not many people recognized him above ground, but below ground, everyone was busy with their own look. Everyone was figuring out who they were, and that didn't leave any time for them to figure out who others were. To everyone in an underworld full of nobodies, he was no one.

Many people walked with dyed hair and painted skin

that matched their surroundings. Fashion was futuristic, colorful and yet mysterious. Clothes were sleek silhouettes, often cropped at the navel and sleeves. Showing off shoulders or stomachs was loudly frowned upon in Questus. It was easy to tell Pagra's influence had traveled below though it never made its way within Questus' walls. Candland wore all dark colors that blended with the darkness in between all of the colors of the Tunnels. His cloak was etched with the only significant and royal detail where the hood was latched together by the metallic rose.

With each step he took from the quicksand passage, he felt the world above, the world of Questus and all the royal responsibilities and duty tied along with it, dampened. Even his missing brother and Maya's death seemed more like a dream. It relaxed him, and what better way to complement relaxation than with a drink? No. Not yet. He thought. His drink wouldn't be alone.

When Ava didn't answer her door, Candland headed to the bridge. It had been Ava's spot, but over time, it had become theirs. Seeing Ava sitting on the bridge with her legs hanging off the parapet calmed him. The glowing plants gave her long, brown hair neon green and purple highlights, and it also made the green Mark on her cheek even more vibrant. It was rare for a Mark to appear on the face—*An unfortunate location even for the cursed* he could hear his mother say—but Candland couldn't imagine the Nylo's symbol to have been placed anywhere else on Ava.

Identical to the green that marked her face, was the

green skin on Axol. He was a mostly white, sparkling salamander with green on the bridge of his nose and circular eyebrows. The jade color was also splashed along his strange external gill-like mane and nimble feet. Axol was the first to notice Candland. The Nylo darted over, white and green sparkles tracing his path like a mist. Like most times, Axol struggled to stop in time and crashed directly into Candland's chest. Candland barely managed to cradle the axolotl in his hands in time to keep the creature from hurting himself.

Ava looked over, and then she smiled.

"Gannick!" she waved.

He waved back and made his way beside her on the bridge.

"Where were you yesterday? You said you'd come then..." Ava bit her lip. She looked as if she wanted to say more. Surprisingly, she didn't.

"Sorry. I had something come up."

"Is everything okay?"

"Don't want to talk about it. Here. I have something for you."

"Deflecting the conversation with a gift... It's working," she smiled.

Candland rummaged in the large pockets of his cloak. He pulled out a small gift and opened his hand slowly to reveal a small sculpture.

"It's Axol!" Ava said. "You made Axol! Gannick! This is amazing."

Candland extended his open hand, and Ava took the

small figurine. It was heavier than she expected. She fingered the smooth, cool stone.

"It looks just like him," Ava's wide eyes zeroed in on Candland's work.

"That's kind of what I was going for," Candland smiled.

"This is... I—"

"If you look underneath, I carved..."

"Our Mark... Gannick. Thank you."

"Welcome."

Candland had spent hours on the sculpture making sure it was just right. Axol had large, innocent eyes that were easy to capture. What wasn't as easy was the way he swam in the air, floating in harmony with the ability to zap away like lightning when he was either excited or scared. It was hard to capture such energy, but Candland knew it was some of his best work.

Ava turned the small figurine in her fingers, her eyes studying every detail and then her eyes would return to Candland where it felt like her analysis only intensified. Making the sculpture took time and effort, but giving it to her was much more difficult. Candland tried to hold her gaze, but trying to mirror her earnestness was difficult. He was typically an honest person. He had never planned on a lasting friendship in the Tunnels—especially with a girl—and so using his great, great, great, great grandfather's name to hide his identity hadn't seemed like such a big deal when they had first met. In fact, Candland had thought it clever to choose that name given Gannick was notorious for not following rules himself.

It was time to tell the truth, to tell her who he was. But as he looked at Ava, her hair spiraling with the eerie underground wind, her rose colored cheeks and lips reflecting the lights from their bright surroundings, illuminating the rest of her face in the darkness... he couldn't find the words. He looked down at the miniature Nylo he had created. Would a small stone carving say what he wasn't able to say himself?

A moment had passed and neither of them had seized it. After some time, conversation eased again. Ava and Candland sat with their backs against the bridge's rails. The gift had been accepted, and the pressures around it finally dissolved. The truth, the intimacy, it had subsided for now.

"I've always wanted to ask about the scar on your hand," Ava finally said.

Candland looked at his hand, smiling at the memory of the young and stupid pain he had caused himself.

"If I say I don't want to talk about it...?"

"I'll never ask you about it again... for at least 5 minutes."

"My brother and I were messing around where we shouldn't have been. That's it."

"Go on..."

"Not today, Ava."

Ava looked out over the bridge into the water. Candland waited. He knew she'd keep trying.

"Are you two close now?"

"We were. But not anymore."

"Why not?"

"We're just... different."

"Still. I imagine it's nice to have siblings."

Candland didn't say anything.

"Enough talking for one day?" Ava asked.

Candland nodded. Relieved.

"Then let's go check out the Blood Parade: the Tunnels' edition," Ava stood.

"Is it much different from the parade up there?" Candland followed, holding the reins of his horse. He had never been able to make it to the Tunnels during the week of celebration.

"Hm, well... I've never been to one up above but from what I hear... Like up there, There's still a lot of red down here. Just replace faith with regret and tradition with disrespect."

"Sounds fun," Candland withheld the fact that he loved parades, while also suppressing the question of whether or not there would be elephants present.

Ava turned back. Her brown eyes flooded into Candland's once again, filling them beyond their brim with attention he could hardly bear. He could see something in her eyes. She was on the cusp of saying something... doing something. He tilted his head.

"What?" he asked. "What is it?"

Ava took his hand, and then stopped. She moved in. Candland's entire body tensed as if he was bracing for something. He felt soft lips press against his along with the tickle of eyelashes, and a tingling that shot up and down his bones. He smelled the purple flowers from her bungalow that hung above her windowsill that he had so often looked out of when they were together. Sweet. Floral. Dewy.

Ava pulled away, leaving Candland looking rather unprepared and rather rigid.

"Your green eyes are just... magical," she said. "And... I like you. A lot. A lot. Really. I like you so much." Her cheeks were red with warmth. Then she danced forward on her tiptoes. Candland didn't have time to respond, though he felt like he was floating and wouldn't have been able to respond regardless if he had had more time. He had wanted to be closer to Ava. He had feelings for her too. He just never thought that anyone would feel this way about him. It wasn't that he thought he was hideous or terrible. Just that he believed the gloom Keyes had always referenced that followed him everywhere he went would scare off anyone that might have feelings for him. However, he raised an eyebrow, if anyone could chase the gloom away from him, it was Ava. And it was that moment, he felt his heart pull towards her with a force he had not felt before.

After a few seconds, Candland had processed what had happened and Ava's intentions and feelings. Finally, he felt his body thaw. He wanted to reach out to pull her in again, to show her what a kiss could be with him when he wasn't half terrified, but before his advancement, Ava jetted off, prancing across the bridge, blushing all the way. Axol zigzagged in unison with his Marked, floating jollily over the bridge.

"We don't want to miss the parade!" she called out sheepishly.

Candland swung onto his horse with a grin he couldn't stop. He caught up to Ava and dropped his arm. Ava took it and locked in. He pulled her up as she swung around and she landed behind him, her arms tight around his torso and her warm cheeks tucked into his back between his broad shoulders. Axol flipped around and found comfort on the butt of the horse as they rode towards the noisy, red streets.

Because the landscape above the Tunnels so abruptly turned to a still desert, the common assumption—not just Candland's mother—was that the place itself was cursed. The people of Questus, which included the majority who followed the religion of the Blood to the drop, did not understand how the Tunnels came to be or why anyone was there at all. But their leaders did not talk about it, so they did not either. The Blood was not concerned with it, so neither were they.

However, many still knew what the Tunnels were

somehow. They never spoke about them. They never visited. They didn't know the specifics of the Tunnels or what exactly they were. But what they did know was that it was where their children went when the poor souls lost sight of the Blood. It was a bad place that kept bad secrets. Candland knew all too well that in the prayers of the religious and loyal, there would always be time to pray for their children, friends, and family who had lost their way and visited the Tunnels. He could almost hear his mother's whispering prayers, asking the Blood to spare him and guide him back home where the grass grew thick and did not light up its surroundings with colors of the brightest rainbow.

Candland had his first literal taste of the Tunnels when he drank their glowing concoctions from within the castle walls. It was a wine-like substance with the power of an ox. A single sip had made Candland's mind float cheerfully towards the clouds only to drop him from such a height so that his brain felt as if it had shattered into a thousand pieces. As someone who often found the days flooding by without a single emotion or purpose to recall, the feelings—great and terrible—left him wanting more. With no friends of any sort and no family with a rebellious drop of Blood, he had no one to turn to. So he found and followed the unseemly people who turned their heads to see if anyone was watching.

And that's how he found the underground city of lost children. That's also how he met Rocky, and eventually, Ava.

What a world it had been. Candland remembered the first time he slid through the sandy passages and his eyes adjusted to a fluorescent garden and neon city. Walking about the city for the first time where the nightlife was the only life, he could still recall the feeling. The people who passed by him with their own hairstyles, piercings, and fashion that made each and every person look as if they had appeared from one of the many worlds that were locked behind West Gate. The energy had pricked the hair on Candland's neck as he suddenly realized the potential of what he could look like, who he could be, and who he didn't have to be.

And now, he walked through a crowd in the upside down Blood parade where everyone below celebrated the Blood Ceremony somewhat sarcastically. They were all rebels to the religion, but they never missed a chance to celebrate. The noises and clusters of people would have been too much for him, and the nausea paired with growing stress would have strained through his veins if it weren't for Ava's hand in his. Her wide-eyed looks, her raw, unrehearsed laughter, the feeling of her fingers squeezing his hand every now and then when she looked back. In a sea of anxiety, he floated on a raft with an anchor that had kissed him on the lips only an hour earlier. He felt warm and fuzzy. And he'd had only two drinks so far.

The Blood Parade in the Tunnels was an attempt to be something different... but Candland found the celebration to be the same as above: an excuse to celebrate. A reason to party. There were red Blood flags with the rose symbol on it. Above ground it was waved with pride, below ground it was waved in a kind of defiance. Wine was drunk above ground with pride and respect; it was symbolic. Below ground, a more powerful potion was sacreligious; it was rebellious. Candland was well aware that the people underground despised the Blood and despised the annual sacrifice made (though they didn't mind to speculate).

And he did not blame them. This is where everything he was taught growing up muddied up in his head, where trying to explain that from the crown's view, the Blood allowed them to drink blood from the Marked. This is what powered the Blood's magic. This is what powered their kingdom. Without it, they were vulnerable to other kingdoms. Without it, they were reliant on manual strug-gles that had become obsolete for a hundred years. For Questus, there was no kingdom without it. The Blood, their religion, guided them this way. It simply was.

Candland did not understand it completely either, but his faith, his trust, had been developed with the history of the teachings he was blessed with as a prince. *A king must do what is necessary for his people—and the people might not always understand*, is what his father used to tell him. Candland had come to accept this: A king must do what was necessary for his son—and the son might not always understand. A king would only make such a sacrifice if it was necessary. . . All of the reasons always started with a king, which was ironic because the only one doing things in today's Questus was the queen.

Ava squeezed Candland's hand, and brought him back. They darted nimbly through the crowd. Candland now walked his horse with the reins loosely held by his scarred hand. Candland saw the many eyes—mostly blue—swim around many other eyes. With the lights of the street, the lamps powered by gels, and the decorations, he had never seen the Tunnels so busy. Ava turned back, Candland saw her green Mark shimmer at the reflection of the parade. With Axol whipping through the air just between them. Ava locked eyes. Ava smiled and Candland blushed involuntarily in return. It was this moment, this look, the way the light reflected off of her body, it was exactly how he wanted to remember Ava. Whenever he would hear her name, whenever he would think of her, whenever she came up, he wanted to think of her in that moment. *What would I name the Ava in this very second, in this very place? Parade Ava? The Most Festive Soul in all of the Festivities Ava? The Squeezes my Hand When I Need Reassurance Ava?*

Candland would wish he had decided sooner—that he had titled that Ava in time, and locked the memory away. Perfect and untarnished by what was about to happen in the next second.

Ava, who led Candland by the hand had turned quickly to share a glance and smile with him. Maybe she had wanted to turn and see him in that very second and very place too. Maybe she wanted a keepsake from what had seemed like the most wonderful night in Candland's life. He had forgotten his brother's disappearance and even Maya's mysterious death—something he would realize with guilt about later.

When she turned her head back towards the direction she was walking, a rather large man had bumped into her. In the chaos of the celebration and the size of the man's stomach, it was clear it was a badly timed accident where the crowd had no intentions of being cautious or careful or delicate, and the man had no spatial awareness or means to have seen Ava coming in the spiraling group of people charging every which way to try and advance on the street. Ava's light, bubbly skipping 15-year-old body had been sent careening sideways. She somehow dodged so many bodies, just grazing past everyone without control, until she crashed into a cart. Even through all of the parade's noise, Candland heard a sharp cracking noise. Candland saw a glittering white and green blur dart after her. Axol. Candland immediately turned to his left and squirmed through the unaware parties. He was only vaguely aware that he had lost his horse in the commotion.

He saw Ava on the ground. His eyes then found one of the long wooden cart handles snapped in half from Ava's body being temporarily turned into a human cannon by a fat man's belly. That had been the crackling noise. Perhaps she hadn't broken any bones. Candland exhaled. The cart owner selling sparklers and other such small contraptions that lit up the Tunnels wasn't as relieved.

Ava was dazed, confused, and slow to get her breath back. It was an accident that could have been a harmless thing if her body or the cart had been only a few inches to the left or right. But the inches were not in her favor. Candland rushed and took her hand to pull her to her feet, but then he dropped it, letting it fall back down to her side. Ava breathed, but said nothing when Candland searched her eyes rabidly for an explanation.

He saw something he had never seen before. Ava's arm had been hurt. Though he couldn't find the source, he knew the cut was narrow but, judging from the blood, it was deep. She had hurt her head too. Blood stained her hairline and flowed slowly down to her eyebrow where it collected.

She bled green.

"IT'S AN ATROX!" the cart owner shouted, pointing at Ava. His hands were pulled up to his face in disgust. Only a few heads turned at first. Candland, who had been crouched over Ava, stood up and backed away. He saw the faces scan Ava's crash landing. They were now realizing what he and the cart owner had realized in real time.

"The Atrox destroyed my cart!" the cart owner shouted again. Everyone surrounding Ava had now locked onto her. She struggled, but finally stood up. The way her arms shook when she pushed herself caught Candland's attention. He somehow knew that that's how he would remember Ava. The weak, shaking girl who bled green and pulled herself out of a damaged sparkler's cart, would be the image ingrained in his mind for a long time. Ava staggered as the crowd had stopped pushing forward to follow along with the parade, and instead formed a perfect semi-circle around her. Axol fluttered around like a fly on a distracted and confused mission. The murmurs of disgust and disbelief grew. Candland looked down at his fingers. A few small drops of green blood had transferred onto his own hands. He looked up.

A man took Ava's wrist into his arm and raised it high over her head, exposing her deeply green blood to the others.

"A bloody Atrox! An Earther!" he said. He spat on her. Another man came in and punched her in the gut, causing her to drop free and keel over. A woman rushed up, bright and blue-eyed like a Questonian native, and snatched Ava by the hair and pulled so that Ava's head was yanked up and she stood up straight again to sustain another blow that sent her back quickly to the ground.

Candland had never seen an Atrox before. He didn't know anyone else who had either. He had only heard the whispers of the terrible breed. The disgusting race. The intruders. The trespassers. The mendicant, stealing, dishonest, dishonorable kind that snuck through the Gatekeeper's portal from a place called Earth. Those terrible people with the green blood.

Candland had frozen just long enough for the most enraged and, thus most fearful, to close in on the Atrox.

The first wave of shock had worn off. When Candland was able to move once more, it was too late. He could not get to her. The people were too many and the need for their own sacrifice, having been robbed one this week already with his brother's failure to produce one, too great. Candland helplessly wrestled and shouted... and after so much struggle as he was swept further and further away from Ava, his angry shouts turned into small, quiet, whimpering apologies. His hand remembered what it felt like only minutes ago to drop her hand after he spotted the color of her blood. It burned as he thought about what the sensations of holding on would have felt like.

Candland somehow stumbled his way back up through the Tunnels, vaguely aware that he no longer had his horse. Numb, he made his way to the river that flowed towards Questus where he stepped onto a ferry. He wasn't sure if he had made it out from underground in a matter of minutes or if he had wandered about in the faceless crowds for hours before finally making his way to the small ferry on the water. His mind had shut down, but he had made it to where he needed to go. He found that he was always quite good with direction, even when he wasn't trying to be.

He had never taken the ferry before though he had heard Rocky mention them. Candland always preferred riding his horse. He winced as he realized he had left the inert animal behind. He did not have the strength to turn back, and he knew it was wrong. But he couldn't go back down to the Tunnels. He just couldn't. And so he rode silently, his eyes staring out in the distance at nothing.

He never found Ava that night. To Questus, an Atrox was even more degraded and repulsive than Nylos and the humans that Matched with them. Actually to the entire Cache, their kind were a disgrace. Their death should have equaled that of a mosquito or wasp—the riddance of an annoying and harmful... thing. And yet, all he could think about was holding onto Ava's hand. The repulsion that had been trained into him from a child was now overpowered by the repulsion for himself. And so he sat quiet, stretching his useless hand, scarred for his brother and too weak to hold onto Ava.

Being the only one on the small raft with the man who paddled him forward, Candland guessed everyone had to still be celebrating, and he was first to leave the nightmare of a party. Still, he was relieved to, for the most part, be alone. The time passed with Candland's body sitting in a tight ball. His head only peeked out when he saw something through the brush. He rubbed his dry, salty eyes for a better look. Metal links... figures. He finally focused to realize he was looking at fences from a distance. Actually, they were cages full of people and animals alongside the river.

"What is that?" Candland asked the ferryman, his only company on the ride home.

"It's the penitentiary for the Marked. The Blood's guard collects them. Never seen them so full."

"I've been out here so many times, but I've never seen them."

"They keep them close to the river for transportation. The royal family likes to keep them hidden away from the roads. It's an ugly they like to forget about until the Blood Ceremony. Say, can't imagine what the Queen is doing without a Marked to sacrifice for this year. Wonder if they'll choose someone by the end of the week? It's always fun when they're foreign. Say, what do you think the Nylo will be?"

"Stop."

"What?"

"Stop the boat."

"It's a ferry."

"Doesn't matter. I'd like to get off here."

"In the middle of the Cages, man? You're not even halfway to Questus."

"Stop. I'll pay you double."

"...And we've reached our destination. Thanks for riding with us today."

The small ferry came to a halt and Candland jumped off as the captain was throwing out guesses of which Nylo would die next with its Matched human. *The flying lion—with the wings last year? That was glorious to watch fall. Such a beast. Too bad they're full of that dark, Bloodless magic.*

Candland marched up to the Cages, a place he had

heard of, seen in paintings and sketches, but never with his own eyes until that night. The faster his legs moved, the less he could hear the speculation of the chatty captain. As weak as he had felt before, when his eyes had cast themselves on the camps of his own royal family, he suddenly felt he hadn't enough muscle for the energy he had left to exert.

He was denied access when he first asked to enter what was officially named The Questus Treatment Center for the Cursed—but more appropriately nick-named the Cages. Then he took a deep breath and bellowed from his stomach, imitating the way Keyes spoke when he demanded something. He showed the throat of his cloak with the family emblem, and the small window slammed and the large door was thrown back.

Candland had concocted a shaky story of being sent personally by the queen to check in on things. It was so early in the morning that dawn was yet an hour away—a strange time to be checked on. But the risk of questioning a prince was too great. So the headmaster obliged, though reluctantly. He walked Candland through the outdoor encampment. His eyelids drooped and his lips smacked when he opened them to speak.

"The Marked are behind the fences. And their Markers are in the cages."

"What about those people? They're in cages too."

"Some Marked have powers that need to be contained in different ways. Some are in cages, some in iceboxes, others in hot metal... whatever it takes to keep them from escaping. Like your majesty, the Queen, asked, of course."

"There are so many," Candland said. "I've seen drawings. I never realized how big these places were."

"Many are Matched, but many of the Nylos we caught in the wild. We know it pleases your Queen when we catch the cursed Markers before they take control of a human. But we're over capacity. Yes. The Queen has approved new plans to build and expand to make up for that. So we make do for now and are grateful for her hand in allowance for more space. The Blood knows we need it."

Candland again compared what he had learned from his education about the Cages to what he saw. The people in cages were covered in dirt and could hardly raise their arms, there was so little room. Candland saw many different emotions across the prisoners: rage, desperation, sadness, nothing. He came across some of the Markings on the bodies. He thought if Ava had been caught in the name of the Blood and his mother, she would be put in a cage like this. It was a good thing she never learned who he really was. Then he thought of why she would *never* learn who he was, and his mood darkened.

There was a large container, plenty big for an inert elephant or bigger. Its metal walls were bolted shut, with blood-soaked chains wrapped around it in a once-frantic manner as if the job had been rushed. Whatever was inside moved, and the walls rumbled. Candland took a step back as he felt the ground shake.

"What's in there?" Candland paused.

"Ah. Don't worry. The beast can't get out. It's our thickest metal. The chains were magicked by one of the Blood Council themselves. That's our biggest cage for the worst of them. Killed a dozen of our men before The Council arrived to close the walls. Look, see. There's no doors."

"How does it... eat?" Candland asked, his neck craned up searching for some opening contraption.

"Someone from the council visits every fortnight or so. He unlocks the chains and tosses in some scraps."

"Don't they need to eat more often?"

"We're in the business of catching them and treating them, Prince Candland. Not feeding them."

"How is he being... cured?"

"This one's been sold already. We will have to move it ourselves, but Makani will take the blood clot off our hands in less than a week. I only wish it had Marked a human already. Then there'd at least be a chance it would be chosen as a sacrifice for the ceremony. What a show that'd be. But it's no surprise. With that kind of temperament, I can't imagine it matches with anyone before it kills 'em."

Candland stopped walking. He thought of Rocky and his crazy flying goggles. He thought of Ava, and her smile as the glow of her Mark shimmered on her cheek. He felt how wrong everything was. If he were being honest with himself, it wasn't the first time he felt it. He had become so good at ignoring it. The morality of his way of life would cross his mind when he spoke with one of his Marked friends, when he snuck into the Tunnels, when he thought of the Blood Ceremony and the year's sacrifice was mentioned...

Questus was his home. The Marked were cursed by the Nylos. They were dangerous. They were a threat. Keeping them in the Cages and using their blood to keep the kingdom running was necessary. Rocky was dangerous. Candland knew that. But what about Ava? What about everyone else? He remembered the last time he touched Ava. He had reached down towards her and started to help lift her up. And then he had dropped her hand. She landed back onto the ground, unable to stand herself. Her eyes had widened. At that moment, she knew he knew. But that didn't matter, Candland thought. What mattered was that she had reached up for him. And he had let her fall.

Candland turned and stared the headmaster in the eyes. "I want you to let them go."

The man laughed in waves, coughing at the end of each interval. He squeezed his stomach tenderly.

"I'm not joking," Candland said quietly.

"It's even funnier because I know you're not. Look here. I wish The Council was here to open the metal box now. You'd see what the truly cursed really look like. Sure, I've seen some Nylos that look innocent enough— even beautiful. But they're all cursed. The Queen is doing a good thing here. We'll reverse the Marker Matches we have, and we'll get rid of the Markers that haven't Matched with any poor humans. Less black magic in the world because of your mother, prince. It's not an easy job, but it's a rewarding one."

"I command you t—"

"Stop right there, I take orders from the Queen and the Council, not the prince—and the second prince at that," the man said. He threw his arm roughly around Candland's shoulder and brought him in close. His drooping eyelids rose slightly. He then pushed Candland back around to the way the prince entered. "It's time for you to go home before I start to take you seriously. Did you lose your horse? Not smart to be losing your horse so near the Tunnels. Someone might think you're coming from that way. Now. I'll get you a horse so you can get home."

Within minutes, Candland was on the outside of the Cages. A set of reins were in his hands, and an inert horse at his service. Candland walked next to his new companion for the first couple of miles, crying all the way. He felt his failings along with his isolation at an alltime high. He had failed his brother for not finding him. He had failed his mother by visiting the Tunnels. He had failed Rocky by not accompanying him to investigate Maya's death. He had failed Ava by letting her go, and now he was no longer sure if he would ever see her again. And all of those shortcomings came with not belonging to either side quite well. Sure, he was a Questonian, but he never felt at home there. Even heading back now gave him no sense of relief. In fact, it only made him recoil. Yet, he continued east because he had nowhere else to go. And to say that he found more comfort in the Tunnels or the company of his Marked friends just made him more of a traitor while his mother and royal family sponsored the Cages that treated the Cursed so poorly. He felt a heaviness he wasn't sure he'd be able to escape.

When his eyes finally dried, he swung onto the unfamiliar saddle and rode home to Questus with a homesickness he believed would never be remedied.

CHAPTER 5

KAVI'S RESEARCH
AVA

Ava was squatting down over the soil. She could see her mother's lips pressed into a warm smile. Ava strained to see more of her mother's face, to repaint her fading memories of her likeness: Thick, black hair that shone like silk, skin the color of amber honey, large black eyes under smooth eyelids without a crease... Her mother held a small bud in place, and Ava's tiny hands swept over the roots with fresh, damp soil.

"You're so good with the flowers," her mother smiled.

"Is it because of Axol?" Ava asked.

"It's because of your mother," a man said with a chestnut mustache and matching brown eyes. He looked at Ava's mom, a twinkle in those eyes. "There isn't a garden she couldn't grow... even in this bloody desert."

Ava's mother laughed, flicking her black eyes up as a warning, but she didn't seem angry...

. . .

Ava woke up. She found herself alone which meant the people had become bored with her body and moved on. It also meant that Gannick had also moved on. She felt the stickiness between her arm and forehead that made a sound at separation that Ava had known to be the crackling of drying blood as she pulled her head from the arm it laid on. Axol, who had curled up next to her, flitted up in response to the slow movement—but movement nonetheless.

When Ava sat up, she looked down to see she had been impaled by a spear that was still stuck through her body.

"Oh, that's not very nice," Ava said out loud.

"I thought so too," a voice startled Ava.

She turned and looked up to see Kavi the unicorn standing over her.

"Oh. You," Ava said.

"I left you alone while you met with Gannick as you requested," Kavi said. Ava had agreed to Kavi studying her as long as they kept their distance from her last night with Gannick. "But I did observe from a distance."

"It didn't cross your mind to help me?"

"Unicorns cannot physically intervene," Kavi reminded her.

"Did you see Gannick leave? Is he alright?" Ava asked.

"He was pushed away by the crowd. He appeared to be unharmed, although I believe he was quite upset."

Ava winced. Was he upset with her? She never told him what she was. Did he feel betrayed? Would he ever speak to her again? Would she ever see him again? Ava pulled herself back looking down at the spear. She had more urgent matters to take care of.

She stood up slowly and the pain from the spear came rushing in. The knife end of the spear grazed the ground as she leaned forward to stand. She then realized bitterly that what was stuck in her body must become unstuck. Ava looked around. She was in a wide alleyway in the Tunnels. Somewhere still in the heart of the city, but off to the sides where the homeless and hopeless resided. In fact, she realized she wasn't *quite* alone. There were other bodies among her in the shadows. Some breathing and some most likely not.

She spun around slowly examining the damage. The spear had completely gone through her body. When she tugged on it, it did not move though she felt immense pain. Her skin had healed with the spear in place. The spear was too thick for her to try and break off the stick end behind her. Without someone's help, it wasn't an option.

"You can't help break the end of the spear behind me?" Ava asked.

"I am part of the Asting. I have taken a vow to never intervene. I would be disowned and my connection to the vastest network in The Cache would be severed at the very least. It is not a possibility."

"A simple no would have sufficed," Ava groaned.

She thought about asking someone. Maybe one of her regular customers would be willing... But she was covered in her own green blood. No one would help her. Grimacing, she walked carefully backwards towards one of the walls until the stick end was square with the wall. She then held her breath and stepped backwards so that the spear was forced forward through her body using the pressure of the wall. Half grunting, half screaming, she made noises the whole way through, taking the steps as quickly and steady as possible so she didn't heal with the spear again.

The spear had passed through until the very end where her back was now against the wall. Her shaking hands were already holding the spear in front of her so the weight didn't cause the weapon to tear through her flesh with gravity. This was the part she had dreaded the most, but by the time she reached the point where she needed to pull the spear out herself, she was just ready for it to be done. Then, she tightened her two hands along the spear that was sticking out just below her chest... and yanked the remaining wood from just under her breast bone. She fell to her knees, her temples white from the pain. She could smell her own fresh blood dripping from the spear, her chest, and her fingers. Mixed with the stench of the alley, she was already feeling sick.

"What's the saying, Axol? If it hurts, you're not dead?"

Axol laughed, which sounded more like a flurry of bubbles being blown into water. He didn't speak her language—nor did he understand exactly what she was saying. But Nylos have a way of communicating through their Match bond. And so he knew her question was searching for the ease of laughter and responded with what would comfort her most.

Ava's torso had already started patching itself up, and her outside layer of skin was already intact once again. Her outfit, not so much. A dazzling dress, the dress she had told Gannick her feelings in, was now covered in the green muck that had launched the crowd into a killing frenzy. Ava was happy to be alive and tried to humble herself by focusing on the fact that, had she not been Marked by Axol, she would have been dead after her Earther origins had been found out. However, there was a childish fire deep within her that she couldn't deny, and it was crying out at the injustices of her last night with Gannick being ruined. She was no stranger to the torments that followed Atroxes when they were exposed, but did the prejudice, fear, and hatred have to come when she was hand in hand with Gannick? Could it not have spared her the night she had pushed her journey for a bastard braid back for?

After a few sideways glances on an empty street, Ava could still hear the crowds, though their volume had faded considerably. The waves of sounds gave Ava the impression that the peak drunkenness had passed, leaving people to fight reality weakly with more drink in the name of celebration or give into the headache that waited for them in this hour or the next. Ava reached up and pulled a side tapestry of a small market tent down as she whispered "sorry" to the person who would wake up to find it missing. More than she had anticipated had come crashing down from the small structure, but she quickly made away with enough material to cover most of her green stained clothes. She headed towards her home, chasing away the ungrateful wishes of more time with Gannick before she lost him.

The neighborhood was quiet. The kind of quiet that came from empty homes—not sleeping neighbors. Everyone was still celebrating and would be heading back soon. Kavi had tried to ask her a few questions about the night on the way back to her home, but she didn't answer them. She was too upset knowing they did nothing when she was attacked. They had been honest about their vow from the beginning, but experiencing this first hand felt different.

Once Ava was home, she drew herself a bath. She slapped the water on the dried green blood, rubbing energetically to remove the remaining stains. Hot flashes of Gannick troubled her head, which made her scrub harder. Had she only left for Pagra when Gears had told her, Gannick would have never discovered her secret. Had she only watched where she was walking and been more careful, Gannick would not have looked at her with such a face. What was it? She wondered if she had misread betrayal for disgust. Did it matter?

She remembered Gannick in so many different ways from that single night. The first time she held his hand. He was like a pup, still growing into his large paw-like hands. The look in his eyes after she kissed him. Like the dark cloud that followed him had evaporated. Her bravery had done that. The feeling of the small carving he had gifted her in her hands. The shock in his eyes when he saw the blood. The way he dropped her hand like she was nothing when he realized what she was. It all kept repeating itself in her head like a foul melody.

She dried herself quickly and changed clothes. It was in the past now. She had lost her chance at love. The boy was gone. Now she needed to not die and get to Pagra. She winced slightly, recognizing the naivety in her choices. She was a day behind staying alive, and had a kiss that had already rotted to show for it. Love couldn't matter if she was dead. She thought of Gannick's face... his emerald eyes, his forest brown hair, and his olive skin with cheeks that warmed red frequently when she said more inappropriate things—No. The boy was gone.

Ava opened her closet and saw the bag on the ground she had packed earlier, ready for the journey to Pagra. She would sleep, and then leave first thing in the morning. That was the plan. Before settling in for the night, she took a slice of bread and cheese and set it on the table.

"Why did Gears give you something to drink to travel out of the Tunnels?" Kavi asked, standing at the table. They didn't seem to notice they hadn't been offered food.

Ava thought for a moment. She didn't have to tell Kavi anything, but maybe talking about it would help prepare her for the journey.

"It's hard to explain. Whenever I've tried to leave the Tunnels... I just never could."

"Why not?"

"I... I don't know. My brain shuts down. I start sweating. My heart starts pounding. I don't remember when I came to the Tunnels, and even though I've tried... I've never left since."

"You cannot recall anything about coming to the Tunnels?"

"Sometimes... Just bits and pieces. Most of it involves... pain. Gears gave me the vial to drink to hopefully calm my nerves and keep my fuzzy memories from overtaking me like they always have. He's offered before, but I never took it."

"Why not?"

"I don't think I really ever wanted to leave. I still don't want to now."

"If you do not go, the Vhyka will get you."

"I'm well aware," Ava's eyes narrowed. "Stupid monsters."

"They were not always monsters," Kavi said.

"...What were they?"

"Mothers," Kavi said with a soft smile. "Oftentimes, a mother pregnant with a bastard was forced to throw the infant out as soon as they were born. They would give them away, leave them in the woods, or end the infant's life themselves."

Ava tilted her head, trying to imagine the Vhyka at her door as a mother at some point.

Kavi went on. "After a time, some of the mothers could never get over what they had done. The guilt began to consume them. Only the desire to try again kept them going. So over the years they transformed into Vhykas, searching for bastard children and trying to eat them to put the cast out children in their bellies again so they can start over and keep the baby."

"...But eating them doesn't make them pregnant..." Ava said quietly.

"They are far beyond reason. Their minds do not work like a normal human just like their bodies have grown stronger from the regret of wanting to do the right thing next time. Really, the creatures are just heartbroken mothers who want a chance to do the right thing."

"That's... so sad," Ava said. "But also, I still don't want them to eat me. How did you know about Vhykas?"

"The Asting knows the history of The Cache very well. I know you are upset because I did not intervene tonight. However, I hope to make it up to you by helping how I can—by offering you any knowledge from the Asting that may help you in your journey."

Ava then nodded at Kavi. That was just how it was. She was still hurt, but she understood. Now, she needed to get some sleep and prepare for tomorrow. She wasn't sure how long it had been, but she knew it had been a long time since she ventured out in the desert. And in her opinion, not long enough.

Ava stood in front of the exit of The Cache. She hadn't planned on drinking Gears' offer, but her nerves were getting the best of her. Standing beside Kavi, and with Axol resting on her shoulder, she uncorked the little glass bottle.

"I hope this works, Gears," she whispered and then tipped the bottle into her mouth. The bottle was so sweet it made Ava's tongue press up against the roof of her mouth. She looked in front of her, studying the way out as she waited for the drink to kick in.

The exit was similar to the entrance. There was a small dune of sand that looked to be under a shimmering spotlight. Scattered sand particles floated slowly above the hill, showing exactly where gravity began to lessen its hold. Ava had seen people leave before. She'd waved off Gannick plenty of times, watching him walk under the silver shimmer and begin to ascend slowly upwards until he passed through the barrier and up into the Wontine Desert.

"I can do this. I can do this. I can do this," Ava said quickly and quietly as she was sucking in air. She could already feel her pulse quicken.

"You can, indeed, do this," Kavi said. "Twenty steps forward and you will begin to float upwards above ground. There is no physical barrier keeping you from the world above, Ava," Kavi said.

"That's... That's a great pep talk. Thanks Kavi."

Ava took a step forward and a memory flashed through her.

She was small. A man held her by the throat, her legs dangling high over the ground. He had a blade in his other hand, and he brought it to her neck. She reached up and grasped the blade with her tiny fingers, pushing the weapon away from her with the little strength she had. Her green blood started to drip from her hands just before she knew she couldn't keep the sharp edge away from her any longer...

"Ava? Are you alright?" Kavi asked.

Ava looked at Kavi, gasping for breath. A drop of sweat fell from her chin onto the ground.

"I can't do this. I can't go up," She said.

Axol flew up to meet Ava's eyes. He flew down to her neck, nudging the bastard braid around her throat, reminding her that she had to leave the Tunnels to get a new one. She had to leave to live.

"Gears' medicine will calm you in only a few moments. Now, I want you to listen to me," Kavi said. His voice was so calm, if not effervescent. "I want you to take three deep breaths. Inhale. One. Two. Three. Good. Exhale. One, Two, Three... Good. Again..."

After a few deep breaths, Ava's fingers only trembled slightly. Axol flew into her arms, and holding him tight, Ava stepped forward. Each step forward, she felt the friction she was cutting through. The dread that made her stomach lurch, and her lungs overwork. The panic within her felt as if it were a resistance band wrapped around her chest, pulling her backwards. But she pressed on. She finally felt the lift of the exit, taking her upward. There was no turning back now. No way to float down. She looked down to see Kavi smiling up at her. They gave her a wave. Then she stood outside. The light was so bright, she had to shut her eyes tight. The heat was so strong, it pressed against her skin as if it were a creature itself. She took a few steps back and opened her eyes ever so slightly to see the largest desert in The Cache.

The Wontine Desert was vast and barren. Like most deserts, it was desolate. At first glance it was empty. But something told Ava that at night it would shed some of its timidness. She somehow knew that sundown was when it would communicate with the rest of the world through plants that bloomed in full twilight, creatures that croaked for romance, and gusts of wind that sifted the sand through its fingers. But in the day, Wontine seemed to keep all of it a secret.

Ava pressed her lips together, checking the status of the moisture remaining. There wasn't much left in the air, causing her eyes to itch. The air was so dry, she could taste the salt in it. When Kavi appeared beside her, Ava took a few steps back and closed her eyes again. They were so white, the sun reflected off of them like it would a cloud.

"You did it," Kavi smiled.

Ava nodded.

"Now what?" Kavi asked.

"Soonja will be our last stop for supplies before we cross the desert."

They began their trek towards the village which

didn't remain silent for long. Kavi was the only being who seemed to ask more questions than Ava did.

"Who is Gannick to you?" Kavi asked.

Ava was tired, but never too tired to talk about Gannick.

"He's... the boy I like. He's from Questus. The son of the sculptor for the royal family. So he lives in the castle. His parents are loyal to the Blood, but he's... too curious to be so loyal. He's kind of got a dark side to him. Quiet. But not quiet like he's mysterious. He's quiet like... he's thinking. Like 'How can I talk when there's so much for me to listen to?' quiet."

"Perhaps he does not seem to talk a lot around you because you talk so much."

"Very funny. I can talk less if you want."

"No, thank you. After last night, do you still like him?"

"Of course I do. I just wish I had more time. I want to tell him that it was wrong to lie to him about what I am, but I hope he understands it was only to protect me. I want to let him know that it's okay that he panicked at first. Everyone does. I wish he knew how I still felt."

"Did he not accept you like the others?" Kavi asked. They were now scribbling words down in a white notebook.

"He just... froze," Ava licked her lips. "I'd just like to see him again. To see if... there's still a chance."

"For what?"

"For him to like me back... Even though he knows what I am."

"I like you."

"You just met me. And I mean in a romantic way with Gannick."

"You are much more talkative than my last subject. This is very beneficial for my research."

"...You're welcome? Okay, that's enough talking for now. Time to save my spit. Let's get to Soonja before you start asking more questions. Oh, and don't mention that I'm an Atrox to anyone. I don't want to have to wake up with a spear through me again."

"Very well, Ava."

Ava stepped within the limits of Soonja. She paused and looked around. Barefoot children, not laughing but running. *Light feet.* There were weapons strategically placed so they were an arm's reach away from most positions a local villager might find themselves. *Always ready.* The adults turned to the west, their hands hovering over their eyes every few minutes to survey the top of the dunes. *Look out.*

"Many are surprised by what they find in Soonja," Kavi noticed Ava's pause. "They expect markets to buy supplies for journeys to be made across the Wontine or to indulge in after the journey has been made. And Soonja does provide this.

"What they do not expect is how militant the village is. Weapons. Combat and survival training. Riders who can make the trip to Questus in record speeds. There are highly trained warriors here all funded by the Questus family whose hand is wrapped around the village. Soonja is an independent entity that has not acted independently in a long time. This place is the first line of defense from Questus' greatest rival, should they ever decide to cross the desert."

"Nobody can get along anymore," Ava muttered.

"Rivalry is quite common in The Cache. Questus aims to save the Marked from their Markers by saving the souls with the Blood. Nevarra wants to save the Marked and the Markers from Questus. Pagra is finally powerful enough to actually be a threat to Questus. Some say ambition alone is why they seek more territory. And of course that is a threat to Questus since they own the most land."

Ava had already stopped listening to Kavi. There was nothing more boring to her than politics, though she nodded politely at Kavi's comments. With Axol tucked away in her robe-like top, hidden from plain sight, Ava walked deeper into the city. At the center there was a market where locals were haggling and the few visitors who had just made their way across the desert were giving up too much money for too little in return because they were far too tired to haggle.

"May I suggest some of those blue cactus flowers with the red thorns and purple leaves?" Kavi asked.

"Rachos. Good find," Ava looked at the vendor. "We'll take three."

"Fifty jun," the vendor said.

"I'll give you twenty five or I'll just get them from around the corner," Ava said.

"Twenty five it is," the vendor said, quickly taking the jun from her hand.

"That is a fair price," Kavi nodded.

"That's why he took it," Ava said loudly so the vendor could hear and put the dried Rachos into her bag.

Ava purchased a few more items for her trip—mainly food. In her pack, she already had a light but large scarf that could be used as an extra head wrap and filter to block the sand and sun, a change of clothes, the sculpture of Axol Gannick had given her, jun—not much but all she had, a jug of Lavi (a juice known for its naturally infused electrolytes), a variety of herbs she had grown herself (each with their own enhancements like focus or endurance), a metal cup, a knife, and forever ice. Purchased from Soonja as Kavi recorded, were dried fruit and jerkies, nuts, three Rachos, cool edible gels, and Sei— a sweet treat in the form of small cubes that tasted like cinnamon and mint dissolving into a cool sugar in one's mouth.

Ava and Kavi headed further west out of the Soonja with Ava's movements casual with the exception of looking behind her for anyone who might be lurking too close.

"Two days to the Shift and then it's smooth sanding from there," she said.

"You are confident about your journey across the desert, Atrox?" Kavi asked. They were the first ones who used the label without any malice. Ava realized when it was said plainly, it wasn't so terrible.

"I am, unicorn," she responded.

The following two days, the Atrox and unicorn surprised each other. Ava surprised Kavi by adjusting well to the desert life. Crossing the Wontine Desert was a journey that not many Questonians could make without full support and guidance. And yet, she seemed more than capable to live in such dire conditions. She pushed through in the darkness, actively pacing her steps in the night, using the layers she packed and the heat of her movement for warmth. She plucked shriveled plants that promised nothing only for the tiny crinkled leaves to pull up thick juicy roots. There were many poisonous plants in Wontine, and many nearly identical to what was edible. Kavi would have interjected had she made a deadly mistake, but they never needed to. Living on the mercies of the desert, Kavi believed that she was quite different from most Earthers who were known for gormandizing on anything they came across. She was keen on desert plants, animals, and seemed more a child of the desert than of her despised ancestors.

Kavi impressed Ava by keeping up. Of course she knew that unicorns were mysteriously powerful. In fact, it was unclear what their powers actually were. All that was really known was that they were powerful and peaceful and would cause no harm. Ever. Not even when attacked. At most, they would use their strengths—whatever they were—to neutralize threats. From what Ava could discern, they hadn't yet taken a drink of anything. They had eaten a single leaf from a single plant.

She also never saw them sleep. When she rested, they sat cross-legged, a dazzling white diamond under the sun, hardly sweating or blistering. When Ava looked at them before she turned in under her cover from the sun, she felt peaceful only because that's all she saw when she looked at them.

They arrived at The Shift after two smooth days on the sand. Ava, though faring better than most, still looked like she had been chewed up and spit out by the desert's unforgiving sun. Her body had grown too accustomed to the darkness of the Tunnels. She was covered in salt from the heat evaporating the gallons of water she had sweat, giving her skin a dry, crusty texture. Kavi, who stayed by her side at all times, looked as wonderful and virtuous as they had the first day they had met.

The Shift was gifted by the all powerful Gatekeeper of West Gate thousands of years ago. It was a different time when Pagra and Questus were healthy rivals at worst, with Pagra hardly qualifying as a threat to Questus. Now, there were a few scattered homes made of clay and small market goods being sold where The Shift started or ended, depending on where one was coming from. There were small umbrellas, giant umbrellas that folded into one-person domes, sun-shielding lotion, sun and sand goggles, large sealing tents that increased in prices based on amenities. For the most part, however, the pit stop was quite barren.

Ava and Kavi walked underneath a large red clay arch to see The Shift. It was an impressively large strip of sand, maybe 50 feet in width and seemingly infinite in length. Ava looked to see all kinds of vagabond groups lined up near where the Shift started. There were also rich travelers with staff surrounding them with luxury sun-repelling equipment. The Shift welcomed all. The first section started at a slower pace. Ava watched a small family of four, holding each other close, quickly step onto the moving Shift. The mother held an infant and pointed at a sack that had been left on the steady, unmoving ground as they shifted forward. The father quickly stepped off the sand in motion, snatched the bag, and had to all but sprint to make it back onto the moving platform to his family.

It was here that Ava and Kavi exchanged jun for passage onto the enormous band of sand that traveled for its passengers. Ava and Kavi stepped up to the wide sandy lane that—at first glance appeared still—was sifting all it carried west towards Pagra.

"How do you feel you are different from Cache-born creatures?" Kavi asked. The two were now sitting on The Shift. Ava was still mostly covered with her oversized scarf, and waiting for the sun to fully depart before she would unwrap herself.

"I am Cache-born."

"How do you feel you are different from non-Earthers?"

"How do I feel different or how am I different?"

"Both."

"Hard to feel different from others when I've never

been anything but what I am. I didn't know I was an Atrox until I was 9. And I bleed green. But I don't think I was around any others like me unless my mother was one, but I don't think so. She… bleeds red. The color of our blood. That's the only difference I'm aware of."

"It is in fact the only logged difference we have in the Asting as well."

"Do you think there are more?"

"I learn best when I have no predisposed assumptions. I do my best to keep it that way."

"So are all unicorns like you? How are you different from everyone else? What's your power?"

"We are alike in many ways and different in others. We were under very strict training with little variation. So in the things we are taught, we are very similar. In the things that we are, we are different. Most unicorns identify by what they choose to study for their lifetime. And as far as our powers go, that, like much information we share through the Asting, is confidential."

"Oh, that's fun. What if I just start saying everything's confidential when you ask questions?" Ava rolled her eyes.

"Then I would put all of my focus into observation. It has happened before. However, that response would surprise me."

"Why?"

"Because you talk so freely."

"We're on The Shift. What else is there to do?"

"Even when we weren't on The Shift. You still spoke a high volume of words."

"If I didn't know any better, I'd think you were complaining, Kavi."

"I am not. I am only stating an observation. I feel lucky to find you are so extroverted and open."

"Alright, well what else would you like to know?"

"How do you know so much about the desert?" Kavi asked.

"I–," Ava swallowed and looked at Kavi with a stern look on her face. "I think it's my home."

"You remember?"

"Starting to. Bits and pieces," Ava said. She reached into her pack to pull out a treat. She handed a cube of Sei to Kavi but they declined. "I sure remember these. And good. I didn't want to share these anyway." She then unwrapped the scarf from her head and settled in as the sun did the same.

"Do you remember why you left the desert?" Kavi asked.

"...No. Just..." Ava flinched. "I don't think it was a good memory."

"Sometimes the mind protects the body by burning the painful memories away."

"I wouldn't know anything about that."

"It is the basis of all healing in the House of Haessig actually," Kavi said. "No matter how deeply physical an injury is, they always start with the mind. With the memory."

"Do you think they could help me remember?"

"I believe they could. I do not know if they would."

"Why not?"

"They would first need to make sure you are ready to dig up the memory."

"I wish I could remember more."

"Perhaps that will be another journey after Pagra. A very different journey."

"How far east is the House of Haessig?"

"It is not about how far east it is. It is about how far north it is. Their headquarters is in the coldest region in The Cache."

Ava's skin shivered just thinking about snow and ice. She preferred the desert sun—the sun she knew in her bones she was born under.

"We have some long, hot days ahead of us. I'm going to try and sleep," Ava said.

"Please. I will monitor your sleep and keep watch. Also, please try to recall your dreams if you can. They might be trying to talk to your memories now that you have returned to the desert."

Ava thought of the memory that her panic attack had recalled when she was leaving the Tunnels. The blade. The blood. The violence. She hoped what she thought was a memory was instead just a dream.

CHAPTER 6

FINGERNAILS
CHINCHIN

Pagra was made up of two parts: the New City and the Old City. Or New Pagra and Old Pagra. New Pagra was cutting edge and not just figuratively. The entire area was made up mostly of Obsidian V, with sharp edges and corners of the stone. Information passed through its surfaces instantly, and it made for the perfect headquarters for Pagra Labs. The Old City to the east was quite the opposite. The Old City had a... well, old feeling to it. It was dusty and slow. The walls were not black, but made of compacted mud and clay that painted its half of the city pastel orange and reds. It made for the perfect place to meet to discuss more private matters.

And so, Chinchin stepped inside a loud tavern in the Old City. No lab coat that evening. She wore a fuschia halter top with the straps tied around her neck and loose beige linen pants on bottom. She looked around, scanning the room. She didn't recognize anyone from Pagra Labs, and if there were any Shadow Scouts, she wouldn't know them without their masked helmets. She walked through the crowd and the chatter they created, and ducked through a colorful curtain. After passing a few occupied rooms in a deep, cool hallway, she found Chauson in a doorless room with a wooden table and chairs backed with colorful patterned fabrics. Chauson was leaning by the window, looking very casual for being the sovereign minister's son. His relaxed state was a stark contrast from Chinchin's. She was more calculated, more accentuated. If he was casual, she was intentional.

"86," he smiled.

The absence of black watching walls put Chinchin at ease even if this meetup had to do with Project 222. "It's Chinchin outside of the Labs. What did you find?"

"So the good news is I found the answer. The bad news is… it's not good." Chauson pulled out a black stone tablet.

"Obsidian?" Chinchin froze. It could be watching them.

"It's okay. Look, it's got no shine," Chauson assured her as he sat down at the table. He tilted the tablet side to side to reveal a glimmer-less surface. "No shine. No eyes. We're working in the shadows."

"Okay. Good." Chinchin noted the matte finish of the tablet in his hands. She continued to stand, leaning over him.

"So, I've seen your activity logging on and looking at your reports on your test subjects all day, every day—"

"My activity? Why are you looking at my activity?" Chinchin said sharply.

"Let me explain. You're looking at your project constantly. Well, your human test subjects, specifically. You've hardly looked at the Nylos they've Matched with though."

"Why would I? I care about the people who are dying as part of this experiment, not the Nylos. I care about Boris, Chasa, James, Tae, Myko and—"

"Maya?" Chauson asked.

Chinchin stopped for a moment, narrowing her eyes. Then she continued, "They're all dead. I only care about saving the lives of the rest of the test subjects. I don't care about the Nylos."

"If I may," Chauson started and then cleared his throat. "They're a huge part of your project, and you're not looking at them close enough. Look at this report I scraped from your files."

Chinchin leaned forward, looking at the matte screen. "It's just Nylos."

"Chinchin. Look. All of the Nylos Matched with the test subjects that died? They stopped eating. If they flew, they stopped flying. Their sleep doubled. Some of them cried out at night. There are recordings the wall took of them clearly in anguish."

"What are you saying?"

"They were... depressed."

"But they're just... Nylos."

"Even inert animals can get depressed. And, anyway, it doesn't matter what they are. They're depressed. They're in literal cages. Their quality of life is making them want to kill themselves, and that feeling is so strong it's bleeding into your human subjects." Chauson ran his fingers through his hair, his breathing was heavier. His voice was raised. It was the first time Chinchin had heard the strain in his voice.

"You really think that's what's happening here?"

"Listen. All of the test subjects that died had Matched with more than one Nylo—something that's never been done before. Take Boris for an example. He had Matched with more Nylos than anyone in the history of The Cache since Maya. But if you look at it from another angle, he was carrying the weight of six Nylos that were all suicidal. They all wanted to die. And synthetic or not, the Marker Match connects them in ways we still don't quite understand... The bond connects more than magic to someone like Boris. It connects their emotions."

"The problem... can't be this obvious," Chinchin said as she took a seat in the chair next to Chauson.

"It's your blind spot. Look at your views. For every 50 times you looked at your human test subjects, you looked at the Nylo reports once. And barely spent any time on them when you did."

"I—they're just the source of magic. That's all," Chinchin gargled. She was starting to feel warm. She was starting to understand... She saw the glimmer in Chauson's eyes, and he didn't hesitate when he saw Chinchin was beginning to second guess herself—something she rarely did when it came to her own work.

"Look, people usually say this about technology. But what you're doing—it's against nature. Nylos always choose their humans. There are going to be side effects like this when you start defying what's normal. Happens all the time with technology too. We run into blockers like this constantly. You just have to keep an open mind. Adapt."

"So what do I do? Build nicer cages? ...Pet them while offering words of encouragement?"

"That's... the right direction. Looking at the data, it looks like the more Matches your test subjects make, the more likely they're at risk."

"It just seems silly that Nylos and their emotions would..."

"You might not think Nylos are truly sentient or even have feelings like some people do. You might think of them the same as simple inert animals. It doesn't matter how you choose to see them. But, Chinchin, if you don't change how you treat them, everyone in your experiment will eventually die."

"You don't know that."

"Actually, I do. It's in the data," Chauson held up his tablet and nodded his head. "I'd bet my life on it."

Chinchin placed both hands on the table flat, with her fingers spread wide. At that moment, she hated his confidence. And she knew she hated it because usually *she* was the confident one. She was supposed to be the one spouting facts, revealing truths, and coming up with solutions. She took a deep breath, aware that her neck was still feeling exceptionally warm. She hadn't been this wrong in a long time. But if Chauson was right...

"What are you thinking about?" Chauson asked.

"There's a legend," Chinchin took a breath. "The Gatekeeper once made a potion that would cause whoever drank it to kill themselves. The process would start the night it was consumed with a dream. Everything in their dream would lose color, and then something would pull them to the ground. It would drag them by the feet where eventually they'd arrive at the edge of a cliff. The weight would continue to pull them down until they were hanging on the edge by their fingertips, digging their nails into the earth. And they would dream that same dream every night until the potion's magic... worked."

"I've heard of that one. Oh! The fingernails. The people who drank the Gatekeeper's potion had their fingernails fall off!"

Chinchin nodded. "That's why they're falling off. With no fingernails, they don't have the ability to hold onto that suicidal ledge in the dream. You're right. It comes down to not having the will to live. To not want to hold on."

Chinchin sat still. Her eyes had moved to the corner of the room on the ground made of tightly packed dirt. She spotted two of the same bugs seeming to climb on top of one another without shame. Never did she see bugs in the corners of Pagra Labs. It was exceptionally clean and cold there.

"If you spend some more time with the Nylos, I think you'll find they're more than just... power packets."

"I'm not really an animal person," Chinchin said. "I'm not even really a people person."

"Dammit, Chinchin. But you care about the people in those Labs. So maybe give the Nylos a chance."

"Do you like Nylos?"

"I don't dislike them. They're incredible creatures."

"They're incredible *resources*," Chinchin countered.

"No, they're more than that. And if you can't see that, then you're... You're..."

"What?"

"Lights, Chinchin. You're stubborn. If you can't see that then you're limiting yourself! ...There's more to them than just being a tool to use for your experiments," Chauson said. He stood up from the table and walked back towards the open window.

"They're not a tool, they're a power source," Chinchin said simply. With his hand in a loose fist, Chauson gently tapped it against the wall as if he had thought about punching the surface, but lost the strength to make solid contact with the wall.

"There's more to them than you give them credit for," he said quietly, turning away from Chinchin.

"Are we talking about Nylos, Chauson?"

"We're talking about you."

Chinchin was stunned by how serious Chauson was. He always had seemed like he was seconds away from a laugh or a shrug, but not now. The boy prodigy was serious. "No, you're talking about you, Chauson. I do give you credit. I've already risked too much sending you the data without the proper steps in place. And it's because I trust you."

"You don't get it, Chinchin."

"What don't I get?"

"I want more than trust," he blurted out. Chinchin couldn't ignore the red that appeared in his cheeks.

"I'm in the middle of an experiment that is killing people, Chauson. People are dying. I don't even have the capacity to think about anything but that fact. This doesn't have anything to do with you."

"I care about you. You're not eating. You're not sleeping. Ever since Maya died, your progress on this project's stalled. And if all you can say is you're not an animal person, then... maybe you're not who I thought you were. Maybe I did waste all of this time sorting out the data."

Chinchin stayed sitting, she took a breath and clasped her hands, interlacing her fingers. This was getting emotional, and she needed to stay poised. Her eyes were still on the mating insects. She remained silent.

"Look, I knew you wouldn't want to hear what I had to say with the data points I collected. But. I didn't think tonight would go like this. I thought maybe you'd even say thank you. I'm going to go," Chauson said.

Chinchin listened to Chauson's padded steps join in

the noise of the bar, disappearing into the crowd faster than she anticipated. She took a deep breath and ran her hands through her ponytail, making her hair flick upwards like a flame. She licked her lips. There was too much emotion in the room, and she needed all of it to settle.

"...I care about you too," she said out loud, her chin held high. But Chauson couldn't hear her. He was too far into the crowd, pacing through the Old City towards the Labs.

Chinchin walked back to her neighborhood of identical black cubed units of living space in the New City, thinking about Chauson's findings which felt more like accusations... even if they were accurate. She saw traces of her reflection on the surface of each unit. Just the colors of her face and the glimmer of her clothing moved from one wall to the next. Without pausing to take a clear look at herself, she knew what she looked like. Dark circles under her eyes, and uncombed, tangling hair pulled back that had significantly thinned out from her constant yanking. She ate little, slept little, and worked lots and between the three, she walked.

Sometimes she would allow the past to creep in when she was literally putting one foot in front of the other. The past where Maya used to walk beside her. She recalled how serious Maya was. How driven. How focused. How passionate. It hurt to remember how much Maya loved Nylos. Chinchin was always indifferent to them, but ever since Maya's death... she had been overly cruel. Far too dismissive. Maya had been Chinchin's best test subject. Chinchin had given her the serum, and the mutation had taken place just as expected. From there, Maya was able to Match with seven Nylos at once—none of them had chosen her like a traditional Match would work. With seven Nylos, Maya had seven Marks on her body. And with seven Matches, she had seven different power sources to channel. Seven different magical abilities she could use at will. Chinchin had believed she found the key to allowing everyone the chance to match with a Nylo, regardless if a Nylo would allow it or not. At the time, she thought Maya was just as excited for the breakthrough. A chance to give everyone power to make their life better. What she didn't know at the time was that Maya was actually there to do everything she could to make sure that didn't happen...

"The mutation. Is it permanent... when subjects Match with a Marker?" Maya had asked, though at the time, she went by her cover name, Kea.

"Seems to be the case," Chinchin had said. All Maya could talk about was the work, and all Chinchin wanted to talk about was how their bodies should never be too far away from each other at any given time.

"If you wanted to reverse it. How would you go about it?"

"Reverse it? We're still trying to get the Match to fully take. Okay, okay. Let's see... Well, first I'd probably start with

funding. You'd have to make your case for Pagra to give you the support needed to even begin researching a reversal. Granted, there's the quick and dirty way, but you could hardly call it a method."

"What is it?"

"Kea..."

"I want to know."

"The Matches made from subjects injected with the serum that causes the mutation create their own individual Marks on the body just like a natural Match would. If you cut out the Marks on the Marked's body, you cut out the contract holding the promise in place. Just like you would do with a traditional 1:1 match."

"But cutting out the Mark doesn't actually break the bond," Maya said. *It wasn't a question.*

"Technically no, especially with natural Marker Matches, but it removes the lock, so to speak. It depends how strong the bond is. And with the Marker Match made by my serum, well, it's not that strong... for now. It's built on an... artificial muta-tion, so for right now, it's not as strong as the real thing. As soon as the Mark was removed from the body, the Marker would be set free and most likely never look back."

Maya had asked so many questions. At first, it was nice for Chinchin to have someone as fascinated about her field of study, but of course, Chinchin finally caught on to what Maya was after. Chinchin was no stranger to hiding her past, and so she picked up on the words and actions that mirrored her own. It took her longer than she would like to admit, but love was blinding. And even after she realized Maya was a spy for Nevarra... it was too late. Chinchin was in love. What did it matter? If Maya would have known how easily she would capitulate for love, Maya could have let her guard down so much sooner. Chinchin could have had more time with Maya—not Kea. Chinchin closed her eyes from the tragedy she was yet to recover from. Maya's death was still too fresh to think about the stolen identities and lies their love had been born from.

She recalled another night, another memory more pleasant and more romantic to feed her spiraling mind. Something happy. Something intimate.

Maya laid on her bed, her head covered in shiny black curls that were wild in volume and elegant in length. Through her thick coiling locks her orange eyes peeked through. Chinchin had seen those same eyes burn red when she channeled one of her Nylo's power. Her stare was full of energy. Chinchin was never sure if Maya was ready to attack or make love, and she was prepared to accept either, as long as she was on the receiving end. In her all black uniform, Maya was professional, keen, and commanding, but when she was bare on top, she was simply striking. Without Maya's uniform, she was less Kea and more herself. Their naked bodies weren't just a more functional state for sex, but it allowed them to be close, just as they were. Without uniforms. Without disguises. And in that, they were able to be in love without duty or whatever it was that would eventually pull them apart.

That night, the only thing Maya wore were loose-fitting pants, tying the top high over her hips. Chinchin could see Maya's four unique Marks (she would bond with three more Nylos and gain three more Marks before her death). Introducing the mutation to her body had gone smoothly. It was hard to believe she had already Matched with four Markers at the time. Then again, now that Chinchin knew she was from Nevarra, a clan centered around protecting Nylos, it now made sense. Her people understood Nylos better than anyone.

When she laid her head next to Chinchin's, Maya's curls sprung up at all angles. It looked as if her hair was in the middle of an explosion, and Chinchin was just happy to be near enough to feel the jolt of what made up the woman she would love deeper than anyone she would ever meet again.

"You know what animal I want to Match with next?" she had asked.

"A fifth already?" Chinchin smiled. Touching Maya's cheek softly.

"An axolotl."

"The salamander? You want a little magical green thumb? Maybe a chance to heal a wound or two?"

"They symbolize rebirth. New beginnings," she had said.

"But here we are. Everything is perfect. Why would you want to start over?"

"Oh, I don't know. What if we met outside of The Lab. What if we could start over..."

"I don't know about starting over. But I do know what I'd like to start... right now," Chinchin placed her hand on her lover's torso, fingering the ribs through her skin. She pulled

Maya in closer and found her lips under the most glorious mane of hair.

She didn't understand what Maya was saying then. She didn't really care to listen then. Now she understood. Now she, too, wanted to start over. She wanted to start with Maya—not Kea—so she had more time with the real woman behind the facade. Chinchin stopped, her body rigid.

"The axolotl!" Chinchin said out loud at her epiphany.

Chinchin turned and ran back to the lab, putting the memories of her dead lover on pause.

Chinchin strung her fingers through her hair with her signature flick. The project review couldn't have come at a better time with the discoveries and limitations she had come across in her project. She had Chauson to thank for that mostly. It had been two weeks since they met in the Old City. They hadn't spoken with each other since, but it wasn't because she was avoiding him. She had been too busy making adjustments after Chauson's findings. And okay, perhaps she was avoiding him a little bit, too.

Despite the casualties, the Marker Matching Muta-tion Project, or Project 222, was still, to Pagra Labs, a huge success. Marker Matches had occurred organically with only a few thousand in The Cache and at the mercy of the Nylos' whims before Chinchin started her work at the Labs. The fact that Chinchin had discovered a way to artificially replicate the Match with her serum she injected into her test subjects was one of the biggest breakthroughs of all time—even though she was still part of the academy and not the Labs at the time.

And in Pagra, where knowledge was the core of their religion, the discovery was an honor under the Light they worshiped as well. The Light was their god. Their north star. Their reminder that illumination in the darkness, learning the unknown, and pushing the limits of what could be done was their pathway to an honorable life that would be rewarded after death. That's why Pagra had built the Labs in the first place. That's why the sovereign minister gave all children a free education no matter their status. That's why she created the academy for those who truly excelled in their learning. Knowledge was enlightenment.

That's why Chinchin had come to Pagra in the first place. She wanted to use science to bring magic to everyone. She wanted to end the days where access to magic depended on having something to trade with the Gatekeeper for a spell (where the wealthy could pay up or the poor could be exploited for desperate offers). It was either that or the rare chance that a Nylo would simply choose them to channel their magic to. Her idea to end magic for only the privileged was something she knew she could only accomplish with the resources and aspirations of a place like Pagra.

But the fatalities were high in a small test pool. And

Chinchin knew all the victims by name, by friendship, by comradery, and even by love. The fatalities, to her, were unacceptable. Anyone with the injection—her injection—was at risk until she could improve the wellbeing of the Nylos... or somehow make her test subjects immune to their Nylos' despair.

She put on her wrinkled black lab coat, and then walked down the hall of the Labs. The halls, like the lab Chinchin worked in, the unit she lived in, and the review room that she was about to present in, were all a dark, polished black. The soles of her shoes echoed off of the walls, just like her reflection. She could feel the walls watching... *Go ahead, watch,* she thought.

"86," a familiar voice cut through her thoughts. It was 546. Chauson. She looked up to see his thick black hair, slicked back tickling his neck and the warmth in his cheeks and in his manner.

"Chauson. Good morning," she said, trying to pretend their last conversation hadn't been emotional.

"Ready for your review?" Apparently he was pretending too.

"Ready."

"Remember, they don't care about humans, and they don't care about Nylos. They care about being the best. You have to come at another angle. They won't easily buy the truth, just like you wouldn't."

"Chauson... You were right. I should have—"

"It doesn't matter right now. Focus on your review," he said. He said it with a smile, though Chinchin wasn't sure if his eyes matched the curve of his lips. She could tell he was being very deliberate with his words and mannerisms. He wasn't relaxed like usual.

"You've got this," Chauson said a little too enthusiastically.

"I know," she smiled. It was rare for her to try to reassure others with a smile, but she wanted Chauson to know they were good. That she was sorry she hadn't tried to contact him since he shared his findings with her. That she cared about what he said. That she cared about him.

Chinchin's eyes sideswept Chauson. Chauson winked in response. She never thought a boy in the Labs would make her neck tingle. And yet... Before she could say anything else, he left. He turned down another hall and walked away. If Chinchin wasn't thinking about her review, she might have blushed.

The review room was large and empty. The room would have felt like one black cube had the ceilings not been so high. Once the door shut, like all doors in the laboratory, the opening sealed, thanks to the fine craftsmanship and expert measurements of Pagra's architects. A solid rectangular block stood closest to the north wall. Chinchin approached it, setting her forearms on top of it with her hands pressed against the top surface, treating it as a podium. She pressed her fingertips into the Obsidian V and watched her fingers whiten under pressure. She faced the north wall, which was only about 4 feet away from the podium. She stood, surrounded in every direction by black mirrors. She could see the ghost of her reflection in the wall facing her. *Just speak their language,* she told herself in a small internal pep talk. *Speak their language. And save lives.*

She saw the silhouettes of bodies sitting on the other side of the screen. For a moment, Chinchin thought about leaving the review room and Pagra Laboratories forever. She thought about walking out past her little neighborhood, out past the city, through the sand dunes where she would never inject another body with a foreign fluid again.

Or maybe she could pass through the mud walls, and like Maya had once dreamed, reset and start over without a single memory of the lives that had been lost because of her.

The north wall rippled from the center, sending waves to its outer edges. The ripples continued past the single wall, spilling onto the surrounding black surfaces, growing smaller and smaller until they disappeared.

"Hello 86. Welcome to your review. We look forward to your updates on Project 222."

"Thank you. I've had some breakthroughs recently."

"Please. Begin."

"PLSA, upload my tray from lab 55," Chinchin summoned a review of her work from the Pagra Labs System Assistant. The ripples ceased, and her work showed up as an outline of stored files on the black surface for all to see. She looked at her work, her findings, her everything. She looked past them and through the wall. She couldn't see the faces of those she presented to, but she could see shapes, outlines of heads of those eager to learn more and willing to fund her project without a second thought. Some of Chauson's data was in these folders as well. His reminder flashed into her mind: *They don't care about humans and they don't care about Nylos. They care about being the best.* The House of Questus came out ahead in land and population—a loyal population that would do anything for the Blood. But Pagra had Obsidian V and every day they came up with new ways to make up for what they lacked in territory and numbers. In the eyes of the leadership within those black walls, they couldn't afford to be second in innovation; but they could afford a few more lives lost.

She needed them to give her their time and money to stop the monstrous effects she had created. Maya had been the queen of persuasion, the charmer's charmer. Chauson thought like the shadows behind the glass because he was literally born to be one himself. He could become political in an instant when he needed to. Chinchin was confident, but not always able to win someone over with just words. But she knew she had a pretty face, and she never missed an opportunity to use it. Chinchin cleared her throat, flicked her hair, and smiled. She could have sworn she felt her gray-blue eyes sparkle.

"I've started looking into species with regenerative qualities. Bees, Costiseis, and flying salamanders. Salamanders being the most impressive healers—though rare—will save our subjects."

"How so?"

"Out of 50 who have taken the jab for the mutation, 9 have died by suicide. All the same symptoms. Irrational behavior, hallucinations, obsessions, recklessness, fearlessness... Oh, and their fingernails: If the subjects don't peel or pull them off themselves, the nails fall off on their own.

"86, we did not authorize this added research. Your focus should be on production speed, the volume of Matches, and the permanence of results as discussed in the last review. We are not concerned with the collateral at this point."

"Well, I did it anyway," Chinchin said too quickly. She focused on her smile, trying to make it dazzle. "And I'm going to tell you why."

"...Continue."

"Of the 50 test subjects that have Matched with healing Nylos, no one has experienced these side effects. In fact, subjects Matched with Nylos that have healing or regenerative properties have a 0% fatality rate. None of them have even become symptomatic.

"It's not a total fix, just a patch until I get a handle on side effects. Healing Markers could mean maybe even an infinite number of Marker Matches with the mutation. That means similar to Questus, we could leverage multiple powers at once. Unlike Questus, the powers wouldn't wear off once the blood they've drunk works its way through their system."

That was what they cared about: how they measured up to Questus. The royals of Questus could bless the blood of the human who Matched with a Nylo, allowing anyone to drink the blood and then use the same power that the Marked human had. This is what the Blood Ceremony was all about—collecting blood from those who had Matched with a Nylo so they had all kinds of different powers they could pass out through their kingdom. Any Questus soldier could drink a blessed vial of blood and have magical powers for the day. It was how they became such a respected Kingdom. Chinchin just needed to tease out having similar abilities to their rival.

"And the added benefit is less deaths in the subjects. Let's be honest, a dose doesn't come cheap. Why not follow this discovery and cut costs and casualties as an added benefit?"

At this point, Chinchin had an image of the axolotl on screen with its small limbs, long body, and strange external gills that looked like what she imagined a lion's mane would look like had a lion been made for the sea. She let the silence linger in the air as she intentionally left out any talk about suicide or depression experienced by the Nylos. First of all, the cause of death was discovered by Chauson. Second of all, even he knew it wouldn't sell in front of this crowd.

"What resources do you need to continue this lead?" 7 asked.

"I need more axolotls. The flying ones have the best healing abilities. And I need them to be extracted carefully. They're extremely rare and extinction would not help our case. I need some, but no more than 5 or 6 or we'll disturb their ecosystem too much. They'll also need to be handled with... care."

"33 will fulfill your request."

"Thank you. The largest nesting area is northeast, above Questus. Somewhere between Questus and House of Haessig." Chinchin didn't want to mention this fact until they had accepted her request. These Nylos were to be found on enemy territory in some hinterland beyond Questus Castle. It wasn't a small ask to capture Nylos so close to their rival house.

"We understand."

"The last update is that I'll be looking into how to make the mutation Matches as permanent as traditional Matches. When we cut out the Mark from the Marked, the subject loses control of the Nylo 100% of the time. When we cut out the Mark from a traditional Match, the subject has a 50/50 chance of maintaining its connection with its Marker."

"Understood. Your research is very valuable to us, 86." The voice paused. There was a side conversation, but Chinchin couldn't make it out. Then the voice continued, "To ensure your research and future research is protected, we will be assigning Shadow Scouts to you. Also, we will be moving your residence to XLVE where we will provide you with an upgraded space."

"Scouts? Look, I don't want to move to XLVE. I want to stay where I'm at with who I work with. I can take care of myself."

"You are a rare and brilliant mind that's essential to Project 222. You will be treated as such with the protection of Shadow Scouts."

"That's not necessary." Chinchin realized that though she had carried the matte stone Chauson had given her which made her invisible to the always-watching Obsidian V walls, they had noticed her absence from their watch.

"Do I need to remind you, 86, that you allowed spies from Nevarra into Project 222? Maya and her partner picked your brain for *months* before they were uncovered by our Shadow Scouts. This is not a request," 33 said.

"No, I—"

"We will provide axolotls for your research. Your residence has been changed to XLVE, unit 145. Scouts will escort you to your old residence, and help you move your things to your new, upgraded home. Your focus for Project 222 will remain as follows: speed of production, volume of Matches, and permanence of results."

"Okay, but can I—," Chinchin began, before the screen returned to a solid black state indicating the call had ended. She was suddenly alone again. She took a deep, slow breath.

"Okay then," she said to herself.

Chinchin opened the door to see four Shadow Scouts waiting for her. They were dressed in all black from head to toe. Even their faces were covered in the material called Ghen that Chinchin was familiar with. It was elastic, flexible, and when needed, it was nearly as solid as the black walls that made up the lab.

"So, if I want to take a vacation before I relocate. Say a week to go to the coast... do you guys come with me, or...?"

"86, lead scientist of Project 222, is not authorized to leave section XLVE."

"A no would have sufficed. No Nylos with you guys? Just the Ghen then?"

"And these," one of the guards revealed a gun. One of the very few things Pagra had modeled after the Atroxes who had entered The Cache over 100 years ago. Chinchin's eyes flickered down at the metallic compact and then back up to the guardian's armored face, another black mirror. She saw the shadow of her reflection in the guardian's mask. She saw a prisoner.

Oh how the landscape of her research had changed. She thought her breakthroughs would give her more freedom, not less. She had finally crossed the line of becoming too valuable—and not without Chauson's help in secret. He must know she's under constant surveillance now. Chinchin began to walk to her new quarters in Pagra Labs, already feeling claustrophobic with two Scouts escorting her on each side as she walked. She could feel the depth in her stomach, the space where dread grew, start to open up. Her face showed no sign of this. Like a porcelain doll, her light eyes and lips were pretty and unmoving. With her emotionless, glass-like face, she began to weigh the seriousness of the increased surveillance. The watching walls she could handle. This? This felt different. And Chinchin was determined to get rid of that feeling as quickly as possible.

It didn't take as long as Chinchin predicted for Pagra Labs to bring in more axolotls for testing. They had brought 20 axolotls back, which sent Chinchin into a fury. They were already an endangered species, and Chinchin was seriously concerned that their axolotl hunting had put them into extinction. And if axolotls were the key to surviving the mutation and the Nylos' depression, they might have just ended the cure before she could confirm it.

When she got the news, she returned to her quarters immediately. Her space was cold and bare. Chinchin didn't want any of the luxuries that came with someone in her position to distract her from her work... and had that first conviction weakened, the idea of deserving anything very nice when so many innocent victims died at her hand did not waiver.

Chinchin entered her bathroom where the black walls appeared to be frosted over. Privacy. She drew a bath. She stood naked over the tub, looking at her reflection. Suddenly the water began to ripple. She was getting an incoming call. She kneeled.

"Chinchin?" a voice said from the water.

"Mother."

"I'm sensing some distress on the other side."

"No distress here," Chinchin sat on the edge of the tub.

"I heard your laboratory collected more axolotls than you intended?"

Chinchin didn't respond.

"You should have killed them for not listening to you. Sweet daughter. Their disobedience is atrocious. If they only knew who you *really* were."

Chinchin sighed, considering the suggestion. "Well, I have the axolotls now. I should be able to neutralize my test subjects. When I know there won't be any more deaths from the experiment, I'll let someone else run things. Maybe I will come home."

"I hope that means soon. I hear they're treating you like a prisoner over there."

"You can always come and get me."

"Your choice is your choice."

"Is it?"

"You're in Pagra. That is not my choice."

"I'll be home soon, mother. I'll work with the axolotls. Then I'll come home."

"Be careful, Chinchin. I'm not there to protect you."

"I know."

The water grew still, and Chinchin slipped into the

black rectangular tub for a soak. Her relationship with her mother was... complicated. She took a deep breath in as she soaked deeper into the tub. It was already done. The axolotls were there. She needed to keep moving forward. Once the experiment was concluded and everyone was safe, she would have found a way to safely allow anyone to Match with a Nylo. It should be up to the human anyway. Pagra might have other plans, but that wouldn't keep her solution from being one for the people, no matter their status or wealth. The warm water soothed her as she combed through her options, and she sunk an inch deeper into the tub. Just as her eyes started to close, Chinchin heard a chime.

"What is it now?" she said out loud. She stepped out of the tub and wrapped a black towel around her. Walking to her front door, the inside stone revealed the visitor: Chauson. She opened the door.

"86," Chauson's cheeks might have turned a shade darker as he glanced at her wet hair. Normally golden, her damp mane was a dusky brown.

"I was busy," Chinchin said as she turned and walked away, leaving the door open. She hadn't seen him since the night of the tavern. Though she tried to act casual, she was relieved to see him.

"Sorry," Chauson stepped in.

"Have a seat," Chinchin gestured towards a rigid block for a chair. She then stepped back into her room to change, "Did you... hear anything?"

"What do you mean?" Chauson called back to her.

"About the axolotls?"

"No. Why?"

"Because they just brought back 20 of them."

"What? That seems like a lot."

"They might have made the one cure I had to the suicides go extinct."

"...So you do think I was right?" Chauson said.

Chinchin walked in wearing all black, just in time to roll her eyes. She sat down across from him, still drying her hair with a towel. "Maybe."

"You think the axolotls will save them?"

"I've made sure the Nylos have better treatment, more space and exercise. More socialization. So I'm not relying on just the axolotls, but I think they'll be the last line of defense if someone starts feeling suicidal again."

"Can I ask a question?" Chauson asked.

"Okay."

"I get why you don't want anyone to die. You're a good person. But why did you set out to create the mutation in the first place? Why do you want to be able to create a way to Match people to Nylos without letting it happen naturally?"

"Marker Matches are rare. Only so many people are *lucky* enough to Match, to have powers. But everyone else... so many people who are struggling just to get by... not so much. I just wanted to try to find a way to give everyone a chance to have powers. I don't want it to come down to luck."

"That's... surprisingly altruistic. And you decided using Nylos was the way to do it?"

"There's plenty of them in the wild. They're just so damn picky with who they choose. It's not fair."

"Sounds like you wish they would choose you," Chauson said.

Chinchin laughed. "That's the last thing I want."

"You don't think it would be fun to have a little power? Maybe the ability to fly? Create fire from nothing..."

"Now who sounds like they want to Match with a Marker?" Chinchin asked.

"I don't deny it. Why wouldn't you want to?"

"There are plenty of people who need it more than I do."

"I never took you for such a softie."

"I'm not soft. Life is just... hard. I just wish the world was more fair."

"You know, I thought you were going to say you wanted to Match with a million Nylos and be all-powerful. You know, like a mad scientist."

"Well, I'm just a scientist."

"Not just. One of the best."

"Well, obviously," Chinchin rolled her eyes again. "What work stuff did you want to talk about?"

"I just wanted you to know how important your work is. I get that you want this mutation to be shared so that everyone will have the right to Match with a Nylo, but it is also going to help Pagra. We're strong now, but a lot of people don't talk about how heavily we rely on Obsidian V. We've bet our future on it and in the last few years realized we're running out of it. Fast. The Old City should have been under construction now and slowly transitioning to the New City. But we just don't have enough."

"I knew there was a finite amount of Obsidian V, I just didn't realize Pagra had already run out."

"We have enough that we have a strong homebase. We could most likely hold off any attack from the East. Even with Questus' numbers, our technology is too advanced. But if we ever wanted to move East... Well, we don't have enough Obsidian to do it."

"Why would you go East?"

"The Labs recently discovered a motherload of Obsidian V."

"Where exactly?"

"North of Questus. Right in the heart of Nevarra."

"How much?"

"Enough to turn every city in The Cache into Obsidian V if we wanted to."

"Do you?"

"No, but we need more to expand into the Old City. You think everyone should have access to magic. I think everyone in Pagra should have access to tech."

"Will you invade Nevarra?"

"We know Nevarra is small, but we're not stupid. We know every man, woman, and child in that forest is brought up to be a Warrior. We're going to try to start negotiations with them soon."

"You think they'd work with us after Project 222? After Maya?"

Chauson shrugged. "Questus is still much more of an enemy to them than we are. Sometimes the same enemy is all it takes."

"I hope you can work it out. We haven't had a war in some time."

"It won't come to that. Oh, and I just wanted to let you know that I'm playing by the rules. I made a request to review your project. If it gets approved, my team could support yours. Maybe we'll officially work together soon. We'll be partners."

Chinchin nodded, a faint ghost of a smile on her lips. Maya had said something eerily similar to her not too long ago. And now... she was gone.

CHAPTER 7

THE CAGES

CANDLAND

There was no news of Keyes. Candland had wondered if Keyes was hiding in the Tunnels, but he knew his brother was too loyal to the Blood to venture that far into the shadows. The question of his brother was like a dull ache in the day, something that he could wonder about, while still getting day-to-day duties completed. It only became something he would despair about in the night, in the darkness where there were no distractions.

But he had competing anxieties. The squeeze of Ava's hand and her jaunty skip haunted Candland whenever his eyes lost focus. Sometimes he would look from the castle walls down into the city and see Ava—her long brown hair, warm brown eyes, her smile, the green Mark on her cheek... He would hold his breath, a second would pass, and he would realize it wasn't really Ava. When he didn't see her, he saw a white and green flash, something dashing through the air. Axol? But after a few seconds, he would realize it was only a simple dove crossing the sky or a paper lost in the wind.

And if that wasn't punishment enough, the cages under his family name took the rest of the space within his head. The people with Markings like Ava and Rocky—the people he was closest to. The Nylos, electric, flying, glowing, hissing, snarling... captive. All to be plucked from once a year for the celebrations if their name was chosen in the Pre Ceremony as a sacrifice.

Seeing the Cages for himself, Candland knew that unlike his lessons had taught him, the truth was that there was no rehabilitation happening. There was trading with Makani who poached some of the rarer creatures or Matches to sell across The Cache. The rest were living captive. The humans Marked by Nylos, sinners by association of dark magic from the Nylos—because no magic could be pure unless it was from the drink of the Blood—were trapped in their cages by order of the Blood and his mother, the queen. It was a prison, not a school. A hell, not a sanctuary. The only thing that hinted at rehabilitation was breaking the bond between the Marked and its Marker. And that was done brutally by cutting out the Mark the Nylos had left on the humans' bodies.

Candland's schoolings were wrong. The Cages were wrong. And after Ava was swept away from him in the underground parade, he could no longer plead ignorant as he had every day of his life before that. Being raised to follow the Blood wasn't enough of a reason. Telling himself it wasn't that bad, wasn't enough justification. The Blood was wrong. His mother was wrong. He was wrong.

And nothing made that more convincing than his last night with Ava. The night he failed her. And if he hadn't failed her then, he thought bitterly, he had already failed her before. He was the prince of a kingdom that held her kind captive. That called her cursed, cut out the Mark from her skin, and locked her up.

When Candland had made it back to the castle after the parade, he closed himself in his quarters. He did not go to his studio. He did not pay his mother a visit to learn if there were any updates on his absent brother. He did not travel back to the Tunnels although the idea of the strong concoctions made there to help him forget everything were tempting. But he couldn't bear the idea of passing through the sand without being able to see Ava. He just couldn't.

He wasn't sure how many days had passed when his mother called for him. Todec was the messenger, his personal guard and friend. When he opened Candland's room, he found Candland sitting on the ground with his back to his bed. Todec threw back the curtains, letting the light pour in, and turned to the prince. There was a dagger that had been tossed a few feet away from the prince, and his forearms and legs were stained with wet and dry blood that the prince had slowly carved out over the last few days. Candland didn't respond to the sunshine. He felt no warmth. He felt nothing.

Without calling more staff, Todec bathed and dressed Candland as if the prince were a doll. He carefully cleaned around the wounds on the limbs of the prince. And he bandaged them delicately. Candland said nothing the entire time, and was too ashamed to look Todec in the eye. Once Candland was fully dressed and sitting on the bed, Todec cleared his throat.

"The Queen and the Blood Council require your presence. She says the distribution must continue while Prince Keyes is away. You are the only one in the kingdom who can bless the Blood and give our people the power they need."

"...I can't," Candland said finally.

Todec sat next to the prince. His fingers were interlaced and resting on his lap.

"You know. My father is a painter. He painted some of the very walls in this castle. When his hair turned gray, so did his eyes. He went blind."

Candland blinked. He heard Todec's voice. He was listening.

"And when he lost his vision, he thought he lost his ability to paint. Lost the ability to be a painter, a husband, a father, a grandfather even. He thought of never knowing what his grandchildren would look like, and he nearly ended his life... But. The Blood had heard our prayers. Westahn heard my father's story. He delivers a small shipment to my father every month. My father drinks it every fortnight, and because of this, he can see. He can paint. He knows what my nieces all look like. Because of those with royal blood who bless it so my father can drink it."

Candland said nothing.

"I know Keyes is supposed to be here. He's supposed to be the one blessing the blood so others in Questus can drink it and feel its power. I know this isn't how it's supposed to be. But Candland, you're the only one who can do this right now. You're the only one who can bring hope and help people like my father."

Candland nodded with a sheen to his eyes. He was close with Todec, but he had never heard that story before.

Todec opened the door from Candland's chambers, and Candland followed him. He felt lost in his own home, and he stayed close to Todec. He wondered if Todec knew how much he relied on him. How much he needed him now. And a wave of guilt passed through Candland's body as he failed to even utter a word of thanks when Todec left him at the entrance of the room of the Blessings.

Candland walked in, hoping his heavy depression—something he wasn't in a state to hide well—could pass as stoicism. He felt sadness as his eyes swept over the room. He saw his mother sitting on a grand chair. She looked... impatient. He saw all 12 of the council, six men and six women, all sitting to the left or right of his mother in their own uniquely adorned chairs, related to their area of governance. He matched a gaze from West-ahn, recognizing a look he rarely received: concern.

"Are you ready to do your duty to the Blood?" Samgal asked as he stood from his chair. He was the councilman over the Blood. *Temples, worship, blood chambers,* Cand-land thought. Samgal walked down the steps, his shoes echoing in the great room. He stood beside the pillow where Keyes had kneeled not so long ago. Candland had been there to witness it.

"The kingdom depends on you," Samgal continued. "We cannot share the Blood's powers without the bless-ings from the direct bloodline of the first king of Questus, King Crotio. We need the power of the Blood to keep our kingdom running. We need it to protect our kingdom. No one can drink the Blood and channel its power unless you bless it first."

"He knows how the Blood works," Westahn inter-rupted. He stood as well. He was The Distribution after all.

Candland knew what came next. He had seen Keyes go through the same ritual when he had come of age. Candland needed to drink blood himself before he could perform any blessings. Next, they would bring different types of blood to bless for Questus. Last time, Keyes had blessed the blood of a human who had Matched with a Nylo who had water-wielding abilities. This gave whoever drank the blood those same water-wielding abilities, albeit temporarily. That batch had been for the farmers of Questus to help prepare for the season well before harvest.

From lessons, he knew the more aggressive Marked with the power of fire or force fields were killed in order to hydrate the Questus army. The Blood Ceremony's sacrifice was the source of their blood. One body at a time, one year at a time. And so each drop was precious. But now that he was getting called upon, Candland knew each drop was bottlenecked without it being blessed by him or his brother. Without a blessing, Questonians could drink as much blood as they wanted, and all they would get was a stomachache.

Candland wondered about his mother. How it must feel to rule the kingdom, but not have the direct blood-line to truly serve her people with the Blood. Did she resent that? She was so close to Keyes, but Candland had never shared that closeness with her. He had been closer to his father before he died. It must have felt strange for her to depend on him like she had to now. It certainly felt strange for him. And now of all times, when everything he felt he was, was simply... wrong. How could he be part of why the Cages existed—the son of the woman who had them built in the first place—and still be the only person with the ability to bless *anything*, let alone the blood of the Marked?

Westahn was now standing beside Samgal with his hand out, welcoming Candland towards the pillow. Candland wanted to walk to them, and lay his head down on the pillow. He felt so tired. He was sure he could fall asleep despite having a formal audience.

"Your father didn't hesitate to help his people when he was needed," his mother said. "You will make him proud."

He's dead, Candland thought. Candland remembered his father in his last weeks leading up to his death. He spent it with Westahn and Samgal on bedrest because he was too weak to stand. When Candland came for brief visits, the blessings didn't stop. Samgal lifted a glass of blood to the king's bedside. His father put his hand on it, his eyes hardly open. He muttered the blessing under his breath—a blessing Candland wasn't allowed to know until now. And Samgal would remove the glass from his hand once his father stopped speaking. Candland remembered his father's hand falling away without the support, and Samgal would bring another large glass of blood up under his father's hand to repeat the process. The Blood of the Marked was like the lifeblood of Questus.

Candland looked at his mother. She feigned a smile.

"I visited the Cages," Candland said finally.

His mothers eyes narrowed. Westahn's eyes widened with warning.

"All of those people. All of those animals—," Candland began.

"Nylos," his mother said as if she was speaking of a poison.

"They're caged. They're being treated like..."

"Like they were cursed? Like the only benefit they serve The Cache is their Blood once they're dead?"

Candland hadn't realized what mood his mother was in. There wasn't a good time to bring up how they were treating the Marked and their Markers, but now definitely wasn't the time. He looked closer at his mother. She was tired. The whites of her eyes were pink with thick veins, and her bottom lip quivered ever so slightly.

"We have to let them go," Candland said quietly.

"What did you say?" his mother asked.

"We can't keep them caged like that. We only need one a year. We don't need all of them like that."

"We pool them together so the council of The Cursed and The Distribution can make sure we have what we need when we need it."

"We have more than we need. We have too much," Candland shook his head, stepping forward. His sadness faded for the first time as anger took over.

"And what if Pagra attacks?" the queen asked. "What if we need more offensive powers? What if our armies need more defense? What if Nevarra invades? What if there is a famine? Who will call upon the rains to grow our food and feed our people without the power to bring a storm to our lands?"

"We have more than enough. The Blood Chambers are filled with blood. You haven't seen it, because you're not allowed. I've been down there with father. We could fill an ocean with blessed Blood."

"Questus needs an ocean of blessed Blood to continue

to be the largest and most powerful kingdom in The Cache. You don't know what you speak of. Now sit down and kneel on that Bloody pillow and be blessed like the little blood clot that you are."

Candland stepped forward, completely dumbfounded by his mother's language in front of the Council. He was slightly surprised that Samgul didn't warn her to watch her tongue.

He looked at Samgul and then Westahn. Westahn nodded. The second Candland's knees touched the pillow, Samgul began the ceremony. Candland didn't expect to be kneeling on that pillow so soon after Keyes. He was supposed to have another year before he would taste blood. He was supposed to be the second prince in the shadows that could do as he pleased. Now, like Keyes and his father before him, he would spend most of his time with Westahn and Samgul, muttering blessings until his final breath. He felt a hatred for Keyes that surprised him then. He shrunk with guilt. What if Keyes was dead and he was developing a newfound hatred for a brother simply because he'd died?

Westahn cleared his throat, and Candland looked up. Samgul held a small glass. Candland could drink it all in one large gulp, which he would have to do. Every drop needed to be consumed. He took the glass. He thought of his brother Keyes who had also taken the glass. Keyes had smiled at him as he held the glass and raised it to him as if to say 'bottom's up'. And then his brother drank the liquid in the same way Candland might have downed a shot with Rocky in the Tunnels.

The liquid shook in Candland's trembling hand. He had not heard a word uttered by Samgul this entire time though the man's voice had sounded grand in the background of his thoughts. Everyone had said "Aye" in unison as Samgul handed him the cup. Candland hadn't said it with them. He didn't need to. He only needed to drink the blood.

He raised the glass to his lips. He heard a laugh. It was Ava. He lowered his head and looked around the room. Marble floors that echoed underneath their feet. Columns. Ceilings high enough for even the biggest Nylos to stand comfortably under. There was no Ava here.

"Drink," his mother said.

Candland lifted the glass again. This time he felt the mist of Axol on his head. He remembered the sensation. It was the opposite of feeling depressed. It was the opposite of heavy. Axol's sparkles felt light. They felt like elephants in a parade or like the feathers from Bern's wings tickling his ear. Candland smiled for the first time since he had let go of Ava's hand.

He dropped the glass and the blood splattered across the floor. The spill was larger than Candland had expected. His mother stood up.

"Candland!" she yelled.

He turned away from her. He turned away from the council.

"Your father would disown you!" his mother shouted over Candland's footsteps.

"Father's dead."

Candland could feel the rage in his mother, but he walked on.

"Then perhaps I should disown you," she said.

Candland stopped and turned around, his brown hair fell forward in an arch, reaching his green eyes. His eyes darkened as he looked back at his mother.

"Then do it. And then pray to the Blood that Keyes comes back to bless the blood. Because he'll be all you have."

Candland walked out and the guards closed the doors behind him. He heard the room erupt behind the doors, and took a deep breath. He wasn't sure if he was doing the right thing, but it was as if he had no choice. He couldn't drink the blood. It felt like an impossible task. And all the while, he was being pulled elsewhere...

His brother was who knows where. Ava was gone. But the Markers and their Marked were only a day's ride away. He knew where they were, and he knew who could help him do what he could not do alone. He just wasn't sure if Rocky would answer his call.

"I want you to know I was on my way to Pagra when I got your message from Berns," Rocky said. "I had to turn around to come and get your ass."

"Thank you," Candland said. Candland rode on a royal horse, while Rocky's Nylo, Berns, was clutching Rocky's leather shoulder harness in his sharp talons so Rocky was flying in the air. At some angles when Candland couldn't see Berns' feet, it looked like Rocky was simply flying through the air with wings.

"...And maybe if I do you this favor, you might reconsider joining me in Pagra?" Rocky asked.

Candland knew this would be the condition. Going to Pagra was still a suicide mission to him, but at this point, that didn't sound half bad. In fact, it felt like it was exactly what he deserved.

"What's wrong?" Rocky asked.

"Nothing. I'm glad you're here. I'm glad we're doing this."

"You can tell me anything."

Candland cleared his throat. Should he ask Rocky where he thought his brother was? Should he describe the surprise of Ava's kiss the night she died? Or should he admit the ignorance he had shielded himself with until he saw the Cages for himself?

"Do you think we can do this?" Candland asked Rocky, though he was asking himself more.

"NG's do it all the time," Rocky shrugged. "We pivoted our strategy as soon as we heard the prince of Questus was leading the breakout... They're excited. And I'm the best NG in Nevarra. So, yeah. We can do this."

"What if we fail?" Candland asked.

"Then some of the Nylos and the people they've

Marked will escape, and that's still better than nothing. Remember, they all have power. As soon as they can, they will help themselves. How many are there? This one was a bigger one. We had it on our radar, but hadn't gotten to it yet."

"Hundreds. Maybe thousands. I'm not sure."

"Can you show me?"

Candland held his arm out, and Rocky flew closer. Rocky took Candland's hand, the Mark that covered Rocky's hand and forearm glowed gold. Candland closed his eyes and thought of the night the headmaster walked him through the Cages. He remembered the people, the Nylos, and last of all, the giant metal box, bolted and chained, dripping in Blood. And Rocky, through the unique power Berns channeled through him, saw it all through Candland's memories.

"The big one's locked with Blood magic," Rocky said.

"How do we open it?" Candland asked.

"Fight magic with magic. Finding someone who can move metal at some capacity would be easiest. I'll ask the NG's to keep an eye out."

"What if there's not?"

"We find someone with the right power to get the Nylo out."

"Okay. It's a plan."

"And what about our plan after this? First of all, your mother..."

"I don't care."

"You will when it's all done. Candland, by doing this,

you're going against your mother. Your kingdom. Everything."

"Why are you my friend?" Candland blurted the question out.

"What do you mean?"

"My family does terrible things to people like you. So why do you even tolerate me?"

"You were born into a family that does terrible things to people like me... but you didn't do terrible things to me. I guess I felt like you were different."

"Am I?"

"Candland. Look where we are. What we're about to do."

"I'm ashamed. Of my family. Of myself."

"You'll feel better tonight. After you've saved lives. Candland, tonight, you'll be my hero."

Hero, Candland thought. Not to Ava though. Still, it was a start.

Candland crouched behind some bushes with Rocky by his side. The Cages were in their view.

"You really ordered your mother to release them all?" Rocky asked as he eyed the front gate.

"She laughed in my face and called me a blood clot in front of the Blood Council."

"Well, she won't be laughing soon. Now remember. I'll start with the people, they should be able to help get their Nylos out. They won't leave without them. I'll look for someone who can help with the big one in the metal box. We'll meet there, and we'll set it free like the rest.

And just be careful. They'll know I'm here to help, but the Marked won't trust you."

"We won't kill anyone, will we?"

"No. Nothing like that. Hey. Look at me. You good?"

"My mother won't let me come home after this."

"Do you want to go home? Candland, if you don't want to, I'll go. The other NGs have my back."

"I want to help them. That's all I know. So let's just go with it before I change my mind."

Candland stood up and dusted himself off. He started walking towards the entrance. It was strange. Before he had not been nervous at all approaching the doors. He had even demanded the headmaster free the Markers and their Marked the night coming home from the Tunnels. Now, here he was again, but the closer he got, the warmer he felt. Candland made his way easily through the front gate.

"You again?" the headmaster said, greeting Candland in the hall. He didn't look happy.

"I wanted to say thanks for the horse. Did she make it back alright?"

"She did. Thank you."

"I brought some wine from my mother. She wanted me to give them to you myself for your trouble with me the other night," Candland looked down not out of embarrassment, but out of shame for his lie. Still, the shame played well into his story.

The headmaster laughed. "That's alright, but I will

take the wine. We eat dinner soon. It's not much, but we'll share the wine."

Candland nodded.

Candland was trained in combat, but he was never a dedicated student—for that topic anyway. In philosophy, languages, and history, he excelled. His tutors could hardly give him enough to read. In lessons he brought up strange ideas or small, obscure moments in history that even his tutors could not speak to, and so Candland was left to his books. He loved the history of the creation of The Cache. It was a time so long ago that fact and myth collided and no one could untangle the two.

In combat, his main motivation came from the desire to avoid pain, but his teacher was long past his battling days and often tired; and so the combat instructor put all of his energy into Keyes' lessons whose favorite classes were Theology of the Blood, Combat, and War Strategy and Tactics. Keyes began sparring at a young age, practicing with sharp weapons sooner than his mother approved. Candland on the other hand showed no eagerness to be armed with real weapons nor use them on anyone. And no one really cared that he didn't because he wasn't the first heir. Second son and in the shadows was a perfectly appropriate place for him, especially because his lack of skill made a position as a general out of the question anyway.

Once in combat training, to understand the feeling of a kill—to pass through the flesh of another living, bleeding creature—the brothers had both been presented Nylos tied down so tightly they could barely move.

Keyes had thrown a spear at his Nylo that landed, and then he finished the creature's life with a single and swift strike of the sword. Candland remembered the moment well. They had both been given weapons, both been presented with their kills. In front of Keyes had been a pig. On his skin, he had patches of scales and other patches of quills like a porcupine. Keyes had thrown the spear so that it had missed the patches and pierced the soft pink flesh of the Marker.

In front of himself was a deer with a thousand long fox-like tails. Candland did not want to learn the feeling of a kill. He refused. Before his teacher could scold him, Keyes had pounced with his sword. The magical deer was dead. Candland remembered the smattering of blood on his brother's cheek, just above a charming grin.

Now, as he strayed from a hall and up the stairs to the third story—which was the highest level of the building—he found himself on top of the stone wall that surrounded the Cages. Beyond the wall, to the west, there had been cages and fences for the low-threat Marked, and already they had been released by Rocky or another Nylo Guardian and were quietly scattering. Candland traced the way from the cages and torn fences to the wall. That's when he saw Rocky. But it was only a moment. Rocky's black coils from his hair bounced softly as he moved from one station to the next. He was fast. His movements made it so that his body seemed just a trick of the light. He knocked out guards before they had any cause to scream or shout. That was the Nylo Guardian way. The Nevarrian style, deep set in assassination and the stealth that was required of it. They were a flexible people who preferred improvised moves over repetitive, trained motions. Candland then realized why Nevarrians were so notorious for their warriors. They were born to sneak, born to shadow, born to do what they must without anyone knowing what was even happening.

Questus had none of these characteristics. Their weapons were big and shiny for show, but loud and clunky for battle. Their fighting style was made up of big powerful motions, but they were not quick. Questus was a threat to Nevarra because of their size and number, but not necessarily skill.

Candland stopped following the traces of Rocky he was able to catch and looked to the center of the walls where the iron box still rumbled occasionally. It didn't look as big from here, though Candland could still see the blood covered chains around it.

Candland walked back down the stairs and took another turn down a hallway of cells guarded by two men. Two Questonian men. Candland approached.

"Sorry, off limits."

"The headmaster said I could walk down and look at them. I wanted to see what you men have to deal with every day." Candland was sure his gruff comment was less than convincing, but the two men looked at each other and then nodded at Candland.

"Don't talk to any of them. And be quick."

Candland walked down the hallway. He didn't have it in him to even knock the guards out, but maybe someone in one of the cells had a power that could help everyone there. He just had to help them out.

He took a few steps down the hall, looking at each cell made up of iron bars. A ragged woman rushed up to the bars, whining and asked, "Wine?" A bald, bull-headed man looked up at Candland and then back down at his hands. Candland was of no interest to him. A scrawny man ran up to the bars and laughed. A teenage girl stood up, but did not approach. She was the least intimidating by appearance, though Candland knew that any Marked could have a power that allowed them to rip him apart in seconds. Of course, she most likely couldn't. The guards wouldn't have let him roam the hall if that was the case... or so Candland hoped was the case.

He walked up to the bars.

"I want to free you," he whispered.

Her eyes got bigger. She was scared, but listening.

"I don't know what your power is, but what can I do to help you?"

"You're... the prince?" she asked.

"Yes. How can I get you out of here?"

The girl walked to the bars swiftly, causing Candland to back up.

"Come here," she said.

Candland looked at the guards who were in their own conversation. Candland took three steps forward and the girl lunged at him. She grabbed his hair and then spun him around with one arm restraining him, the other hand holding only what Candland could guess was an antler with a razor sharp point. He hadn't seen it before. Where had it come from? He could feel the blood drip from where the point pressed into his neckline. Or was it just sweat? The guards ran towards him, clanking on their way down the hall. He must have yelled when she grabbed him. One guard turned and yelled for backup.

"I want to free you," Candland squeaked.

"Not more than I want to free myself," the girl said through her teeth. "Come any closer and the prince dies! Keys. Now!"

The guards were not highly trained. This was not a high-risk hall. These were supposed to be prisoners who could do no harm at an arm's length, which was generally the case. The other prisoners screamed and shouted out into the hallway. The girl unlocked herself from her cage. She threw the keys onto the ground, and Candland kicked them to the next cell just in time before he was dragged out by the once unassuming Marked. The two walked out into the hallway with the prince acting as a shield.

More guards rushed in, but stayed their distance when they saw the prince held with a point to his throat. Once Candland and the girl made it to the main grounds, it was chaos. Marked were running and flying, Markers were traveling in a dozen other various ways. It was a stampede of cursed creatures and the humans they had

Matched with. The gates were open and everyone was escaping in the chaos. The girl threw Candland to the ground, and he fell flatly on his back. Candland watched the girl run towards one of the openings as another Marked stepped on his hand on their way out. Candland grabbed his hand in pain and quickly stood up. He saw the headmaster guiding three guards. They were all yelling at each other, but nothing was being done. What could be done? Rocky and the other NGs (who Candland disappointedly had yet to spot) had done their job well.

Candland sat for a moment, squeezing the pain in his hand. He was in awe of the Nylos he saw. A crow-looking bird flew across with a dark shadow following behind it, leaving traces of a darkness behind him. It was as if the crow was followed by or even leading the dark. Another animal was hurtling forward, clenching onto the earth in handfuls and throwing them behind it as it crept forward at an incredible speed. It looked like an alligator. It paused in front of Candland, and looked at the prince. For a moment Candland was transfixed. Then spikes jutted out of the animal every which way, that caused Candland to fall backward. The alligator-like Nylo's eyes glowed red and then the creature moved on. The next thing Candland saw was a sphere of light, darting to and fro. It resembled a floating gel more than any inert animal Candland could think of. In fact, for a moment, he wasn't even sure if the bubble-like creature was a Nylo at all.

Rocky. Candland remembered they had agreed to

meet at the giant metal container. Candland gathered his astonishment and put it away for another time. He headed to the iron-walled cage where Rocky waited for him. A woman was standing beside him, a white bat flapping above her head.

"Good, you're here," Rocky said. "This is Elise."

"Elise. Okay."

"She can walk through walls, and she can bring people—and Nylos—with her."

"That's great!"

"I'm worried about what's inside," Elise said.

"Candland and I will go with you. We're both powerful Marked. We're just trying to get everyone out of here," Rocky said.

Candland looked at Rocky, catching his lie. He wasn't powerful or Marked. Then Candland looked at Elise, he nodded, growing the lie.

"If things go badly, I won't wait," Elise said.

"You don't have to worry about that," Rocky smiled. "Let's go. The quicker, the better. The guards have probably called for help by now."

The three walked up to the metal wall. Elise, in the middle, clasped her right hand with Candland's and her left with Rocky's. Candland took a breath, his soul searching for the reason he stood in front of what might be his death. *To not be... bad anymore.* The words floated in his chest. Then Elise walked forward and they walked through the blood-chained wall with her.

Inside was a creature with eyes the color of frozen lightning. It had large, triangular ears, a black nose, and teeth the size of Candland's hands. The beast was covered in reddish brown and white fur with a stripe of white fur running down between its eyes. It growled at the sight of the three poking through the opening, and stood with its legs backed up to the very back of the container.

It took Candland a moment to remember what it was he was doing there and why. It took him a moment to realize he was there, and it was too late now to not be there. So, frozen in place, Candland shouted. "You have to leave now! You're running out of time! Come with us!"

The giant wolf spun around. Elise and Rocky ducked, but Candland was knocked back into the metal wall. He slid down, hitting the ground hard. Elise panicked. She turned around, trying to yank herself from Rocky. Instead, she pulled them both onto the other side of the wall. Candland was left alone with the beast, sprawled on the ground.

"No, no, no," Candland said, banging on the wall as the air came back to his lungs. He could vaguely hear someone banging on the other side. Rocky? Was Elise gone?

Candland didn't have time to wonder. He spun around, acutely aware of his new predicament. The Nylo was on all fours, its head tilted down. Its lips were raised in jagged lines to show off its even more jagged teeth, and a low growl vibrated against the walls. The beast's breath alone was enough to send Candland back to the ground. Candland looked into his blue eyes and remembered that the creature was only fed once a month.

"I was—am—just trying to help you," Candland said carefully. "I was just trying to free you from this place."

The wolf's stance had not changed.

"And now we're both stuck. Why... am I not surprised."

The wolf stepped forward, and Candland froze. Its nose, the size of Candland's head, sniffed in his scent. The nose moved forward, brushing up against Candland and tickled his chest. Candland held his breath, noticing the heavy, panting breath smelled even more terrible up close. It was the scent of filth and rot. Candland, in all his fear, felt pity for the beast. To be stuck in this metal prison which was clearly never cleaned was punishment enough. And the Nylo was only waiting in it until he was traded to Makani where who knows what waited for him. The wolf then abruptly turned, as if he could read Candland's thoughts, and curled up sitting in the back corner.

"Not tasty enough for you?" Candland tilted his head. He leaned back on the metal wall. "No. That's not it. You're not in the mood. How could you be when you're locked in this windowless cell." Candland never had an appetite when things were bad as well.

The wolf blinked.

"It would be cool to see what your power is. I'm

guessing the chains are keeping that from happening, but we'll get you out of here. Rocky won't leave us here. Then we'll see what you can do."

A second later, Candland heard banging on the wall. He heard Rocky's voice. Very muddled. He was shouting.

"What?" Candland shouted back. "What are you saying?"

Then a few words registered: "...Blow this... Move... back... 3... 2..."

"No, no, no!" Candland spoke before rushing to the back of the metal crate, wolf or no wolf. He hadn't made it all the way as he hesitated when he was thrown from the explosion against the metal wall.

"You okay, prince?" Rocky coughed, waving his dark hand through the smoke. Candland was planted flat on the ground, but awake and making a poor attempt to sit up right. The wolf jumped towards Candland before Rocky could approach, picking him up by the collar with his teeth, and leaped through the busted wall and over Rocky's head. Rocky turned and watched the Nylo escape, a blue glow around the beast now that the chains had lost their hold on the creature.

"It's up to you now, prince," Rocky smiled to himself.

Rocky stepped out of the giant damaged crate. He called out for his Nylo as he ran back into the remaining chaos of the Cages. He saw Berns's feathers out of the corners of his eye and then jumped into the air and Berns caught him by his leather straps. Candland's friend took off like a rocket, flying low over the land ensuring his fellow Marked made their way to the river uninterrupted where rafts were waiting.

Candland was seeing a lot of the ground while being carried by the Nylo. He would strain his neck up to get a look at where they were going, but he would only get flashes of trees and greenery. He guessed they were going some direction east, but he couldn't be sure. It wasn't until the sun was low that the wolf slowed down and lowered Candland onto soft, long grass.

Candland was on all fours, trying to keep from vomiting from the rough ride. He turned and sat, with his head pounding. Candland looked up. The wolf sat beside him. They were surrounded by thick grasses and tall, bushy trees. It was cooler, wetter. They had gone Northeast. The air was moist and a thick misty rain sprung upon them.

"I guess you rescued your rescuer," Candland finally said as his head stopped spinning. He had seen inert wolves before, but nothing like this. Its appearance nonplussed the prince. This creature was so large that it made Candland question the species. The fur seemed so thick that a single strand from its coat might pierce through his flesh. And the outline of his frame was red, a stark difference between the rest of his white fur and blue eyes. The wolf's eyes were a deep, dark blue, reminding Candland of a starless night. Looking at the paws, claws, and long snout, Candland knew he was inches away from what could be the end of his life, and yet he still felt lucky to be close to something as majestic as the Nylo that sat beside him. Candland could smell the heavy breath of the wolf and wondered how many others had been so close?

Then the wolf's tongue rolled from its mouth, peeking out and then tucking itself back in. Candland had expected a snarl, a growl, a show of teeth. Seeing that the tongue was pink like a pup surprised him. He would have laughed had he not still feared for his life. Then a blue beam of light struck him suddenly. Candland dropped to the ground limp, where he would dream that he was sculpting the creature who had just filled him beyond his capacity with an energy he had never known before. It was a vision that he felt deep within his soul— trying to capture the energy of a lightning bolt in the shape of a stone. It felt impossible. And yet, suddenly within him, it felt absolute.

Candland woke up to the feeling of wet sandpaper sweeping heavily over his face. He lifted his hand slowly and involuntarily wiped the drool that laid thickly on his cheeks. The smell almost knocked him out a second time. He heard the sound of running water as he stirred, trying to remember where he was. He opened his eyes slowly seeing the pink tongue that had prefaced the flash of light and was brought back to where he had fallen unconscious. He let out a weak yelp, and scooped his body further backwards to make space between him and the giant nose in front of him.

A dark blue glow from his heart caught his attention. Candland looked down to find a Mark on the right side of his chest. The Marking glowed a blue that was not striking for its brightness, but for its flexible nature of being able to look anything from a stormy silver to a blue only the deepest oceans could replicate depending on how the light and shadow reflected from his body. The Mark on his chest, just larger than his own handprint, then extending over his shoulder and down to his bicep, was a collection of odd patterns. Hexagons were stamped blue together near his pectoral. More rough edges with sharp corners were repeated as if they were a chain or rope, wrapped around and around his shoulder and bicep. Strings of different patterns were wrapped around his right side almost as if the Mark had been a magical rope of armor. Some of the patterns reminded Candland of hot spinning metal gears or a piece of honeycomb. Could it remind him of both at the same time? He had Matched. He was Marked. Totally awakened by the incredible situation he found himself in, he looked up at the wolf.

"My mother is going to kill me."

Looking at the Nylo, the Marker who had lived up to its name and Matched with him, Candland saw things he didn't before. He had noticed the size of the paws, but not the fluff in between the wolf's toes. He had noticed the sharp body of the fur, but not the way the giant tail waved back and forth as if swaying to its own melody. He had noticed the pink tongue, which still reminded him of the very puppy-like way it peeked out and returned and sometimes didn't return immediately back behind the teeth of the Nylo.

"Proru," Candland said. The wolf looked at him, tilted its head, and then howled into the sky. A blue beam shot from Proru's mouth upward towards the clouds.

Candland staggered back, his forearm shielding him from the brilliant glow of his Nylo. When Proru quieted, Candland's worries seeped back into his mind.

"Proru, we have to get away. We have to go home. Home! We can't go home. Look at me!" Candland tore at the opening of his tunic, lifting and raising the front button to the wolf in accusation.

Candland began to pace, both his hands scratching around his head. Proru followed while Candland recalled the last conversation with his mother. He had asked her to free the Nylos. To free the Marked. And she had laughed in response.

There was a small drop of hope that his mother would take him in. Wouldn't she prefer a Marked son than no sons at all? But he knew the answer. He would be locked up in the Cages and counted for dead the second she saw the symbol glowing from his chest—and that was a best-case scenario. She would send Proru into a thicker metal cage with more blood-covered chains. She would sell him to Makani. His mother would not receive him. This wasn't just him escaping to the Tunnels every now and then. He was now one of the sinners of dark magic. The enemy of the Blood. He was cursed. He could have easier traveled to another world through the West Gate's portal than he could travel back to a place in The Cache that would feel like home for him. His home was no longer.

Candland plopped down at the realization, sitting in the soft grass with his knees bent as the sun made its final appearance. He took a few deep breaths while he pulled at his hair and fidgeted with the bridge of his nose. When he felt somewhat calmer, he looked up into the indigo eyes of the creature that was now connected to him in a way he had never been connected to anyone or anything before. The wolf looked back with his head cocked to one side, clearly amused by Candland's temperament, but also slightly concerned. Candland wondered at the thought of how he could possibly have Matched with a Nylo, and one that even the elephants from the Blood Parade would scatter from.

PART II

CHAPTER 8

A CHANCE ENCOUNTER

AVA

When Ava arrived in Pagra, she was already thinking of the Tunnels. She was homesick for a home that she knew wasn't really her home, and her heart ached for a boy that—had circumstances been different—she would have liked to have kissed more than just the one time. She stared out at the strange new land. Half of the city was made of Obsidian V, with sharp corners, sleek edges, and tall buildings. The other half was made up of common materials: water, clay, hay. Ava had heard of the black half, New City, and how it contrasted with the creamy, water-colored Old City, but seeing it was something else.

"You must get a new braid soon," Kavi said. "Or else the Vhykas will come for you. I fear they are close."

"Do you know where I can buy one?"

"In the Old City. Further west."

"I've never been this far from home," Ava said as she took her first steps into Pagra.

"When you say home, where are you referring to?" Kavi asked.

Ava looked at them without an answer and then started on her way to the Old City. So Kavi continued with more questions that were easier for Ava to answer as they first traveled through the black city. Axol stood out in his sparkling white body, looking extremely out of place. At the same time, they both felt it safer that Ava cradled him in her arms, and so he returned to her bosom where she stroked the back of his head.

Walking through the New City, Ava had never seen so many identical buildings in one place. There was something eerie about the duplication of the city. Something almost egotistical. Like the creator of the new city had decided the best structure had been discovered and only that structure—smooth black, reflective walls, seamless doors that gave them the appearance that they appeared from nowhere—was worth building.

When they reached the Old City where no two doors looked the same, Ava felt her shoulders lower and her ankles loosen. She wasn't afraid to make noise, and Axol must have felt it too because he fluttered out of her arms and began to explore a bold distance away from her. It was as if something had been watching her, and she had finally traveled to where its gaze could not follow.

"How did you manage to save such a fortune?" Kavi

asked. It was one of 50 questions they had asked since they had entered the Old City.

"What small fortune?"

"A bastard braid ranges from 6,000 jun and up. And that price would only get you so far for so long."

"What?" Ava stopped. Her mouth opened, closed, and then opened again. "6,000 jun? I don't have that kind of money."

"Ah. That is why my question to you did not make sense: because you do not have a small fortune."

"That's exactly what I don't have."

"If you do not purchase a braid soon, you will most likely be brutally injured by a Vhyka. I would estimate you have less than a week."

"I thought I had more time," Ava said.

"The good news is, you have proved to be quite impossible to kill. With the Vhykas, I see that as no different. They will only try to kill you and eat parts of you again and again... But you will not die."

"Not helping." Ava had now turned down a narrow, but naturally lit alleyway. She looked up at the clothes hanging from the lines through the open windows. No screens to keep the bugs or dust out, just wooden doors that would be closed for privacy in the night. She closed her eyes and began to rub her eyelids.

"Sand in your eyes?" Kavi asked.

No, just hopelessness, she thought. "6,000 jun..." Ava said in more of a groan than anything else. Axol hovered over Ava's troubled head. His eyes were watchful, sensing her frustration. He opened and closed his mouth a few times, making a strange, bubbly sound that only Ava thought was adorable. She could feel the glittering mist from his path sprinkle over her. It was refreshing after traveling through the desert heat for over a week. But it didn't help the fact that she was about 5,000 jun short.

Then she heard a strange noise. A small grunt like Axol had run into something. She raised her head and opened her eyes. Axol was gone. She turned to see a man in black sprinting down the alley. She could see Axol's white sparkles tracing his path.

"The Shadow Scout captured Axol," Kavi said.

"Axol! Kavi! He's got Axol!" Ava screamed as she scurried after the Nylo-napper.

"This is bad. I cannot physically help you," Kavi said. They were casually sprinting behind Ava. It was clear that this lung-wrenching speed for Ava was a leisurely pace for Kavi by the way that they spoke.

"Kavi, I'm losing him. Follow him!"

"I cannot physically intervene," they reminded her.

"Axol!" Ava clenched her teeth and pushed harder. She put all she had into her next strides and found that she was not chasing one man, but three men dressed in black, who were already disappearing from the next courtyard. Kavi followed behind her, close enough to observe, far enough to not get tangled in the action. She had made slight gains being just one weaving through the busy streets versus the three men trying to run in a unit. But then the three men split up. Without stopping,

Ava followed the white and green glitter floating a left turn where the men had split. She kept pushing.

Just as Ava was about to lose sight of her Nylo, her friend, her companion, her other half, she saw an owl dive for the head of the captor, causing the man in black to duck. A boy jumped from the roof, his feet used the man's back to break his landing. Just as Ava was coming upon them, the boy bent down and snatched the netting Axol was trapped in. He took out a knife, and Ava screamed. The boy turned around to see Ava reaching out.

"Don't hurt him!" she screamed.

With one swipe, the boy cut the net and Axol flew freely into her arms, shaking in shock. "Wasn't gonna."

"Th-thank you," Ava said.

"You cry *again*," Kavi said, writing down more notes in their book as they studied the tears in her eyes.

"Get used to it," Ava said, wiping the last of her tears.

The boy approached. She noticed his eyes were glowing a fiery gold. There was also a flicker in his eye. She thought it might be a spark of recognition—like he thought he knew who she was for a moment. It made her wonder if they had crossed paths even though she was almost certain she'd never seen him before. The owl appeared again, landing lightly on his shoulder. The weight still caused his shoulder to slant down.

"Are you alright?"

Ava caught herself staring. The golden glow of his eyes meant that he was using the powerful second level of Marker Magic. She had only seen this done a few times. Most Marked only ever experienced the first level of magic their entire lives—herself included. She had only seen a handful of people who had reached the second level with the glow in their eyes when they used their magic. And she'd never met someone who had unlocked the third and final level of the magical bond. This also made her a little wary. If his eyes were glowing, he must be using his magic in some way... but she didn't notice anything magical going on. Was he reading her mind, maybe? What could it be...

"Don't worry, the shadow scouts are gone. My name is Rocky. Your Nylo is safe for now."

"My name is Ava."

"And who's your bodyguard?" Rocky eyed Kavi.

"This is Kavi. They're *not* a bodyguard."

Rocky's eyes returned to Ava when she emphasized what he wasn't.

"Nice to meet you, Kavi."

"Likewise. Are you a Nylo Guardian?"

"That I am. I guess we're not as sneaky as we think."

"Nylo Guardian? From Nevarra?" Ava asked.

"That's me. How could you tell?" Rocky smiled.

"I had heard things about a golden owl through the Asting network. Rescuing Axol was another clue. I was not certain though. You are far from home," Kavi said matter of fact.

"But glad you're here. I don't know what I would have done if they had gotten away," Ava added.

"Keep him hidden while you're here," Rocky said. "I've heard the lab is looking for axolotls and salamander-like Nylos. They started with incentive programs, but now the Scouts are just taking them. Hide him... and hide your cheek. They know to look for a Mark like yours to find that type of Nylo," Rocky pointed at her cheek.

"Why would they take Axol?"

"I'm not sure yet," Rocky said. "But they've been failing miserably on their hunt for them and other Nylos since I got here."

"Kavi, do you know?" Ava asked.

"I do not have information on that yet. I will let you know when information on Pagra Labs and their interest in axolotls and salamanders is updated."

"What are you doing so far away from the Tunnels?" Rocky asked.

"I—um. I'm taking care of some personal business," Ava said.

"She is here to purchase a bastard braid," Kavi added.

"There's nothing wrong with a replenish," Rocky said. "I was actually heading the same direction to the markets now. I'll walk with you."

"So, you're after a braid. What about you, Kavi?" Rocky asked. They were headed towards the side street shops, and as they traveled downhill, Ava noticed they were also closer to the border of the New City. Some of the tall, black buildings rose above the Old City's smaller, but more charming structures. Ava couldn't help but feel the Obsidian V was looming over them.

"I am observing Ava as my topic of research."

"Oh? So you're from the Asting. I should have guessed from the robes."

"All unicorns are from the Asting."

"That's what they want you to think. What research are you in, Kavi?"

"Um—What are you doing so far from Nevarra?" Ava blurted out to change the subject.

"I have some unfinished business here, but seeing how aggressive the hunters from the lab are getting... saving little guys like Axol has taken precedence. I've never seen them take so many like they are right now. I've had to call in for reinforcements." It was clear from the ease of his walk and the bounce of his hair that he was wild and ready to get physical if needed. But when he spoke about the Nylos, a softness came about him that made Ava ache.

"Pagra Labs is known for cultivating the newest Marker Match mutation," Kavi added.

"So you unicorns do know a thing or two," Rocky smiled.

"What mutation?" Ava asked.

"It's a mutation that allows a human to force a Match with a Nylo. And now they're taking it one step further. It now allows a human to Match with more than one Nylo —all by force," Rocky said.

"More than one Nylo?" Ava asked, petting Axol.

"They're enslaving Nylos for multiple Matches to leverage more than one type of power at a time," Rocky said. "Pagra Labs is at the forefront of this so-called 'innovation.'"

"How is that possible?" Ava asked.

"Still not totally sure. There's a new scientist from Pagra Academy. She isn't leading the project, but she was the one who created the injection that triggers the mutation. I think it's all connected to the increase in all of this Nylo-trapping. All I know is that, one, Pagra Labs is Matching one person to more than one Nylo which isn't what nature intended and, two, the Nylos are somehow being forced into the Match against their will."

"Kavi, you don't know more about this?" Ava asked. "Those poor Nylos."

"No confirmed information. Though, the scientist who created the mutation—," Kavi stopped speaking. They turned around.

"What is it?" Ava asked looking back. There was nothing in the path behind them, but Ava knew something was wrong. Was it the Vhyka? They were so close to a new braid. Would this be her end? So close to a replenisher, only to die thirty feet away from where she could have been granted 15 more years of never having to worry about a Vhyka and their bastard-craving appetite. Ava heard a noise in front of her and turned quickly back around only to find Rocky had disappeared.

"Rocky?" Ava whispered. She squeezed Axol tightly

and slid sideways so that her back was against a wall. "Kavi, where did Rocky go?"

"His owl took him. I believe he knew we were surrounded."

"By what?" Ava asked. Had the Vhyka gone and brought *more* Vhykas with it?

Men wearing all black appeared at both ends of the alley. They wore smooth black masks over their faces. Though Ava was agitated with fear, she felt somewhat relieved to see arms and legs of regular size. These were not Vhykas. They began to walk forward, closing in on Ava and Kavi.

"Kavi, will they hurt us?"

"It is likely."

Ava took to the first door in the street. It did not open. She took to another, and it opened. Axol flew forward from her arms to lead the way, and Kavi followed behind them. Axol led them to an open window. Ava climbed through clumsily, and Kavi followed with a quiet grace. They ran through the street and Axol stopped at another door. Ava tried it with success. They went through another window and then took to another narrow walkway. She had no idea where they were going, but she was trying to create as much distance as possible.

Something grabbed Ava by the hair and yanked her back. She fell backwards, looking up to see her reflection in the hard black mask above her. The Shadow Scout dragged her backwards by her hair, with her struggling to keep her feet under her. Axol looked back, pivoted towards her, and Ava screamed.

"Go Axol! Fly away!" she shouted. "Kavi take Axol and go!"

Axol didn't listen and neither did Kavi. Axol flew to her, buzzing around the now four men surrounding her. Kavi stood and watched calmly with their hands by their side.

"No Axol. Go. Please go!"

Rocky, with the wings of his owl, floated swiftly down to the ground. He took out the first man in four quick strikes with his hands. He received a hit to the shoulder by the second man, and then responded with two silent strikes while he closed the distance between him and the scout. Rocky held onto the scout's helmet and slammed it against the wall. Ava watched in amazement at the speed of Rocky's movements. He took the third down with a kick to the head. The last man standing with a handful of Ava's hair, took out a gun and held it to Ava's head. Without a pause, Rocky threw a dagger that struck through the man's hand and then heart, pinning his arm. A shot had still been fired, but missed Ava's head but not her ear.

The man went down and Ava, deaf to Rocky's words, realized in a panic that there was most likely a green splatter from her now regenerating ear. Rocky, not much taller than her, took her hand and guided her to a clear opening. She looked back to see what looked like an infinite amount of men in black coming after them. She looked up to see more shadow men on the roofs of the buildings. They passed Kavi, who followed slowly behind the action. Ava's hearing came back, but it was accompanied by a loud ringing.

"You Asting are bloody useless!" Rocky shouted as he hurried forward with Ava. Ava was too stunned to voice her agreement. Then again, what had she really brought to the table herself in this mysterious disaster?

As she wondered this, she felt a piercing pain through her shoulder, followed by more shocks to her body. Her body jolted forward, and she looked down to confirm that she had been shot. Many, many times and with large bullets. Rocky looked down at the wounds. He quickly turned around and threw an explosive that shook the ground and walls. The smoke rose and Ava's lungs burned. Rocky supported her onward, holding her up for there was not much of her core intact to stand up on her own. Her entire stomach was overflowing with her green blood pouring through her clothes. Rocky used his shoulder to force open a door and set her down in the corner of a modest kitchen. Kavi stood like a white ghost haunting their dire circumstances.

Rocky found a blanket and covered Ava who was now crouched in a corner with Axol on her lap, clearly in shock. Rocky looked down at her. He took her shaking hands in his. His orange eyes were large and alert and glowing a bright golden hue, but Ava's brown eyes were fading.

"Listen to me, Ava. They want me. You're going to

hide here. You and Axol must be quiet. Focus! Listen! Be as still as you can. And when this is all said and done, come find me and give me what is mine. Candland will help you. Okay? Come find me, Ava!"

Ava looked down, she was healing quickly, but never had she seen so much of her body missing. She began to worry. What if the power Axol provided her didn't cover giant sized holes? What if she had used up all of the healing juice and this was it? So much of her was gone. And though Rocky looked serious and concerned and most definitely was saying something important, Ava couldn't help but wonder why he hadn't reacted to her green blood the way every single other person had when they saw it. There was no time to ask, and she didn't have the energy to speak.

Rocky covered her with a blanket and then leapt out of the window as Kavi stepped back into the shadows, somehow harnessing enough stillness to seem invisible to the human eye once again. Ava, in a foggy state, then heard footsteps. She tried to stop breathing, but the shock was too much. Instead she just focused on breathing slower. So many footsteps shuffled through the house and then through the window tracing Rocky's path. It sounded like hundreds of Scouts had funneled through. Ava thought about it, before she was shot, when she had looked back... there had been so many, it was almost as if the border of the New City, in all its blackness, had broken apart into figures and come to life.

Finally, the silence came. And Ava let it come. She

must have sat still for hours after listening for more footsteps just to be sure.

She removed the blanket from her head and looked around. There was no one else there. There were only the normal objects that seemed so peculiar to scan through after a dizzy near-death experience: a stove, a basin, a bag of grain. Then she saw Kavi, standing in the corner on the opposite side. They had been so still, she passed over them the first time.

"You were still for so long," Kavi said. "I thought you might have..."

Ava stood up, holding onto Axol who was clearly still in a state of panic. The dizziness closed in. Her mind was flashing with visions... hallucinations. She saw death. She felt it. But it wasn't coming for her, it was coming for everything she touched.

"Kavi... I don't feel... right."

She collapsed, and the visions were abruptly taken over by a black darker than Obsidian V.

CHAPTER 9

RESIGNATION

CHINCHIN

When Chinchin left her residence, she was escorted to the Labs and down the halls of her workplace by four Shadow Scouts. Her days had been identical for the last week. She woke up before the sun and was escorted from her pod to The Lab by scouts. She stood by and monitored her team while all of Project 222's subjects had their fingernails checked. Then she sat in her office, facing a broad window where she could watch the sun rise as she cleared her head.

While her every move had been monitored not only by the Obsidian V itself, but by the Shadow Scouts, Chinchin had been thinking of ways to escape Pagra without giving up on her research. She hadn't come all of this way to be babysat, but at the same time, she couldn't just leave Project 222 behind. Her mission to make the

Nylos' magic more accessible was still dear to her heart, and too many sacrifices had been made so far for her to leave it all behind. But it was getting harder and harder to work on Project 222 when she felt like she was being treated like a criminal in a prison.

"Do you get tired of watching me in my office?" Chinchin asked without looking away from the window. "Can't you just tell 7 I don't need babysitters?"

"7 is busy today," one of the Scouts commented. When they were first assigned to watch over her, they hadn't answered her inquiries, but now they entertained her every so often.

"That's hard to believe," Chinchin sighed.

"That Nevarrian punk was captured last night."

"Come again?" Chinchin jerked her head around.

"The Nevarrian spies," another guard chimed in. "Remember Kea? The one who snuck in right under your nose?"

More like under my sheets, Chinchin thought. "Yes. I remember. She's dead."

"We have her brother. He's going to go through the mud wall today so we can extract his memories. Then he'll join his sister."

"Should at least make our Nylo hunting easier with him out of the way," another shadow man said.

"I hate their little sneaky ways. Living in trees like Nylos themselves. Just like animals," said another.

"I want to see him," Chinchin said. She realized she might have said it a little too quickly.

"You want to see the brother?"

"Not a chance," another scout said.

"When is he going through the mud wall?" Chinchin asked.

"Preparations have already started. Ironic. His Nylo's power inspired the mud wall, and now he'll be passing through it himself."

Chinchin stood up abruptly and pushed past the scouts to the exit.

"Where are you going?"

Chinchin turned, "That asshole almost cost me my career. Like hell I'm not going to watch him get his memories drained." She then charged forward. The guardians all looked at each other, shrugged, and then followed in uniform. She took a deep breath when she realized they bought her act, but she needed some excuse to see Rocky for herself.

Chinchin had missed the sound of her steps against Obsidian V on their own. Now all she heard was the heavy clunking of shadow feet shuffling behind her like some kind of robotic army. At least they had finally let their rigidness down. They spoke to her casually when at first their exchanges had just been official reports. No one called her Chinchin though. To them, she was 86.

She made it to the observation room for the mudwall's procedure. 7 was there, standing in front of a large black glass window. On the other side were the mudwalls, collectively and officially known as the Source Wall.

"86. Welcome," 7 smiled.

"No invitation?"

"I didn't want to interrupt your morning routine."

Chinchin smiled and walked up to the dark glass.

Chinchin looked through the window and saw two shadow scouts bring Rocky in. Rocky was different. Chinchin had never seen a face so filled with fear that he was almost unrecognizable. What had they done to him? He was a Nevarrian assassin, not a fearful child. Chinchin wondered why he didn't fight back. It was unsettling to see the guards dragging his feet, while Rocky's gaze wandered around like a lost animal that was both aware of a threat and yet helpless. Something seemed off. Maya's brother would never be dragged in like that.

The Source Wall was a large room with many walls dividing the room into little hallways, almost as if it was a maze, except there were no twists and turns, just wall after wall after wall. Chinchin and 7 were observing from a lookout point higher up so they could see down most of the maze on the other side of the stone.

Chinchin had rarely come down to the lower chambers where these kinds of things took place, but she had to see Rocky for herself. He stood in a zombie-like state, staring into the wall that swallowed any colors around it. Chinchin had forgotten how the wall oozed, giving it a muddy texture (and its nickname) that made it look... alive. In fact, it looked more alive than Rocky did at the moment. It pained her to see him so afraid. She had lost Maya and though she had no idea how they caught

Rocky, she suddenly felt responsible for him. For his life. She couldn't bring Maya back to life, but maybe she could help Rocky...

Rocky looked at the ground where the wall connected, and sure enough, the wall was spilling onto the floor, and while the shadowmen held him firmly in front of the wall, Rocky's bare toes began to stick to the ground as they dragged. Chinchin knew Rocky. He was an uncontrollable flame. The fact that he wasn't flinging insults and laughing at his captors was strange. Had he been so defeated? What had happened before this? Or had he been like this since he lost his sister? She hadn't seen him since the day of Maya's death, so maybe she was looking at his new normal state. Maybe his sister's death had broken him. Maybe this was what Rocky was like when he was broken. She couldn't blame him.

Chinchin stood with the poise that came through a straight spine, but on the inside, she felt a sense of doom. Even more dreadful was the moment Rocky realized the wall wasn't bare—that he wouldn't be alone. There were other bodies buried in it. Some of the victims' limbs poked out of the sludge-like tar, but the bodies were too far gone in the sticky wall to be able to move on their own. Each head poked out, completely covered in a large mask with no glass, just a solid black covering over their faces with a large tube attached that led up to a large tank above. *Oxygen?* Chinchin wondered. The tube was pumping upwards and away from the heads, so it wasn't oxygen. Memories, Chinchin realized. It was pumping memories up, up, and away. There was a smaller tube paired to each larger tube she hadn't seen before. That was the oxygen. It was small and couldn't have been providing very much air.

"What is the survival rate?" Chinchin asked.

"Don't worry," 7 said, "I've instructed them to ensure his breathing tube is clear. Suffocation would be too easy for a Nevarrian shit."

"Have you settled on a method of execution?"

"Still deciding. Why?"

"I want to make sure the punishment fits the crime," Chinchin swept her hair back with the flick of her fingers, trying to feign a casual, but dark tone.

"He and that sister of his made us the fool. We will take the information gathered here today so that his death will begin the undoing of Nevarra. We'll know exactly where their base is located and find out exactly where their Obsidian V can be mined."

"How did you catch him?"

"He was interfering with our hunters who were actually looking to catch more axolotls for your project. I got wind of his return, and I decided I wouldn't make the same mistake twice. I sent every Shadow Scout we had after him. Sometimes, 86, it's respect for an enemy that allows us to defeat the enemy."

"Mmm."

"But then again, having a little too much *respect*, like you did for his sister... That can be just as blinding. Am I wrong?"

Chinchin looked down and remained quiet.

"Unfortunately our Labs have not found the cure for *dumb love,*" the last two words were said with emphasis. 7 did not look at Chinchin as he said it, but she had turned to look at him. He smiled, knowing his words had cut.

Asshole.

Chinchin stood silent, now turning her attention back to her dumb love's brother. The parallels of the mud wall to being buried alive came through as Rocky started to scream and fight. He pushed back, and kicked, and bit. It was a reckless attempt with no grace or strategy and confused Chinchin even more. A Nylo Guardian of Nevarra trying to *bite* his way out? He was weak, and the guards easily handled his tantrum, taking him to an open area on one of the many walls where a body was being enveloped to Rocky's left and another to his right. Chinchin would have looked away if she were alone, but instead she stared straight into his heart, wondering why he wasn't truly fighting back. *Do something,* she thought.

She eyed the pumping wall in front of Rocky. Giant black veins connected the wall to the ceilings, pumping precious memories from the wall up to the main black artery that went through the ceiling. Rocky screamed, he swore, he pleaded. Even cried. The guards turned Rocky so his back was to the wall, and lifted him so his feet were well off the ground, pressing his body into the sticky, wet surface. Attaching him to his fate.

And there go all of Nevarra's secrets. Chinchin took a

deep breath. Taken by Pagra and soon to be exploited. The sacred tradition of Nylos, the location of where raw Obsidian V could be harvested on their lands, assassin secrets... all sucked up through a tube. And like Maya's death, Chinchin placed this reckoning on her shoulders.

She watched the immediate suction of the wall grip Rocky. Pump, pump, pump, squeezing his body with each contraction. The sludge was everywhere, quickly flooding over the front of Rocky's body, locking his hands in. Rocky was being swallowed by the wall. He took 8 more struggling breaths, and then the guards pulled the large black mask over his face. There were no holes for his eyes to see through. Nothing. Rocky's face was gone, and he was left with the darkness and what might be a tiny airway to allow for a chance of breathing.

Chinchin had played around with the Obsidian V in the current state of the Source Wall months ago. She knew he felt like he was suffocating while being pulled from every direction. Whatever he had known, whatever he had felt, whatever he had feared... would soon be transcribed in a Pagra Labs report that would include rough illustrations. And he would be left with something less than nothing. It was a "feeling and thinking" nothing, but with the torturing and acute awareness that there had once been *something*. That he had once been *someone*.

"How long does the extraction take?"

"Ten hours for the average person. With someone with a memory like his? Could be days," 7 said.

"Is his Nylo here as well?"

"Why?"

"A Nylo in the memory category. Could be something there that might help me strengthen the bond between multiple Marker Matching."

"Interesting. I'll have the owl sent to your lab."

"Thank you. I'll be waiting," Chinchin turned to leave.

"And 86?"

"Yeah?"

"Don't taunt the Scouts for doing a good job keeping you safe."

Rocky's owl was in front of her desk when Chinchin arrived. She looked at the owl. It was large, filling the large cage it was in without effort with its golden wings. She stared into its bright yellow eyes, and it stared back. Nylos were no different to her than the gentle, inert animals of The Cache. They didn't have human intelligence, and so she equated a Nylo to that of any other animal. Cows were livestock for feeding humans. Nylos were livestock for powering humans. She did not feel anything for the owl in its cage, but she had studied Nylos and their Marked enough to understand that Rocky would not leave this place unless his Nylo were escaping with him. She understood the bond was strong. So to be clear, rescuing the owl was purely done to make Chinchin's next order of business easier for herself.

Chinchin pulled at her hair, watching the owl closely. Her four Scouts stood at the door of her lab. She had not planned on escaping today. She didn't have the supplies... or the ammo. She didn't intend on leaving the test subjects until she was sure they were okay. However, they had the axolotls and the team of scientists knew what to do next. They didn't need her around to make sure the axolotls Matched with the test subjects to keep them safe. It was in the last minute she had decided an escape was in order, that Rocky's life and the secrets of Nevarra mattered more. It was the only thing she could do to truly honor Maya's death... she just needed help.

She took the elevator down to Chauson's floor, and found him in his office with the door open.

"I need to talk to you. Privately," she whipped her eyes behind her at the four Scouts.

"That's alright, Scouts," Chauson nodded. "You can wait just outside."

The Scouts stepped outside and the door closed. The walls turned matte, leaving them to talk.

"I need help," Chinchin said.

"What kind of help?"

"I need to get out of Pagra Labs."

546 raised an eyebrow.

"Because of the Nevarrian boy? He'll be dead by the end of the week after his memories are gone. What difference does it make if you stay or go?" Chauson said coldly.

"It makes a difference to me."

"Why?"

"I need to leave, and they won't let me. Will you help or not?"

"And what do you need from me?"

"I need a blind spot again. The Shadow Scouts took my last one when they moved me to my new pod."

"Where are you going to go?"

"Away."

"But what about Project 222? What about making The Cache fair?"

"The other scientists will figure it out. They have everything they need."

"If I help you leave, Project 222 will move at half the pace it's moving at now. It's one of the most important projects in the Labs. The city has been counting on it. We're running out of Obsidian V to support the city, and if we —"

"This was a mistake. I shouldn't have asked," Chinchin turned around.

"Chinchin, you're asking me to go against my parents."

"I thought you said it was your *job* to rebel against your parents."

"This is different. Your work is so important for this city, Chinchin. We need more of V to support everyone here," he said quietly.

"...So you're choosing to keep me here against my will."

Chauson paused. "Of course not. I just want to make

sure you know what you're doing before you do something impulsive. I know with Maya—"

"Don't."

"Chinchin. If you go, you can't come back."

"I know."

"Then that's it?"

"That's it."

Chauson looked at Chinchin. It was quiet, the air between them straining for what that really meant. They weren't just talking about Project 222 even though that alone was enough to be a monumental loss. They had become close over the last few weeks. Chauson had helped Chinchin time and time again, and now she was asking even more from him.

"I couldn't make you stay even if I tried," he said quietly, a faint smile on his lips.

She didn't want it to mean the end of their friendship, but Rocky was losing precious memories as they spoke. Chauson opened his drawer and pulled out a small matte stone. A blind spot.

"Here. Hang on to it this time. And here."

Chauson handed her another black stone, triangular with a hole in the center.

"...What's this?"

"It's a copycat. With it, the walls will think you're me."

"...But..."

"And anytime I press my hand to the wall and use a special word—"

"A spell?"

"...A password," Chauson smiled with a twinkle. "When you use it that way, a secret elevator appears. It goes all the way to the roof, but more importantly, it goes underground. Go down. It will get you out of here. Fast."

"They'll know you helped me."

"That's why you're going to tie me up, and punch my lights out. You'll have to get rid of the scouts outside though. The copy cat only fools the stone. I can't help you there."

"I know you wanted me to finish the project," Chinchin said, looking down and biting her lip.

"You wouldn't though. You would have been forced to do it. And the project wouldn't get done. Your work would suffer... And despite how charming I can be, you'd hate me."

"But I don't hate you." It was the closest Chinchin had been to admitting there were any feelings at all. She noticed Chauson was holding his breath, and then he noticed as well.

Chinchin stepped forward before she knew what her body was doing. She pressed her lips to his. What she was sure was a quick peck, became more. She felt her tongue outstretch for more, surprising herself. Her fingers were grazing Chauson's cheek, and she felt his fingers digging into her hair in response. They both paused, and she smiled, her lips still touching his. She felt the tingle at the back of her neck. She never thought she had feelings for Chauson—not because she didn't feel a connection—but because she felt it was a betrayal to Maya. However, her body, and now her heart, was acting on its own. She opened her eyes, and Chauson's eyes were gazing into her own. There was a fire there that stood out from his regular casualness. She recognized the look. She could nearly read his mind. "I knew it," he was thinking. "I knew you had feelings for me too."

"It's time for you to go," he breathed out. "We'll find someone to replace you anyway. Someone smarter."

"I highly doubt that."

"There's always someone smarter, Chinchin."

"Maybe."

"If anything, maybe we can use Rocky's memories to tie everything together. That data will be... gold. The Light will shine. So today won't be a total loss."

Chinchin's eyes diverted. Chauson hadn't thought Chinchin was going to try to get Rocky out of the Labs with her. And then Chinchin knew he saw it in her eyes now. He realized he was making a mistake.

"*No.* Chinchin, you can't take him—"

Chinchin punched his lights out. She let his body collapse, but caught his head so it didn't hit the stone floor. She laid his head gently. She kissed two of her fingers and placed them on his lips, again, before she realized what she was doing. She looked at the mark her fist had left.

"I'm sorry, Chauson."

She turned to the door and exited quickly.

"Back to my floor," Chinchin said to the Scouts.

In all of this, the most complicated piece of the escape was the owl. Would he cooperate with Chinchin or wouldn't he? She was back in her office, staring at the creature. She injected the owl with a sleep serum and then pulled him out of his cage.

"Shadows, can I get a hand? I need to measure his wingspan. Here, hold this wing. Extend it, but make sure not to overstretch it. It needs to be the natural length of the wing. Yes, like that. Thank you. Can you hold the body? He's heavy and I need to take down these measurements."

All four guards were propping up the oversized, napping owl. Chinchin spun around to get the length of the other wing, quickly taking out the first scout by sticking him with a needle. She put him to sleep just like she did with the owl. The second scout leaned over, and Chinchin gave him a swift punch to the face, catching him off guard. She finished him with the needle. There were two left who had now realized something was wrong as the first two Scouts had fallen to the floor. The third scout was fast. He went for Chinchin's hair, grabbing her ponytail that had been tied back. She first tried to loosen his grip, and then changed course by kicking him between his legs. His uniform had protected most of him, but still caused him to let go of her hair and bend slightly forward. She cupped the back of his head, forcefully guiding his nose down to her knee. He slid down.

The final shadow scout pulled her gun out as a last resort. Chinchin knew she didn't have time to hesitate.

She kicked it out of her hands with her right leg. The woman ducked Chinchin's punch and countered by a hard strike to Chinchin's gut. With a grunt, Chinchin took in the pain. It had been too long since she had been in hand to hand combat. Straightening her spine, she quickly approached the scout. After directing a few jabs to the scouts shoulder only to be blocked, Chinchin threw her weight onto the Scout, sending them both onto the ground. She didn't waste a second, using their momentum to spin around the Scout with her arms forming a triangle around her neck. She tightened her hold, pulling back with her core until she felt the body lying on top of her go limp.

Four down now... but a sea of scouts to go once she left the room. Chinchin slid the bodies behind the lab counter so that anyone poking their head in would not see them. She was carrying the blindspot, but the scouts would be found soon. She then put on the woman's uniform, mask, gun, and all. Then she quickly made a mixture, pouring the concoction into two small bottles. They weren't exact measurements, but in record time, she had made 2 multi-purpose bombs. She then returned the owl to his mobile cage, grateful it was large enough to warrant the wheels below it, and headed to the elevators with the blindspot activated to hide her from the walls.

She pressed the Obsidian V near the elevators, first indicating she wanted to go up. When the first of four elevators arrived, she pressed the wall, directing the elevators to the top floor. Then she stepped back, shook up one of her small vials, and tossed one of her makeshift bombs into the elevator and let the doors close. The bombs headed up towards the top level, the 90th floor. Then she quickly pressed the wall again, indicating she wanted to go down, and another elevator arrived swiftly. Chinchin entered, rolling the golden owl in with her. A man in a lab coat, a fellow scientist, was standing in the elevator when the doors opened. She stepped in with her disguise, helmet covering her face, and the cage on wheels.

"Owl?" the man in a black lab coat said.

Chinchin nodded.

"Must be, see you're coming from the 50s."

Chinchin nodded again.

"They let 86 do whatever the hell she wants. Three floors for one scientist's project—did you know she's just an intern really? It took me a decade just to get my own corner of a single floor!"

"Maybe that's because 86 is smarter than you," Chinchin said.

The man looked at her, cocked his head. He opened his mouth, and the elevator stopped. The doors opened to his destination. He didn't move. His eyes narrowed.

"What floor are you—," he began, before an explosion above shook the elevator. The man staggered, trying to keep his balance. Chinchin gave him a swift kick to the chest, sending him skidding across the black stone floor. There was alarm in his eyes, but he was unable to get another word out before the elevator doors slid shut again. Chinchin placed her hand on one of the stone walls, directing the elevator to accelerate to its destination. She wished she could use Chauson's emergency escape right then, but she couldn't leave Rocky.

Chinchin jumped out of the elevator once it reached the floor the Source Wall was on. Shadows were swarming every which way. Some were heading up to investigate the explosion, others were heading to the nearest exit.

Through the chaos, Chinchin calmly walked to the observation room where she had visited 7 earlier. It was empty with everyone responding to the explosion. She left the owl there, and took a door to the mud walls and hurried down a set of stairs, toward the oozing wall. She rushed to Rocky's body, which was now completely enveloped by the Obsidian V goo with the exception of his head. She pried and pulled, careful not to get trapped herself. There was progress, but it was slow. She could have made a concoction for this, but she hadn't planned on separating anything from the Mud Wall until a few hours ago. She pulled a knife from her uniform's belt and began cutting at the strands of goo that stubbornly held onto one of the most notorious Nevarra NG's. The progress was still slow going. She eyed her gun, but knew if she used it, she'd most likely harm Rocky in the process.

She had his entire upper body out from the goo, but his hips and legs were still well in. She checked his pulse. He was still alive. At this rate, her chances of escape were decreasing by the minute. She had only used a direct spell once while she was in Pagra. It was always a risky move, but she had no choice; she was in a risky situation.

"Pali Palar si havavala," she hissed. The wall of tar suddenly melted into a soft wax and Rocky, along with several other bodies that had been cocooned into the wall, peeled off. Chinchin caught Rocky while the other bodies crumbled to the sticky floor. The mask was too much to fuss with so she cut the tube it was attached to and left the face piece on Rocky. He was unfortunately just as asleep as his Nylo. Chinchin took him over her right shoulder, and awkwardly made her way back up the steps to the owl. He wasn't the largest human in The Cache, but he wasn't the lightest either. For his size, Chinchin was surprised how heavy he was. She hadn't planned to be taking a body and an owl with her when she made her escape. She grunted under the weight of her dead lover's brother.

She entered the observation room where she could look out at the Source Wall once again. 7 stood there waiting for her. He was alone.

"How did you do it, 86?" his voice sounded... amused.

Chinchin said nothing.

"Tell me how you wiped his memory clean before the mud wall, and I can make your punishment less... severe."

"What are you talking about?"

"We'd been at it for some hours now. Nothing has

been extracted. Tell me how. 86, I won't make this offer again."

Chinchin didn't respond. She placed her hand on a wall with the copycat stone hidden under her palm. A door opened nearly instantly. Chinchin threw Rocky's body through the opening onto the floor. 7 looked at the cage that stood between them. Chinchin wanted to leave the owl so badly. She thought about it. She could almost feel her feet leaving the ground and following right behind Rocky into safety.

"I'm not letting you go," 7 said.

"Pali Pala havavala," Chinchin said quietly as she ran to the cage.

The soles of 7's shoes had melted to the stone he stood on. It gave Chinchin just enough time to reach the cage, drag it back with its tires screeching and throw it through the opening waiting for her to enter.

"My shoes!" 7 shouted as he clumsily untied his shoes. "What is this?"

Chinchin stared at him from the getaway elevator doors.

"Please accept my resignation," she smiled.

The doors closed and Chinchin felt a whoosh as the escape pod began its emergency escape. Chinchin's smile still lingered, a bold and beautiful front to cover other emotions that were bubbling up. Two spells in one day. She hadn't been this desperate since she left home... until now.

Rescuing the son of a Nevarrian general had not been

a part of the plan. Fluffy, sleeping owl in a huge cage had not been part of the plan. Chinchin hadn't had a moment to really think about what she was doing. She knew it was her emotions that put her on a smooth black escape route. And now that she couldn't take back the things that she had done in the last hour—kissing *and* knocking out Chauson, stealing Rocky and his Nylo, casting two spells, and running away—she needed to stop leading with her heart and start leading with her sharper asset: her brain.

And her brain told her to wake Rocky up. As the pod slid seamlessly through a maze Chinchin assumed was underground, Rocky laid unconscious with the face mask still attached to his head. Chinchin kneeled over him, and after a minute or two, was able to loosen the mask and pry it from his skin. He coughed and then moaned in response.

"Good. You're awake. Here's the plan. Once we get out of—"

"Who are you?" Rocky rubbed his face with both hands. His voice was wheezy from the mask.

"...Don't you remember? Maya was on my team at the Labs."

"Maya?" Rocky asked.

"Your sister. Maya."

"I'm sorry. I don't know who you are. I don't remember a Maya."

Chinchin knew the mud wall sucked out memories, but she had expected there to be a lot more of Rocky's memory left. He had only been on the wall for less than three or four hours. For someone like him, the memories would have been more difficult to extract. Then she thought of what 7 said. *"Tell me how you wiped his memory clean before the mud wall."*

Maybe his brain was wiped before the wall somehow... But that didn't make her situation any better. She was hoping he would wake up an assassin who would be able to take her lousy escape plan and run with it. Looking at him, still leaning back, dazed and confused, she thought she'd be lucky to get him to stand up without vomiting. He was in a complete state of torpor that didn't seem like it would wear off any time soon.

"Do you remember the owl?" she pointed to the cage.

"Owl?"

"He's your owl. I forgot his name. It was something like... Fire? Or Fireball or something."

"I don't... remember anything."

"He's your Nylo. You two are connected by a sacred bond," Chinchin said this sheepishly. She knew it was sacred to them. To her, it was simply a chain of events that took place between the two organisms.

"Sorry. The sacred bond isn't really ringing any bells... What's my name?"

Chinchin sighed. "Rocky. Your name is Rocky."

"What's your name?"

"Just call me... call me Soti."

"I... I can't remember anything."

"Look, I know this might feel... scary, but we're in a

lot of danger. We need to be ready to run when this thing stops. We need to get out of Pagra."

"Pagra? And go where?" Rocky asked. His eyebrows came together. Chinchin saw he was on the brink of tears —one of the most dangerous killers in The Cache, and there he was sitting in a puddle of fear.

"Your home. Nevarra."

CHAPTER 10

THE KINGDOM IN THE TREES

CANDLAND

For being so large and spread out, Nevarra was well hidden. The first huts were built into the trunks of the larger trees and blended well with the forest that was as impressively tall as it was vast. Even the smaller trees were hundreds of feet high. And height was no issue for the Nevarrian residences either. Their homes were set in gigantic branches, connected to their neighbors by light wood and rope bridges.

Someone unaware of Nevarra might walk through the forest without even knowing they were walking through a city. And still as Candland saw the first doors speckle the trees, he thought about the Nylo Guardians this tree-house city produced. Some of the most lethal people—including Rocky—were born and made among these very trees. Nevarra was so withdrawn, so unimposing. And in that, it was very misleading.

The days leading up to the arrival had been thrilling, exhausting, and special in a way Candland felt he couldn't put into words. Proru had communicated his name to Candland upon their Match. From then, a friendship that had been missing Candland's entire life had begun—but it wasn't an easy beginning.

Because Nylo magic wasn't magic blessed by the Blood, it was considered dark magic to Questus, and so Candland's teachings of how it all worked had been more focused on the fact that it was evil than what it actually was in itself. He had always been the odd one in his family, but now he was something that left him wondering if he still had a family at all. Still, he felt an energy within him—a humming in his chest that hadn't been there before. It might have been the power his people feared, but he didn't feel afraid. He only felt... inadequate to receive it. It was like a growth spurt that led to much needed height but with no way to control the limbs that came with it.

Proru's eyes would sometimes light up or he would howl a blue phantom-like beam into the sky, making the fields around them ripple... but Candland did not know what it meant. He would watch the beam shoot up into the sky many times over, but he did not know what it did or didn't do. What was Proru trying to say, if anything at all? Candland had thought that after he spoke Proru's name as if he had known it all along, the rest of the understanding to be had between them would flow as naturally. However, he found he could not communicate with Proru like that at all. In fact, even understanding how the Nylo's general emotions like happiness or sadness were expressed was foreign to him. He could only work off of what he knew from inert animals. He would see small resemblances here and there with the wag of the giant tail or the direction of the wolf's pointed ears.

The first night they spent together, Candland slept on the opposite side of the fire. He would never admit it to his Nylo, but there was still a large part of him that was afraid to be eaten. Though his experience with Berns and Axol had been positive, the stories that circulated the castle walls growing up only spoke of betrayal and chaos from dark, magical beasts. Any creatures with magic outside of the Blood were not to be trusted. And Proru didn't have the most approachable manner or size either with his giant paws and pointy, blood-seeking teeth. But the same had been said and taught about the creatures' counterparts: the Marked. They were just as sinful in those teachings he had been subject to growing up. And Candland was now Marked. Did this mean that he was now a traitor? Contaminated by evil? Bad? Cursed? Was the Mark a result of his decision to help the Marked break out of the Cages? Was it fated to him before as punishment for letting Ava's hand go? Or was it more random than that?

On the third night of travel to Nevarra, the night brought on a wind and chill that kept Candland from lighting a fire. Someone with more skill and experience could have started a flame rather effortlessly, but Candland was only working off of what he had learned from tutors. As a prince—second in line for the crown—his lessons only briefly covered wilderness and survival. Candland had actually surprised himself the first two nights by being able to come by fire the way he had been taught briefly many years ago.

The forest not only grew cold without the flame, but it grew more frightful. Candland laid across from Proru, only to begin to tremble from the mixture of fear and cold a half hour later. The unfiltered wilderness, unstopped by wall or window imposed its true threat when Candland was left in the darkness. He had appreciated the fires before for their warmth, but now he found himself wishing he had their light for safety.

Proru stood and walked to his Marked, and Candland was too overwhelmed in the darkness to move. The wolf curled around Candland, his large tail wrapped back around the large wolf body, making a blanket for the prince. At first, Proru's warm breath was so close to Candland's own that he stayed up, calculating the milliseconds it would take for Proru to chomp his head clean off. However, in the following nights, Candland discovered quickly that he could only fall soundly asleep if the humming of Proru's rough exhalations were near enough.

On the fourth night, Candland had mounted Proru for the first time which allowed them to travel much faster. He was still getting a hang of where exactly to sit and where exactly to hold on, but he did stay on Proru for the most part. They had yet to come to an agreement on the dismount though, as Proru only seemed to buck Candland off of him when in a flowing river or on the edge of a lake. Candland still rode Proru often, but continued to get soaked when the ride came to an end. If he hadn't known better, Proru looked more amused than confused when Candland tried to explain to him he wanted to not be drenched in water when it was time for Candland to jump off and walk again.

There was no better way to get to know one another than to be far away from the homes of each—traveling and living amongst the trees and under the moon and stars. By the time Candland found they had reached Nevarra, Proru had gained the nickname of Pror. Candland had created a special whistle that sounded almost as if two whistles were harmonizing that he used to communicate anything to Pror. The whistle meant it was time for dinner, other times it meant it was time to make camp, other times it meant to come find him. The whistle was identical each time, but Pror understood.

It was only a full seven days later that Candland realized he hadn't been weighed down by his thoughts. He had been so focused on the present moment with his new companion that he hadn't thought about his brother, Rocky, or Ava. Slowly, however, those relationships came back to him as he rode on Proru's back. He hadn't seen another person in the last week. His brother might have been found by now, but he would have no idea.

And Rocky. He hadn't had a chance to say goodbye, but Candland knew he was surrounded by other Nylo Guardians during the jail-break from the Cages. He didn't have to worry about him, and now so many Marked were free with their Markers. It had all happened so quickly, that it was only after the fact that Candland could marvel at all of the different Nylos that were making their escape. Some Nylos were nearly identical to the inert animals he had seen scattering around. It was only the way their eyes lit up when they used their powers that gave them away. Others were entirely magical species that didn't cross over to the inert animal family—this included fire-breathing dragons, lions with wings and talons, and something he'd never seen before which he recalled to be simply a sphere of light.

And to see their Marked alongside them now felt different too. Candland knew they would help the Nylos they Matched with to escape the Cages, but now that he had his own Nylo—his own Marker Match, he couldn't imagine the pain they must have gone through by simply being caged separate from each other. He couldn't dwell on that long. His mother's disappointment arose in his mind. She would know it was him. And she would not forgive him. Just like how she would not forgive him for being Marked. And at that moment, Candland wondered if he truly wanted her forgiveness.

He never found an answer as Ava then drifted into his mind. The feeling of her hand. The look on her face when her true identity was revealed. An Atrox. He had lied to her about his name and who he was, but he had no idea she was doing the same. He wondered what became of her. He didn't imagine her surviving the angry mob that had taken over that day in the Tunnels when they saw her green blood. And while part of him imagined her lifeless body somewhere in the shadows underground, there was the smallest part of him that wondered if she was somewhere in the Tunnels... alive. But even thinking about Ava with the perception of hope brought him shame. He had let her go. And the current of those livid faces had swept her away and drowned her when he was her only lifeline. Could he have saved her? Could he have used his princely title and ordered them to step back? He would never know, because he had frozen.

As Candland and Proru walked through Nevarra, people began to appear, one by one, head by head, as Candland entered their home with the giant wolf beside him.

Candland was unsure of how to announce himself. He had been to Nevarra once before and remembered the way to the temple, so he decided to head there first. The Nevarrians began to follow him, like the shifting of leaves through the wind, their chattering grew. This made Candland nervous. First, because he hated crowds. Second, because he was, in fact, the prince of Questus, a kingdom that had banned Nevarrians. Rocky's father, Obigon, had welcomed him when he was a young boy, but would he welcome him now?

What calmed him as he continued forward were the

many Nylos that made an appearance. There were, of course, Nylos in the Tunnels, and he had seen plenty in the Cages under captivity or fleeing. But here, he saw them in the wild. Alive. Free. And his mouth remained open for the rest of his walk. He came across many Nylos he had never heard of. A shark-like animal that broke open the earth and appeared from under ground gave Candland a start. Proru's teeth were much larger, but this Nylo's teeth were pointed outward in chaos. He saw a phoenix float from one large tree to another, its long fiery feathers ruffling across its many layers. Candland could feel the heat from its wings. He saw a tiny lizard cross his path, only to increase in size by 50 fold so that it went from harmless gecko-like creature the size of his hand to a full sized alligator. It turned to look at Candland and Proru let out a low growl, after which the scaled creature turned back to continue on its way.

With a crowd behind him, Candland made it to a hidden temple made completely of black marble with white and silver veins. Once he made it up the steps, Obigon greeted him at the large doorless opening. It was large enough even for Pror to fit through comfortably. The way he had been waiting made it clear that word had gotten around quickly, and Obigon knew Candland was coming.

Candland kneeled in respect to the general on the steps, aware of the audience that had accumulated behind him. Obigon stood for a moment. He was a lean man with deep lines in his forehead and large, toned veins in his arms. His skin was dark, but his eyes were bright orange just like Rocky's. He was middle aged, but it was still clear to see where Rocky and Maya had gotten their vibrancy from. Candland had no doubt that this man could kill him in 100 different ways, each within three breaths.

"Prince Candland," Obigon said with a smile. "And you've brought a friend. Follow me."

The general led them inside the temple, through a few immediate turns, funneling them into another long passageway. The black stone was carved intricately throughout, with full stories of Nevarrian history carved into the length of humble furnishings as simple as benches or tables. As a sculptor himself, Candland examined the details and took longer to walk through the halls than most. The increased humidity and echoing of their steps gave the temple a cave-like feel. He could smell the dampness. Candland could tell Pror liked the feeling of the cool stone under his paws and the dim-lit hallways. The wolf's eyes glowed blue.

The temple was open, even the smallest hallways were wide, and the lowest ceilings high. It held a strange balance between holy and eerie, with the quiet peacefulness contained in the same structure that was outlined with whole black-stained windows that let the light seep in to emphasize the shadows even more. Rather than be afraid, Candland was comforted. It was the opposite of being in the middle of a loud crowd. It was quiet, peaceful, and spacious.

They finally reached a large room. The front of the space, opposite from where they stood, was curved into a large half dome that made up seven tinted windows that showered the dim of the sunlight onto the most beautiful life-sized carvings of different Nylos. In the center of the half dome was a stone figure standing in a black robe, with the hood covering the figure's face. The statue felt powerful and unforgiving. It reminded Candland of Maya while immediately recognizing the figure to be a Nylo Guardian.

As Candland approached the front of the room, he noticed that Obigon's hair had a few streaks of white, similar to the white streaks in the temple's stone. Obigon turned and looked at Candland—letting the look become a stare. His face was angular, with high cheekbones, a sharp chin, and a wide nose. He had the angles of a stern man, but his face softened with the prince, and he lifted his hands up. One hand wrapped around the neck of Candland, and the other clasped Candland's forearm. He was less formal now that there wasn't a crowd.

"Welcome, Prince Candland. We are glad you are here," he smiled.

"Thank you, Na Obigon," Candland bowed again. Candland used the formal Nevarrian word for combat general that Rocky had taught him.

"And you somehow found our hidden temple. I imagine that might be thanks to the Moon Wolf that travels with you. I can sense you two are connected. A Match," Obigon said.

Candland pulled down the neck of his shirt to reveal part of the Mark on his chest that glowed indigo like his Nylo's eyes.

"It happened after Rocky helped me rescue the Marked and their Markers from the Cages. After I was Marked... I wasn't sure where else to go. My mother..."

"I understand. You were right to come here. Does anyone know you're here?"

"No. I just came here because... I don't know the first thing about Nylos apart from what I've been taught in Questus... and you know how they feel about them..."

"You have certainly Matched with a powerful species. It only makes sense for a prince."

"...Can you teach me?"

"What do you want to learn?"

"What does this mean? Why did I—a Questonian—Match with a Nylo? And then I don't know where to start with the rest. What powers do I have? How do I use it? What powers does Proru have? How do we communicate? How do I know he's okay or... happy?"

"A lot of questions, but then again, you're coming from the dark," Obigon said. Candland thought of his mother, and how she would be telling him he was a lost cause, a child traveling into darkness.

"I don't want to be a burden. I don't want to cause any trouble," Candland added, again thinking of his mother.

"You can stay with us. You will attend some of our Nylo trainings. You know so little about Nylos, so we will start you from the beginning. In return, you will not let any outsider know you are here. Questus will only be able to interpret your presence here as our prisoner, and it will put us at risk."

"Thank you, Na."

"Your Match is very powerful indeed, Candland. I hope you understand the seriousness of your training. It's important to learn how to control your powers and not let them control you."

Candland nodded.

"Draya. Take Candland to his new quarters. Candland, you are a friend of my son's. You are welcome here as long as you would like."

A young girl appeared from around one of the Obsidian corners. She bowed to the Na with a small nod and the joining of her hands. Then she turned to Candland and used her hand to communicate that he should follow her. As she walked in front of him, Candland noticed a large spider resting comfortably behind Draya's ear.

The next morning, Candland was woken up by Draya. His new quarters were within the temple, made from the same raw rock with humble wooden furnishings: a bed, a table, a chair, a small basin of water. Draya said the first lessons would only require Candland, and that Proru could come later. At home in the den-like coolness of the room, Proru remained still although Candland hesitated at first.

It was the first time Candland had been separated from him since they had Matched. He gave the wolf one more long glance, and the wolf nodded his head once slowly. Candland couldn't help but notice a small pain in his stomach the moment he passed through the beaded exit of his room. Draya led him to one of the main halls of the temple where food was being served on low wooden tables with thin pillows on the ground for chairs. Everyone ate sitting on the stone floor, quiet and meditative.

Draya led Candland to a buffet style setup with humble offerings of rice, vegetables, aromatic sauces, and bread.

"Only take what you can eat," she said as she handed him a bowl. He thought he saw one of the legs of the spider holding onto her ear wave at him, or perhaps emphasize Draya's suggestion.

"Can Pror eat?"

"We have sent food to him already."

Candland tried to restrain himself, but had brought back a mountain of food to the table with Draya. He noticed her glaring at his portions. He had managed to catch fish mostly and that was with Pror's help. They did come across a minberry bush once that Candland ate from until he was forced to lay flat. Other than that, he had traveled with sparse meals. His princely trainings had barely been enough to keep him fed.

He watched Draya eat with her fingers, squishing the rice between her fingertips. He followed her, using his fingers and pinching at the vegetarian plate. It was delicious, though noticeably absent of meat. This would not be acceptable for a meal in Questus, but vegetarian meals were the only meals in Nevarra. Two lands... Candland couldn't imagine them more different when they weren't even geographically that far apart.

After breakfast, Draya and Candland took their plates to a large wooden bin. Then Draya led him through a series of dark hallways, lit with purple and green gels floating above them. The gels—small bubbles containing a gel-like substance made from a spell made long ago by The Gatekeeper—glowed red in Questus. The soft purples and greens reminded him of the Tunnels... just less vibrant.

The light brought back memories of the last day he had spent in the Tunnels with Ava. The warm glow of the flora and fauna, the city lights, all reflecting off of her cheek and the light in her eyes. And then Candland remembered how he had left her, how the crowd had rushed in over her and shut him out. He felt cold and he instinctively raised his hand slightly, searching for Pror's fur that was too far away for comfort.

Draya stopped at another beaded curtain hanging at an entryway—Candland was just now realizing there weren't any actual doors in the temple. Draya gestured for Candland to enter by holding out her hand. When he walked in, she did not follow. Inside the humble-sized room were children. He hadn't been around children often, but he guessed they were all younger than 6 years old. They all sat with their legs crossed. Many of the children had visible Marks on their bodies. Nylos rested on shoulders, on the tops of their heads, or in their laps. Some children didn't seem to have a Nylo. Candland wondered if he just wasn't aware of them because they were small like Draya's spider or if there were some that simply hadn't Matched with a Marker yet.

A boy Candland's age sat facing them. His hair was cut so short; fingers could not grasp it. His eyes were large and gentle. He had a Mark that started on the left side of his forehead and temple, clearly continuing onto his scalp though his tight black curls grew over it. His lips thick, almost puffy, even when the edges turned up into one of the biggest smiles Candland had ever seen.

"Prince Candland. Obigon mentioned you would be joining us. Please. Sit."

Candland only paused for a moment, awkwardly looking at the children he towered over. He sat in the back, quietly crossing his legs. The boy then continued with his lesson.

"Everyone has their own version of the beginning. Our clan has the Nylos' version: The Sky was the first of the brothers to be born. The Ocean, the second. The Land, the third. Three brothers. They were in the darkness. Then came their sister, the Light (the direct descendent of The Gatekeeper). Now illuminated, the Sky saw the Ocean and wanted his waves. The Ocean saw the Sky and wanted his clouds. They fought wildly, creating the weather. The Ocean created glaciers to make the Sky jealous, and so the Sky created the stars.

"The Land, starved for attention and companionship while his brothers quarreled, created the animals that roamed it to keep him company. He grew forests to feed them, rivers to hydrate them, caves to shelter them, and eventually fire to keep them warm.

"Suddenly the Sky and the Ocean noticed the flame. The Sky tried to blow away the Land with tornados and hurricanes, but the land did not give in. The Ocean tried to drown the Land, but could not maintain the waves it took to submerge his younger brother for long. The attacks, the first signs of any attention given to the Land, angered him. This led to the first volcano.

"The volcano filled the sky with smoke and the sea with burning lava. It was such a powerful rage, the Sky and Ocean surrendered, fearing for their lives. The Land stopped, seeing how he had hurt his brothers. But then the Land looked at himself, realizing his rage had killed the animals that had kept him company when his brothers had ignored him. The Land had never known such pain, such guilt, and such loss.

"In grieving, the Sky brought the moon for his brother. And the Moon Wolf was the first to return to the place now known as Questus, and then the others followed. The howl of mourning with the moon was the first animal sound after the first volcano. And the Ocean pulled back and revealed lakes, islands, and canyons. And so the world continued.

"Many humans and animals perished amidst the gods' quarrel. But where did the survivors like the wolf come from? Well, some humans had found refuge deep underground in tunnels. And not only that, but they had led many animals underground with them. When the rumbling above stopped, the humans led the wolves and other animals out of the tunnels—not knowing some were Nylos and had immense power.

"In return for the kindness, generosity, and protection the humans had shown them, the Nylos blessed the humans with their sacred powers. This is known as the first Marker Match or the Semel."

It was the last part that strayed very far away from Candland's history and theology lessons. In the version he knew, the humans fought the lava to protect its people with the only liquid stronger—the Blood. The animals all abandoned the world, hiding like cowards in the caves and accidentally stumbling across the path to an evil underworld where they were cursed for their cowardice with dark magic and put under the control of darkness where they hid until the humans had defeated the volcano—proving humans were a match for even the greatest rage of a god, and thus proving the Blood was in itself, more powerful. From that day on, Questonians followed the Blood, the champion of the war with the volcano, and left the worship of the defeated gods—the land, sea, and sky—behind them.

But the lesson was not done, and the teacher continued:

"The first Marker Match was between the leader of the people who hid in the cave, a brave and generous man named Croat. The Nylo was, of course, the elephant Zona."

That wasn't right, Candland thought. The first leader was Crotio.

"He was granted the power of fire—as that was what he brought with him in the caves for his people. Many of the men and women who helped care for the animals during the battle of the gods found Matches that day or in the coming weeks, but Croat's brother, Crotio, did not find a Match that day or any day after.

"Upset, ashamed, even fearful, Crotio wanted power like his brothers and sisters, so he went to other sources in The Cache that had their own power. Where do you think he went?"

"The unicorns!" a child shouted.

"That's right. The unicorns first, but of course the creatures of the Asting turned him down. They do not meddle in the lives of others, they only study. So he went to the only other source of magic other than unicorns and Nylos. Which is...?"

"The Gatekeeper!" another child shouted.

"Right. He went to see the most powerful being in The Cache—the only one who can cast spells: The Gatekeeper at West Gate, the guardian of the portal to other worlds. There, she listened, and she made a trade for one of her spells. He had to follow instructions carefully, and if he did, the Gatekeeper explained, he would become powerful just like his older brother Croat.

"Crotio returned to the village—now known as Questus—but at the time, it was still small with lots of growing to do. And Crotio did the unthinkable in order to gain his power. He killed his brother Croat and drank his brother's blood as The Gatekeeper instructed. This gave him the power of his older brother's Match, fire-wielding, and the throne. Every year, he drank the blood of a Marked to maintain his power. He sired a son and taught him the secret to power and so the tradition of the Blood began.

"Of course, he didn't want anyone to be more powerful than him, so he outlawed Marker Matching soon after. Those who were already Marked fled north to safety, founding the very place we sit today and building a community created to protect Nylos and our families.

"The murder was never discovered... by humans. Zona knew of the murder and knew her powers were being used by Crotio. Zona knew and so all Nylos knew. It wasn't until Gannick of Questus was able to communicate with his Nylo on a much more complex scale, thanks to his Match's magic, that the truth was finally found out. Interestingly enough, Gannick was from the royal family and spilled the ultimate secret before he was executed. He was the last Questonian to match with a Nylo... until today."

The teacher's eyes found Candland's, causing the

prince to look away. All of the children turned to see Candland. Questus was a people of pale skin, blue eyes, and blond hair. Candland stood out there for his olive skin, green eyes, and sandy brown hair. Here he stood out amongst the many children with thick black hair, dark skin, and brown eyes.

"What is your Marker?" a young boy asked the prince.

"Don't tell him," the teacher said quickly. "See if you can guess. Prince Candland, would you mind showing us your Mark?"

Candland unbuttoned his shirt slowly to show his chest. The children leaned forward. Candland pulled his shirt apart to show the full blue-glowing Mark.

"Does anyone recognize the Mark?"

"The circle on the right side of his chest is made up of chains... Like a Moon. It's a Moon Wolf," a little girl said. "Like the first wolf that howled at the moon!"

"Yes, Dasa. Very good. It's a wolf," The teacher smiled. "What is the Eme of the wolf?"

"Seeker," Dasa said.

"What does Eme mean?" Candland asked the teacher.

"This is a good segue into our next lesson. Markings. Prince Candland, the symbol or Eme of the Wolf is 'to seek'. Their powers correlate with that symbol or theme. Your wolf's power will have a strong connection with its symbol. And in more ways than one, so will yours. Now, let's identify the 100 most common Markings..."

The Markings lesson lasted an hour. Candland had first felt out of place for being so much older than the children in the room, but it wasn't long after that he felt out of place for knowing so little about Nylos compared to his younger peers.

The history taught was so different. The history he knew was centered around the Blood—completely absent of Nylos except for a line or two condemning them due to their contamination from the dark underworld due to their lack of bravery. The Nevarrian history was centered around Nylos. And their knowledge continued around them. The children could identify countless Markings, linking them to their symbols and themes, and even making educated guesses on what powers could be generated from certain Nylos, though apparently every power was as unique as the individual that wielded it.

After an hour of learning Markings, the teacher—Candland learned his name was Noro—started teaching several other lessons: Communication (how to communicate with your Nylo), Care (how to care for your Nylo), and the last class was a physical class called Caprice (unpredictable and impromptu movement).

Caprice was the strangest class. There seemed to be no instruction on what to do other than simply move. The more chaotic, the more unpredictable, the better. Candland had only been taught to control his movements, to control his thoughts, to control his feelings. For a class with such a simple objective, he felt it hard to grasp. He moved, but jerked around, held down by the expectation of what his body should be doing. Noro was kind to him, but Candland knew his Questonion roots had never been louder.

Draya came to pick Candland up at the end of the class and escorted him back to Pror. Without her guidance, he would have surely become lost in the halls of white-veined marble. When he passed through the beaded entrance to Pror, Pror nearly crushed him in all of the excitement. Candland turned to thank Draya, but she was already gone.

"C'mon, Pror. Let's go stretch your legs," Candland said. Pror was able to find the exit of the temple with ease. From there, Candland jumped onto his back, wondering how Pror's magic was connected to a seeker.

CHAPTER II

NOT MYSELF

AVA

Ava was warm. The sun was bright. She was above ground. Tucked into a ball, sitting in the dunes of the Wontine Desert. She was tired, hungry, small... but not alone. Axol was there with her, tucked in between her small chest and knees. She was glad he was there. He helped dull the pain that came with missing her mother and father. Missing the garden. She wanted to go home, but she had to wait. Her mother told her to wait as long as she could. To wait long enough for all of the other children to return first. To wait until she was the only one left in the desert. And then, only then, could she come home.

Something poked Ava's shoulder, and the blanket fell from her head. Ava was startled awake by a woman holding the end of the broomstick. Ava looked around. She was in the woman's home, clearly a trespasser, and the woman was more scared than she was. Axol loosened from Ava's arms. He flew up between Ava and the offending cleaning tool, ready to defend his Marked at all costs.

Ava slowly stood up.

"Sorry. We're not supposed to be here. This was an accident," she lifted her hands and slowly scooped up Axol from the air. He was in fight mode, but she was still drowsy.

"Get out of my house, Atrox," the woman said. She was trying to be more brave than rude, Ava thought. Ava looked down at what was left of her shirt, it was stained in her green all-telling blood. Ava slowly sidestepped with her Nylo held close to her chest. One arm was still up in surrender and sorry. Then Ava found the door and leapt out just a second after she saw a large white blur around her peripheral. Kavi.

The three walked down the alleyway. Ava was the slowest.

"Did they get Rocky?" Ava asked.

"They did," Kavi said.

"There were so many of them."

"There were."

"Why would they take him?"

"Pagra began testing on Nylos, and Nevarra has become their enemy ever since."

"Why are they testing on Nylos?" Ava asked, rubbing her head.

"They believe in innovation. They are the first ones to learn so much about Obsidian V—even before the Asting.

They could almost call themselves another source of power with what they have been able to do with the stone solely through science and technology alone. Naturally, they wanted to start exploring other powerful sources. Nylos are one of them, and easier to capture than The Gatekeeper or a unicorn. Are you alright?"

"My head hurts," Ava continued to rub her temple. "I don't remember having a headache since I Matched with Axol. I wonder if it means that I'm not healing anymore."

"That is not the way Marker Matching works," Kavi said.

"I don't know. The hole in my stomach was so big, I wouldn't be surprised if patching it took up all of the magic Axol had left."

"So what should we do now?" Kavi asked without any concern heard in his voice.

"Well, I still need a bastard braid. So that's still first on my list. After that, we'll head for Nevarra. We need to let them know Rocky's been taken. So. I guess the plan to not die is still number one."

Ava looked down to see her stained clothes again. She looked up to see some clothes hanging on a line—there didn't seem to be any kind of shortage of clothes lines in the Old City. She looked around several times and then swiped a few pieces of material. She dumped her old clothes along the wall, quickly changing, and emerged with a purple linen dress and burgundy headwrap that she wrapped around her neck and then up around her face to cover her cheek.

"How will you make money to buy a braid? You do not have much time left."

"I could beg. No... that would take too long... I could steal it," Ava said. Axol looked at Ava, jerking his head back. "No, you're right, Axol. That's a bad idea. I'm not that sneaky... Kavi, what should I do?"

"If you sold Axol to the Labs here, you would have enough for five bastard braids," Kavi said.

"I said what should I do, not what would be the worst idea in the world," Ava said.

"You could sell the carving Candland gave you. The stone is valuable. It could give you a braid of about 4 weeks."

"What else?" Ava said quickly.

"I thought he abandoned you to an angry mob. Why do you want to keep something he gave you?"

"He was just surprised. He's just processing. When you like someone, you'll understand. Now what else?"

Her head began to pound again. Her vision grew fuzzy. They weren't normal symptoms for someone who healed almost instantaneously. It was the stress, she thought. The bastard braid, the Vhyka, the hole in her stomach from the gunshots, Rocky and the one million shadow-people that came for him... It was all getting to her. She needed to distract herself from the chaos. Then she smelled something. It was earthy. Damp soil. Fresh greens. It smelled like her mother's garden. She looked around to find the source, but there was nothing but the red clay of the Old City surrounding her.

"Are you alright?"

"Just tired," Ava shook her head. She needed a distraction. Something for her to focus on. "Kavi, you never told me about the other Earthers you researched," Ava said as she focused on a steady walk.

"You never asked."

"How many Atroxes are there out there?"

"Less than one percent of the humans in The Cache are Atroxes."

"How many have you studied?"

"Eleven—two being Earthborn."

"What happened to all of them?"

"They all died."

"Of natural causes?" Ava swallowed.

"No. All of them were murdered," Kavi said.

"When they were found out?"

"Yes."

"What were the Earthborn like?" Ava asked.

"One of them killed everything he touched," Kavi said softly. "He killed the humans that hurt him as well as the humans that helped him. He killed the lands they lived in. He killed all of the livestock that fed him. He used up everything or destroyed it and then moved on. He was completely and utterly unsustainable."

"Oh..."

"The other was kind. She was loving, brave, and generous. She was the opposite of the other Atrox."

"That must have—"

Ava began seeing the hallucinations again. A slit

throat. A body dropping to the ground. The sound of a blade being unsheathed. It was all happening so fast. Ava stopped and leaned onto the wall.

"What is the matter, Ava?"

"I'm sorry. I'm just having these strange... I'm seeing strange things."

"Like a hallucination? Tell me more. Has this ever happened before?"

"No. Never. They're vivid. Almost like visions. I'm usually hurting someone. No. I'm usually killing them. And I'm angry. Kavi, it's like I'm seeing into the future. I'm not a girl anymore, I'm this woman. And I'm not hiding. People are hiding from me."

"Are you sure it is the future?"

"No, but it has to be. It's not who I am now. So maybe it's who I will be."

"Is that who you want to be?"

"I know I don't want to hide anymore. I know I don't want to... to... be afraid. To have to be impaled every time someone sees me bleed. To have Vhykas on my back because a piece of jewelry is expiring... I hate that things are so hard for me, and I hate how apologetic I am for being what I am."

"Interpreting dreams... It is not so much what the dream means to tell us, but what we *think* the dream means to tell us. I feel the same may be for these visions of yours."

"But they're not dreams. They're clear. They're full of

emotion. They're so real," Ava said. "What else could they be but visions of the future?"

"You did not see these before meeting Rocky?" Kavi asked.

"No, not until I woke up after he was gone."

"His Nylo is a golden owl."

"What does that have to do with anything?" Ava raised an eyebrow, feeling more irritable with the headache.

"The owl symbolizes memory, Ava. I am not certain the extent of his powers, but his eyes glow when he uses magic and his Mark expands, which means he can fully channel his Nylo. That he's a fully ascended Marked. My hypothesis is that he gave you these memories. In these memories, are you Rocky?"

"No, no. I'm not Rocky. I'm a woman. I'm... I'm..."

"I do not think you are yourself. Pay attention in your next hallucination, Ava. I am confident you will find you are someone else. This should support the hypothesis that what you are seeing is quondom."

"Quondom?"

"Erstwhile."

"Erstwhile?"

"From the past, Ava, and not something yet to be."

"You use such strange words sometimes. Kavi, Rocky said something else that might have something to do with all of this. Before he left, he said *'Come find me and give me what is mine.'*"

"Did he give you anything?"

"He only laid a blanket on top of me. And then he was gone."

"Did he say anything else?"

"He said... Candland would help me."

"Prince Candland of Questus?"

"I don't know. He just said he'd help."

"Then perhaps Candland knows. He should have answers. I do believe—"

"Shh," Ava put her hand on Kavi's chest. It was the first time they had touched. Ava quickly shuffled to the side of the small pathway so that her back was against a wall. It was just one more turn and they would be on the bustling main roads with rolling carts and shuffling feet kicking up dirt. Ava looked back to see a strange head poke out from around the corner.

"A Vhyka?" Ava tilted her head.

"I had not detected it at first. I apologize," Kavi said. They watched Axol fly away from Ava's shoulder and hover over them. Axol normally stayed close to his Marked or flew about to explore. There was something about his hovering over Kavi that caught the unicorn's attention.

"It's... for me," Ava said. Her head tilted again strangely. She pressed her fingertips against the wall to crouch forward. Kavi noticed she was moving in such a way that he had never seen before. She was attached to the wall, taking steps without making a sound. It was as if she was stalking her prey. Her head was leaning forward, staying near the shadows.

"There are too many people here. We need to get away from here to a private location where it is safer. Remember Vhykas only eat when they have an audience."

"I don't run," Ava said, her teeth clenched. Kavi was now the one tilting their head in perplexion. Kavi looked curiously at Axol. The Nylo stayed back where Kavi followed, spacing himself out behind Ava. The axolotl and unicorn watched Ava walk towards the Vhyka. Kavi noticed her hips moved side to side with more width, her spine was thrown back in a rigid manner. Suddenly Ava opened a door, disappeared inside, and returned in less than 20 seconds with something bound in her hand. The Vhyka's long body shuddered in excitement at the sight of its fresh meal reappearing. Just like before, the beast was salivating for its bastardly treat with its whole body and moving with its angular rhythm—all without taking a single breath.

The monster charged towards Ava with its legs that resembled a spider in speed, but human in skin and general anatomy. Ava sped up towards the beast, and just steps before colliding with the Vhyka, she leapt onto the wall, sprinting up it with three large steps. She landed on the monster's shoulders, with its head between her legs. She quickly released a long cord from her hand and hooked it around the monster's neck.

Ava leaned hard to one side, causing the Vhyka to stumble sideways. The cord wasn't meant for strangling, it was meant for steering it into the ground. The sound of the animal fighting for balance made Ava feel both satisfaction and nausea. Seconds later, the Vhyka fell heavily to the ground. It wriggled free, shuddering in agitation, and before Ava could get onto her feet to re-hook the cord around its neck, the Vhyka ran away in sharp jagged movements. Her necklace still had trace magic remaining apparently. There was still time yet, or the monster wouldn't have turned around. It would have attacked. The weighted thud from the Vhyka's fall echoed in Ava's mind as she turned around and walked back towards Axol and Kavi who remained still. She saw the look on Kavi's face and turned, dropped the wiry cord onto the ground, and vomited.

"You seem to have developed more... agility," Kavi said. Ava took Axol back the way a young girl might take back a stuffed animal. Her own Nylo looked up at her face, uncertain. She clutched onto him. More hallucinations came from combat. Ava saw blood and pain, and what was even stranger, she remembered how it felt. Not what it felt like to kill things—that was still nauseating —but what it felt like to not be afraid. To feel in control. And then there was still the scent of her mother. The perfume of her hair, the savory vegetables she grew, and the soil her mother spent so much time on each day she was alive.

"We'll pick up the bastard braid first thing. Then we find Rocky," Ava said in a low tone. Axol again retreated back to Kavi, floating above their shoulder, near their ear.

"You still need money, Ava."

"I'm an Atrox, aren't I?"

"Yes."

"Then we just need to start in the shadow markets," Ava said, before pressing onwards out to the main street. Hesitating for a few moments, Kavi followed with Axol by their side.

Not far away from where bastard braids were sold were the body tents. It had never occurred to Ava to sell her blood. It was a deviant trade that could end badly, but her fears and doubts had taken a back seat. Her body moved as if it wasn't her own, and suddenly without having anything to say, she would hear her own voice talk out loud. It was like hearing someone else's thoughts out loud and having no choice but to listen.

Ava ducked in the first tent with Axol on her shoulder and Kavi behind her. The tent was large. Never ending even. The material of the structure was heavy, dusty, but perhaps once rich with color. Ava found herself among items that were all body parts or once were. Jars with brains, perfume bottles with fingers, and eyeballs set into the design of a silver hand mirror. Though the collection was horrifying for her to witness with her own eyes, the smell was the most offensive. Axol began to venture out from her arms, but Ava squeezed him in closer. She did not want to start the trade off with a broken glass full of bone marrow and bubbles caused by Axol's tail. In fact, now that she was here, she didn't want to start the trade at all. Had this really been her idea?

"I never seen a unicorn in a body tent," a man said in the center of the large tent, at its highest point. He sat low on a cushioned bench with a wooden counter top encasing him on each of his four sides. "Name your price for your horn, lad. I know you have one when you transform," he wiped a small jeweled dagger in his hand carefully. He was cleaning it with a tongue.

"My horn is my honor. I would never sell it."

"I'm the one here to make a trade," Ava said. Her voice surprised her yet again.

"Well, I'm more interested in the unicorn, girl."

"May I?" Ava asked, gesturing for his weapon. The man raised an eyebrow but then leaned forward and handed the dagger to Ava. Ava raised her hand and dug the dagger steadily into her flesh, letting the green of her blood peek through for a few seconds before her skin sealed itself. The man's entire body that had seemingly been collapsing into each vertebrae one year at a time, straightened up to reveal a bear-like height. He stood, and from what Ava could tell, it had been a while since he had exerted this much energy so involuntarily. Ava turned to see Kavi had also stepped forward and raised their hand... but said nothing.

"One ounce for 500 pieces," Ava said.

"What? That rate is unheard of," the man's eyebrows lowered as the red in his face rose.

"So is the blood of an Atrox, basically. Right, Kavi?"

"It is rare, if that is what you are asking."

"Exactly."

"It's too much."

"Do you think that's what all of the body tents are

going to say along this alley? Look, I don't want to waste my time. It's an ounce for 500 pieces and not a bit less. I'm not here to bargain, but I'll collect bids if I have to," Ava felt her stomach flutter as she listened to herself.

"Fine. Fine! But I want more than an ounce," the man said.

"How about 20 ounces?"

He sat down, clearly upset. He looked around, trying to see as much as he could without moving. He found a large glass with notches on the side and slammed it on the table. Ava raised her wrist and cut her skin open with the dagger again. Her skin healed quickly, so she was forced to make the same incision multiple times over the course of filling the container. Sometimes the cut made her wince, sometimes she hardly reacted to it. Kavi had to hold Axol who squirmed at the repeated self-inflicted wounds. Though Ava was sure Axol couldn't make sense of what was happening, he knew she was in pain and wanted to make it stop.

The 20 ounces were given and a rather noisy bag of coins in exchange. Ava left the man with her blood and a frown on his face, but she didn't waste any time. She moved through the markets in Pagra quickly to the tents filled with braids. There were all kinds and all styles. Some braids were made with spikes so that the illegitimacy of the child was made clear around their throat. Other braids were similar to what Ava's braid had been, covered in other metallic designs on the outside to disguise its purpose. Many assumed that the thicker the chain, the longer it would last, but it was actually quite the opposite. The thinner, lighter designs were more expensive by nature and the expiration date was added after the fact. The duration of the necklace varied by the strength of the Gatekeeper's spell that was added to it when the craftsman created each piece of jewelry.

Ava chose a silver chain so thin that she could barely feel it when it was placed on her neck. It was barely visible by the human eye so it needed no disguise, with only its brief glitter in the sun making it noticeable. It was almost as if there was a small part of her collar bone that was made with a sliver of gold.

Shortly afterwards, Kavi followed Ava to a taller clay building, spotted with open balconies that were stacked randomly onto each other. Its design was just another way to contrast the perfectly symmetrical architecture of the New City. They walked through the large arched entrance made without doors but given prominence as it was situated between two large red pillars. The lobby was large and equally red and made of clay as the rest of the structure. There was a man who sat on a colorful rug on the floor. He was smoking something that smelled like plum.

"What can we do for you?" He stood up nimbly and approached them with his hands behind his back.

"One room for the night. On the top level. I like a view. Two baths immediately."

"I will not bathe," Kavi said. At this point, Axol was resting within Kavi's robe, well hidden from Scouts.

"Make that one bath. And send a tailor up please. Does the unicorn eat?" Ava turned to her companion.

"Yes, of course. But I will find my own food."

"I'm still starving. Send enough food up for two," Ava said. She lifted a bag that contained a small fortune and placed three coins into the man's open hands. Ava had been speaking most of the conversation, but the man's eyes never left Kavi. The host received the payment with two hands as he bowed.

"Jeremonie. Guide our guests to their room."

A boy maybe three or four years younger than Ava came running barefoot. He stopped, his eyes searching around their knees. He looked clearly at a loss when he realized their belongings were too few for him to assist. He then stopped and stared at Kavi.

"*Jeremonie,*" the host coughed.

"Yes. Of course. Follow me," Jeremonie said, remembering himself. He turned towards the large central staircase that took them to the fifth level. The doors they passed were not doors, but layers of large, thick, hanging rugs that absorbed the sound significantly better than the average door. Jeremonie stopped at a rug that had a unicorn in its winged horse form, complete with a horn, woven into the center. Jeremonie grinned when presenting the incredibly relevant design to the two guests. Ava exhaled a small laugh, and Kavi said nothing.

"I will have the bath prepared for you immediately," Jeremonie said as his guests entered their room.

"Good. And send the tailor up."

Ava and Kavi listened to the footsteps chafe against the sanded ground as Jeremonie sprinted away for the tailor.

"You know, it's really hard to command a room with you standing next to me," Ava eyed Kavi.

"I do not understand."

"Everyone is so distracted by the unicorn, they hardly notice me telling them what to do."

"Ah, yes. We are rare. It is natural that they stare."

"They used to stare at me."

Kavi turned their head, concentrating on their subject.

"You speak differently," Kavi said.

"By different, do you mean better?" Ava asked.

"No. Just different."

"Maybe you've been studying me a little *too* hard," Ava said. Three women called out before entering with vases of hot water. They walked through a beaded arch, where they emptied their vases. Ava saw the steaming pool of water carved into the ground as they silently exited.

"I'm going to be in here for the next hour. Please. Unless it's the tailor, I don't want to be bothered," Ava said as she walked through the thin bead barrier. Axol, Kavi noticed, remained with them.

A half hour later, a tailor was holding out different materials for Ava to pinch between her fingers from the bath. Axol still remained in the other room with the unicorn. Ava was drawn to blacks and purples that reminded her of movement in the early hours of the morning. The materials were all tight, elastic, and silent —all made for moving in the night. She chose a dark gray scarf and a purple one—long enough to use as a hood and face cover. Her Mark made her a target in Pagra with the Scouts after axolotls. And her Mark being on the cheek was basically an advertisement to all. Adding to the accessories, she chose lightweight, fast-drying boots and a larger pack that would not only fit her new wardrobe but also had enough additional room for Axol to hide in.

Once Ava was done with her bath and continued customizing her wardrobe with the tailor, Kavi took only a few moments using fresh hot water to wash and dry their clothes by hand. Ava noticed the clothes only took a few minutes to dry before they were back to being the spotless pure white robes that Kavi scholared in.

Later that evening, Ava stood on the balcony with a little round covering offering her little shade from the low sunset. She wore a nude-colored dress that hung loosely from her frame since she was waiting for her new wardrobe to be outfitted. She looked out where the New City crept its way up to the border of the Old City. She took a few large gulps of wine in a wooden cup. Kavi sat inside, studying the Atrox from a distance. Axol rested on their lap. Kavi was careful not to pet him.

"I know you are wondering the same question," Kavi whispered to Axol. "Where has our Ava gone?"

Ava stood in darkness with a small hunch that she was asleep and finding herself within a dream. Colors came and went, revealing the past. One memory in this strange dream was of Axol as a little larva. Her father had found him while working at the edge of the desert and brought the small Nylo to her. Her mother hadn't been thrilled at the idea, but her father and Ava had perfected a pleading look her mother couldn't refuse.

Ava reached out to touch little Axol, resembling more leaf than animal, and Axol, along with the entire environment, disappeared and left her in darkness once again. She missed Axol now. Where was he? She looked around, but there was nothing but infinite darkness. She felt as if she were weightless, floating in the blackness between stars. She felt ghostlike. She was sure she must be in a dream.

Another memory soared by, and Ava absorbed it. There were two long swords in her hands. She moves at an impressive speed. The swords swished in the air with flashing silver reflections appearing for half a second. Ava felt the flesh give under her sword. She heard the release of blood and also the grunts of men soon to fall who would never get up again. Her hands reached out, catching her victims and laying them down softly so their bodies reached the ground to die without a sound.

Ava pulled back from the memory in repulsion and returned to the darkness. She remembered this just like she remembered baby Axol, but she did not *know* it like she knew her Nylo. She could recall it, but it wasn't hers. The hands that held the sword were not her own. And yet, somehow the memory was inside of her, recalling for her as if it were her own.

She heard a voice. It was benevolent, peaceful... Who was it? Her memory log loaded... Kavi! It was Kavi. Their pure voice cut through to her like a siren. Ava closed her eyes and held her breath to decipher their words.

"Are you feeling alright?" he asked. "Where are we going?"

"Kavi!" Ava screamed. "Kavi!"

She paused, shaking in the blackness. She wasn't trembling from the cold, but from the weightlessness— from the way she felt separate from her body. She didn't know what else to shout. Where was she? What was happening? Where was everyone and everything? She wanted to speak to Kavi. Like many victims of a nightmare, she wanted to wake up. She screamed, and then she was back.

She was sitting with Kavi on the ground. They were looking at her. It was one of the rare occasions they didn't look annoyingly benevolent. She was wearing a tight purple top and black pants to match. She looked at her boots. They were so new, they were still shiny.

"Ava?"

"Kavi!" Ava said, as if she had been holding her breath this whole time. "I was stuck in a dream. It was dark everywhere... What happened? Where am I?"

Axol flew to her bosom like a shooting star where she squeezed him tightly.

"It is you!" Kavi exclaimed, watching Axol flounder in Ava's arms. "We are heading back east to Nevarra. We still haven't reached the Shift."

"Nevarra?"

"You wanted to find Rocky."

"What happened?"

"I think my hypothesis was correct. Rocky shared memories with you. Are you sure they are not his?"

"Not entirely. Everything is jumbled in my head, but I keep thinking about killing all of these people..."

"Whoever's memories you have, they know how to fight."

"Rocky told me to give him back what was his..."

"Perhaps they are his memories after all," Kavi said. "Pagra takes all of their prisoners through The Source Wall. As a Nylo Guardian, he would not have wanted Pagra to extract information from him. He might have given them to you."

"Rocky's memories?" Ava asked. "I'm not sure..."

"It would explain your fighting skills. Muscle memory can go a long way. Your fighting style *was*, in fact, Nevarrian from what I observed with the Vhkya. And if he gave you all of his memories..."

"Kavi, what is it?"

"Your identity could be at risk. You are having a literal identity crisis."

"You mean..."

"Consider this. If you have all of Rocky's memories, half of the memories that make up you are from him."

"I do feel like I'm losing myself," Ava admitted. She held her hand to her head. The whole situation was a literal headache.

"How did you come back? Only a few minutes ago, you were certainly not yourself."

"I just... I thought I was having a nightmare. I got scared and tried to wake up."

"Intense fear."

"Well—"

"Ava, it is imperative that you remember what you did to come back. You will have to do it again."

"I was just scared."

"Intense emotions then, perhaps."

"Isn't Rocky in Pagra?"

"My network tells us he has already escaped. The entire city is looking for him. You were certain he was heading back to Nevarra."

"Well, Nevarra is the right place to be heading for us too. If Rocky is there, we can find him and give him his memories back. Then I'll get to be myself—without anyone else—right?"

"Just be careful," Kavi said. "Memories work in mysterious ways. We are only a day from The Shift. We will stay here for the night, then—," they stopped. "Someone is coming."

Ava turned to see a group of three approaching on horseback. Their walk was imposing, intimidating, and their Nylos crawled, flew, and slithered along with them.

"They are desert bullies who are all Marked," Kavi said. "Once they find out we do not have much to take, they should leave us alone."

"If only they were so lucky," Ava said with her eyebrows low.

One of the men spoke first.

"We're taking donations to ensure your safe passage to The Shift," he said. The back of his hand glowed red from his Mark. Ava saw the sharp corners of a triangle glow from his wrist, and a large hog stared at Ava and stuck twin tongues out to sense the tension.

"Funny. So are we," Ava said. Kavi gave her a sideways glance as she stood up. Ava's hands were on her hips, her stance wide, and one eyebrow was now raised. Axol had returned to rest on Kavi's shoulder.

"You're going to make sure *we're* safe?" A woman with pink hair asked, grinning. Ava couldn't see her Mark. It must have been under her clothing, hidden away.

"Sure. Some extra food for the night should be enough," Ava said. "Surely you know a unicorn could obliterate the three of you in a few seconds."

"Unicorns? They're too afraid to get their robes dirty."

"Fair. Well, just me then. I'll keep you safe for some dinner."

"We do the negotiating. And you're coming up short."

"Then come get your donation," Ava picked up the

new sword she had purchased only two days ago and unsheathed it. *When did I get this?* She wondered.

"She's got an axolotl," a man with greasy hair said to his two companions. His Mark peeked from his bare shoulder, glowing violet. "No offensive powers. And we could sell the Nylo to Pagra for a small fortune."

"Go," the man with the hog said.

Kavi took a step back at the same time Ava took a step forward. Two Marked dismounted from their horses and ran forward. The man who Ava thought needed to wash his hair had a chain in his hand, and a small yellow bird flapping above him. The pink haired woman had a spiked ball on a stick. The first man threw his chain that Ava easily dodged. She skidded under the long weapon for an easy but messy swipe under his legs. He went down onto one knee. He was forced to let go of the chain to use his hands to stable himself. Ava used her sword to send the chain sliding across the dirt. A second later, she heard the chain dragging across the ground. It magically retracted back into the man's open hand. He was standing now and ready with a grin. He flicked the metal, and it hit Ava's upright arm with a weight that had her stumble a few feet to the side. She had braced for the blow, but hadn't blocked it very successfully.

The pink haired woman spun, a dagger in each hand. Ava had barely been fast enough to leap backwards, dodging the first two swipes. Ava took a breath, sizing up her opponents properly. Then she stepped forward. She swung her sword in long swift motions, knowing the daggers were at a disadvantage as long as she kept her swings flowing forward. Ava dug her back leg into the dirt as she went for her target. She drew blood on the outside of the woman's shoulder just before sidestepping to the left to dodge an overhead swing of the first man's chain. Without hesitating this time, she charged forward, swinging her sword deep under the man's ribs. She meant to go deeper, or at least a part of her wanted to cut deeper. She felt herself pull the weapon away as she pulled away from the desire to make her enemy a dead one. She couldn't explain the conflict happening in real time. Part of her could care less about the life she could take in that moment. Another part of her resisted the urge with all of her might. The cut was still enough to send the man down and maim him. The decision to kill or not kill faded as the confidence in her abilities grew. She could still inflict enough damage to do what she needed to do.

Ava turned to the woman. With a twist of her sword, she had thrown one of the daggers from her hand as she heard her opponent curse. Then she nicked the woman's shoulder again, just an inch below where she had tagged her before with her sword.

Ava's mind flashed. The strikes, the grunts and groans, the feeling of flesh being cut... this would be a new memory like the other foreign memories that haunted her. Except in this new memory she was making, it was clearly her body. It was her hand doing the striking. But she couldn't control how her body was moving. It was like she had no control. And though it was alien to her, even the enjoyment of inflicting pain was hard to distance herself from.

Then, suddenly, pain.

The hog had landed on her back. She felt her bone crack. The third drifter had dismounted and joined while she was distracted, and his Nylo hadn't wasted any time. She then tried to somersault away to get a better read of the group, but her body didn't roll into the tight ball she had planned it to. She bounced awkwardly on her shoulders, feeling the cracked bone give even more before it could heal. She fell clumsily onto her backside, and dodged a heavy club by mere inches. Goosebumps crept up her neck as she felt the air rush from the swing that had just missed her.

She clambered to her feet. There was a tight rippling under her skin; her bone was healing in real time. It was painful, but she felt her arm reach full strength again once it was back to being completely intact.

The expectations of her untrained body had made a statement. She—or Rocky or whoever—had overestimated their physical abilities in this fight. She needed to end this. She lunged forward after another swing from the clubbed man, slicing him in the leg. Then she jumped, twirling and slashing, using the length of her sword to take on all three and then some. The final strike was a kick to the last standing, the woman with pink hair, that resulted in a knockout.

Ava didn't wait. She emptied their pockets before

exploring the sacks they dropped before the scruffle. She walked back to Kavi, richer than before, and with two extra daggers.

"You did not have to do that," Kavi said.

"They didn't have to go looking for donations," Ava said.

"Where is Ava?"

Ava paused and looked at Kavi. Then she touched her finger to her temple and tapped twice. "She's in here, pissing her pants and thanking the heavens I'm here to handle people like this."

"Rocky, this is Ava's body," Kavi said.

"Rocky?" Ava lifted an eyebrow.

"Is that not who I am speaking to right now? The memories of Rocky?"

"That's my brother."

"But that means..."

"That I'm Maya. The most deadly assassin in The Cache, at your service," she gave the unicorn a curtsy.

"I did not know Rocky had a sister."

"Well, *had* a sister. But my memory lives on thanks to him," she smiled.

"I want to speak to Ava."

"Me too. This body," Maya said. "It's slow, soft, weak, and totally inflexible. It almost got us killed just now. Lucky for me it heals."

"I want to speak to the owner of the body."

"Yeah? And what are you going to do about it,

unicorn? ...That's what I thought. Not a thing. Let's go. We can make The Shift in two days if we keep going—especially with one of their horses," Ava started to pack up.

"Fine," Kavi agreed. They did not smile.

It only took Ava a few minutes to pack a white horse with brown speckles on its back, she mounted the horse.

"Are you ready?" she asked Kavi.

Kavi closed their eyes. Their bones moved, and their skin changed. Ava watched a horn as white as a string of pearls grow from the peach-colored star that was stamped on Kavi's forehead. It only took a few seconds for Kavi to shift into a glorious white horse with thick, long, and feathery wings. Axol flew above the magical unicorn and then found a comfortable napping spot on Kavi's back.

"Well, that's something you don't see every day," Ava said, clearing her throat. "Let's... let's ride."

***

Ava's body was not ready for the trek to Nevarra that Maya had planned. Her fatigue overcame her incredibly quickly and with not much effort. She could not run for long, and her wobbly core made even riding the stolen horse a challenge. The soreness in her legs and hips that followed even a few hours on horseback was upsetting to her, to say the least.

Quickly realizing she would never be able to catch up to Rocky with Ava's level of fitness, Maya switched gears and decided to take her time in getting herself back to Nevarra. She knew Rocky. He would get there on his own just fine. But if this was the body she now inhabited, it was the body she would need to mold and shape in a way that worked for her... and as quickly as possible so she wouldn't struggle in taking down three mediocre drifters.

She began training. She ran long sprints until it felt like the air was going to claw her lungs out. She started with body weight exercises where, to no surprise, she found her maximum number of pushups to be five before her arms began to tremble. Endurance at fast speeds was low, strength as well. Those could be built up over time. But the biggest threat to limiting her physical abilities was flexibility—on the battlefield, yes—but it would also be limiting in more personal areas of her life too. This would simply not do.

One night, Maya sat in front of a fire with the quiet unicorn sitting across from her. The sun had gone down, and the moon and stars glistened brightly. Axol also preferred to stay closer to the albino than his own Marked. It had been that way since she had stolen the inert horse.

"You don't say much," Maya rolled her eyes. Clearly bored.

"Ava never thought as much," Kavi said.

"I get it. You and Ava were close. You don't have to be so bitter about me being here."

"Oh?"

"What would you do if you were me? Get a second chance at life and throw it away?"

"I want to talk to Ava."

"And this body. What a waste. It's soft. Immoble. Stiff as a log—wait a second," Maya jerked up. Her eyes running through an impulsive plan. "I could fast track that."

"What do you mean?" Kavi asked.

Maya ignored the unicorn. They wouldn't approve. She kneeled onto the ground, leaning forward. Then she slid her legs apart, her left leg forwards with her heel in the dirt, and the right leg backwards with the top of her foot pressed into the ground. Her hips were still well over a foot away from the ground. It was a sorry attempt at the splits.

"See, this is where Ava's body stops," Maya said and then took a deep breath. With an exhale, she pushed down suddenly on her body, pressing her hips to the ground. She heard the pop of ligaments and felt the tear of muscles and a scream escaped her from the burning pain. Her head bowed down, buried under the pain and alarm her body was feeling. Kavi didn't move as they watched her. Axol fluttered up, but did not get any closer to Ava's body. Maya flipped her hair up, giggling as she rose with a straight torso. She flexed her legs straight, and felt her body mend itself with her legs laying opposite of one another.

"We can do full splits now," Maya smiled at Kavi.

"This body has no idea of its full potential. It's bloody limitless."

"Nothing is limitless," Kavi responded. They held their hands facing up towards the sky in their lap so Axol could rest on their open palms. Maya ignored them, and continued to even out her lengthened legs on the other side.

The next day, Maya and Kavi had made it onto The Shift. They sat patiently, letting the shifting sand take them east.

"Does Ava see what is happening?" Kavi asked.

"Why would I tell you anything?" Maya asked.

"Can you hear her?" Kavi continued.

Maya didn't answer.

"I thought you were Rocky," Kavi said, looking out at the sand they were slowly drifting over.

"Rocky is here too," Maya said, "But he locked his memories away for himself... The way he transferred my memories... it's clear he wanted her to stay out of my way. As for him, he's a very private person."

"When we get to Nevarra, will you give Rocky his memory?"

"Yes."

"Will you leave Ava's body?" Kavi asked.

"I don't have anywhere to go," Maya said.

"You admit you do not plan on leaving Ava."

"The body's healing properties are useful. I was actually going to try to Match with an axolotl next. This just saves me a step."

"If you do not leave, you will be interfering with my research."

"And if you have any intentions of forcing me out, you will be tampering with your research and interfering with my life," Maya responded.

A silence passed. Maya watched the top layer of sand get swept up into the air and float back down onto the surface in a soft sprawl.

"Why Atroxes?" she asked.

Kavi hesitated for only a moment before answering.

"I believe they are misunderstood here in The Cache."

"They begged to be let in through the West Gate. And when the Gatekeeper let them in, they came in like a disease. Little leeches. They are the worst part of all of us. What's misunderstood about that?"

"You see them as leeches just as I see you as a parasite. They came from another world and another culture. We do not know their story."

"Neither does Ava. She hardly understands what it is to be an Atrox. She only knows she is hated. You're wasting your time with her. She's too naive to be insightful."

"You do not know her."

"I know her better than she does. She's locked in, but

I'm not locked out. She thinks the love of a prince of one of the largest kingdoms in The Cache is actually attainable for her—a bastard hiding in the Tunnels."

Maya was smiling, but Kavi noticed a tear slide down her cheek just the same.

PART III

CHAPTER 12

A SMALL PIECE OF REDEMPTION

CHINCHIN

The doors and small windows, creaking bridges, and ruffling leaves surrounded Chinchin and Rocky. Chinchin slowed her walk, taking in the hidden details of Nevarra. She had realized and accepted that the clan might want her dead. That was okay. She had done right by Rocky, but wrong by Maya. And as she literally took careful, calculated steps, she wondered when Maya's footsteps had last walked where she was walking now. Even though this was the furthest from home she had ever been, Nevarra felt familiar to Chinchin. Maya felt close. The wild power in Maya's eyes was present in the air between the trees. The leaves growing every which way reminded Chinchin of Maya's hair. The height of the trees, the way Maya stood confident and erect at all times. Never at ease, only alert. Everything that made up Maya now surrounded

Chinchin, and it hurt. In fact, she would be okay to lay down now. One of the two Nevarrian generals' children killed because of her, the other free because of her. She would at least die knowing she had done *something* she was proud of.

Before she was able to dwell on her guilt any longer, people began to appear from every direction. Some clung to the ladders on trees, some looked down from tall branches, and most stood, appearing suddenly through the forest fog. Maya always appeared out of nowhere in the same way. Chinchin smiled at the painful memory.

"Who are you?" the man said, looking at Rocky and back at her. Chinchin could tell it was Maya and Rocky's father from the way his eyes studied her. His face was just familiar enough through his children.

"I've brought Rocky here. To his home."

"My son, an NG, does not need a guide."

"He doesn't have any memory. He was captured in Pagra and passed through The Source Wall. He doesn't remember anything," Chinchin said calmly.

"Is this true?" the man looked at Rocky.

"It is," Rocky said quietly.

"You're the scientist, aren't you?"

"I am."

"You work for Pagra."

"Worked. I don't work for anyone at the moment."

"Why did you save my son?"

"I—I..." Chinchin cleared her throat, "I created the

mutation that killed your daughter. I'm the reason your daughter is dead."

"Maya killed herself."

"No. She suffered severe side effects from my experiment. She was not the only one."

"Do you seek forgiveness?"

"I only wanted to return Rocky. I don't have any other expectations."

Rocky started to open his mouth, but his father raised his hand.

"We do not want your life, if that's what you think. We want information. All of it. Tell us more about the curse you have created, and you are free to leave tomorrow morning."

"I don't want to stay here," Chinchin's voice shook. Maya was everywhere, and so was her death.

"It is not a request," the man said. He walked up to Rocky and put his hand on his son. It was clear Rocky did not recognize him. "Ahma, take my son. Draya, show Chinchin where she will be staying."

Chinchin had thought she was in the heart of Nevarra when Rocky's father, Obigon, had first appeared. She was not. With Draya alongside her, the group walked deeper into the forest where the trees were so abundant she could barely fit between the trunks. Then suddenly, the trees opened up to reveal what actually looked like a city. The structures were still built with nature rather than against it, but there were wide paths for the traffic of people, and larger roofs for city gatherings.

Though it was still a distance from the clearing, Chinchin also eyed an edifice centered in the city. It stood out immediately because Chinchin recognized the material. Obsidian V. It was covered in white veins, left in its raw, natural state. The group dispersed as Chinchin and Draya made their way into the busier areas and as Chinchin guessed, she was led to the city center.

It was strange to see Obsidian V so untouched. In Pagra, it had been sanded, processed, recast, and redesigned so that it could morph at top speeds. It made up Pagra's core tech that consisted of smooth surfaces and abrupt edges. It was like a land made up of black mirrors, and she had never known there was another side to it. She remembered Chauson talking about how they had discovered there was an abundance of the material in Nevarra. She wondered if he had actually seen it. It was incredible. She then thought of Chauson and how the last time she had seen him she had knocked him out. It was for his own good, she reminded herself, but she couldn't help but feel the guilt seep up from her chest.

Chinchin was prompted to remove her shoes before stepping onto the dark surface of the temple. She took her first step onto the black rock, surprised to see ripples the color of lightning extend from her foot. Chinchin looked at Draya who walked forward, circular lightning ripples lighting up around her feet as well. As Chinchin walked up the steps, she felt the uneven slab under her toes, etchings and all.

The edges were raw and, in its roughest form, even

jagged. In Pagra, the rock had been molded to match the structure, manipulated to match its purpose. Here, the structure was molded by the rock. Chinchin walked through the entrance. There were no pillars, no clear doorway, but a simple wide opening as mysterious and one-of-a-kind as any sacred cave.

The deeper into the mouth of the building, the darker it became—but it was only with each step's bright rippling that she was able to see in front of her—that and the purple and green gels above. She walked slowly, and Draya patiently waited for her. It was still possible that they had the intention of taking her life, and the darker it became, the more afraid Chinchin realized she was. She thought of her mother for a moment before pushing forward. If she died here, would her mother ever find her? She doubted it since her mother never left home. Through a maze of darkness, Chinchin was led to a humble-sized room with a small black boulder in the center. Draya gestured for her to sit in on one of the wooden benches surrounding the center piece. If this had been Pagra, Chinchin thought, the boulder would have been a sleek cube, connected to the ground and ready to morph at any point into meeting room furnishings.

Obigon came from the darkness as Chinchin sat. Another silent Nevarrian entrance.

"Tell us everything we want to know," he said. "And then you can tell us what you want us to know."

Chinchin resisted the outpouring only for a few

seconds, but she knew this is why she had come. The words came flooding out of her mouth.

"I'm a Mutations scientist with an expertise in human biology. I wanted to use science and technology instead of Gatekeeper spells to... I was trying to create something that made a Nylo's power accessible to everyone.

"When I created the mutation, I wanted it to be the door for anyone—rich and poor, lucky or not, *chosen* or not—to experience what it was like to have power. To feel what magic was like. It wouldn't be just the rich and powerful who tipped the scales in their favor when it came to a Nylo choosing who would get their power."

"What happened with the experiment that killed my daughter?" Obigon asked.

"We experimented heavily on Nylos to figure out how to make them Match with any human. It didn't matter if the Nylo wanted the Match. It only mattered if the human wanted the Match. We had a lot of success. More failures. We tested on regular people who didn't have power first. Then we started testing the mutation on people who already had Matches so a human could channel more than one power. That's when the side effects started. Along with irrational thinking, suicide became a common side effect of anyone who took the mutation who already had a Marker. The more Markers they had, the more likely they were to self-destruct. We believe this is because the Nylos were becoming... depressed," Chinchin tried not to wince at this last word.

There was shame there she hadn't come close to unpacking.

Obigon nodded gravely.

"We started using salamanders with their healing properties to subdue the depression, which was proving to be very contagious, and it worked. But I was too late with Maya. She took on 7 Nylos before she died. It was too much. I should have never let her, but she wanted to try. She wanted to know how it was done, and if it could be undone... And the scientist in me also wanted to know."

Obigon remained silent. At this point, Chinchin realized he wasn't the only one in the room. The room's darkness was slowly fading, and she realized it wasn't as small as she had first thought. There were many shadows that were revealed under the gels as she continued to speak to the growing audience.

"The axolotls were the key. I didn't want to take as many as we did, but as soon as Pagra Labs realized they were needed to allow someone more than one power with immunity to the suicidal tendencies, they started to hunt them aggressively. If they're not an endangered species already, they will be soon. So many took their own lives. It wasn't just Maya. It was a side effect of the Nylos' sadness. It wasn't because she was sad. I think it's important that you know that."

"All of this coming from you wanting to give everyone magic?" Obigon rubbed his forehead and then looked at Chinchin.

"I wanted everyone who wanted to be Marked to be able to Match with a Marker. I wanted to close the gap between the Marked and the un-Marked, but I only made it worse," Chinchin finished.

"And my son?"

"He was caught trying to save a healing Nylo. I know he has no memories, but they did say they weren't able to extract any information from him even though he was attached to the mud walls for a few hours."

Obigon turned to Ahma who stood a few feet behind him.

"Let our NG's know that Nylos with healing capabilities are in danger. They're rare enough as it is. Have Rocky meet with Noro to go over memory transfer—he must have given them to someone. Let it also be known that Chinchin is no longer working for Pagra Labs. She is an outlaw to our enemy and on our side—"

"I'm not on any side," Chinchin interrupted.

"Are you on Pagra's side?"

"No."

"Then you're on ours."

"There's also something else you should know," Chinchin said. "Pagra knows you have Obsidian V here. And they are running out. I'm not sure they've already tried to negotiate with you, but it will happen if it hasn't. And soon."

"Thank you, Chinchin. Ahma, set up a living quarters for Chinchin. She has saved my son, and I believe was a fair match for my Maya," Chinchin blushed. So he did know there was something between her and his daughter. Then Obigon turned to Chinchin who, despite her best efforts, let a tear escape her eye, "Thank you for your courage. I am glad to have Rocky back. Pagra must be stopped, and the Marker Matching must remain sacred and natural. It is no surprise that artificial, synthetic mutations to force a Match have already been punished by nature. Your mutation can only lead to forced partnerships. To slavery. It is as we feared: the Nylos and their freedom are at risk. They are in danger."

Chinchin stood out over the paneless window of her own guest hut in the Nevarrian trees. The rustling of quiet people came through along with the light smoke of incense in honor of Rocky's unlikely but welcomed return. Below her, she would have thought it was just trees blowing in the wind and the leaves making their own natural shuffling music, but now she had seen these people. She knew where to look, and she could see them all moving through the gigantic branches, lightly over the dirt, and everywhere in between.

She had thought she would visit Nevarra not long ago. She didn't think it would be without Maya. It had grown easier to distract herself with her science so she wouldn't think of her dead lover. And not thinking of Maya usually made it so that she forgot Maya was gone.

When Maya was not in her mind, Maya was simply off somewhere, being Maya. Now Maya was fully present in her mind in Nevarra, which meant that her death was fully present in her mind as well. All of this led back to her guilt.

Chinchin stripped the dirtied, bloody Pagra uniform from her body. She decided she would not wear black for a very, very long time. She climbed into a large wooden tub full of steamy water and laid back. She took a breath, and exhaled the last tears that sealed the fact that Rocky's rescue would not bring Maya back. It was something, but would never be close to enough. She settled in —the water was up to her collar bone. All the good in the world, all the revenge, all of the wrongs made right that she could do, that she would do... It would not bring Maya back.

And that was not okay for Chinchin. But still she bathed. Still she would sleep. Still she would eat. And still she would breathe. But it all seemed useless. Sleep without dreams. Food without taste. Air without life. That was what it felt to be Chinchin without Maya.

Chinchin walked freely (with the company of Draya, of course) on the grounds of Nevarra. She walked through the trees, until she came across running water that led into a lake. And then she found herself following the sound of children. She came upon some type of schooling happening in front of her. Small black children stood lined up, their Nylos next to them. A teacher spoke, he must have been around Chinchin's age, maybe slightly younger, but Chinchin was too far to hear what he was saying.

What was most peculiar was the sight of a green-eyed teenager—also about her age—standing in the group, a couple of feet taller than anyone else, if not more. He was obviously older, but seemed to not notice. He was serious, focused, and meditative. His excitement, if it existed, was reserved while the other children were moving, chanting, laughing constantly. Chinchin looked to his right to see the largest wolf she had ever seen. She recognized the species. An original Moon Wolf. She had never seen one before until that moment.

"Who is that next to the Moon Wolf?" Chinchin asked.

"Another guest," Draya said. "A friend of Rocky's."

"Do you have a lot of visitors these days?" Chinchin asked.

"Never in my life. At least none that we let stay. And now two at once," Draya said.

"Let's get closer."

"If you wish," Draya changed direction. They made their way downhill through the grass and sparse trees. They got so close that Chinchin could now hear the teacher. A child appeared from nowhere and whispered something in Draya's ear.

"I have to go. I'll return here to pick you up," Draya said. What Chinchin heard was don't move until Draya was able to come back. Too bad she was never a great listener.

The older boy's face was flushed, and it was obvious why. Every child was performing a small show of magic. Their Marks on their bodies glowed brightly with extra power flowing through them. His did not. No magic flowed through him into anything notable. His Mark glowed in its natural state through his shirt, but nothing more was happening. He was clearly blocked.

"Think of the color blue like your Mark," the instructor said quietly to him. "And focus on that color."

The boy's eyes were steady, hair falling over his forehead, down just past his eyes. His body shook from effort, but nothing came from him channeling the color of the wolf's eyes. The class ended, and the children and instructor left. The older student found a quiet corner and sat. He wiped the sweat from his forehead, drank from a large wooden cup, and then, giving into his anger, he threw the cup on the ground. The water spilled onto the damp grass and he sat with his fingers loose, his elbows resting on his knees. The wolf laid by his side, his tail slowly flowing from one side to the other as if he had unconsciously assigned himself to be the official duster of the Nevarrian forest.

Chinchin walked from the shadows. The boy looked up, clearly surprised to see someone without the dark Nevarrian skin or perhaps it was surprising to see someone who wasn't half his age. He blushed, most likely remembering his outburst with the cup only a few seconds earlier.

"Did you Match with your Marker recently?" Chinchin asked.

He wiped his mouth. "Yes."

"The instructor is wrong," she said. "It has nothing to do with thinking about color. That's bullshit."

"Bold to contradict a Marker expert from Nevarra, don't you think?"

"Not if I know what I'm talking about. And it didn't seem to be working anyway."

He said nothing. He stood up and picked up the cup that he had thrown earlier. The wolf went from laying to sitting, watching Chinchin carefully.

"It's not color. Using magic from a Nylo is much deeper than the color blue," Chinchin said. "Besides, I don't think you're blue."

He crossed his arms, clearly hesitant.

"Get the idea of blue out of your mind. Your Mark is a stamp. Its purpose is already served as soon as you glow a color for the first time—it's just the contract binding you with your Moon Wolf. It's not the core of your objective. It just reflects a bit of who you are. Instead, think about something important. Something that brings up emotion. It sounds silly—so close your eyes. It helps. Think about something that makes you feel... any emotion, but just a lot of it."

He closed his eyes. Chinchin watched as his thoughts seemed to scurry through memories until he landed on something. She could tell by his breath. He had landed on something worth a pause. Worth emotion. Was it admiration, fear, courage, doubt, sadness, desire...? She wished she could know.

The ground beneath the two began to tremble. He opened his eyes. Chinchin had quickly widened her stance to catch her balance. His Mark glowed brighter through his shirt. His eyes widened more in shock, and the ground stopped. Chinchin smiled.

"You're connected to the earth. It means you're stubborn, maybe not great with change. With a seeker, whatever you're looking for, you'll find either way."

"Who are you?" he asked.

"Doesn't matter. I'll be gone soon."

"No instructor has been able to get me to do anything."

"I've studied harnessing magic from Markers to Marked very closely."

"Are you Marked?"

"No. I just like the science behind all of it. Not all magic has to be mysterious."

"Will you teach me more?"

"I think it's time we get back," Draya said. The boy and Chinchin both spun around. Neither of them had heard her. "Candland, someone will be here to take you back to your quarters soon. Chinchin, are you ready?"

"Candland?" Chinchin asked. "You can't possibly be..."

"Chinchin, follow me please," Draya stepped forward.

Chinchin turned around and followed Draya. She turned back and stared at the boy who had sad eyes and a Moon Wolf. A prince from a kingdom that had banished Nevarra and an ex-Pagra Labs scientist. Nevarra was in curious company these days.

CHAPTER 13
THE REUNION
CANDLAND

Candland learned Nevarra's version of how the world of The Cache came to be—how his kingdom, Questus, came to be. He had learned more about Nylos and their magic in a single day sitting with the Nevarrian children than he had his entire life in his own home. He had even started to be able to move more freely during Caprice, which he felt bled into how he thought and felt.

However, the progress he had made as far as harnessing Proru's power had been slow. And the only progress he had was thanks to the other mysterious guest, not any instructor at Nevarra. Chinchin was a striking young woman. Had she not the most symmetrical face, thick lips, sharp chin, and mesmerizing blue-gray eyes, Candland admitted he might not have immediately started listening to her advice the first day they had met.

She was the first person to help him make the ground shake. So when he saw her walking along the river again, he didn't hesitate to be the first one to speak—a rare impulse for him.

"Hello," he said. Behind him, Proru took a step into the river and began to drink by unnecessarily submerging half of his snout into the water.

"Prince Candland," she bowed her head slightly.

"I didn't get your name."

"It's Chinchin. How is training coming along?"

"Not well."

"No surprise there."

"Any advice?"

"Maybe think about who your teachers are."

"What do you mean? I'm learning from some of the most knowledgeable people in The Cache when it comes to Nylos."

"Exactly. So why aren't you making good progress? Is it you?"

"I wasn't exactly born to be Marked," Candland said.

"Or... You're the prince of a kingdom that goes against everything your teachers stand for, and they don't want you to be able to make the ground shake beneath their feet. Why should they trust you?" she asked.

"...I guess you have a point. I would never do anything to hurt Nylos."

"I believe your intention. But do they?"

"Why did you help me the other day?"

"I think everyone should be able to use magic. Had I known you were a prince, I might not have been so inclined seeing as you don't need it. So, what *is* the prince of Questus doing here?"

"I was Marked," Candland said, pointing to his chest. "I didn't know where else to go."

"Is that why you're so sad?"

Candland thought of his brother, Keyes. *There it is. The gloom!*

"No. I've always been this way—even when I did have a home."

"They have spells for that."

"Magic doesn't fix everything," Candland said. It sounded like he was speaking from experience. He kept his eyes on the river. "What would you do if you were me?"

"Learn what you can here, but don't stay too long. They clearly don't want you to learn too quickly. Probably means you're a threat, which I would take as a compliment."

Candland laughed. Never in his life had he ever been considered a threat. In fact, it was strange that he was even considered at all.

"Where would you go?"

"Have you ever heard of The Almra?"

"I thought they were just a myth."

"So the Blood says, but they also think Nylos and Marked like you are cursed—which really is just their way of making sure faith in the Blood is never lost. Okay, my turn. What would you do if you were me?" Chinchin asked.

"I don't think I'm the right person to give you advice," Candland felt warm suddenly.

"That's just all the more reason I want your advice."

"Well, given that I know nothing about you other than the fact that you've helped me, most helpful people I've come across forget to help themselves. I guess I would say to make sure you help yourself."

"It's too late for that," Chinchin smiled as she looked away. Candland watched her gaze fall onto the water. Was she a little gloomy herself?

"I disagree."

"Oh?"

"Life's too unpredictable and confusing to know if we're too early or late. As far as we're concerned, maybe you're right on time."

"Who's the optimist now?" she smiled.

The next day, Candland was even more excited to attend lessons as Noro chose to teach the class outside that day. Candland had thought that all humans who Matched with a Moon Wolf had his same Mark, but that wasn't the case at all. In fact, the magic was constructed a lot looser than he had imagined. Noro explained that color was the first place to start. Every human was Marked with a color of the rainbow. The color they were Marked with spoke to their unique character: red for courage, yellow for passion, orange for adaptability, green for resilience, blue for peace, indigo for compassion, and violet for intelligence. It wasn't as simple as it sounded though, Noro had warned. Just because someone's Mark was blue, representing peace, that didn't mean they weren't dangerous. It was simply an indicator of their trait that was more prominent than others. He had mentioned that even the Blood killed and caged Marked in the name of peace. So, perspective was key—even if intention was true to their color.

Next, what seemed rather basic to all of the other children but was brand new for him, was the Mark itself. He learned that every single Mark on each and every human was unique. No two Marks were the same. However, the Mark of one color would share a similar feature. Noro described them quickly, and thanks to Candland's love for his history and philosophy lessons, Candland was able to follow closely.

Red favored triangles. Candland remembered Maya and her red Mark. The design was made up of triangles that started just above her knee, echoing with that same shape up and down her leg, stopping at her shin and her upper thigh.

Rocky's Mark was yellow—which made total sense. He was as passionate as anyone. Especially when it came to the Nylos. Yellow resembled fire. Rocky's arm was marked with long, nearly-tangling swirls that ran from his forearm all the way down to his pointer finger.

Green was Ava. Candland's stomach dropped slightly when he thought of her Mark. He hadn't noticed when he first met her, but there were small blooming flowers with soft petals and green leaves delicately placed on her cheek. Green Marks were always intricate and organic—including things like vines or leaves or flowers. How fitting, he thought sadly.

Orange Marks were heavily influenced by circles and dots. Blue Marks, he learned, echoed waves or clouds with large, round curved Marks, and violet Marks heavily utilized pointed stars. His color, which he initially thought was simply blue, was actually indigo. Links were always present in an indigo Mark. He had never thought about it before, but the hexagons and other layered cornered shapes he dawned were a pattern that were all linked together like a chain wrapped around his chest, extending over his shoulder and bicep.

Noro had pulled out large papers with different Marks to test them with. Unfortunately, Draya put her hand on his shoulder calling him away. She, once again, had appeared from what seemed like nowhere. Candland cursed under his breath, getting tired of the ever-silent Nevarrians. Proru, who had been laying out on the grass, lifted his head. Candland met his gaze. Proru was tracking him with his blue eyes.

"Is it my brother? Has he returned?" Candland wondered aloud. Every day, he had asked Draya if there was any news, but she always confirmed their spies had not heard of his return. Perhaps that was it.

"No. Someone else has though."

"Who?"

"You'll see soon enough, Prince."

Candland ran his fingers through his hair in anticipation. Pror had caught up with them now. Draya led them back to the temple, through what felt like a maze in the trees, before they reached a large gathering area. There were many empty tables, with one large table at the front of the room. Obigon sat at the head of the table, and Rocky sat on the table with his legs hanging over one side.

"Rocky!" Candland smiled.

Rocky turned to see Candland and did not return the smile. Candland paused at the blank face.

"He doesn't recognize you. His memory has been wiped by Pagra," Obigon said. "We've been trying to get it back, but..."

"Wiped? Rocky, it's me. Candland," Candland walked up to his friend, placing a hand on the table.

"I'm sorry. What he said is true. I don't remember you."

"I was hoping a friend with some fun memories might bring something back," Obigon said. "I'll leave you to talk."

Obigon left the room. Rocky looked down at the ground. Finally he looked up at Proru.

"He's your Nylo?" Rocky asked.

"Yes. All thanks to you, actually," Candland took a seat next to Rocky.

"I have an owl. Apparently his name is Berns."

"I've seen you fly with him," Candland said.

"I don't even know how that would work."

"He's carried both of us at once. The physics doesn't really make sense, I guess," Candland admitted. After a pause he continued. "Rocky what happened? What do you remember?"

"Nothing."

"What's the earliest thing you remember?"

"Chinchin pulling me from a wall that was trying to eat me. We ran away from Pagra."

So that's why she's here, Candland thought.

"We came here. She said it's my home," Rocky shrugged.

"She's right. It is your home." Candland was dwelling on the fact that Chinchin was able to save Rocky and escape Pagra without even being Marked, but decided to keep things focused on Rocky.

"It doesn't feel like it."

"Here. Touch my head," Candland said.

"What?"

"Touch my head. We always did this. You'd touch my head, I'd think of a memory, and you'd see it."

"I don't know how."

"You just have to touch me. You like to hold hands to embarrass me, but I think hand on head is a good start. Just try, Rocky."

Rocky placed his hand on Candland's head. Candland closed his eyes and thought of a time when they were in the Tunnels. They were young. They were flying over a field of glowing flowers. Well, they were sort of flying. Rocky's straps were in Bern's talons, but Candland was holding onto Rocky so that Berns wasn't able to get too much air because they were so heavy. They only left the ground a few feet at a time. Berns would lower them back down to the ground, and Candland would kick his legs up to get more air. Rocky's laughter was squeaky when it wasn't airy, and Candland's was high pitched and unembarrassed. Both boys were still soft and thin in their features... They were very young.

Candland opened his eyes smiling. Rocky looked at Candland.

"We're friends."

"Yeah. You're my best friend. You're the reason I found this guy," Candland pointed to his wolf.

"He's pretty cool. Thought he was going to eat me when I first saw him."

"He can always change his mind," Candland winked. "Do you want to go smoke?"

"I don't think that's allowed here."

"Wow. You really don't remember much about yourself, do you."

There was some noise coming from the hallway. It sounded like shouting outside and both Candland and Rocky turned towards the exit.

"What is it now?" Candland asked. He looked at

Rocky. They stood up and followed the sounds, stuttering through a few wrong turns like blind mice with Proru following behind them, and then finally made their way outside to the main entrance. They looked down at the black marble steps where the noise was coming from.

There was a crowd of people surrounding something or someone. Rocky led the way down the steps, with the natives shuffling to the side when they saw it was Obigon's son who was trying to get through. Candland came up behind Rocky to the center of the commotion where he saw a tall albino boy who stood with a poise that made Candland feel all of his physical shortcomings as a prince. Standing next to the white stranger was... Candland froze. His mouth fell open and went dry. His lungs froze in place while his heart started pounding so hard, he thought his eyeballs would pop.

"Ava," he said. Then louder, "Ava! Ava!!"

She looked his way and her smile disappeared. Her face froze in place as if she were trying to remember who he was. Did she not remember him? Or was the reaction *because* she remembered him and the last time they were together?

"It's a unicorn," Rocky said to Candland. Rocky hadn't even noticed Ava standing next to the unicorn. "Obviously I can't remember if I've seen one before, but it feels like the first time."

Ava glanced at Rocky, and then locked onto him. She broke into a large smile and came running towards him with her arms open. She wrapped him in her arms, nearly lifting him off of his feet, and he returned the embrace out of politeness. Candland was unwillingly given a front row seat to the smile on Ava's face during the welcome. If he reached out, he could touch her. It was at this moment, he realized how different she looked from the last time he had seen her.

Her skin was the first thing he noticed. In the Tunnels, her skin had always been so pale. It wasn't until he saw her bronzed skin that he realized she was born of a people that were meant to be above ground and under the sun. Her dark skin glowed with warmth in a way he had never seen. Her face was leaner, her cheekbones high when before he'd never even noticed cheekbones under her warm brown eyes. It hadn't been that long since he had last seen her, only a full cycle of the moon, and yet she looked older. Even her hair was unmistakably longer. He noticed her arms around Rocky were indented. More firm rather than soft. It was his sculpting eye that saw this. And it was the rest of him that came to the conclusion that she was more beautiful than when she first kissed him.

"You two... know each other?" Candland asked.

"Of course, Prince Candland," Ava said as she pulled back.

"Y-You know who I am?" Candland asked again.

"How could I not?" Ava smiled. She took Rocky's hand and pulled him forward up the temple stairs. "Come. Where is father?"

"Father?" Candland mouthed to himself. He had now

stopped saying his questions out loud when everything stopped making sense. The people pressed against him to get a closer look, but this time he was with Pror. Candland did not give an inch and did not let Ava out of his sight. Not this time.

Obigon stepped forward, and Ava embraced him with a familiarity that confused Candland. Did they know each other? She said something to both of them. They stood there for a few moments exchanging words, and then they walked forward together towards the temple. Candland began combing his brain from what he knew about Ava's past. She had no parents—or so she said. She had never mentioned where she was from before the Tunnels. Was it Nevarra? She didn't look the part. Her skin was light brown, but not as dark as a true Nevarrian's. Maybe she had some Nevarrian blood in her? Her eyes were large, similar to a Nevarrian, but sharp, wide, and slanted slightly up, like a desert native or even islander. It occurred to him that he had never asked where she was from. She could be Makani-born for all he knew. And then he remembered the green blood. Was there some place in The Cache they hid?

Axol came flying by and swished in front of Candland. His gills fluttered with a high pitched greeting. Candland caught him in his arms, lifted the creature to his face, and the axolotl gave his nose a warm nuzzle.

"Axol. At least someone missed me," Candland said. He patted his old friend gently on the head. He looked up and saw Ava, Rocky, and Obigon further up the steps.

Candland followed them all the way to the opening. Obigon turned and saw Candland taking the steps two at a time.

"Candland, please give us some time to welcome the visitor privately," Obigon said with a slight nod.

"Ava's my friend. I'm not going anywhere," Candland said.

"It would be better if you gave me space," Ava's eyes were lowered, but lifted to look him directly in the eyes when she spoke the last word. There was a defiance in her that shocked him.

Candland stopped. He took a step back, stunned by the words and the look. She knew he had abandoned her. That he had left her to die. Of course she wouldn't want him near her.

"Ava, I need to explain—"

"Can it wait?" she asked. But it wasn't really a question. Her tone was sharp. Candland had never heard her sound like that before. She had never cut him off before. He took another step back. He had never let her die before either, he reasoned. Axol floated around him in several circles as if to keep him from falling. He watched them walk into the temple, disappearing into the black stone. Axol lingered a while longer. It was strange for him not to be hovering over Ava's shoulder as if they were attached by an imaginary string. Candland nodded, and Axol zoomed ahead to catch up to his Marked. As Ava got further and further away, Candland felt himself shrink, feeling less and less.

"It's time you get back to your quarters," Draya said. *Where had she come from?* Candland wondered. And always at the most inconvenient times. Candland had followed her prompts up until this point to try and be a humble guest. He wasn't in the mood this time.

"No, Draya. It's time for me to take a walk. Alone," Candland turned and walked down the steps. Proru stared at Draya for a few moments as if to emphasize Candland's tone and then followed his Marked down the steps and through the forest.

How did Ava know Rocky and Obigon? How did she know who he was? How did she come to be here? Would she forgive him? Even if he wanted her forgiveness more than anything, did he have a right to even bring it up? And then, how was she even alive? These questions and more floated about him as he walked the edge of a stream, but the answers were far from his reach. He was numb. Numb from Ava hardly reacting to seeing him again. Numb from the image of her, walking next to a unicorn... There was something different about her. Her shoulders were rolled back, chin set and proud. It was like seeing a color transition from its pastel form to a bold, powerful royal pigment.

"Got rid of your babysitter?" Chinchin's voice startled him. Maybe it wasn't Draya. Maybe he just was easy to sneak up on. She was wading in the small stream, her loose orange pants rolled up to just below her knees. He noticed she was always wearing something colorful—even flashy. In contrast, her cropped pink shirt hugged her body, ending so that Candland could see the bottom of her ribcage press against her skin.

"For now," Candland responded, looking over his shoulder to see if Draya had caught up to him. The little stream reminded Candland of the water he and Keyes used to play in when they were little. He could almost hear Keyes' hardy laugh alongside the dancing water. He hadn't thought of Keyes in a while, and he started to feel guilty.

Chinchin looked at him and her face changed. "You look terrible."

"Thanks."

"What is it? You're... pale."

"Nothing."

Chinchin shrugged. "Any more earth shaking break-throughs?"

"Still just making the ground shake. Pror likes it. It's like a massage for him when he's lying down."

"Give it time... or just wait for that life-or-death moment. That seems to work too. Though I doubt it would work for you."

"Why do you say that?"

"People with suicidal tendencies aren't always moti-vated in the best of ways in life-or-death situations."

"I'm not suicidal."

"Your scars say otherwise," Chinchin nodded towards the scars on his arms.

"I'm not suicidal," Candland rubbed at the white scars that criss crossed on his forearms.

Chinchin shrugged again.

"Not anymore," Candland said. "I couldn't do that to Pror. This was a long time ago."

Chinchin reached into the water and pulled out a smooth pebble.

"Why are you here? What's your story?" Candland asked.

"Just another visitor passing through."

"Seems to be a lot of them these days."

"What do you mean?"

"My... friend... and a unicorn just walked into the temple."

"I'm more surprised about the unicorn, but you seem more surprised about your... friend."

"Well, I don't know what the unicorn's story is, but... I thought my friend was dead."

"That's what it was."

"Huh?"

"You looked like you had seen a ghost," Chinchin said, stepping out of the stream.

"Where are you going?"

"I'm going to go see what the unicorn is doing here. Want to come?"

"Obigon didn't want me around."

"Suit yourself. Should I ask about this not-dead friend of yours?"

"Just tell her I want to talk to her."

"She sounds special," Chinchin smiled wide.

"Just... tell her I'm waiting for her. Okay?" Candland's cheeks warmed as he looked away, clearly flustered.

"Okay! I'm leaving, I'm leaving," she said with her hands up. She could tell Candland didn't want to talk about it.

Candland sat on a good-sized boulder. He watched Chinchin leave and then turned back to see Pror splashing in the water with his paws and blowing bubbles into the water through his snout. He thought of the surprise of seeing Ava on the steps. Specifically the surprise that she was alive. Then he thought of his lesson that day. Her Mark glowed green. What did it represent? That's right, he remembered. Resilience.

Proru could sense Candland's restlessness. Standing by the stream, listening to the moving water wasn't enough to calm Candland's nerves after seeing Ava. And Proru knew it. He crept forward towards Candland and bowed his head, welcoming his Marked to climb up onto his back. Candland smiled as he took a handful of fur and hoisted himself up. As was typical with Proru now that Candland had been more accustomed to his temperament, Proru didn't hesitate to dart forward. The second prince of Questus welcomed the rush of air around his ears and the sound of breaking twigs and torn up dirt under his Nylo's paws.

Chinchin's conversation had stuck with Candland

while he was in Nevarra. If her assumptions were true about Nevarra not fully trusting Candland, then he had needed to take more of his education into his own hands. Without really knowing where to start, he took small steps. First, he started asking more questions. While before he had been content being an intent listener, he realized that it was up to him to fill in the gaps. If Noro was going over Nylos, it was up to Candland to ask about Moon Wolves if he really wanted to gain more information that was more applicable.

He had also found the Nevarrian library. While it wasn't as vast and impressive as the one at home—and many of the ancient texts were found scrolls in languages he couldn't understand—he still was able to glean a lot of bits and pieces of information that caught his interest. And a lot of his interest was in understanding his Nylo better. In one of the first lessons Candland had sat in, he had learned that all Nylo species were tied to an Eme—something their being and power and connection would return to time and time again. For Proru and all Moon Wolves, they were known as seekers. At first, Candland had thought that simply meant Proru was good at finding things—similar to how inert wolves were good at hunting and tracking. And while that was true, it was in his own studying through dozens of scrolls that Candland realized it was more than that. Seek was the Eme, but like the colors the Nylos showed with their magic, Emes could be interpreted many ways.

While those who were Marked by Moon Wolves were

more capable of finding objects or people they were looking for, there were other ways their Eme revealed itself. For example, Moon Wolves were often known to be seekers of truth. If those who were connected with a Moon Wolf were seeking a truth, they were most likely to find it. And that could mean a truth that was a mystery to them, a truth that was hiding from them, or a truth they were wrestling with. At the end of one scroll, Candland had read a line that seemed to resurface in his mind: Whatever a seeker or its Marker looks for, they will find.

Somehow that seemed related to Ava. As if ever since he Matched with Proru, the Moon Wolf's Eme had known that Candland longed to see Ava again, and alive at that. It felt strange to think he had found her given that she had arrived in Nevarra on her own accord, but knowing his Eme... he couldn't help but think their paths crossed because of a pull from somewhere beyond coincidence.

Proru had gone up through the Nevarrian forest to higher ground. The wolf hunched ever so slightly to the left, and Candland leapt off of his Nylo, rolling to his knees. He hadn't perfected the landing yet, but they were both definitely making improvements. One being Proru didn't look for a body of water to throw Candland in. And two, Candland mainly landed on his feet and not his bottom.

Candland stood up and looked out over the forest. Proru had found a good look out spot where the trees had thinned out. However, looking down into the heart of

Nevarra, it was still nearly impossible to know there was an entire people inhabiting the space. And only because Candland knew where to look, did he see where the temple was located—its raw Obsidian V looking more like the edge of a natural rock formation than any man-made structure. Ava was in there somewhere. Talking to Obigon. Talking to Rocky. Candland let out an abrupt huff. Proru turned to his Marked. And Candland just shook his head. How could he explain any of it to Proru?

Somehow though, Proru seemed to understand. He seemed to accept and absorb the anger and regret Candland was feeling. The wolf knew Ava was special to him. It was as if he could feel everything Candland was feeling. And Candland seemed to be feeling everything. He turned to Proru, and realized Proru was waiting. Proru had known all along that Candland was bottling up emotions that couldn't be bottled up.

"What, right now?" Candland asked his Nylo. "Just... Just do it?"

Proru looked at him, a blue flash in his eyes.

Candland looked out over the forest. He widened his stance and after a deep inhale, he surprised himself by shouting out into one of the enchanted forests of The Cache. He felt the threads of his heart escape through his throat. His temples seemed to be trembling on his own. His eyes had closed from the expenditure. He felt the ground shake. He opened his eyes. A small crack appeared in the ground between his legs. The earth below him had shifted slightly. Candland staggered back, losing his balance for a moment as the ground returned to its stillness.

"Woah," Candland said. This was more than just a tremble. He looked down at the crack in the earth. It was wide enough for him to fit both of his hands in. It was the first time his powers had actually left something permanent in the ground. Proru, with no manner to wait, then howled into the sky, his blue beam coursing through his siren-like call of the Moon Wolf. Candland brought his hand up to shadow his green eyes from the light. It was then that Candland knew that Proru felt his pain. Felt his regret. Felt everything.

It was also then that Candland looked at the beam of light his wolf made knowing truly it wasn't just a blue, but an indigo. A light of empathy. A light that could find anything. *Seeker.* And even without finding a scroll with all of the answers, Candland knew in time, he would uncover the mysteries of Proru. Like the wolf did with him, Candland would feel everything he felt. And in that moment, just like Proru could seemingly split the sky with his light, Candland felt he could channel that energy to one day split the earth.

CHAPTER 14

THE SECOND CHANCE

CHINCHIN

Chinchin walked towards the temple to learn about the unicorn after seeing Candland so flustered. She had heard of the first heir of Questus. He was often included in the news from the East and sounded very... princely. He was described as handsome, generous, adventurous, charming... She knew Keyes had a brother, but she had actually forgotten because he was mentioned so seldomly. He was no threat to Pagra—no warrior, as some second sons were known to be and took up a commanding position within a crown's defenses. She had known next to nothing about him, except that there was nothing to know. And now that she had met Candland, she had found the second prince of Questus unexpectedly refreshing. She found his brooding and dark humor to be a puzzle she wanted to solve. Maybe that was the scientist in her.

She reached the temple and lightened her steps in an effort to not bring any attention to herself. She walked through the entrance on the balls of her feet, and made her way through the temple with memorized twists and turns to the main hall where she heard voices bouncing softly off the stone.

"That's where the axolotl comes in," Chinchin heard a woman's voice.

"I would like to check in with Ava and make sure she is alright," a calming voice chimed in.

"She's fine," the woman's voice answered curtly.

Chinchin walked into the room. She saw the unicorn first, nearly glowing white among the black stone with his long flowing hair and robes. Then she saw a young woman with dark brown hair, warm, angular eyes, and a lean on one leg that came from impatience. Her stance reminded Chinchin of someone...

"Chinchin," the brunette said immediately. She rushed towards Chinchin.

"...Have we met?" Chinchin asked, not expecting such a warm greeting.

"We have. I was just in another body," she said, taking Chinchin's hands and squeezing them. Chinchin pulled them back. She was vaguely aware of a white and green axolotl floating near the unicorn.

"Who are you?"

"It's me. Maya," she took Chinchin's hands again. They went limp.

"...What are you talking about...?" Chinchin looked past the stranger, to Obigon, Rocky, and the unicorn.

"Rocky transferred my memory into this body before he was captured."

"But how—"

"That's why he doesn't remember a single thing. He wiped his brain clean before he was captured. He knew they would put him through the Source Wall as soon as he was caught," she said. "His memory is in my head too. I just have to give it back."

"How do I know it's really you?" Chinchin asked, her guard still up—protecting the months of mourning she had started. She couldn't go through it again.

Maya smiled with her chin tilted slightly down so that her doe eyes looked even more mischievous. She brought her fingers up to Chinchin's face and traced her jawline delicately.

"That night. We snuck out of the lab. We went to the Old City. It was the first time we kissed. That's when you talked about running away. You were wearing orange— like burning embers. It was the first time I'd ever seen you wear a dress. I should have listened to you that day..."

Chinchin's lips trembled, and a tear slid down her cheek as she choked in disbelief.

"What's this?" Maya's finger wiped the tear with her thumb. "No tears, my little scientist."

"Maya..." Chinchin said her name and her lips were met with Ava's. All of the grieving fell away. Maya's hands were again on her—just in another form. She had done right with Rocky, and here, somehow, she had been given a second chance. Maybe she had done just enough to deserve... hope.

"I have so much I have to say," Chinchin pulled away for a moment—regretting it as soon as she felt Maya's lips leave hers.

"Okay, getting Rocky's memories out of this head is the first step. I can't think straight. I'm literally going insane. After we've prepped him and he can extract himself, then we'll talk. *Really* talk."

Chinchin nodded. Maya could say anything and Chinchin would be nodding, receiving, accepting. This was Maya. *Maya.*

<hr>

While Maya—in a stranger's body—continued to work with her father in getting Rocky out of her head, Chinchin gave them the privacy they wanted and went back to her quarters to bathe. She had no curiosity for the unicorn. Maya was alive. What did a unicorn matter?

Before Maya's death, she had kept up with herself. Before going into the lab where she would work with her secret lover, she would wash. She brushed her hair, she added color to her face, jewels to her neck, and chose the colors underneath her black uniform carefully. She kept herself clean. And when she did so, she knew she was able to catch the attention of anyone. She only cared about Maya's attention, but the double takes leading up to her interactions with her test subject didn't hurt either.

After Maya's death, Chinchin hadn't been so attentive to her appearance or cleanliness. Her hair was often pulled back to set the tangles behind her face. Her skin was often stained—not her lips or cheeks with rosy hues—but of smudges of dirt. Her clothes were filthy, albeit colorful.

Not today. Today she bathed. Sitting in the tub of water, she scrubbed the dirt away from her arms and legs until she was a few shades lighter. She dug the tips of her fingers into the roots of her caramel hair, and twisted the long locks between her fingers. She washed in places she hadn't made time for or thought of in months like between her toes, behind her ears, and her ashy elbows.

When she stepped out of the bath, she splashed herself with water soaked with fresh-picked flowers that had gone untouched since she was at Nevarra. She dressed in new clothes delivered by Draya, a long, wispy dress that would drape her body in whites, pastel and peachy pinks. When she slipped it on, the fabric hugged her chest, her waist, and hips, but flowed freely around her arms and legs.

She sat and stared into the small mirror as she combed her hair. How long had it been since she actually sat to comb her hair? Since she could actually run her fingers through her locks without them getting snagged? How long had it been since she hummed while she brushed? She left her hair down and then applied color from the earth to her eyelids, cheeks, and lips. She licked her lips thinking of the kiss.

It was strange to be embraced by a stranger, but also strange to be embraced at all. The body that hosted Maya couldn't have been more different from her lover's. The straight hair was so orderly and plain when Maya's curls had been so wild. The eyes were wide, large, and round, so wide open, and innocent. Maya's were always constantly shifting, searching, planning. Mysterious. The high cheek bones were overwhelmed by the roundness of the stranger's face—the softness of the chin, the nose, the eyebrows. The shapes and shades were... submissive to the rest of the features. Maya's face was made of sleek, direct lines, and sharp corners. Dominance.

Chinchin licked her lips.

The new lips were light, thin, as if they gave into smiling on a whim. Maya's were thick, plump, heavy—it took a lot to turn her lips from anything but a neutral pout. The new body was smaller, compact. Wide, strong shoulders. Short strong legs. They moved cautiously. But Maya's had been long and loud. Her steps meant something when she wanted you to hear them. Her hand reaching out for a pen or knife meant something important. Always. Everything about Maya's movement was intentional.

Chinchin wanted to take longer to prepare for their next meeting, but she could wait no longer. There was a strange, irrational fear. What if she lost Maya again? What if Rocky accidentally took Maya's memories with his own? What if there were some temporary rules to his power she didn't know about? What if the body she now inhabited was due for a heart attack and collapsed to the ground along with what was left of Maya? No. She had seen the Mark on the cheek. The green floral print. She was Marked, and it was the axolotl she was Matched to. A healing Nylo. Maya was protected. Chinchin took a deep breath in, and let her irrational anxieties fall away... for now.

Chinchin hurried out the door and down the spiral steps that outlined a giant tree trunk. When she reached the ground, she saw Candland. He looked at her and froze.

"You look... different," he said. She had looked completely different from their last encounter by the stream. He was petting Proru, his hand reaching up to get behind the wolf's ear. Hours ago, Chinchin had wondered about the prince. How curious was it that the first heir had gone missing and this younger brother came upon a Marker as powerful as Proru? How curious was it that Nevarra was trying to block him from realizing his powers?

It had been curious. Very curious. And the scientist in Chinchin wanted to know more. The scientist wanted the answers to her questions. But there was one thing Chinchin was more than even a scientist, and that was Maya's other half. And Maya's other half did not care to find any of this curious. Maya's other half only cared that Maya was alive—that they had more time together. That she could say sorry for letting the experiment get so far out of her control...

"I have to go."

"Did you tell her that I wanted to talk to her?" Candland asked.

"Tell who?" Chinchin asked, already walking away towards the temple.

"Ava. Did you tell her I need to talk to her? That I'm here?"

"...No. I didn't get the chance."

"Please. If you see her. Tell her I need to talk to her."

Chinchin nodded without any intention of following through, and walked away. She had already forgotten Candland's request again and was feeling the way her stomach was moving in and out the closer she came to the temple. Closer to Maya.

Chinchin and Maya had walked hand in hand through the trees until they came upon a small hilltop—one of the edges of the city overlooking a lake on the other side. Rocky's memory transfer had been very slow going. They had hardly made any progress when he demanded a break from exhaustion. If Maya hadn't had Chinchin to go to, she might have denied him that break.

Maya hadn't had the time to clean up like Chinchin had, but she started to look more like Maya every second. The way she walked, the way she looked at things, it was how Maya walked and looked at things. She wore tight black pants that stretched with her stride and a dark green tank top that covered the top of her shoulders but left her arms exposed. She looked good.

They looked out over the land and finally Chinchin attempted to explain herself, to apologize, to express her love.

"When I came to Pagra, I wanted to see if I could make it so that everyone could Match with a Marker so that everyone could have a chance to feel powerful."

"I know," Maya smiled.

"It was naive. Pagra Labs was letting me run with my idea so they could take it when I made it real. I think they're more desperate for Obsidian V than they let on. It was mentioned a few times. The scarcity of it. They knew Nevarra had some."

"I heard about that issue too. It was definitely something they were trying to keep quiet... running out of the thing they had put so much time and effort into... The one thing that makes them powerful. Don't worry. They won't find us. Now, what else do you have to tell me so badly?"

"In Pagra, you wanted to push the boundaries with the experiment, and instead of thinking about the why's or the why not's—like a true scientist—I just wanted to impress you. I knew you were a spy—"

"You did?"

"Once you had Matched with your third Nylo."

"Ogis."

"I thought you were just ambitious like me. But you kept asking for more Matches. I could barely keep up…"

"You still gave me everything I asked for even though you knew?"

"I love you, Maya. Of course I gave you everything you asked for. I wanted you to know you could trust me. I wanted a way to tell you I was on your side without giving you away."

"We lost so much time dancing around, pretending in front of the Labs."

"I knew you were a spy, but it wasn't until the day you died that I learned you were a Nylo Guardian. I kept wondering what you had really thought of me. The situation was this Bloody loop. I would have never gone so far as to Match more than one Nylo had it not been for a sexy test subject that wanted to see if the impossible could be done. And the only reason this sexy test subject wanted to see if it could be done was to learn how to keep it from being done ever again. We created evil by trying to prevent it."

"I wish I could have told you who I was earlier," Maya said.

"Instead, we pretended to be people we weren't. And along the way… You died because of me, Maya. I'm so sorry."

"Don't blame yourself. I pushed you. My death had nothing to do with you."

"And now Pagra Labs… they have enough information to recreate the mutation. And they know how to deal with the side effects now with the axolotls. They'll be able to make humans who won't kill themselves or die. Marked, with multiple powers and sources. They'll be unstoppable."

"But now we're together again," Maya said. "And this time, we don't have to hide ourselves. You're the best Marker scientist in The Cache. I'm the best NG in Nevarra. We have all of Pagra's secrets. We can stop them together. Stronger than ever."

"Two girls?" Chinchin asked.

"Two *women*," Maya smiled. "And maybe we can convince that prince to help us. Maybe we can get Questus behind us."

"I don't think he has Questus behind him. He can barely motivate himself right now."

"We'll motivate him."

"He's an outcast to his family. I bet you, beyond looking like they're searching for him, the kingdom is doing nothing to get him back."

"Outcast or not. He may be the sole heir with Prince Keyes missing," Maya said. "And he's here, with us."

"If Keyes comes back, it won't matter."

"*If* Keyes comes back," Maya emphasized.

"Don't tell me you have him."

"I wish I did. No. I have no idea where he is, but if we get to him first..."

"Candland's an outcast, not a villain. He's not going to be okay with his brother being murdered."

"He doesn't have to know."

"Maya…"

"I'm just exploring our options. Chinchin, Prince Keyes could already be dead. You don't have to look so concerned."

"I'm not, but I just—"

"Do you like the prince?"

"Don't ask stupid questions."

"Oh, my love," Maya put her hand on Chinchin's head and ran her fingers through Chinchin's floral scented strands. "Don't you worry. Oh, and I have a unicorn too."

"I had almost forgotten. What's a unicorn doing here?"

"They're very attached to this body," Maya shook her head. "Technically they can't do anything about it, but we need to keep an eye on them. A unicorn is much better as an ally than not. Their wealth of ever growing knowledge is something we could use."

"What happened to the person in this body before?" Chinchin asked.

"The poor girl. Rocky found someone that was hardly there in the first place."

"Is she still in your head like Rocky?"

"Yes, but her memories are put away thanks to Rocky. Thank god, her mind is so impaired. Some accident when she was little. She's hardly present, just static. Once Rocky is able to get his memory back, I'm going to have her removed too. It's so hard to think straight, and with a lame mind she couldn't do much with the body anyway.

This way we are putting it to good use. Wouldn't you agree?" Maya leaned in.

Chinchin saw the green glow of the Mark on Maya's cheek. She suddenly remembered Candland's request... but the memories she was most interested in were standing right in front of her.

"Are you ready to kick Pagra's ass?" Maya asked. It was as if they had traveled in time. They were together again. Maya was coming up with her big ideas, and Chinchin was the brains, laying down the groundwork of how to put these ideas into a plan. What she loved most was that they were both always part of executing the plan. They could dream, they could talk, but they could act on it all. Nothing that came out of Maya's lips was something she wouldn't do herself.

"What's the plan?"

"We need to get Rocky back. I can't handle his memory-less mind any longer. I need him back. But I knew we needed to talk. I needed to see you again," Maya placed her hand on the nape of Chinchin's neck and brought her closer. Chinchin felt the heat rise from her chest to her neck. Her breath quickened. Even in a different body, all it took was a touch from Maya. Still, it was a different body, and Chinchin wasn't getting over that any time soon. She pulled back with a smile.

"I miss the curls," Chinchin admitted.

"We'll figure it out," Maya smiled. "Just give it some time."

CHAPTER 15

BATTLE OF THE WILLS

AVA

The thing about having Maya in Ava's head was that when Maya was in the driver's seat, Ava was sitting in the background—much closer to all of her own memories that she couldn't previously recall and without the distraction of living in the now. After the kicking, screaming, and fighting for control that she inevitably lost to Rocky's lock he had put on her within herself, she found memories she had long forgotten about. Memories that were so blocked or over-powered by the trauma of when she first learned she was an Atrox that, had Maya not fought to keep her in the background under Rocky's mental lock, she might not have found them.

While Maya was trying to talk some sense into Rocky, when she was analyzing how to get the unicorn on her side, or holding Chinchin in her arms, Ava was gardening with her mother.

The desert, a desolate place to most, was a paradise to Ava's mother. She grew such things no one thought would grow in a desert. And anything that would grow in a desert, thrived under her care. Ava watched herself and her mother. She watched her past self with her small toddler hands that could barely scoop up a proper handful of dirt. When her mother would pat down on the earth around a new young plant, little Ava would follow with a few light and caring pats herself.

"Every plant wants to grow," her mother said. "They just need a little help."

"Are you their mother too?" Ava had asked.

"In a way," her mother smiled. "And as long as your love is true, every plant gives you something in return."

"Like what?" Ava asked again.

"Flowers, fruit, shade, a place to nap, protection, shelter... So many things, my love."

"What if your love isn't true?" Ava asked. She was at the age where her most prized skill was asking an unending amount of questions.

"The plants will know, and they will not grow. And they will die, along with all of their gifts."

"And then we die?"

"If we're lucky," she smiled mischievously. "Now. What is this seed?"

"It's an Ora bush seed."

"Yes. Tell me more about the Ora bush."

"They grow white flowers that slow bleeding. The fruits can be eaten to relieve pain. The thorns, if cut by one, cause temporary paralysis."

"Anything else?"

"...They're home to Azza bees. Their honey can speed up healing or give you an energy boost."

"That's right."

"But Sky says after the boost, you crash hard."

"He's right. That's why you shouldn't rely on them for energy every day like Sky does."

"I'll let him know," little Ava said.

"Yes, please do," her mother smiled.

This time, the older Ava smiled too. She knew Sky was her father now, an Atrox, her mother had fallen in love with. She had forgotten, but now she remembered. She wanted to tell her mother right then, *I know who he is. Who I am. What I am. It's okay. Don't worry, mama.* But her mother was just a memory.

Ava flowed through these memories without order, the way scenes might take place in a dream. The details, however, were so much clearer. Without the distractions of living in the present, the essence of her own memories were so easy to grasp. The feelings, the smells, the melodies, they were all crystal clear. And, hardly aware of herself and her own existence, Ava had no desire to be anywhere else than with her mother once again. After all of those fleeting and scattered memories she had dreamed about, she had thought she lost these precious moments forever.

It wasn't until she heard Gannick's voice that she was yanked into the present moment and present state of things. She hadn't thought about what was beyond her memories until hearing his voice, and unable to get to him, Ava felt trapped. Her world of memories wasn't a hiding place anymore, it was a prison.

"Ava's my friend. I'm not going anywhere," his voice echoed around the blackness that surrounded her. Ava stood up, looking for his voice. Was this a memory that was coming through to find her or was Gannick somewhere out there where Maya was controlling her body?

"Gannick?" she said quietly. Could he hear her? She felt like a whisper herself, like a faded, static memory that would completely disappear in time. For a moment she wondered if this was what Kavi felt like. A witness, with all their actions contained. It was draining. Diminishing even.

"Gannick, I'm here," Ava said quietly. Did she even believe what she was saying? What was *here*? Ava closed her eyes, standing in the middle of nothing. She took several deep breaths as she accepted the reality of her next actions: to search for Gannick in the present, she had to stop searching for her mother first.

She turned and saw her mother working in the garden, calling her over to try the sweet Ag fruit. She was smiling with her perfect crooked teeth and sunburnt skin. *I'll be right back*, Ava said. The pain, the loss, the death. It all came back as she watched her younger self run towards her mother. Her current self did not follow. She remembered everything now—even the memories of her father's death.

She needed to speak to Gannick. She needed to get out. She couldn't stay here, a ghost of her own memories.

"What the hell are you doing?" Maya's voice came through the darkness. Ava looked, and though Maya was not whole, parts of her came through. Ava saw some fuzzy curls bounce around Maya's shoulders. She saw Maya's thick lips pressed together tightly. Her dark skin came and went as Maya stood with her hands on her hips, a mental phantom.

"Maya?" Ava said.

"Why are you trying so hard to come back? Don't you want to play with your mother here?"

"...I heard Gannick. Is he here?"

"You're getting your memories all mixed up. You're going crazy."

"No, I don't think so. His voice was so clear."

"You're really losing it. Look, just a little longer. Then Rocky's going to move my memories to another body. A better body. And you'll have your body back. Who knows if you'll be able to see your mother as clearly as you can right now. You don't have much time left here. Do you want to waste it?"

"No. I don't want to lose her again."

"Then stop getting mixed up in your memories with Gannick."

"I just thought he was here."

"Why do you even care about him so much? He left you to die," Ava winced. It had been unsettling knowing someone else could sift through all of her memories, and this didn't help.

"If he would have tried to fight that crowd, he would have died too. And *he* wouldn't have come back to life."

"You know why I think you like him so much? I think it's because no one else showed you half as much attention as he did. You're latched onto him because you have no one else that's even close to liking you. It's any wonder how you Matched with an axolotl—"

"Axolotl," Ava said. She looked away, straining her thoughts. Her cheek began to glow green. "Axol!" She remembered him. How had she forgotten? Why was he missing in all of the memories she had been dwelling in? He should have been there with her and her mother.

"Shit. Looks like she just undid Rocky's lock," Maya said under her breath. She looked at Ava, her tone remaining casual. "Look. He's fine, but you need to stay here. Your memories with your mom will be lost if—"

"AXOL!" Ava yelled.

Ava flung up from her bed and sat up. There was no fogginess around her. There was no mother. No garden.

No earth to pat down and truly love. She was in the here and now. She looked at her hands, they were her own. Not as dark and cool as Maya's midnight skin, but tan with warm, desert undertones. She was herself. Ava looked around, and there was no one. No Axol. No Kavi.

Ava stood up. Her legs were stronger, firmer, and more elastic. Her bare feet felt the ground in a way that not only allowed for walking but for seeing. Her body was her own, but different. How long had she been lost in her memories? How long had she been in the garden with her mother?

She walked to the corner of the dark room where she found an opening through a beaded curtain—just as she suspected. She was able to pull from Maya's memories. That's how she knew where the opening was. That's also how she knew Axol was in the guest quarters with Kavi where they stayed since Ava had been lost in her most precious memories. Ava paused at the exit. She turned and walked to the wooden table where a large pouch of coins sat. Moving slowly and trying to be as quiet as possible, she slid the pouch off of the table. Then she turned and walked down the hall without having to hesitate before making a turn in the darkness.

There was no door to Kavi's room, only wooden beads that made plenty of noise for anyone who might want to discreetly track the coming and goings of a guest. Ava pushed aside the beads. She saw Kavi, sitting with their legs crossed on their small bed. Axol was lying next to Kavi. He raised his head when he saw her, but did not dart towards her. It was strange not to be greeted with an excess amount of energy from him. Ava thought of everything he must have been going through with Maya in her place. She rushed to the bed and scooped him up in her arms.

"Axol. You're okay! I'm so sorry."

He looked first at Kavi with wide eyes. Then he closed his eyes and purred warmly as he rubbed his head deeper into her chest. Ava took a deep breath in. She could still smell her mother's garden, but the scent was being overcome by little Axol's own smell. A combination of fresh river water and wild grass. She had missed his constant fluttering, his sparkling mist, the way his head tilted side-to-side.

"Ava," Kavi stood so quickly and quietly, it looked as if they floated to their feet.

"It's me," Ava said. "It's *me*-me."

"The fact that you are even acknowledging Axol already gave it away. I am glad that you have returned to us. Are you well?"

"I think so. I have Maya in my head, and she doesn't like me leading. I don't know how long I will manage to be... out here."

"That must be strange. I would like to hear more about it."

"Well, first, is Gannick here? I heard him inside my head... I need to talk to him. And then we have to leave."

"Who is Gannick?"

Ava paused. Maya's memories were mixing with her

own. She heard the name Candland echo in her mind. She felt her heart quicken and then sink. The boy she had liked was a prince? "I mean... Candland? Is Candland here?"

"He is in his quarters now. It is very late or very early rather."

"Then we'll wake him up. I have to leave."

"I am glad you plan on leaving. They would not let me study you as closely as I would like."

"It kind of sounds like you missed me. But we seriously need to get out of here. If we stay much longer, there won't be anything left of me to study. Now let's go," Ava turned, pulling apart the beads as she walked.

"You know where Candland sleeps?" Kavi asked.

"Maya does," Ava said, still churning Gannick's true identity in her heart.

Ava only had to travel down three long hallways to reach Candland's room. She pulled the curtain of beads back and let herself in.

"Who is it?" Candland asked in unison with Pror's growl.

Ava stopped, seeing most of the room was filled with a Moon Wolf. That was new.

"It's me. Ava," She said, her voice shaking at the size of the beast.

"Ava! Come in. Did you get my messages?"

Ava didn't come any closer as she eyed the wolf. "No. None of them. Gannick—I mean... who are—"

"I can understand why you wouldn't want to see me

—," Candland was now out from under the blankets and standing up to begin his apology while still half asleep. Ava noted that his chest was bare first, and that it was Marked second. He had changed. His body was firmer, stronger... Her skin tingled, and she licked her lips. She was glad it was dark, because she could feel the warmth in her cheeks turning her skin scarlet. Gannick was a prince. Her own identity was at risk of being lost to Maya the longer she stayed in Nevarra. And all she could think of was how warm the prince's skin might feel had this been a different moment—a moment where he welcomed her touch.

"Of course I want to see you," she said.

"You do?"

"I've been trying to find you ever since I heard your voice. But your chest. You're Marked? And... Your name isn't...Gannick?"

"I'll get to that... but Ava, how are you even alive?"

"I guess I'll get to that too. Candland, we don't have much time. I need you to listen to what I have to say. And I have to say it now."

"Okay. I can do that," Candland nodded.

"Maya is in my head."

"What?"

"I met Rocky in Pagra. He gave me his sister, Maya's, memory—all of it—and put it in my head. She took over, and I got stuck somewhere in my mind—deep in my own memories. I couldn't get out. When I arrived here, it wasn't me. It was Maya."

"That doesn't sound like Rocky… but also makes so much sense. Wait. Did he give you his memories too?"

"Yes. But he was able to transfer his memories back to him. Now it's just me and Maya in my head. He didn't take them back. But we have to get out of here. They want Maya to keep my body, and get rid of me."

"Get rid of you?"

"Erase all of my memories. Well, all of the memories that make up me."

"Rocky can do a lot of questionable things, I'll give him that. But he'd never do that. Besides, he's not even himself right now."

"I told you. He has his memories again now. He's himself. That's what they're going to do."

"You don't know that," Candland said.

"Maya and I share a head. I have all of her memories. That's her plan, and her father and Rocky are on board."

"From what I have observed," Kavi stated, "Ava's suspicions are not unfounded. It would only make sense that Obigon and Rocky would do anything to bring back their family—especially considering Maya was the best of the Nylo Guardians. Another supporting factor would be Ava's Mark. Chinchin confirmed that axolotls could possibly be the key to the synthetic mutation she created. It would be logical for Maya to want to keep Ava's body if she intends to try the mutation again," Kavi spoke matter-of-factly with that benevolent smile Ava was just now realizing she had missed.

Candland looked at Ava and then back at Kavi.

"You can stay here if you want, but I can't. I can't risk getting... erased," Ava said.

Candland stared at the ground for a moment.

"Fine. I-I don't blame you for wanting to stay," Ava said. She turned to leave, her heart sinking.

"I don't think Rocky would do that, but... I can't let you go on your own. I owe you that much," Candland said.

Ava's trembling stopped. Her bluff had worked. She would have never been able to have gotten far knowing Candland was in Nevarra. She couldn't leave him. Not only did she have some big unanswered questions, she felt a pull towards him. She felt something that made her wonder if it was even possible that Candland didn't feel it too. She wanted to yell at him. She wanted to ask why he lied about who he was. She wanted to ask him how he was Marked. She wanted to ask him if he had ever thought of her since the last night at the parade. But there wasn't time. All of her questions and the emotion behind it all had to wait.

"Follow me," she said.

Candland and Ava swept through the beaded curtains from where she came, Kavi, Axol, and Proru following after her. She glanced back to see Candland's face illuminated by Axol's white shimmer. His hair was long and shaggy. The green in his eye was more electric than usual with the color coming off of Axol's body. Candland moved steadily in a way that she was not accustomed to. Nevarra looked good on him. She felt a sudden twinge of guilt for taking him from this place. She froze for a moment, second guessing everything. Then Ava felt Candland's hand around her arm. His hand squeezed her just beneath her elbow. It wasn't done in a romantic way, but still it brought back familiar feelings. It was, Ava decided, hopeful. She continued pushing forward in the dark, her Nylo, a unicorn, a prince, and a Moon Wolf following behind her.

Once they reached the outside of Nevarra's center and the trees began to grow sparse, Ava finally raised her voice from a whisper. While the sun rose, she had explained they would head to the House of Haessig where the best healers lived—and where Gears had once practiced medicine. The journey was suggested by Kavi. The Asting network that Kavi was always connected to, thanks to their unicorn horn (though only present in unicorn form) had intel on a lot of healing work done there, cross referenced with memory control. If anyone could do it, it would have to be the healers of Haessig.

The first stop on their way north would be in Du, neutral ground between Nevarra, Pagra, and Questus while they got their bearings. With a long way ahead of them, Ava could hardly contain her thoughts. Where would she start? It was time to catch up with the prince.

"Gann—I mean, Candland. Why did you tell me your name was Gannick?" she asked. She had meant to sound more casual, but her voice was soft. Delicate, almost. She thought Candland might not have heard, but his green eyes tracked hers. Not unlike old times, he had been waiting for her to break the silence.

"I didn't want anyone to know I was a prince," Candland said. "In the Tunnels, I liked not being a prince. And I didn't think I'd really meet anyone that I'd see over and over again. I didn't think we'd become friends like we did."

Ava nodded. She had known the reason. Of course he would hide his identity to not draw attention. She just wanted to hear it from him.

"You're not... mad?" Candland asked.

"No. I mean, you were hiding who you were when I was hiding what I am," she said. "If anything... I actually owe you more of an explanation. And I don't think it can wait."

Suddenly the questions inside of her stilled. She realized it was time for her to share more. Kavi deserved to know more of her history, and Candland deserved to know more of her. Talking to both of them felt natural.

"I wasn't born in the Tunnels. I was born in Soonja... I had forgotten that. I couldn't remember anything before the Tunnels. But I found all of my memories after Maya had taken over my body. Memories I had perhaps buried.

"My mother was sweet, open, generous. She spent most of her days in the desert gardens, and even grew some things that shouldn't have been able to grow in that climate. She could grow anything. Except for a baby,

I guess. It took her a long time to have me. Finally, I came. My—er—well, we'll call him my father for now. He was the Woh, the leader of the tribe. He was all about two things: protecting Soonja and constantly scouting and tracking the desert. You know how Soonja is. You were giving me the backstory earlier when we passed through, Kavi."

"Had I known you were born there, I would not have," Kavi said.

"That's okay. It was a nice reintroduction. I hadn't been back since… Well, I'll get to that. When I was born, my father knew I might be the only child he would ever have. So I was trained from the second I came out of the womb. Like all Soonja children, I learned survival first. We learned all of the secrets of the desert. How to live in it. How to defend ourselves in it. How to kill people with it. Mainly though, the first few years of my life were about not dying. There were only small windows of time that I got to spend in the garden with my mother—I still remember those times better than any of my training.

"My father as the Woh had the most land in the village. So he had the most servants. My father didn't care for the land literally and figuratively, but my mother did. So she managed most of our staff at home.

"There was one servant in particular. He was always kind to me. Funny. Made everyone around him laugh. He was the main servant for the gardens so my mother and he naturally spent a lot of time together. His name was Sky. Or at least that's the only name I ever heard him called. He was the one who brought Axol to me on my sixth birthday. I couldn't believe it was a Marker. Soonja isn't under Questus law, but we're heavily influenced by it. It was an unspoken law that we followed the rules of the Blood... even if we believed in something else.

"But that was how Sky was. He did what he wanted. My mother wasn't happy about it, but Axol and I Matched instantly. There was nothing she could do. I was Marked from then on, right on the cheek. We hid it when I went out with scarves at first, but eventually my father found out. He never said a word, he only looked disapprovingly at my face and the 'little white ghost' that floated alongside me. It brought shame to our people because Questus would not approve. But he never did or said anything. That was it. Just disappointment from afar.

"Now, I never realized it until now, but my training in combat was lighter. No one dared attack the daughter of the Woh with the intention to draw blood. My father wanted me to build confidence, and my mother especially didn't want me getting hurt. She was extremely adamant about pushing it off for as long as possible. Now... I understand why she was so careful with me. I was so annoyed then. I thought she didn't think I had what it took, but now I know she just didn't want me to bleed."

"...Go on," Kavi encouraged Ava when she lost herself to the gentle buzzing of the meadow.

"I turned 9 and my father decided it was time to

really push me in the combat training because I was clearly falling behind. I was never really good at it. At 9 years old, there was no other child who could keep up with me out in the desert, but I wasn't great with hand to hand combat or weapons because I was never allowed to fight seriously, but that changed. Every year in Soonja there is a tournament. Every child needs to stay out in the desert, alone, for a week."

"I have heard of this ritual. Did you succeed?" Kavi asked.

"I had returned after a month—everyone but Sky had thought I was dead. Many parents said I wasn't technically alone because of Axol, but if I'm being honest, the desert is not his natural home. He felt more like a liability and another mouth to feed. But his company, and of course power, allowed me to stay out for so long.

"After that, my father said it was time for true combat. I started training with real weapons, and even sparring with blunt weapons that were still fit to kill if they made a direct hit. I remember my mother and how afraid she was for me. She begged my father to wait.

"One day, I was put up against a 15-year-old boy named Lon. The best in the village. Many were still apprehensive when it came to trying to actually hurt the daughter of the Woh, but this boy hated me as much as I hated him. We were thirsty for a duel, weapons or not. I was in over my head, but I didn't know it. Within two minutes he had knocked me down and without hesitation, drew the spear down on me. He demonstrated what little self control he had, and the arrow of the spear dug into my shoulder just deep enough for the spear to stand up on its own for a few seconds before he stepped away, leaving the weapon in my body before it fell to the ground. He must have remembered my father, the Woh, was watching—along with the entire village.

"It might be hard to believe that I had not bled until 9 years old. If you had seen my mother and how careful she was with me, you would. I had had minor cuts and scrapes, but nothing like this where the blood flowed freely from my body. And the Woh was never around me much otherwise to notice what color I bled through those minor injuries. I remember the Woh stood up and my mother stepped forward towards me. Her face... I wish I could shake the look she had on it. The look of one who accepted a fate they didn't have enough time to get away from.

"My father ordered everyone to leave. My opponent left with his parents. The murmurs were so loud, and I wondered what had happened. My father was clearly not happy, my mother distraught. Had he believed I would never lose a battle? I thought this is what it must be to truly let him down. I didn't realize that the reaction was because I was an Atrox. I didn't know what an Atrox was. That he would hate me from that moment on. He turned and grabbed my mother. She screamed... I've never heard anything like it. And he dragged her into our home and there was no doubt in my mind that his intent was inimical.

"It was like I saw something go the wrong way and I knew it was going to end badly. It wasn't too late to do something, but it didn't feel possible to do something. It didn't even occur to me to move. So I just watched from the ground and hoped the bad feelings were just feelings.

"Finally, I sat up. Sometimes I wonder if I should have followed them in. Could I have stopped him? But I couldn't move. The entire situation seemed unreal. Like I was in a dream and my mind and body were not connected in a way that was needed for even the most basic movement. I'd like to think that there wasn't enough time, that before I could react, I was swept up by strong bronze arms. But, still, I think there was a second where I could have followed my mother."

Ava wiped a tear from her cheek. She looked at Candland. He nodded silent encouragement to continue.

"Sky had me in his arms. My limbs hung numbly, not like a desert child, not like a Soonja warrior, just a child. We rode one of the horses reserved for emergency runs to Questus—our fastest. He said things that didn't make sense for someone who was always joking, always funny, always so relaxed. He only spoke about serious things, and he was not good at it. He told me it was okay. He told me I needed to hide. He told me I needed to stay with Axol, and that he would come for me when it was safe. We rode further on, and he gave me more vague instructions that were more like weak motivational phrases speckled with declarations of my feelings: You're okay. You're very special. You're just fine.

"In the back of my mind, my survival brain had taken in what it needed. Survive until Sky comes and finds you. And had what was about to happen next not happened, it would have been the perfect plan.

"In the last few minutes of Sky's life, his words changed. He gave me directions to the Tunnels. The directions were in the form of a story. How a horse fell through the quicksand near a stack of boulders and found an underground oasis where it could hide from all of the bad.

"That's when I told him, horses were coming. He wasn't trained like me to listen for them. He was just a servant. 'How many?' he asked. There were only three. The desert spoke to me just as the sun was setting. My father, his brother—my uncle—and Lonna—the mother of Lon and the first battle leader after my father.

"The sun had met the sand, and we were overtaken. Sky stopped. He got off his horse to face the three Soonja warriors. He was not a warrior. He was only part of the garden staff," Ava stopped. The tears had reached her lips and she licked them. She looked at Kavi and Candland and smiled. They all knew how this ended. She had never told the story to anyone, and she realized she had never been able to recall the memory with the acceptance of who Sky really was... until now. She had buried it all deep down where if she had only looked at it plainly, she would know why he swept her up into her arms that day.

"My once-father, the Woh, said something. Betrayal. Dirt. Earther. Sky only asked about my mother. 'Was

Minnia okay?' My father responded with a sword straight through Sky's throat. It was a quick death, but he twisted his sword out so that Sky's face took the shape of a torn mask when he dropped to the ground. As terrible a sight as it was, it was the sounds that were beyond terrible... The flesh and bone, the twisting of the Woh's hand, and the last sounds that came from Sky: tense, broken... formless. The opposite of what he was to me. The way a real father should never sound.

"What surprised me was that Sky bled green just like me. An Atrox, just like me. Then my father came to me. I hadn't spoken since I had been pierced to the ground by Lon. I hadn't called out for my mother. I hadn't shouted threats at my father. I hadn't questioned Sky. I had been silent. I looked up at my... who I thought was father then. I could not speak. He took a dagger from his belt. He picked me up by my neck and lifted me to his eyes. I lifted my hands to defend myself from his weapon.

"I had no will to live, but my training to not die had kicked in. I wrapped my fingers around the blade he held at my chest, pushing it away from my body. I couldn't tell if I had surprised him with my strength or he had a change of heart, but the dagger did not advance forward. I was sweating clear liquid. But I bled, a thick green liquid flowing from my hands as the edges of his blade cut through my skin. My father's eyes had been on mine, with my own eyes focused on the blade and his soul—two places that might be key for my survival. But when his eyes caught sight of the color of what I was, his strength returned. He dropped me.

He smashed my head in with the blunt of his sword—perhaps looking into his soul wasn't an entirely bad idea. I lost consciousness and was unable to leave my eyes open for him to see his reflection in them. And I don't recall this, but he stabbed my 9 year old body multiple times. I know this because of the cuts in my clothing and the stains I woke up to.

"The Soonja Woh and his closest council rode away thinking they had removed the dirt of The Cache from existence, two leftover Earthers. But he didn't know—and neither did my mother and true father or I know at the time—I could not die... Even if I wanted to... because of Axol's unique protection. I had never bled like that until that day."

"That is why you wear the bastard braid," Kavi said.

"I'm a bastard—an Atrox bastard no less."

"You lived alone in the Tunnels all of this time?" Kavi asked.

"I was too afraid to leave. I had tried many times. Candland, I tried to go with you a few times."

"I remember. You went into a panic every time," Candland said gently.

"I couldn't remember why I was supposed to hide in the Tunnels. I had blocked all of it out. But now I remember... And now... I'm not afraid."

"That's how you survived the mob that day in the parade... Was it hard sharing that story with us?" Candland asked.

"I needed to say it out loud. And I needed to tell you

both. Candland, you found out what I am in a way I'm not proud of. I want you to know who I am, and on my own terms."

Candland paused and looked back at Proru. The large wolf stepped forward and bowed his head down. Ava watched carefully as Candland scratched behind Proru's ear and then extended his hand towards her, his eyes a gentle invitation. Without hesitation, her hand found his. He helped guide her up Proru, showing her where to step on his shoulder to swing her other leg around. And then without even having to use his arms, he kicked off of Proru's shoulder and jumped onto his back, just behind Ava. Both of his arms came around her to hold onto Proru's fur in front of her. And before Ava could pretend to be unphased by his arms basically wrapped around her, her body reacted instead. As if she had imagined it a thousand times in her head, she found her leaning into him, her Marked cheek pressing into his bicep. She couldn't believe how warm he was. Axol settled onto Proru just in front of Ava.

"Can you keep up?" Candland asked Kavi.

"Yes, I can," they responded. Kavi closed their eyes. Where the coral star on their forehead was, a horn grew. Their nose elongated. Their chest became broader, longer. Before their eyes, Kavi transformed to their most primal state. Some would argue their true form, wings and all.

"Bloods. That's neat," Candland said quietly. Ava smiled at his young, rugged surprise. He was always curious. Always impressed. In a way, it reminded Ava of how young they were. They were still discovering themselves. Still in awe at the magic of The Cache.

Proru didn't wait a second longer. He jolted forward so suddenly, had Candland not been behind her for her to brace against his chest, she would have flipped backwards off of the Nylo. Candland was holding on tight. Ava guessed he was used to this kind of take off that launched them forward towards Du. Though she was reluctant to, Ava was able to finally lean forward a bit to regain her balance. She realized she had closed her eyes from Proru's launch, and slowly coaxed her way into opening them.

The rush of Proru's speed was unlike anything she had experienced before. The sparse trees from the lingering Nevarra border were blurred pastels of woody browns and bushy greens. The smell of dewy leaves and wet mulch on the ground flew into her nostrils. The scent of the forest was intoxicating. And the whip of the wind roaring past her face, a cold sting on her cheeks. Her body, which had gone stiff since Proru had charged forward, became aware of its rigidness on the wild ride. And she suddenly thought, *I'm riding a wolf. I'm riding on a Moon Wolf with Prince Candland.* And she shouted into the forest. It was a deep noise that came from within her chest. A carefree volume she rarely used. She heard Candland laugh behind her. So close behind her. Then he shouted as well. Loud. Untamed. And Proru followed with a short but powerful howl into the air, complete with a blue beam that shot up into the sky for a few moments.

Ava squeezed tighter, looking down at Axol who was tucked tightly in her lap. It might have been the only instance where he looked like he thought he was moving a little too fast. Ava giggled.

———

After a long stretch of sprinting with Kavi not far behind, the trees had completely cleared. Proru had stopped by a small stream. Candland had leapt off with a confidence Ava was still getting used to. Proru then bowed, and Ava felt Candland's sculpting hands on her torso as they supported her dismount from the Moon Wolf. Proru then proceeded to step deeper into the water and dunk his head into the water. Axol joined the wolf, splashing in the running water.

"That was..." Ava said. It was the first time in a while she felt speechless.

"Ava. There's something I have to say too," Candland started.

"Oh. Alright then."

"I know what you are now. I know your past. And I don't care if you're an Atrox. What I do care about is that I haven't said sorry, and that has all I have been since I last saw you. The day of the parade. In the Tunnels. I saw that you were an Atrox, and I panicked. I'm sorry for how I reacted. If I could go back, I wouldn't have let you go. I would have stayed with you. I would have held onto you."

"Then I'm glad you can't go back. You would have died," Ava said. She was not looking at him though she would have loved to meet his eyes, but she knew her heart might give way to too much emotion that way. "I'm a rare breed. I understand why you reacted the way that you did."

"It doesn't mean it was right."

"My mother used to say, the first reaction comes from the garden you grew up in. It's the second reaction that reveals what kind of plant you really are."

"I'm still sorry. And I lied to you too. I lied about who I was."

"You told me you were Gannick. I didn't tell you I was an Atrox, born from ancestors from Earth. We're here. Safe. Together. That's all I care about."

"You still care about me even after all of it?" Candland asked, exasperated.

Ava turned to face Candland. She took a step towards him. "Maybe even more. You're here with me... after all of it. That's what's important."

"But I'm... I'm a part of the Blood. The kingdom... and what it does to the Marked..."

"You're Marked. And you've only been kind to me."

"You're... too kind," Candland said, his gaze dropping.

"Hey," Ava said, her fingers nudged his chin so he looked back into her brown eyes. "You are important to me. I think we both understand our actions... our words... our why's. We're here now. We just need to get Maya out of my head. And then... and then we can..."

"What do we do?"

"Let's just take it one day at a time," Ava sighed. She didn't have an answer either.

"You're right. Before I saw you in Nevarra again. I thought... I thought I had lost you," His voice cracked. His eyes closed.

"I'm right here," Ava reassured him. She placed her hands on his chest. She felt his heartbeat firing against his shirt, into her palms.

"I can't lose you," Candland whispered.

"I'm here," she again reassured him.

She lifted her hands to his face. She closed her eyes and brought his forehead to hers so they touched. She could hear his breath. Feel his warmth. Smell the musk of wilderness from his skin. She felt a sparkle in her chest. There was a tingle that started at the pit of her stomach, rising into her chest, up to her throat. There was that undeniable energy again. The pull. Did he feel it too? There was one way to find out.

Eyes still closed, she lifted her lips to his. The touch sent shivers down her spine as she tentatively kissed him. She wanted more, but needed to know if he felt the same and so she moved slowly. A small panic shot to her head, wondering if she was alone in her feelings. Had she just messed everything up? Was this not what he wanted too?

His idle arms found hers just before the doubt could settle. She felt one hand on the edge of her face. His thumb grazed against her Marked cheek. His other hand was at the low of her back with more force, pulling her closer gently against him.

That was all she needed. She reached up with confidence and dug her fingers into his long shaggy hair. He wanted more too. She could feel the impatience with every touch. What had started as a careful inquiry had now transformed into an impossible-to-satiate desire.

Reason. Fear. Worry. It was all gone. There was just the urgent feeling of arriving home. Being held. Belonging. Ava let her weight fall forward into his hold, completely surrendering any caution she had been clinging onto.

More... More... More!

"Eh hem," Kavi cleared their throat. Ava pulled back to see Kavi standing less than two feet away from them.

"Kavi!" Ava jumped. She stepped back, alarmed by the false sense of privacy she had fallen victim to.

"I do not mean to interrupt, but I have pressing news from the Asting's network that I feel Prince Candland will want to be aware of."

"What is it, Kavi?" Ava asked, her fingers touching her lips that were now stinging for more contact. She looked up to see Candland looking awkwardly away as he ran a hand through his shaggy, sandy brown hair.

"Prince Keyes has returned to Questus. And he's made an announcement. He's looking for you, Prince Candland."

CHAPTER 16

THE RETURN

CANDLAND & AVA

Candland felt the parts of him deep inside roll outwards. His cheeks burned, and his eyes felt like they were getting bigger with each heartbeat, pulsing even. He turned to Ava. Her large eyes didn't need to search his for very long before she spoke.

"You want to go to your brother," she said quietly.

Candland nodded in a daze.

"Ava, both you and Candland as Marked are not welcome there. You could be arrested and put in the Cages the moment they see your Marking—which is on your face, might I add," Kavi stated.

"I'm aware. Thank you, Kavi," Ava gave him a small smile. "Candland, what's the plan?"

He wasn't a leader. He wasn't even a planner. Candland only had tugging emotions that occasionally cut through the numbness he roamed within himself. As someone who sometimes felt nothing, a tug was all he needed to see an emotion through. His brother had returned. His brother was looking for him. He was relieved that his brother was alive. Happy that he returned. But he also harbored something close to guilt that was souring his emotions. He was ashamed he had left when Keyes might have hoped he would be there waiting for him.

"Do you know why he was looking for me?" Candland asked the unicorn.

"Of course he's looking for you. He's your brother," Ava said. Sometimes her feelings towards him could be slightly coddling. Candland only nodded in return. He was no planner, but Ava was now looking to him for a change from their somewhat vague plan.

"I need to see my brother." Candland thought about saying he wanted to see his brother—which was also true—but needing to see him was more true. He wanted an explanation. He wanted answers. He wanted to know what had happened.

"We'll get you there. We'll wait for you on the border," Ava said after some thought. She was already planning for his return after the reunion with his brother. But what if he didn't return? What if being Marked was okay, and he wanted to stay? Or worse, what if they held him there against his will?

"You can come with me. They won't hurt you in Questus if I'm there with you."

"Are you sure, Candland?" Ava said. He could read her

doubt all over her face. It wasn't one feature that gave herself away, it was everything. He only needed to see her lips or an eye or hear her voice to know how she was feeling.

"They won't be happy, but you'll be safe. Especially with Keyes back. I'm sure tensions will have gone down with him home," Candland said. He swung on top of Proru, and stretched his hand out to Ava. She took a few steps forward, clearly unsure about the plan. But Candland felt it. When he held out his hand, it was like she felt him reach through the airwaves. He was reaching out for her. He could almost feel her need to answer him.

She placed her hand in his, and he pulled her up. She landed in front of him, and he wrapped his arms around her. Axol landed softly on the wolf's behind, relieved to rest while they journeyed. Kavi transformed into their four-legged other self. They were stunning, to say the least. Candland would never get used to it. The magical horse bowed slightly, their wings stretching out and flapping twice in what looked to be a warm up.

"How—," Ava started, but Kavi leapt in the air, taking a few galloping steps as he flapped his feathery wings higher and higher.

"Rude," Candland said, a smirk coming through his awe-struck face.

"Very," Ava nodded. "Okay. Let's go see your brother."

Proru darted forward, and Candland wrapped his arms tighter around Ava.

Candland had not realized what he had missed about Ava until they were together again, talking at a normal volume now that they were on their way to Questus. Even after she had filled him in on all she had been up to when Proru slowed to a reasonable pace, she continued to talk about everything. Candland never had to fill an empty silence, and yet everything that Ava talked about was something she cared deeply about. When she pointed out a cloud, it was because she was in such deep awe of the voluminous shape. When she pointed out a flying insect, it was because she was fascinated by its wing speed. Candland imagined she would still talk out loud even if she were the only one left in The Cache. She was that impressed with the world around her.

When they eventually reached the countryside along the border of Questus, Ava pulled a scarf that had been circling her neck over her head so that it covered her hair and then, wrapping it around her head horizontally, covered everything below her eyes. The green glow of her Mark was still somewhat visible, but she wrapped the material around her face again and again until the glow had all but dampened. She couldn't hide her darker complexion or the way her eyelids folded over differently from Questonians, but being seen as a foreigner was much less of a nuisance than being seen as a Marked in Candland's birthplace. Axol found a hiding place under her robe, popping his head out and leaving floating sparkles around Ava's chest as he looked about from the opening of her top. She looked down at her not-so-camoflouged Nylo and up at Candland with questioning eyes, and he only nodded to assure her he was not riding her into danger.

When they reached the heart of the kingdom, Candland and Ava had slid off of Proru and walked beside him. People paused. Even when Proru wasn't glowing… it was obvious he was a Nylo. Candland was sure the majority of people would tell themselves it wasn't actually a Nylo. They wanted to believe it was just a wild beast. But those who didn't believe what they wanted to, would kindly report the animal to the Council as a loyal civilian. Candland decided it was best to get to his home fast.

Now that he was home, Candland's excitement of his brother's return was fading. He began to remember more of his recent past. He had freed those who were captive… from his mother. It must have cost his mother a fortune with the people and Nylos she could have sold to Makani. It was only a short second that he worried that he had brought shame to the family, but he knew his mother better than that. The truth would have never reached the city walls. In such a disaster, it was easy to blame the wicked for the wrongs her own family had committed. She would blame the Marked on the escape to cover up what he had done. That he knew. But what he didn't know was if she would be happy to see him.

The people in the streets began to follow them slowly. Proru's size alone was too much, and Candland quickened his steps to the inside of the castle, his home. But it didn't matter. Guards of the Blood approached them on their way to see his brother, and after a quick and unsettling exchange, they escorted the prince and his unlikely visitors. When they reached his home, Candland took the hood off of his head. He wasn't as recognizable as Keyes, but the guards still knew his face. They did not relax, but yielded when Candland assured them all was well.

They made it into the main hall. Everything was rather quiet. Some might even call it peaceful. The palace was made up of many levels, a balcony on every two levels all the way to the top. Each balcony was decorated with satin curtains that could be drawn when desired. It was familiar to Candland, and though he was still nervous, he was reassured by the sound his shoes made on the ground. The polished echo he had known since he could walk. He was home. Perhaps he had been wrong to think it didn't exist for him when his skin was tattooed with a magic contract.

Candland found a servant before the servant could make himself unfound.

"Tell my mother and brother I'm here. We will wait out here on the balcony."

The servant nodded, staying only long enough to hear the request, and then scurried away from the prince and his friends. He was clearly afraid he would become Proru's next meal. Candland cut through one of the satin curtains and walked out into the open air. His friends followed him.

"Candland... are you sure..." Ava started. Her voice slightly muffled through the layers covering her face. She wore a loose one-piece with pant legs. A belt with Nevarrian-style tassels at the ends tied everything together. The headdress, however, made her head look as if her head had become a small, layered pillow. Axol was still hiding in the folds of her many layers. He wanted to come out, but Ava rocked him gently to see if he could afford just a little more patience. The two would have been more inconspicuous if Axol's glitter didn't leave a trail as she moved.

"It's my family," he said. It came out harsher than he had intended. Ava only nodded in reply—a rare response from her. Kavi stood quietly. The Asting was taking everything in just as they were taught to. They looked out over the city, recognizing the kingdom's popular landmarks. They curled their hand into a fist and knocked on the banister of solid stone. Not Obsidian V, but stone from Questus' own mountains to the south.

"My son," his mother's voice cut through the curtain seconds before she did.

"Mother," he smiled.

Her smile disappeared as swiftly as she had walked in. Her eyes were locked onto the wolf. She stepped back, clearly startled.

"What is that?" she asked.

"It's a Moon Wolf. His name is Proru."

"His name? It's... It's..."

"It's a Nylo," Candland said and then sealed his lips as if he were protecting his tongue from the backlash to come.

His mother's mouth opened. Her eyes left Proru and fell onto Candland where they stayed.

"He's my Marker."

His mother still said nothing.

"Candland!" Keyes exclaimed as he joined everyone on the balcony. He looked at Proru as if he acknowledged a servant, and then his gaze returned to his brother. He sped past his mother and embraced Candland in a way Candland was sure he had never been held by his brother before. After the embrace, Keyes stared at the unlikely group of visitors.

"I am Prince Keyes," he said to Ava and Kavi.

"Ava," Ava said with a small, unpracticed bow.

"Kavi of the Asting," Kavi said. They made a deep bow. "I am honored to meet you, Prince Keyes."

"A unicorn. I think you may be one in a dozen that I have ever seen in my life. Wonderful. Wonderful!"

"Keyes," Candland finally said. "I'm sorry I wasn't here when you returned. What happened? Are you alright?"

"Apology not accepted," Keyes said seriously. Then he laughed heartily, the sound echoing from the balcony. "Now, I want to fill you in on everything. Everything! But let's save it for tonight. I'm sure you and your guests are tired. The Blood knows I was when I came home. Let's let you all bathe first. You're just absolutely filthy! Then we can have a proper dinner tonight. Then tomorrow, Candland, I'd like to take you to the Blood Chambers. There are important and... private things I need to share with you that I cannot do over dinner with your friends. Excuse the secrecy," Keyes said with a nod to Ava and Kavi. Ava lifted her hands quickly to show she meant, *Oh, we understand.*

"That sounds good," Candland said. "We're exhausted."

"Let's revive you. Revero. Please, lead Ava and Kavi to our guest quarters and see to it that their every need is met. Start a bath for them. Do you need clothes?"

"Yes, actually," Ava said, slightly ashamed that the first impression of her would be one of her in need, but she agreed with Keyes. With the exception of maybe Kavi, they were filthy. And she hadn't thought to pack properly when they snuck out of Nevarra.

"I do not," Kavi responded.

"Very well. It will be so. Candland, you haven't forgotten where your bedroom is, have you?" Keyes chuckled. "I'll see you all for dinner once you have had time to settle."

There were very few things Ava could imagine better than a hot bath after traveling, and with very little supplies. Had she not been eager for food, she would have sat in the porcelain tub for a few more hours. Instead, she worked quickly, washing her hair with lavender scented soap, and scrubbing her body until her elbows were red. Of course, she left time for Axol to submerge himself and blow enough bubbles for him to feel satisfied.

When she stepped out of the bathing chamber, she saw clothes had been set on the bed. A red dress. She preferred pants when she was on enemy territory and also when she was on edge... It was much easier to kick in breeches than a skirt if Keyes changed his mind and decided her guest quarters should be in the Cages. But on the other hand, she had never owned anything so nice. And then, Candland hadn't seen her in anything so fancy. She felt a flutter as she recalled the sensation of Candland's fingers in her hair, answering her question on whether or not he had feelings for her too. She fingered the silky material of the dress. This trip was dangerous and too risky in her opinion, but imagining Candland seeing her in something other than runaway robes almost made it all worth it.

Looking in the mirror after managing to put most of the dress on before she would need to call for help, she realized it had been a long time since she had studied her reflection. Her thick brown hair now grew down her back to her elbows. She remembered the feeling of her hair being yanked back when she was in Pagra when they had been ambushed by the Shadow Scouts. Quickly shaking her head to lose the memory, she refocused her gaze.

She felt stronger in a strange way. Strange, though

good. Red was such a bold color—something she'd never choose on her own. But she liked the way it looked regardless. Perhaps *looking* bold was enough. That was a feeling she was too embarrassed to share. The neckline was high, with the top lace tickling her chin. The short sleeves ran longer than average, just above her elbows. And the skirt was made of two layers. The first layer was solid red, the color of Questus. The second layer was the same color, but of fine lace in rose pattern and long. Actually too long. It dragged on the ground. It was a traditional modest cut for Questus, which was the norm in fashion for the women. The red clashed a bit with the green and white of Axol, Ava noted with a frown as he fluttered to her shoulder.

You're kidding yourself if you think you can pull that color off. A voice cut through the silence. Ava looked around. There was no one else in the room. It was then that she realized the voice hadn't been out loud. She had heard Maya in her head.

I'm ignoring you, Ava responded in her head.

Well, maybe you shouldn't, because coming here of all places was an idiotic idea. You're putting both our lives at risk.

Candland needed to see his brother.

You should have had him come alone.

Ava closed her eyes. Her fingers rubbed her temples. She knew Maya was right, but she couldn't leave Candland's side. They were together. Together together too. And outside of the Tunnels. Under the sun. He had invited her to his home. She looked good in Red. Maybe his mom would even... like her.

You stupid, naive girl.

Not listening...

If we die here, it's because of you.

There was a knock on the door. Three women slowly came through the door, all dressed in red. Seeing Ava was nearly dressed, they sped up. Surrounding her, they started to fasten her dress by pulling the lace that gathered around her spine. Somehow they managed to hem the dress at the same time. The length had been dragging a few inches on the floor, and when they were done, the dress simply brushed the marble as Ava walked. It made Ava appear more graceful when she moved. Ava took a few steps closer in front of the mirror.

While her skin was definitely tanner, her brown eyes were lighter. Her long hair had naturally been highlighted by the sun as well with some golden hues. Her tan had become more bold. But it was the shape and feeling of her face and body that she really saw. Without testing her body, she knew she had a wider range of motion. She felt flexible and strong. Maybe even an inch taller from the way Maya had sculpted her body.

Ava disappeared in the mirror, and Maya's face appeared in the reflection. Ava froze. She saw Maya's golden eyes just before they began to glow red. Her black curls. Her thick lips. That smirk.

Admit it. I suit this body better than you do. I deserve it more than you do.

"Are you alright?" one of the ladies in waiting asked.

"Y-yes. Yes. I'm ready for dinner," Ava said, hoping eating would give her enough strength to keep Maya at bay. She also needed to find Kavi and let them know she was starting to lose control of Maya... or that Maya was simply ready to take the reins.

One of the women guided Ava through a large corridor. Ava studied the golden crown moldings at the edge of the high ceilings. Everything in Questus was big and grand. The rich colors gold, white, red, and even black made their way through the interior. And Ava couldn't walk more than ten steps without seeing another rose, thorns, or emblem of the crown weaved into the floors, walls, or even the sconces. It was the one place, Ava noted, that fire was used more than gels.

The woman guiding Ava through the palace finally stopped at a large, but intimate dining room with a long table. Everyone was already sitting down. Keyes sat at the head of the table, with Candland on his left and his mother, the queen, on his right. Kavi sat to Candland's right. Candland smiled at her arrival. She couldn't tell if he was impressed by her appearance, and suddenly she began to doubt the dress she was dawning. The plate setting for Ava was next to Candland's mother. Ava's pulse quickened. Knowing Candland's mother was just a human, and yes a queen, Ava would have preferred sitting next to a Vhyka.

The dinner was quiet, except for Keyes. He was animated and talkative—asking questions and hardly waiting before answering them himself. *How was your journey?—I'm sure long and exhausting. What's the wolf's name? Proru? Did you name it that? No? Oh. What about the Asting? Tell me all about it...* The guests were hungry and didn't mind not having to pause from their food to interject.

Ava studied Keyes' face at the table. At first she hadn't seen it because the brothers' colors were so different. Keyes' hair was golden above his bright blue eyes. The contrast of his moon-white skin, light hair and bright eyes from Candland's features was striking. He had a light freckling over his nose and cheeks that, Ava thought, made him look more approachable. But it was just such a stark difference from Candland's olive undertones, green eyes, and brown hair.

However, the outlines of the brothers were nearly identical. Had Keyes had the same palette of skin, hair, and eyes, Ava might have thought them to be identical.

She was taken by Candland. Though it was clear there had been a comb to his head, his longer hair still managed to fall into his emerald eyes. He wore a red shirt, thick enough to be a jacket that crossed over and was buttoned closed. The final black button at the base of his throat was the family emblem. It was strange to see him in such formal attire. The material looked stiff, and Candland pulled at his collar every few minutes to scratch an unreachable itch on his neck.

His skin had not burnt under the sun, but took on a deeper tan that was hard to come by for Questonians with their typical blonde hair, blue eyes, and fair skin. It wasn't that Ava was unfamiliar with his features, but they stood out so much more when Candland sat in his own home. She also noted that riding Proru must have forced him into shape, as hugging the beast with his thighs and hanging on with his arms wasn't an easy task. And lately they had been riding more than ever.

There always seemed to be a darkness to him though, Ava knew. Somewhere where his hair wildly framed those emerald eyes, there was something there that Ava always wanted to know more about. A shadow maybe. Was it pain? Was it something else? She never knew. Regardless, she saw him pull at the collar of his neck again, and realized perhaps it was the fact that in becoming stronger, his clothes had fit just a tad bit too tight. Ava thought life outside the castle suited him better as she blushed and remembered that she was sitting beside the mother of the boy she was gawking at.

Proru wanted to hunt, but Candland was too nervous to let him out of his sight. At Candland's request, Proru was fed from the livestock and seemed rather unimpressed with his food readily prepared for him. Proru took small pieces of his dinner every so often, sitting just behind Candland. His mother wasn't happy about the arrangement, and he noticed her unwavering gaze whenever Proru's teeth snapped together over a piece of meat. Axol stole bites from Ava's plate, and sometimes her fork. He may have been trying to be sneaky, but as soon as his teeth would sink into something, he'd forget his incognito intentions and chomp loudly which made Candland chuckle.

"I'm sure, Candland, you have some stories to tell. Some new scars to share. Oh, by the way, did he ever tell you how he got that scar on his hand?" Keyes looked at Ava, "Let me tell you. It's such a funny story."

Ava looked at Candland, he glanced at her, and then quickly back at Keyes.

"We had snuck out past curfew and snuck into the blacksmith's workshop. My idea. I was such a naughty little boy then, but I had wanted to make a sword. I was 14. Candland was 9. Trying to make a sword. Can you imagine? We did quite well for ourselves until a certain point.

"Candland was a grand assistant. He followed instructions as if his life depended on it. But then I saw him looking at the sword we were making—it was just a glob of burning red at the time. He had the strangest look in his eye, like he was possessed. He reached out to touch the molten metal! I couldn't let him burn. Mother would kill me. I moved fast, but too fast. The sword fumbled, and by reflex, I tried to catch it... with my own hands.

"My scream woke the blacksmith up, and we were returned back to our angry parents. Father was furious. And I had this to show for it."

Keyes held out his hand to reveal a scar very much like Candland's on the inside of his left palm.

"Like all older brothers. I took the fall and kept Candland out of it—but he wouldn't let himself stay out of it. The next night he showed me his raging purple scar. A mark he had stamped upon himself by roasting some old useless sword on display over the hearth. I looked at him and laughed. We never spoke of it again. But I can't help but think of that story now. How you, Candland, were so drawn to the fire. How you Marked yourself then and now you come up, Marked on your chest."

Keyes laughed. His mother followed with a short chuckle. Shortly after, a servant shuffled over to Keyes' side and whispered something. The next king of Questus excused himself apologetically from the dinner table when he was called away for other duties. Candland tried to hide his disappointment in time with his brother getting cut short. He couldn't get a good read on Keyes, but he was reluctant to see him leave. The queen followed shortly after, having said nothing the entire meal. Candland assumed she had gone to do more praying in the temple after her two sons' safe return.

Ava didn't eat very much, and stranger, she didn't say much either. Candland had dismissed the servants so that Ava felt more comfortable. He could tell she was more aware of her Mark than ever, and wanted to take that worry away. Candland had eaten his favorite dishes when Keyes had been going on about their childhood. It was when he took a bite of a roast chicken mixed with whipped starches and cream that he realized how much he had missed Questus. How far he had gone when he Marked with Proru after never having left the kingdom before. He had run away and survived. It was more than he had expected if he were being honest.

"What did you think about my brother?" Candland asked. It wasn't often he had to start the conversation, but it usually only took a question for Ava's mouth to gain momentum.

"He's... really different from you."

"Mmm."

"You two are complete opposites... It was nice though. How excited he was to see you."

"I actually didn't know if he would be or not. You know, with Pror. He's as devout as they come to the Blood. He didn't even hesitate."

"Maybe that's it."

"What's it?"

"Just something seemed... strange," Ava said.

"Strange?"

"Do you think your brother's okay with you being... one of us?"

"I wasn't expecting a dinner like this on the first night if I'm being honest."

"I'm just surprised, but I don't know your brother."

"I am too. But we don't know where he's been all of this time. Look how much I've changed since you last saw me. Maybe he did a lot of changing himself."

"Maybe."

"Do you like it here?"

"It's really beautiful. Just, you know, in any other circumstance, I'd be put in a cage."

"You're safe here. My mother and brother understand."

"...What are the Blood Chambers?"

"It's a sacred place. Only the royal family is allowed. It's where we store—," Candland stopped.

"Store what?"

"The sacred blood from the Blood Ceremonies." Candland looked down at his food.

"So that's where you keep the remains of the Marked your family murders."

It was a strong word. *Murders.* Candland clenched his teeth when Ava said the last two words. He had never murdered anyone. He wasn't even old enough to speak at a ceremony. What did she expect?

"It's a sacred sacrifice. The Blood protects the kingdom." He was on Ava's side, but suddenly he felt the need to defend his brother and mother.

"I know you were born and raised here. I know having Pror is still new to you... But you're one of us now, Candland." Ava stood up. She walked towards the exit.

"You're finished?" Candland asked.

"Not hungry anymore."

Kavi stood up and bowed before they followed Ava. Candland remained sitting. He looked down at his plate. A home cooked meal that he hadn't realized he had been craving all of the time he was away. If he didn't eat it, he felt he was wasting the meal that had been specially prepared for him. All of his favorites were still hot and inviting. If he did eat, he felt he was letting Ava down. And not just Ava, but Rocky, and Proru, and all of the prisoners he had freed just before he had left for his adventure to Nevarra.

Before he had time to make a decision, his mother walked back in. At first he thought it was Ava, but tensed when he saw his mother's outline. She walked slowly, with purpose. Her chin was high in the air, it was a posture of confidence she had tried to teach her two sons her whole life. She had only succeeded with one. Candland liked to keep his chin down; it was easier for Candland to avoid eye contact when his head was lowered. The queen sat.

"I thought you might not return," she said.

Candland couldn't tell if her quietness was coming from a gentle place or elsewhere.

"Two sons. Both missing," she went on.

"I'm sorry. I didn't know if you would want—"

"When you left, the kingdom began to talk about two missing sons. I was with no heir. I looked the fool. Now you return with that cursed beast. And you brought him *here*, cursing our family. And with that... girl... who is just as damned. A Mark on her Bloody face. I don't look the fool, Candland. I *am* the fool."

Candland now recognized the tone. How quickly he had forgotten...

"This wasn't planned—," Candland tried to start again.

"You were born so different from Keyes. I was so hard on you because of the shadow. First it was within you, but it showed on the outside too. Brown hair. Green eyes. Your olive skin, always a few shades darker than the rest of the children. A child who liked to hide in the dark. The Blood couldn't find you. I couldn't even find you in the darkness. Did I ever tell you that when you were born you had blonde hair? Blue eyes? Skin as white as Keyes?"

"Mother, what are you trying to say?"

She paused as if changing her mind. "When you ran away after Keyes, I prayed that you'd never come back."

The words were sharp and heavy and hit Candland like a weight against his Marked chest. His throat dried up and his lips parted. He was thirsty for something. An escape? A response that would feign her words had fallen short—that her prayers were of no interest to him?

"I always told you praying was a waste of time," Candland said, slamming his hands on the table much harder than intended. His emotions had spiked, and he felt the ground tremble. The silverware and porcelain plates made a brief noisy chatter as they shook. His mother's face paled. It offered a strange satisfaction for Candland to see her like that, almost afraid. Before he was just a strange little boy who couldn't fit in. Now, with Proru, there was something more. He was more. He used the same exit Ava and Kavi had used only a few moments earlier. He had also lost his appetite.

"Kavi, did you feel that just now?" Ava asked back at her guest quarters.

"I do. I believe it was a mild earthquake."

"Are they common in Questus?"

"Not in the slightest. But it may be from Candland, given his Mark."

"Maybe we were too hard on him."

"*I* did not speak at dinner," Kavi pointed out.

Ava glared at him. Then she sighed.

"I should go talk to him."

"Candland cannot control his powers yet, and has no grasp on the amount of power he channels from Proru. I suggest you let him calm down before approaching."

"I hate waiting," Ava said. Sitting on her bed in her own chambers, she tucked her knees into her chest feeling much too childish for the red dress she wore. Her eyes closed and her teeth clenched slightly before she opened them and her jaw relaxed.

"What is it?" Kavi asked, noticing the strain on her face.

"It's Maya. She wants... to be in control... now."

Candland hadn't gone back to his quarters, and though he didn't want to be near his mother anymore, he also wasn't ready to face Ava yet. So naturally he found himself in his studio in its lone wing with Proru tracing his steps. His sculptures—clay and stone—all inert animals—were there to greet him. If he ended up staying home longer, he hoped that Axol wouldn't be the only Nylo he sculpted.

"Maybe I'll sculpt you next," Candland said as he put his hand on Proru, a faint smile on his lips. Why did the idea seem almost impossible? Keyes had welcomed them with open arms. Keyes saw him, his brother, cursed with a Nylo, and didn't stop. Why? Candland wanted to believe this was how it could always be, but there was something in his gut warning him.

"Do you feel it too?" Candland asked Proru. "And even if I feel it. What do we do with that feeling? Borrow worry from tomorrow?"

"Doesn't sound very appealing," a voice cut in.

Candland looked up to see Westahn entering the studio, always that sparkle in his eye.

"Westahn!" Candland exclaimed.

"You left in quite a fury last time I saw you."

Candland remembered the premature ceremony he didn't complete. He was about to apologize, but then he stopped. He wasn't sorry.

"That's quite alright," Westahn smiled. "It seems you knew the path you were on already—and it didn't involve drinking the Blood."

"It didn't feel right."

"It's clear why," Westahn said and then looked at Proru. "Magnificent creature..."

"You mean... cursed creature, right?"

"Both can be true," Westahn nodded.

"Now I'm cursed too, apparently," Candland said.

"It does put you in a rough spot, doesn't it, Prince Candland?" Westahn didn't seem troubled.

"I would have thought so. Keyes doesn't even seem to acknowledge I'm now... cursed."

"Do you think you are?"

"I'm more concerned about what he thinks. Mother has made her feelings clear."

"Change isn't easy for anyone, but I'd wager it's hardest for Questus. We're a big kingdom. And perhaps with the exception of your Moon Wolf, big things commonly move quite slow around here."

"Why do you think Keyes hasn't condemned me already? The Blood's teachings are his life," Candland asked.

"I'm not quite sure. Sometimes it's the Blood's most loyal who are most faithful in its plan. Keyes trusts the Blood. He trusts what it allows to happen and not happen. Perhaps this is the case with you. He doesn't understand it, but he knows the Blood has allowed it."

"What do you think about it? Me, being Marked? Surely the councilman who oversees the Blood, blessings, and allotment... feels some kind of way about it," Candland asked.

"The Tunnels aren't supposed to be here in Questus, but they are here. You were certainly not supposed to have Matched with a Marker, but here you are. Just as the

Tunnels belong to Questus, so do you. There is a place for the Tunnels, and there is a place for you."

"What place is that?"

"I'm not sure, my Prince. But I hope I am lucky enough to see it for myself."

"I wish everyone felt that way."

"A valid wish."

Candland took a deep sigh.

"Do you still have that special clay I brought you the day of the Pre Ceremony?"

"The clay from The Cache's core? Of course."

"May I recommend you keep it close to your person?"

"I always have. It's a small pouch just here... Why?"

"It's not just for sculpting, Prince Candland."

"What else could it be for?"

"For when you're ready to seek a place for you."

Candland paused, looking at Westahn. *Seek.* Did he know the Moon Wolf was a Seeker? Was that a coincidence?

"I best get going. I hear they're making those sweet potato buns I like in the kitchen. They're best when they're hot."

"Westahn—"

"If you'll excuse me," Westahn interrupted. "I'm so glad you returned. Good day, wolf."

Westahn turned swiftly and made his way down the spiral steps. Candland pulled the pouch of clay from his waist, feeling the weight of it in his hand. He'd never examined the gift before. He felt the urge to pour the soft stuff into his hand, but decided he wasn't ready to seek that place yet. He returned the pouch back to his belt, and walked to the balcony of his studio—staring out in wonder. What did Westahn mean really?

***

The next evening, Candland was preparing for his meeting with Keyes. His older brother had been so busy since their arrival, Candland had hardly seen him that entire day. It made sense, given he was gone for so long. Candland guessed a lot of the time went into blessing Blood for the people to drink. The thought of drinking blood made him shudder. Still, he was excited to get some time with his brother—Keyes was obviously more excited than his mother about his return.

Proru was too large for the Blood Chambers. Candland pressed his forehead to the wolf's head before leaving. It wasn't a farewell. Though Candland was excited, he was also nervous, and wanted to smell his Moon Wolf. The scent reminded him of a cool running river in a forest. He could almost smell the leaves blowing through the trees. The beast that once terrified him was now his greatest comfort. Candland pulled his head back up.

Everything. All of the answers. They were only a few moments away. His mother had made her feelings about Candland's return clear. It had made even the most familiar things like his favorite dishes or his own bedroom feel like nothing when he thought it all might still have a chance at feeling like home. Keyes was now his only shot at that feeling now that he had Matched with Proru.

Candland stepped forward in front of the Blood Chamber's entrance, but the guards kept their eyes forward. Their eyes were steadily on the beast behind Candland. The second prince of Questus coughed politely, and the guards refocused on him. They pulled the heavy stone doors forward, the bottom of the rocky barrier grinding against the ground.

Candland was seven years old the last time he was in the Blood Chambers. His father had brought him down, wanting his son to "feel the protection and power" in the Blood that surrounded them. The royal family, the Blood Council, and, on a rare occasion, very, very limited guests were allowed into the Blood Chamber. It was one of the most sacred places in Questus. The stairs went deep into the earth, where it was cool and safe for the sacrificed blood to be stored. Once Candland reached the end of the steps, he found it to be harder to breathe from the pressure of the cave. Deep, wide holes were dug into the walls, fitting vase after large vase, each full to the brim with blood. The containers were each the size of his entire body when he was last there as a young boy, the color of cool rubies that slept in the shadows. He stared at them quietly, noting how the dust on the glass gave the bloody vases a frosted look.

This blood is ours, son, his father had said. The blood did not scare Candland. As a boy, he would have skipped in the cave if it were allowed and not seen as disrespect-ful. This was the first time his father had taken him anywhere alone—no mother, no brother—just father and second son, together. *By the power of the Blood, only we can touch the containers. Only we can open them. Only we can pour it. Only we can do what we will with it. Not even the Blood Council can obtain the blood and its powers. It's because of the royal blood—my blood— that courses in your veins, just like your brother. You, me, and Keyes. Without us, this kingdom would fall. We're the link between the power needed to protect this kingdom and those we deem worthy to wield it. This blood is ours. Mine and yours."*

Candland felt the coolness meet his cheeks under-ground. No sunlight, just like the Tunnels, but they couldn't have been more different. The gels inside the chambers were golden, making the blood in the containers look lively inside. The vases did not seem as giant as they had when he was little, yet they were still large enough to make him feel squeamish now. He looked at the liquid behind the dusty glass—the Blood's magic protecting every drop all of these years from all kinds of threats to the reserve: robbery, natural disaster, or betrayal.

"Brother," Keyes said softly. Candland turned to find his older brother sitting on a bench carved out of fine gray marble. Candland wondered how long he'd been sitting there. Keyes looked like an angel with the gel's golden light shining upon him in the holy cave. Keyes was looking down at the ground between his feet.

"Keyes," Candland said. His brother still did not look up.

"I'm so glad you came," Keyes spoke softly. He was not the same person Candland met yesterday. This version was somber, troubled, quiet—much more like himself. And Candland didn't like it.

"Of course I came. I wanted to learn where you've been. Why you left. Hear about your adventures."

"Then let me answer quickly. I went to the Alcalus. I hadn't planned on running away. I left with nothing, but I didn't need much. I only needed to discipline myself. To make sure I was worthy of this kingdom, but more importantly, to make sure I was worthy of the Blood."

"The Alcalus? Why did no one find you there?" Candland wondered. He should have been easily discovered in the Questus monastery in the southern mountains.

"Because the Blood didn't want me to be found then. The priests and priestesses respected their wishes."

"Why did you leave?" Candland pressed.

"Because of you."

"Me?"

"The Blood was testing me. That day of the Pre Ceremony, I held the petal in my hand and read your name on it. *Candland.* I had no voice. I couldn't read it out loud, knowing what would come next."

"How is that possible...? I wasn't Marked then. The sacrifice is always a Marked."

"Because the Blood knows all. And now you're Marked, damned like the rest of them. If I had called your name that day like the Blood wanted, you would have died with honor. Today, your death will be covered by a lie. And that is my fault, brother." Keyes quickly wiped a tear from his cheek. "I was too weak to do what the Blood was asking of me, and because of that weakness, you've had to suffer. Look at you. Marked by that monster. Cursed. I'm so sorry, Candland."

Keyes stood up, and he drew a sword. Candland stepped back—it was an involuntary reaction. His voluntary reaction would have been to run, but he could not call his legs to act. The knowledge that Keyes was 100 times the swordsman he was, was the reason he needed to flee. Keyes' eyes lifted to meet his brother's for the first time. There was a cool determination about them. Candland looked into his blue eyes, and knew Keyes had replayed this moment in his head many times before. It was the moment Keyes had returned to Questus for. It was why he wanted Candland to come back home.

"I wanted us to have a perfect dinner. One happy meal together before tonight."

"No. Don't do this. Keyes. We're brothers!" Candland said. He remembered the story of betrayal between brothers in Nevarra's version of how the world was created. It felt too close to his reality. "Let's talk. Let's sit down and talk. I've learned so much since I've been away. I want to share it all with you..."

"Share your disease with me? Your... Your curse? Candland. It's too late. The Blood has given me one chance to make this right." Keyes shifted his position quickly to block the only exit.

"How will you explain my death to Mother?"

Keyes stopped. "Explain? You're as stupid as you are damned. She's already getting the story of your death prepared. The girl you brought ambushed you. The Nylos turned on you. In refusing to succumb to their ways because you are *loyal* to the Blood, they killed you. It's time, Brother. Please know, I'm doing this for Questus, for the Blood, but most importantly, I'm doing this for you."

"What about you? Questus... The Blood... Me... What about you?" Candland said, shaking his head. "You'd kill your own brother?"

"A small sacrifice for the safety of Questus. You would understand if you were meant to be a leader like me. It takes more than you will ever know to be king. Now. Things will be easier if you kneel."

"Things? You mean killing your own brother? Wh-why here?"

"No witnesses," Keyes said quietly.

Candland's legs were finally free from the reality of his situation. He skidded along another wall made in the cave, hollowed out holding vase after vase of blood.

"You're going to run?" Keyes asked. "You're throwing away your chance at a sliver of honor that's still left for you to die with?"

Candland pressed his back against the wall. There was nothing in the chambers except glass too heavy to lift and magical blood he could somehow drink but had no idea how to use. The ground beneath him trembled somewhat—or was that just him? He had been able to do little more than make the ground shake, and all that would do is lead to an arguably more painful death than what Keyes was offering. At least his brother would die with him then... That idea didn't escape Candland.

Keyes reached out, grabbing Candland's arm, pushing him off the wall. He was an angel with murder in his eyes, square with Candland. With no weapon, Candland was defenseless. Keyes swiped once, Candland jumped back. Keyes thrust his sword forward, and Candland dodged the deathly jab by mere inches. Candland was able to strike Keyes in the face, surprising even himself. It was clear Keyes hadn't expected Candland to take a swing. The punch was more of an insult than anything, and brought on Keyes' anger. Combat was his one outlet outside of religion that he had grown faithful to over the years. Candland now wished he had spent more time sparring and less time arguing with his philosophy teacher about the worlds beyond The Cache and the portal The Gatekeeper guarded.

In a blur and both a piercing and dull sense of pain, Candland found himself on his knees, his face bloodied. The blood that flowed above his brow, flowed into his eyes, making it hard for him to see clearly. He wiped his forehead with his hand and felt the sting. He couldn't believe how much blood was curtaining his vision. How did he get on his knees? Would he not see his death coming? He looked up to see a flash of silver and raised his right hand in a sorry attempt to block what was coming. He felt the blow, the sting of freshly sliced flesh. It was like a clean fire swept through his arm. He fell onto his back and turned, shocked to see his right hand and part of his arm laying several feet from the rest of his body. His elbow was now sprawled on the floor. The blood glowed golden on the ground from the light, making his fluids look rich and magical—almost celebratory. A fitting end for a small, unimportant prince, Candland thought. Keyes would appreciate the lighting approved of his actions. Like their mother, Keyes always liked when things looked the part.

Candland looked up, though it was hard to focus on anything. Keyes was walking slowly around him. Was he savoring this moment where he proved his loyalty and faith to the Blood? Or was he hesitating? Did he feel something for Candland that slowed down his mission to repentance for not killing his brother sooner? Candland didn't wait to find out. He closed his eyes.

He would soon be dead. His brother Keyes was lost to the Blood. He had led Ava into his home where he promised her safety. He had let her down again. If he could just make the earth shake enough for the walls to come down, Keyes might get away still... but the Blood of the Marked wouldn't. And Candland was going to die anyway. He heard his father's voice again. *Only we can open them. Only we can pour it. Only we can do what we will with it.*

Focus. Focus. *Focus.* He thought of Chinchin's one-time coaching. He had to bring up emotions... Well, not this time. He was already emotional. His brother had betrayed him. Ava was in trouble. Proru... Proru. Candland felt his heart break. He couldn't think his anger. He could only feel it.

First there was a shaking. Then he felt the rocks beneath him begin to crack. Candland opened his eyes. He could see the indigo glow from his chest reflecting off of Keyes watchful eyes. Keyes stopped and looked up to see parts of the earth sift from the ceiling.

"What are you doing?" Keyes said. It was the first time Candland had heard Keyes' voice waiver, but Candland was weak and needed to concentrate. He closed his eyes again and tapped into the rage that had been hiding, perhaps, not so deep within. He needed to feel *everything.*

One of the dug-out shelves that housed a row of vases collapsed. The glass shattered, and the blood spilled. A wave of blood flowed out and splashed onto the floor. Keyes looked at the blood on the ground that the sand quickly absorbed. Years of strategically chosen sacrifices, gone in an instant.

"You're destroying everything our family built!" Keyes shouted. Candland held his upper arm, or what was left of it, but he felt whatever it was keeping him alive, that energy, was quickly dwindling. He pushed everything that was left of him out, breaking the vases. If he was a curse to the family, then he might as well do some damage. He opened his eyes just once to see more blood quickly seeping into the tightly packed earth below. Then he closed his eyes again and thought about who his brother really was. The world shook even more. Keyes widened his stance to stay upright, and then lifted the sword high into the air for a final blow. This was it, Candland told himself. Keyes needed to put a stop to him.

A knife flashed through the air, and Keyes' sword was knocked from his hand. He turned to see Ava running towards him from the staircase with the unicorn following behind. Keyes pulled out a dagger from his belt just as Ava sidestepped a large rock crumbling down. Ava pulled out a second knife, smaller than Keyes', but she didn't seem to mind. She glanced at Candland and saw more blood than body. Axol was zigzagging above him in a flustered state. One look at Candland, and she knew she needed to be quick.

"Get Candland and get out of here!" Ava yelled at Kavi.

"You know I cannot do that," Kavi responded.

Ava rolled her eyes. *Goddamn unicorns.*

"You haven't been around many unicorns, have you?" Keyes asked, flustered and yet still amused by Ava's appearance. Ava changed the grip on her knife for a quick exchange, and approached Keyes with steady, calculated steps.

Ava lunged quickly. With every jab or swipe of the knife, she stepped forward, covering ground and putting Keyes on his back foot. She worked fast, leading with offense. She sliced the side of his cheek, and the playfulness she had seen from him just a few seconds earlier disappeared. The cut was deep, and the blood ran down his cheek. He clenched his jaw. Keyes blocked another swipe from above that was aimed to kill, and found himself blade to blade and eye to eye with Candland's mysterious and well-trained friend. He looked at the glow of her cheek, and his concern was overcome with hate.

He pushed her off, and Ava landed with an athleticism that he did not expect. She used her fall as a jumping point, and in one step leapt forward, putting all of her weight into her blade that was quickly closing in on him. He blocked the blade, but not without losing his footing where the ground had come apart from Candland's doing. Ava saw the opportunity and pierced him in the shoulder, feeling his muscle tense up around the blade. She lifted her blade again to finish him off, and got another quick stab near the heart, but flew backwards last second to dodge a horse-sized boulder that came crashing down on Keyes' leg.

She wanted to finish him herself, but Candland needed her, and she didn't know what condition he was in. Every second was critical. Ava quickly turned and ran to Candland, leaving Keyes anchored down by the boulder. The chambers shuddered. The whole cave was giving in. Another large boulder fell onto Candland's lower half. Ava had to jump back to save herself. She looked through the dirt that was falling from above to see the boulder had landed on Candland's right foot, just below the knee. Dammit. She stood up, spreading both of her hands on the boulder. She pushed.

"I'm dying," Candland said. "I'm dead. Go."

No. She ran and snatched Keyes' sword and returned to Candland's leg or what was left of it. Without any care for the pain she would add to his misery, Ava stuck the sword into Candland's leg where the boulder crushed his limb. She cut into his skin, ligaments, bone. All of him. But she also made her way under more of the boulder. She put all of her weight into the hilt of the sword, and the sword broke as the rock rolled just enough to reveal more of Candland's leg.

Ava wasn't thinking. She was acting. She reached down, holding just below Candland's knee and pulled. She pulled and pulled. She was now screaming in defiance. She fell back. The boulder released Candland's leg. The boulder budged a few more inches, revealing the rest of his foot. She threw Candland over her shoulder. He was heavy, and his body was awkwardly positioned, but there was no time to readjust.

"Axol!" she screamed. "His arm. Get his arm!" Then she pushed past the ghost-like presence of Kavi, taking the steps up to the surface in twos. She could still hear Keyes shouting angrily: *Candland had left the kingdom defenseless!* His brother's voice was seething with hatred, disgust, defeat even. When Ava reached the fresh air, she continued to run even though her lungs felt as if they had no air left and her legs had reached their limit. She pushed hard, knowing she was still slow going with Candland's weight. Though the quakes had stopped, loose earth was still giving way. She had to push through.

When the earth finally seemed to settle, she flung the second prince down. She ripped Candland's belt from his body and wrapped it around his leg—or what was left of it. His foot was still attached. How? She wasn't sure. Maybe it was a shred of a ligament keeping it together. Maybe it was the last of his leg bone. Either way it was still there. She pulled her shirt off and tied it around his arm. His arm was completely unattached. Axol had carried his arm, barely managing from the weight. He dropped it gently beside them. Ava looked at the prince. There was so much blood. Ava's breath started to catch. Candland's eyes weren't closed, but they weren't open. They were rolling. They were such large wounds, getting rid of Candland's life with the force of a waterfall.

"Kavi!" she screamed. "Tell me what I have to do to keep him alive!"

"I will advise to the best of my abilities. First, tighter. The belt needs to be tighter. Once it is tight, continue increasing the tightness. And repeat the same thing for his arm."

Screaming in frustration, Ava pulled at the belt, pulling as hard as she could. Her arms already burned from pushing the boulder and carrying the prince. She was afraid she wasn't strong enough to stop the bleeding.

Proru had found them. He howled into the air, a loud cry that shot into the sky. The thunderous sound echoed through the air. Ava and Kavi turned to see the rest of the Blood Chambers implode on itself. Ava returned her focus to Candland's side, with Proru sniffing and licking Candland's good leg affectionately.

"Wake up, Candland. Wake up! Kavi. What should I do?"

"Take him to the castle infirmary. It is his best chance."

"Proru. Up!" Ava lifted Candland and threw him over the back of the wolf, laying him limply on his stomach. Axol flew nearby, zipping nervously. Ava took Candland's arm and jumped onto Proru's back, holding Candland's foot so it didn't fall from the rest of the leg, and also holding onto Candland, making sure he stayed on Proru's back. On the way there to the castle entrance, Ava couldn't help notice Proru had managed to soften his stride. She leaned over once to try and figure out how the wolf was doing it. In the second she was able to lean, she thought for a moment that she saw the earth soften underneath the Nylo's feet—as if he were commanding the ground to absorb the shock each time he put a paw down.

When they arrived at the front gate of the castle, Ava was met with more than fifty guards blocking the way.

"Let us pass. The prince need's help!" Ava shouted.

The soldiers stood their ground. So she swung off of Proru, and approached the first guard.

"The prince is injured. Let us pass. It's Prince Candland. He needs aid. Now!"

"We have orders. We are not to let you back into the palace."

"Then take the prince. We don't need passage," she said, desperate.

The guard hesitated. "Those orders include Prince Candland."

For the first time since she entered the Blood Chamber, she paused. "Does the Queen know he will die? Take him to the Bloody infirmary! He needs a doctor!"

The guard looked to the ground. Ava pushed the guard, and the group unsheathed their swords in unison. Ava opened her mouth, but then eyed the queen, watching from above at the top of the overpass.

"He will die if you don't let him in! He needs help! He may be your only son left!"

The expression of the queen did not change. It was as if she were looking at a stray dog, frothing at the teeth from a disease. The old woman turned and walked away until Ava could see her no longer.

"Arrest her and put her in the Cages with her lizard," the queen said. "Find Keyes."

"He's your son too!" she shouted. "He needs you!"

The guards did not hesitate, their eyes on the wolf. It was clear they were willing to stand their ground, but not quite sure how to make the arrest with Proru there. Ava could wait no longer now that the queen was gone. She turned back to Proru and swung upon his back. They could still force themselves through, but it was a risky bet to think the infirmary would work on him given they could be killed if they interfered—which Ava didn't put past the queen.

"Kavi. Direct me. How do I make sure he's okay without the help of Questus? House of Haessig?"

"It is too far. Much too far."

Ava's eyes scattered as she scanned her brain for any answers. Then it came.

"If I can just make it to the Tunnels, we can save him! Kavi, do you know the Kleen Root? Is there any on the way? They often grow near water…"

"Ah. Yes, the Kleen Root. Known for temporarily putting a human into a sleep paralysis, ultimately resulting in slowing the body down. In this case, it would help stop the bleeding and stabilize Prince Candland."

"Yes. Yes that one! Proru. Head towards the Tunnels. Kavi, where can we find the root?"

Proru had jolted into a full sprint.

"The Asting confirms there is some that grow near the river leading toward the Tunnels. Ava, it is a worthy attempt to save your friend. Once you give Candland the Kleen Root, what will you do in the Tunnels?"

"Find Gears!" Ava shouted.

The last time Ava had been in the Tunnels, she was impaled by a spear, and she had visited Gears who had sent her to Pagra. Now she found herself again running through the dusty hallway that always seemed so narrow to her, but seemed to bend outward to accommodate for Proru—which was a good thing because it had quickly become apparent that Proru was not going to trust Candland to human company without his own presence there ever again. She had failed Candland. She had failed Proru.

And even after finding and administering the Kleen Root like her mother had taught her, she still feared she was too late. The plant had slowed his breathing and his bleeding. But he had lost so much. She refused to think of what was at stake as she came through the opening into Gears' operating space.

"Gears!" she screamed before they even reached the large laboratory. "Gears, I need you!"

She scanned the room, finding the best thing they had to a doctor bent over a few medical instruments wearing a welding mask. He turned, flipping his mask up over his blonde hair. His blue eyes looked at Ava, the unicorn, then the wolf, and the body on top. He walked swiftly to them as Ava slid Candland's body down. She had no idea if he was even still alive, but they had ridden as fast as they could.

"Gears. Save him. Please."

"Bring him here. On the table." Ava helped half-lift, half-drag the prince's body to a metal table with a thin white cloth. His body made a loud bang as they placed him there to rest. Gears examined Candland's body. He turned away and came back in seconds with two proper tourniquets. He started with the leg, squeezing above Candland's knee until Ava was sure his leg would simply pop off. Her shoulders caved in, realizing she hadn't made the belt even close to being tight enough. Gears did the same with the arm, capping off his blood just below the shoulder, around the bicep.

Ava watched Gears work. She looked around, vaguely aware that there were others. Other patients. Other people in pain. She felt guilty that she didn't feel guilty that Gears was at Candland's table. He needed Gears. She needed Gears. Gears took a needle and injected something into Candland. He took five more needles, repeating the process.

"What happened?" he finally said.

"His brother attacked him. And then a boulder fell on his leg. And... I couldn't get him out... So I kind of cut his leg so I could get enough leverage to move the rock... And then I had to just pull his body out from under the rock."

"How did his leg even stay on?"

"I... I tried to hold it in place. We gave him some Kleen Root on the way."

"He's stable. For now. He lost a lot of blood. The Wolf is using up a lot of energy to make sure his heart continues to beat... but I don't know how stable he would be without his Marker. I gave him something for his heart, something to help him rest, and something for the pain. When he wakes up, he'll be in a great deal of pain, Ava."

Tears streamed down Ava's eyes in relief. She could deal with pain. He could deal with pain. As long as he was alive.

"We need to give him a blood transfusion. The arm is a clean cut. Good job keeping the arm. I think it might be possible to reattach. But not here. I don't have the equipment. And... I don't know if we can keep the leg."

Who cares about keeping the leg? Ava thought. *We just need to keep him.* But then she thought of Candland. He would never walk on his two feet again. There had to be a way...

"It looks like some bone's been missing from wherever you came from. I can't even tell how long his leg should be at this point. I could use metal, but I don't know. I don't think it would work..."

"S-someone told me," Ava wiped a tear from her blood-stained cheek, "That fire and metal could be persuasive. Gears. I love him. Be persuasive."

"I did say that, didn't I?" he murmured. "Do you really love him?"

"...Yes. Yes I do." She felt so many things at that moment. This wasn't how she was supposed to fully realize her feelings. This wasn't how the first words of love were supposed to come out.

"We can work with that," Gears offered a smile for comfort. "I'll go get the fire. In the meantime, do you have a memory of him? A happy one? One with no stress or trauma?"

"Yes. Yes I have lots of them."

"That will definitely come in handy."

Ava waited while Gears worked. She walked to the table every so often to check in on the progress. She never knew what she was looking for. She saw metal, fire, bone, and blood. Then she would return to sit with Axol and Proru who lay in one of the laboratory's dim corners. Kavi sat beside them, writing in their Asting journal or sometimes accompanying Ava as she made her rounds. She had started to check on the other patients, making sure everyone's illnesses and ailments weren't urgent. She tried to be helpful, but she felt like she herself was running out of energy.

"You should try to rest and perhaps eat," Kavi said as she returned from making her rounds.

"Rest? How can I rest when Candland—," Ava's voice broke. She broke. She knew Maya had stepped in to save Candland. Where had she gone now? Or did Maya feel the same? Did it matter? Ava leaned her back against the wall, and slid down until she was curled into a little ball. She crossed her arms over her knees, ducked her head between her knees and let out a muffled wail.

Candland had been so excited to return to his family. To see his brother again. So sure that his mother would come around to accept who he was. His mother had turned her back on him. He had lost his home. Whether Keyes was dead or alive, Candland had lost his brother. And if that wasn't enough, he had the physical wounds to remind him. His arm. And his leg. Would he be able to walk again? Would his arm be able to be re-attached?

Ava sobbed into her knees, her chest shuddering as the waves of everything came crashing down on her. She felt the physical burnout from carrying Candland and being too fatigued to properly take care of his injured and unattached limbs. She remembered the howl Proru had released into the sky. The sorrow. The anger. His howl made her feel like the ground would implode on itself. It was the only sound that could follow such a betrayal. Had Candland heard it? Then, Ava thought he might die in her arms. The only person who stayed by her side after discovering what she was. The only person who deserved the best... nearly bled out.

And how would he be when he woke? And he would wake up. What would he think of his arm and his leg? What would he think of his brother and mother? How should Ava be? What should she say? If he wondered why he wasn't in the Questus infirmary but underground in more of a makeshift healer's quarters... Would Ava tell him? Would she tell him that his mother left him to die?

No. No she wouldn't. She lifted her head. Because Candland needed her to be strong now. She had lost her home once. She had lost her parents too. She had been left to die. She had been alone. Candland would never have to go through this alone. Ava wiped her nose, snif-fling as she slowly stood up.

"C'mon, Axol," she said. "Let's go get something to eat."

With food for Gears and Candland—if he woke sooner rather than later—Ava and Axol made their way back to Gears' place with full stomachs. Ava could feel Maya's presence. Before entering the Blood Chambers, Ava had felt under control. Maya couldn't get control. Ava was able to block her out. Ava could feel the shift in her head. Maya wasn't in control at the moment, but it was because she hadn't taken control. Ava was weak. She was tired. And she knew Maya was only biding her time. Was Maya waiting for the right moment to take over again? But she couldn't worry about that right now. She would be there for Candland, and fight the battle with Maya when the time came.

When they returned, Gears was sitting beside Cand-land. To Ava's surprise, Candland was awake. She dropped the food she carried into Gears' lap, and nearly fell over Candland. She stood over him. Then she looked at his arm. It was in a full cast. The cast thickened around where his arm had been separated. Something was underneath the cast, holding his arm together. Then Ava looked at his leg. She did her best not to react. From his knee down, there were metal bars of varying length of thickness driving through his leg. It was a kind of metal cage that not only surrounded his leg, but pierced through it countless times. The lower leg had been wrapped multiple times with bandages, fresh blood stains surrounding each metal bar that protruded from his leg. Ava knew Gears had been their best option, and she knew he was good at what he did. But what she looked at... what she saw... it could only be described as a mad attempt at keeping Candland's leg attached to his body. She almost felt as if it would have been better to sever the leg altogether.

"Ava," Candland smiled. Tears slid from the sides of his eyes and onto the white linen underneath him. His teeth were clenched and his forehead was wet with sweat. He was clearly in pain.

"I'm here," Ava said, hoping he didn't catch her staring. "Everything is okay."

"I'm so sorry," he said. "I should have never—"

"Everything is okay," Ava shook her head. "I'm okay. Axol and Proru are okay. You're okay. Nothing else matters."

"My brother almost killed me."

"But he didn't," Ava said.

Gears cleared his throat. He had already eaten the bread, cheese, and smoked meat Ava had brought.

"How is your pain?" Gears asked.

"...There's a lot of it," Candland said.

"We will work to get that under control. I'm going to tell both of you where we're at," Gears said.

"Can it wait?" Ava asked.

"I'd rather him hear it before I medicate him," Gears said.

"It's okay," Candland said quietly to Ava.

"Your arm will heal. If you can get to the House of Haessig soon, you're looking at a good chance of a fair recovery. Of course, it's hard to say.

"Now your leg. Your leg is in bad shape, my friend. I probably should have cut it off."

Ava's breath caught. She wished Gears could work on his bedside manner.

"But I decided what did you have to lose? Besides the leg, obviously. As long as you can keep it from getting infected, you might as well try to keep it attached until the healers at Haessig can have a looksee. Now, the way it is now. You're going to be in a lot of pain. We'll try to keep that under control, but you won't be comfortable."

"Can't you just up the dose on the relievers?" Ava asked.

"I have. But some injuries will just hurt. And, I don't know how you got hurt, but it's clear that the way in which you were hurt and by who... was also painful. And no medicine can take that pain away." Gears put his hand on his heart, "Now, my prescription is to get to House of Haessig as soon as you can, and with as little movement as possible. Don't move your arm, and don't move your Bloody leg. Do not walk on it before you get there. Do not walk on it even after you get there. Don't try to stand on it. Don't put any weight on it. Rest today, I'll build you a little... sled your wolf can pull you on. If anyone can save your leg, it's the House of Haessig."

"Thank you so much. For what you've done," Candland said.

Ava looked at Candland's leg. It was hard to feel grateful at that moment. Candland was kinder than she was.

"You'll thank me more in a minute," Gears smiled. "Ava. I'll need you to assist me here in a moment."

Gears turned, walking past many strange machines that were not made of what medical machines were made of, but he had made them all medical machines nonetheless. He stopped at an open metal shelf where he picked up a small snail shell that was clear with white flecks.

Gears returned to the table, standing over Candland. Ava took Candland's hand. He squeezed it weakly in return. His hand was damp and trembled slightly. He must have been in so much pain. Gears tapped on the snail shell over Candland the way a man might tap his finger on a salt shaker. White beads, moving and swirling in a fluid shape so that they appeared more liquid than solid, floated out from the shell above Candland. The beads began to collect in certain areas above him. There was a cloudy cluster floating above his arm where Keyes had severed it. There was another swirl moving like a swarm of bees above his ankle and shin. More around his head, and the rest over his chest.

"His heart is broken from betrayal," Gears said, "That will be the most challenging injury to overcome."

Ava remained silent, regretting ever letting Candland

return to his so-called home. She turned to see Kavi now stood on the other side of Candland. They were quiet and though they still had that unicorn lightness about them... they were more somber than ever.

"Close your eyes, Ava," Gears said. "Think of a happy memory with him. It doesn't have to be the happiest. What's most important is that there is no bad. No stress, no anxiety, no discomfort. It must be free from pain, suffering, or sadness. Think of your memory over and over, and don't stop until I say."

Ava's eyelids fell. She slipped past Maya, who still just seemed to be waiting for her moment just below the surface... It was rare for her to be quiet, unmoving when Ava looked within. They both knew there was common interest in keeping Candland alive, and Ava was the only one who had pure enough memories with Candland to help.

Ava found herself in a meadow. Glowing fern-like plants waved slowly as if they were underwater. The Tunnel's city lights were a cluster to the south. Axol, so near and so full of energy, was the brightest thing there. He rested square on Candland's head, illuminating the prince's green eyes and bringing out the golden hues in his dark sandy hair and skin. The ever-glittering Nylo left a cloud of magical mist around the prince, his tiny fingers sticking to Candland's temples like a baby frog might hang onto a rock. When Axol had nested on top of his head for the first time, Candland's eyes had rolled up only to see the white sparkles tinkling into his vision. He had laughed as he reached up and gently tried to nudge Axol's body one way or the other only to realize Axol was set on his new resting place. Now that Axol had found his head of hair many-a-time, Axol rested light like a feather, and Candland did not look up or try to re-adjust the Nylo's placement. If anything, it sometimes looked like Candland tried to glide more than trot with his lanky legs for a smoother ride for his friend.

It was just hitting midday so the sun's rays were directly hitting the desert floor. And for an hour, The Tunnel's top layer would let in some of the direct sunlight. Like a pastel sunset in a smoky sky might be for those who lived above, the midday rays that stretched behind the crackling dirt and endless sand was a routine wonder. The light seemed to make the air buzz. Candland's hair was outlined with the alpenglow that only escapes when the sun feels bashful.

Candland had come down to the Tunnels earlier that day. He knocked on Ava's door. When she opened it, already knowing who it was from the way Axol was trying to pry the door open with his little fingers, Candland had looked up at her, asked, "Meadow?" and then his eyes darted away, lacking the courage it took to wait for an answer.

It had been hours since they walked out the door, and neither of them had said a word since. They had walked about the meadow, hopped, danced, and laughed. Ava had shared some traditional Sei she had packed, and they nodded at each other when they had finished the last of them.

Ava imagined what it would be like to walk above ground with him. What it would be like to spend a long day with Candland and come home sunburned. Then midday had hit, the sun came through, and Ava didn't wonder anymore. Why wonder when the golden outline of your best friend was right in front of you, beside you, around you?

And that's when Ava realized she wanted to be close enough to Candland to smell the horse ride he took from Questus. She wanted to know the soft and hard parts of his hands. She wanted to know what he saw when he looked away from her gaze. All of the space between them suddenly became visible. She wanted—no, she needed—to be closer. That's when the pull she felt towards him had started.

It was all similar and entirely different from when she Matched with Axol. She felt herself attaching to everything that made up Candland in the same way she had done with Axol when she was younger. The Marker Match with Axol had felt transcendent, freeing. However, this Match with Candland was overpowering. It was so strong, it almost hurt. Freedom was not a word that came to mind. Instead, she felt exposed and vulnerable in the same way one might feel when everything is *too* perfect, *too* lovely, *too* good.

Candland turned to her in the meadow as if sensing a change. It was her eyes that scattered now. Could he feel her discovering this kind of love for the first time? Was it such an event that could not be quietly felt? Could he hear her heart? Could he smell her desires? Did he hear her body cry out from the small distance between them? She looked at him again. She tried to say it then, with her stare. With her eyes. With her smile and the shine of the sun: I'm devoted to you.

"Ava. Come back."

Ava looked up. She was standing beside Gears. Candland lay in front of her. She noticed the subtle tremble he had taken on was gone. His eyes were closed, and his face looked... peaceful. His eyebrows, one thin line without the wrinkles of pain.

"This is the best he will feel in a long time," Gears said. "Let him rest. Tomorrow, you'll begin a long and painful journey."

"Thank you," Ava said. Still pulling away from her memory, aware that Maya was smirking at her past. At her weakness. At her strength. At her love.

CHAPTER 17
THE 100
CHINCHIN

When Chinchin didn't hear from Maya early the next day, she had assumed Maya was up with her father trying to get Rocky up to speed. When she realized that Ava had left, taking Maya with her, she didn't hesitate. Although Rocky's memories had been fully transferred back, he was still settling back into his body and recovering. Obigon sent the Nylo Guardians out to search for Ava, with the lot not quite knowing why it was so important to find her. But Chinchin knew.

She packed her things and took off. Chinchin wasn't the sit and wait kind of person. Maya was gone, but not dead. And Chinchin wouldn't lose her like that again. She knew it was Ava who had left, not Maya. And if Ava thought anyone could sever Maya's memories from her brain, it was House of Haessig. She knew she could be completely wrong about Ava and her intentions, but she had to act. She had to move. She just hoped that the Nylo Guardians would cover the ground she wasn't if her hunch on Ava's whereabouts was off.

The first main city heading north towards House of Haessig was Du. It was a rich city with a landscape made up of water, mountain, valley, and greens that not many other settings could compare to with the exception of Questus. Du was a few days' ride north of Nevarra and was made up mostly of immigrants from the House of Haessig and refugees from families who were torn between quarreling geographies. Du was claimed as Haessig territory, known for being a neutral zone for any two opposing sides to communicate or negotiate when the need arose.

More importantly to Chinchin, as an extension of House of Haessig which was headquartered so many thousands of miles north, it was an independent land. It was free and safe, and any type of violence was not tolerated there. Enemies could quarrel, but they couldn't attack one another. Its peace had been respected by visitors and natives for hundreds of years. In fact, even Chinchin didn't really know what happened if someone were to break those rules.

Her first steps in Du had reminded her of the days before Pagra, just after she had run away from her own home. She was more mischievous then. Less afraid.

Unaware of the consequences to be had from actions, no matter how good her intentions were. She was careless, bold, and looking for trouble. On the first night in Du, Chinchin pickpocketed enough for a new outfit, a hot dinner with plenty of drink, and a place to stay for the week within her first 15 minutes of being in the heart of the city. It was so easy, it made her sick.

Maya never knew this side of her, Chinchin thought as she took a bite of fresh cooked duck served on an assortment of steamed vegetables on a lavish platter next to a full glass of wine. The company was loud and crowded and yet somehow scattered. Old men toasting, young ladies raising and lowering their eyes and skirts at opportune times. No, Maya never knew this side of her. She only knew her as a scientist, not as the runaway rogue.

After that first dinner, Chinchin decided to stay in the city for a couple of days just in case Ava hadn't made it through yet. The days passed by quickly. There was something about the running water of the Du river, the largest river in The Cache, that told her to stay longer. The river seemed to promise it would point her in the right direction, and Chinchin was listening. She stayed in Du a third day.

Rumors of Prince Keyes' return landed near her while she was searching for Ava's face and Maya's memories. The whispers were about him returning from a much needed vacation that was turned into a missing prince story by mere miscommunication. She thought of the second prince, hiding in Nevarra, hardly able to understand the power he now had within him. She had liked him. Then she laughed to herself. Of course a prince whose entire kingdom was against Marker Matching would find himself Marked, while others with nothing went scouring The Cache for a Nylo to give them a chance at making a better life and would still end up with nothing. The prince who didn't need it and probably didn't want it... got it anyway.

On her third and final day in Du before deciding to head further north, Chinchin decided to take the long way back to the inn she was renting a bed from. She walked along the river, and then deeper into the solace of the trees, wondering if the river would suggest she, yet again, stay longer. The rustling leaves made her think of Nevarra and her good deed in returning Maya's brother home. *See?* She told the river. *I'm not so bad.* But then she thought of that last time she saw Chauson. How in return for helping her, she had hurt him. Physically. Emotionally. She wished she could have left a note or some kind of symbol so he knew she was sorry, but anything that could look like a friendship between them would have made it look like he had helped her escape. She wondered how he was doing... but then decided it didn't help to wonder.

She heard the snapping of a branch. It was a strange snap. Not the careless break that an animal might make. No, this sound was sneaky, quiet, and full of regret.

Chinchin turned around quickly, but she was too late.

She was knocked to the ground. She scrambled backwards to create space between whatever it was that struck her. Then she heard laughing and saw shapes begin to form. The shade gave into color and Chinchin realized she recognized some of the faces. Test subjects from Project 222.

"Hello 86. Remember us?"

"Rox. Kara. Tara. Dela. Boz."

"You always were good with names."

"I remember people I care about," Chinchin said as she pulled herself up. "Why did you knock me down? That hurt."

"Sorry. That was Span," Boz said. A small, round creature with skinless, exposed muscles on the exterior appeared. This was the heavy Nylo that had knocked her down in the first place. A Cohmo. They were one of the uglier Nylos, where all of those external features you might think of existed on the inside of its sphere. On the outside, it was muscle that acted like armor. Span looked almost like a human brain, but with a less slimy, much more rigid appearance.

"What are you doing here?" Chinchin asked.

"You know too much about the Labs to be roaming without Scouts," said Kara.

"We need you to help make more of us," Tara said.

"A lot of us have died without the axolotls, and we can't find any more of them," said Dela.

"And it's your own Bloody fault, 86. So you need to come back and fix it," Boz said.

"Pagra Labs and I have creative differences," Chinchin said. She noticed more creatures among the trees, more on foot. Nylos. She was outnumbered 5 to 1 in humans using her mutation and 0 to who knows how many in Nylos since they all were probably Matched with multiple Nylos at once. All five of her former test subjects were Shadow Elites that had joined the experiment. Chinchin knew they were all skilled fighters. She knew their files. They were ruthless. Being so far from home, she was out of her depth—and it wasn't often her calculations came back with that result. Chinchin looked around, she had spied several axolotls varying in color. They had made the match with the healing Nylo, they had more than one Nylo, and they hadn't died. *I created a nearly-impossible-to-kill army for Pagra with unlimited power. I'm such an idiot.* She thought.

"We won't kill you," Rox said. "I mean, we are on neutral ground here in Du. Besides, you're wanted. Alive. 546 was pretty clear about that."

Chauson.

"How many of you are left from Project 222?" Chinchin asked.

"100 even."

"Who's in charge here?"

"We are," Boz said. His lip curled slightly.

"Who's giving orders?" Chinchin asked.

"Number 7. He misses you," Rox said.

Span leapt up, spinning in the air like a self-possessed cannon. Chinchin dodged him this time. She threw a metal star into the shoulder of Boz, a weapon courtesy of Nevarra. Hearing him grunt in pain gave her no joy. She didn't want to hurt any of them. In a way, Boz was right. They were all her fault. She was responsible for them. And she felt that even now.

The fighting escalated faster than Chinchin hoped. Chinchin was able to do some more damage from a distance, throwing more of the sharp weapons she had taken with her from Nevarra that hindered but did not kill, but then the Nylos closed in. And she couldn't keep them all off for long. They crawled, rolled, flew, charged, and Chinchin was on her back, kicking at the ground and sometimes at the air, and sometimes at a Nylo. There were so many, she wasn't even able to classify all of them as they attacked. Her right calf burned. Her left shoulder was cut deep by a claw, causing blood to drip from her fingers. She saw the blood from her own body stain fur, scales, skin, and raw muscle. Whatever indifference that had slowly been turning into fascination for the Nylos during her time in Pagra had quickly soured into hatred as she spit out the blood filling her mouth.

The five Marked had hardly moved when she found herself a couple of feet deep in the river water, pushed into the waterbanks by the pure force of an animal that looked half goat, half tiger. She was out of stars to throw. She held a dagger she had unsheathed from her thigh. There were enough Nylos to make her feel dizzy, but the Nylo in front of her had a horn on each side of its head, the lime-colored fur, black stripes, and whipping tail of a tiger. It took a few calculating steps backwards as Chinchin inched deeper into the water. The creature charged forward with the impact, throwing her body back deeper into the river.

She swallowed a mouthful of water, clawing frantically to find the surface. Her eyes were wide, searching through the chaos of blood and bubbles in the water. She was losing.

Dear mother, she thought. *I'm sorry I didn't make it home. In fact, in a sort of poetic way, I died by my own creations. I wanted to do better. I wanted you to be proud, truly. In that kind of I-didn't-know-this-would-make-me-a-proud-mother kind of a way. I thought I knew what The Cache needed before it knew what it needed... But I didn't even know what I needed. I was naive to think tending to others' needs before my own would fix everything. I was naive to think more would mean enough for everyone. More isn't associated with words like fair or equal. More is associated with greed—*

Chinchin broke the surface of the river, finding herself waist deep. She half-swam, half-waded into more shallow water so it was only up to her ankles. The Nylos had backed off. Her test subjects closed in on her.

She wiped the blood from her brow that was making it extremely difficult for her to see. She would go down, but not until she couldn't get up. She widened her stance. It was weak and visibly wavering. Between the streaks of blood coming down over her thick, damp lashes, she could see the smiles of her enemies as they saw her sorry attempt at looking ready to give or take another hit. She realized she was only looking out of one eye. Her other eye had been swollen shut.

"Lights! If you're going to kill me then at least one of you do it. I'm done with those Bloody Nylos!" Chinchin shouted venomously.

"We're not going to kill you. Remember? You're coming with us alive," Boz said.

In the midst of pain, Chinchin had forgotten they were told to keep her alive. She felt some relief, but not enough to lower her hands. Even if her life wasn't on the table, her freedom was. And she would fight for it with everything she had.

But before anything else happened... something took Chinchin by surprise. Literally. She had the wind knocked out of her. Gasping for breath, she became painfully aware that her shoulder blades felt as if they were on fire. A second later, she also caught glimpses through her bloody vision to indicate that she was not on land any longer. In a sudden rush, she found she was airborne. She turned her head to try and figure out what had happened, but all she could see were golden feathers here and there. The feathers were... vaguely familiar. She was too exhausted to recall where she had seen them before. Or maybe she was too angry to come to the fact that she was clearly being rescued by none other than a Nylo.

Chinchin woke up. She was lying in a neat bed, her wounds cleaned up and bandaged. She started to sit up, but then stopped. She felt pain ring through her entire body. She looked around. The room was airy and clean, and modest in what it contained. She liked it.

"There you are."

It was a familiar voice in an unfamiliar tone. Chinchin turned to see Rocky. He sat by the window, back to the wall, chin up, head relaxed, throat exposed—carelessness in the form of arrogance. Immediately she saw *him*. He was himself this time. The days he had spent with her on their way to Nevarra, he was like a body with new muscles and no name. Slow, confused, anxious. Now he was back.

"Rocky?"

"You know, I don't know if Maya would have fallen for you if she saw what you looked like with only one eye able to open," he smiled.

"What are you doing here?"

"Well, I saved you. So that's what I did here. Well, technically Berns saved you, so you should probably thank him before he holds it against you. He *lives* for recognition. And now I'm here because I have some news."

"You found Maya."

"Obviously. You thought you could find her before me?"

"When I left Nevarra, you weren't... *you.* Where is she?"

"Not here. Now, you and I didn't get a chance to talk once you heard Ava—er, Maya— left with the prince. I want to tell you what happened. Fill in the blanks for you before anything else happens."

Chinchin sat up despite the pain. She was eager to hear what he had to say.

"Before we tried to escape the Labs for good, Maya was acting funny. She was saying stuff that didn't make sense. She was coming up with plans that would kill us— even if we succeeded. Something was up, so I took her memory. All of it. I never told her...

"She killed herself. We now know that's because of whatever you did to her with your *science.* But I had her memories in my head. I was captured by the Scouts, and I knew I'd be put through the Mud Wall, so I gave someone all of the memories I had before I was taken."

"That's why Pagra Labs didn't get anything from you. That's why when I got to you, you were blank. I wasn't late, you just didn't have any memories. You gave them to that girl."

"A friend of a friend. I locked up my memories before I gave them to her. You know, privacy. I transferred Maya's into Ava's head freely. Just all of Maya into another body. I knew she would know what to do."

"I don't get it though. That would be too much for a cerebellum to process. It wouldn't work. It would just destroy the original processor and brain circuits. Anyone would go insane."

"An overloaded system, right? Well, with this person —whom you met—she has an axolotl for a Nylo. You saw her Mark. It was lucky to find someone with her abilities that could handle a full download of memories like that. I took a chance. Better all of my secrets die with her rather than get sucked into that Bloody wall."

"And?"

"And it worked. A healing Marked was the perfect vessel. Maya came back. Different body, same bossy, know it all, I'm-the-best, leader of the NGs, Maya."

"So it worked."

"I honestly wasn't sure if it would. But you've seen her. She's herself."

"Where is she?" Chinchin asked again.

"She was last spotted in Questus with Candland and the unicorn."

"Questus." Chinchin hid her disappointment in being wrong about where Ava would head to first. "Maya had mentioned something about using Candland... I didn't think she would be stupid enough to go to Questus."

"The thing is, Ava left before we had time to... make arrangements. It wasn't Maya that left, it was Ava."

"I knew she was lying," Chinchin said quietly.

"Who?"

"Maya told me Ava was brain dead before her memories were planted. That the body didn't really have anyone occupying it when she... arrived."

"She knew you wanted to hear it," Rocky shrugged.

"I'm not an idiot," she sighed. "It would have to be a very strange case for a person with that Mark to suffer a brain injury and not heal."

"Why didn't you tell her you knew she was lying?"

"When your soulmate comes back from the dead, you don't waste time on that kind of stuff."

"Well. I'm glad you feel that way... because I need your help."

"What do you need me to do?" Chinchin cocked her head. She didn't trust Rocky completely, but she knew they had similar goals.

"I'm not going to sugarcoat it the way your soulmate did. I'm going to find Ava and remove her memories from that body. Nevarra needs Maya to protect Nylos from Questus, Pagra, and now, frankly, the 100 that just messed you up—that's what they're calling themselves now, anyway. You saw them and what they can do. They attacked you in Du of all places. They clearly don't think they need to follow any rules anymore. They're powerful. We need Maya back—and not dealing with a weird version of schizophrenia. For whatever reason, Maya couldn't keep Ava under control for long enough. And because of that, Ava got away, and the prince and unicorn went with her."

"Where do I come in?" Chinchin asked.

"I thought you might want to talk to her... and I could use a little help. Removing Ava's memories would generally be frowned upon by NG's. It's not entirely ethical—if it were anyone else, we'd never do it like this. But it's our leader. My sister. The lives of our people, of who knows how many Nylos will be saved by Ava's sacrifice. It has to be done. My father sent me to do this without involving any other NG's, but it's not exactly a one-man job."

"Is the girl a fighter?"

"No, but like I said, she has Maya's memory—and that includes muscle memory. I've never beaten Maya in a fight. Candland just Matched. He has no idea how to use his power, and he's not really a man of action so I'm not too worried about him. Oh, and there's a unicorn—"

"Well, that shouldn't be a problem."

"Obviously," he flicked his hand and rolled his eyes. "Unicorns, am I right? Anyway, I just want this to go smoothly and quietly. Ava with Maya's muscle memory and Candland with some very untapped potential... could make it difficult. There isn't any room for a mistake here. I just want to have some backup. So. Do you want to talk to the love of your life again or what?"

"When do we leave?" Chinchin asked.

"Easy. You still need to rest. Berns is going to keep tracking them. Last we heard, they left Questus and are heading right for us."

Rocky opened the window. Berns flew in and Rocky's eyes burned gold in response to the owl's presence.

"You've already reached the second level with your Nylo at such a young age... How old are you?"

"Fifteen. It's a good thing I'm a second level Marked,

or I wouldn't have been able to save Maya. Berns makes it easy though. He's the responsible one."

"I could never replicate what you have with that bird with my mutation. The bond was never very strong."

"That bird is my Nylo. Of course you couldn't replicate it. What Berns and I have is... Well, you wouldn't understand."

"That's what Maya used to say."

"Well, she's right."

Berns made a long, winding screech.

"Oh, Berns says he's sorry that he hurt your back. He usually snatches my leather straps that I wear," Rocky pulled at the leather bands across his chest and around his back and shoulders, "But you didn't have any like that so he just had to grab whatever he could. Your back got pretty ripped up."

Berns screeched again.

"To be fair, he says you didn't look great when he arrived anyway. Now, give him a good scratch just there behind his head. It's the least you could do after he saved your life."

Berns flapped over to the end of her bed. He faced the window so that the back of his head was easily accessible for Chinchin. She wasn't convinced that the owl wouldn't try to peck her eyes out. He must know who she was, and what she had done. The owl's head spun around, his eyes wide. Chinchin got the message. She reached over slowly and started to scratch under his golden feathers.

. . .

Dear mother,

I can't come home yet. I have to help the woman I love first. Oh, and I just made a new friend. I think. He's a Nylo. Imagine that.

Love your daughter,

Chinchin

CHAPTER 18

WHAT WILL IT BE?
AVA & CANDLAND

When Candland woke up, he didn't say anything. He didn't ask where he was or what happened. He didn't ask about Keyes or Questus. He only looked at the oversized cast around his arm and then, straining, below at the cage around his leg that looked like it was made out of giant needles. Ava opened her mouth several times, but she didn't know what to say. She couldn't know what he was feeling. Even Kavi knew to withhold their questions and/or explanations for the time being. Ava once tried to reach for him, and Candland retracted. It hurt Ava enough to leave him alone so she stood up and left to give him space.

Proru was the only one who dared come near Candland after that. Gears had given Ava as many bottles for the pain as he could spare for the trip. Then he presented them with a rickety, metal crate, stuffed with spare rags and other soft stuff for Candland to lay on top of. Underneath were straps to attach to a makeshift saddle for Proru. Upon looking at it, Candland had said it looked like a coffin.

Ava had thought she and Gears would lift him into the crate, but Gears insisted that Candland sit up himself and, using a cane, hop into the contraption. Candland stood up and his eyes filled with tears. It took a very long time for Candland to make his way over to where he would be sitting for the next week. Ava and Gears helped Candland inside. Ava noticed Candland was reluctant to take their hands, but did so when he realized there was no other choice.

He laid flat while Ava and Gears nearly failed in lifting the crate onto Proru who lay (unhappily) on his stomach. When Ava's hand slipped and Candland's crate jerked forward she swore. Then she looked over her shoulder at Kavi who was jotting something in that Bloody journal of theirs. *Goddamn unicorns,* she thought. They could have done something. They could have helped Candland when he needed it most. Gears secured the straps and showed Ava how to do it.

Gears stepped away from Proru and turned to Ava. He mentioned that it was important that Candland sit up, stand up, and move—though he should not touch the ground with his caged foot—to ensure his blood continued to circulate. He warned that Candland would not want to because it would be painful. Especially as the medicine wore off. Ava looked up at Candland who lay defeated in the crate, his eyes closed, his jaws clenched in pain and surrender. How was she going to motivate him to move through pain?

Ava turned back to Gears. His crazy blonde hair, his crazier eyes. He hadn't hesitated when she came to him. He hadn't rested when he wasn't tending to Candland. He had helped others who needed aid. He ate to keep his strength up, he slept so he could be awake when needed. He was there for those who needed him. And shame on House of Haessig for letting him go. Ava swore she would let the people at House of Haessig know their mistake when they arrived. Gears was *good*.

She hugged him, surprised by how thin his body was under his heavy coat. How light his bones were under his skin. She felt a pain inside her well up. He helped everyone that needed him, but who helped him? She handed him the bag of coins she—but really Maya—had made from selling her blood. When Gears refused, Ava said to use it to help more people. Gears took it, and as Ava walked away, she wondered how such a thin boy managed to carry such a heavy bag of coins without toppling over.

They left the Tunnels and made their way above ground. Ava didn't hesitate this time as they floated to the surface. When Maya had been in control, her own memories had revealed themselves to her. She knew how she ended up in the Tunnels. She knew her past. Her heart didn't lock up like it once had. It simply beat louder for the ones that died for her to make it to the Tunnels the day her identity was discovered.

Proru carried Candland in the crate—which Candland had already started exclusively calling his coffin. Proru prowled forward gracefully, seeming to understand that any turbulence greatly increased Candland's pain.

When night came, they decided to set up camp near a lake. Ava helped Candland down from his coffin and helped him lay on the blankets she had laid out by the fire. Though she could tell Candland didn't want her help, they both knew he needed it. His dependence seemed to upset him as he laid on top of the blanket, but this was the only time Proru was able to truly be able to connect with Candland. Proru laid so close to Candland at night that parts of Candland's body were hidden in the Moon Wolf's fur. Ava was worried Proru might accidentally lay on top of Candland, but knew better from her own bond with Axol than to say anything.

That night by the fire, Proru licked Candland's uninjured arm. Candland looked up, but he didn't see the stars. He saw nothing. He felt a shame deep within him that he could not face from being less than a whole body. He felt an abandonment from his family he could not deny. And yet, he still somehow felt as if he needed to mourn his brother. Sometimes, he presumed Keyes to be dead, buried under the ground Candland had called upon, and it brought tears to his eyes. Other times, he knew Keyes wasn't so easy to kill, and swore he'd kill Keyes himself if he did actually survive the earthquake.

"Let me know if you need more medicine. Gears said it was easier to stay ahead of the pain than to play catch up," Ava said. She was massaging Axol's head in her hands. It was a strange thing they did. She would make a circle with her hands and Axol would float his head inside the circle and wait for her to gently squeeze his head, which inevitably turned into a full body massage.

Candland didn't say anything. Kavi refrained from speaking as well. They had been rather quiet since their new journey started, but they still had been taking diligent notes in their peach-colored journal. Unable to turn over, Candland laid on his back, waiting for sleep he knew wouldn't come.

***

He would never have been hurt if I was in control.

Ava looked up, but Candland lay idle and Kavi sat with their eyes closed, meditating. It was Maya.

What did you say? Ava asked in her head.

If I was in control, he would never have gone to Questus. He'd be able to walk. He'd be riding Proru, not riding in that Bloody goddamn coffin, Maya said.

Leave me alone, Ava said.

Why? So he can get his other arm cut off? Maya asked.

"Shut up!" Ava screamed. She realized she had

screamed it out loud. She was standing and Candland and Kavi were both staring. "...Sorry."

Ava walked out to the lake they had camped near. She knelt above the water.

It's cute. How much you love him and how little you can do to actually take care of him.

What do you want?

You know what I want. I want the reins.

It's my body.

And you're wasting it. I'll be a good case study for Kavi's research—a Nevarrian in an Earther's body would be a breakthrough for the Asting. And I'll protect Candland. I'll help protect Nylos like Axol. All that and more.

Stop. I know I can't protect him... but I can love him.

Is that how you'll feel when he's dead? His brother wants him dead, and he's the next ruler of Questus. You don't think Keyes will see it through?

Do you think Keyes survived?

I've seen enough battles to know the ones you want to die the most are the hardest to kill. Candland's a curse to the family. He's a stain on their name. Even if Keyes is dead, Candland will be dead by the next full moon by his own mother's doing if you don't let me do what I can to help. They will come for him, and they will kill him.

But... I love him.

Then watch over him. And let me protect him. And if love's what you're worried about, I can give him some of that too.

Get out of my head, Ava said angrily.

Getting jealous, Ava?

Leave me alone!

Don't you mean... leave Candland alone?

"Are you alright?" Kavi's voice chased Maya away... for now.

"It's Maya."

"I understand. You have been keeping control well. Even under stress or fear.

"Ever since Candland showed up, I felt like I needed to be here..."

"What is it?"

"Candland wouldn't have gotten hurt if Maya was leading."

"Perhaps. And then again, why would Maya protect Candland at all?"

"She said she would. She wants to use his position. She said she would have kept him safe. He'd be whole if she was here."

"Do not confuse claims and promises as action, Ava. She might have use for him, but can you truly trust her?"

"I feel confused about everything," she said. "Sometimes I can't tell which thoughts are mine. I can't tell if what I'm feeling is her or me. I can't keep things straight."

"It is not easy, but you must not give in to her sophistry—even if it is a voice inside your own head. You *know* what is you. I *know* what is you... That does not make it any less scary, I know."

"You know, Kavi, the one good thing about being an Atrox is it brought you to me. You're a good friend."

"The Asting does not have friends."

"That's the Asting. I know what is you, too, Kavi. And you're my friend," Ava smiled. She had been hard on them since Candland's injuries. She knew she had redirected her anger at them even though Kavi had always been honest about their inaction from the beginning. They weren't to blame. Kavi smiled, looking out at the water. She stood up from the shores of the water.

"What is next?" Kavi asked.

"Du. And then House of Haessig."

"And then?"

"I don't know."

"You are still so quiet."

"I'm listening to Maya."

"What is she saying?"

"That I'm a coward."

<hr>

It was two days later that Kavi spoke in the forest; Candland was yet to start a conversation. They were only a couple hours away from Du. Candland was lying in his coffin, riding on Proru's back.

"We are not alone," Kavi said.

The group stopped and began to look around. Ava tried to quiet her heavy breath.

Let me out! I'll protect you! Maya shouted from inside Ava's head.

"Candland!" a voice said. The screech of an owl followed.

Rocky appeared. Berns had flown over and dropped him at their feet. The group exhaled. It wasn't Keyes, and that offered some relief. The owl perched aggressively onto Rocky's shoulder, causing his shoulders to slant, as usual, from the weight of his Nylo.

"You didn't say goodbye to me before you left," Rocky said. Candland sat up onto his elbows slowly as Chinchin stepped out from the trees.

"Bloods, man. What happened?" Rocky said, looking at Candland. "What in the Lights happened?"

"Keyes cut off Candland's arm with a blade when trying to kill him. Then a boulder fell onto Candland's leg," Kavi answered.

"That's cold." Rocky crossed his arms.

"What are you doing here?" Candland asked.

"Well, Ava took something that doesn't belong to her. I'm here to make that right."

"I didn't *take* her. *You* put Maya into my head. I never wanted her here," Ava said.

"Well, then, it's time to take her back. Don't you want her out of your head?"

Let him come. I'm so over being in this body.

"I'm not an idiot. We share the same memories now. You want to erase me," Ava spoke.

Chinchin began to pace, eying Ava.

"Who are you?" Ava asked.

Chinchin, Maya answered quietly.

A flush of memories of her came over Ava. She saw her breasts, heard her moans, smelled her skin, tasted her tongue. Maya was reliving a flood of memories.

"Chinchin," Ava said involuntarily.

"Is it you?" Chinchin asked.

"It's Ava," she said, shaking her head.

"Is Maya there?"

Ava remained quiet. It was a battle inside her mind. When she had been in the backseat reliving old memories, it was when Candland had first appeared outside of herself that caught her attention. It was remembering Axol that empowered her to take action. Now Maya was answering the call of her brother and lover and Ava couldn't hold her off much longer.

"She's there," Rocky said, getting closer and closer to Ava. "I know she is."

"I want proof," Chinchin said.

"Come here, Ava." Rocky set his hand out for her to take.

"No," Ava said, stepping back.

"Candland, tell her it's okay. I'm a friend."

"She doesn't want to," Candland said. His arms were shaking from holding himself in a somewhat seated position. He pressed both hands down firmer into the coffin to stay sitting up. Proru took a step forward, though he couldn't move too much or too quickly without hurting Candland on his back.

Rocky shook his head, rolled his eyes, and sighed. Then with lightning speed he took Ava's hand. She yanked it away and Rocky laughed.

"Calm down. I just took a glimpse into Maya's past. The first time she stayed over at your place Chinchin was when 7 yelled at you for wanting to limit Marker Matches to 3."

"Maya," Chinchin breathed. She walked to Ava and quickly reached out. Ava put her arms up, deflecting the first attempt.

Chinchin swung her fists forward with a speed that surprised both Ava and Maya. Ava was able to block the first punch, but she missed the second, and was hit squarely in the face. She was thrown a few feet back, but her feet were able to stay under her thanks to Maya's natural reflexes. Candland shouted. Proru lunged forward, and Berns left Rocky's shoulder. He swooped down in front of Proru's face with his claws out. Proru had to pivot and duck at the same time, sending Candland sprawling out of his coffin onto the ground. Candland screamed. Everyone looked his way from the shrieks of pain. Candland was helpless. Immobile. Proru took a defensive stance around Candland, guarding his suffering human.

Give up.

Rocky had circled so that he stood behind Ava. Berns swooped down again towards Candand this time. Proru easily kept Berns from hurting him with his claws or beak, but it was enough to keep Proru from leaving Candland's side. Chinchin stood in front of Ava who was trying to keep track of Rocky. Chinchin unsheathed a dagger from her thigh. She shuffled forward and then lunged as she drove the blade near Ava's shoulder. Still moving forward, gaining ground on Ava as she shuffled backwards, Chinchin pushed the dagger in deeper. She left it buried in Ava's shoulder. Ava instinctively reached for the dagger, forgetting for a moment that Rocky was behind her. Without hesitating, Chinchin took Ava's head square between her hands and rammed her head against her own forehead. Ava instantly collapsed.

Give... Up

Candland was still unable to move. Unable to help. He was only keeping Proru from being able to do more.

"...Go," Candland said. His teeth clenched together. "Protect Ava." But Proru didn't listen.

Chinchin was kneeling on the floor with an unconscious Ava pinned to the ground. Rocky kneeled on the other side of Ava and reached for her hand. A touch and a handful of minutes, that was all it would take to have his sister back, and in a pertinacious body. She had been the best warrior in The Cache. With this Marked body, they would free every single Nylo that Pagra and Questus had tried to contain, had tested on, had sold, had "rehabilitated". With Maya in full control, Rocky and his sister would free them.

But something grabbed his hand before he could make contact with Ava. Rocky turned to see Candland was still failing to even sit up properly after the pain from the fall and Proru hunched over him. Rocky looked down at his own arm and saw a white hand wrapped tightly around it. The white fingers felt cool and implacable. Rocky looked up to see Kavi standing over him.

"You can't touch me. You're a unicorn!" Rocky shouted. "Let go of me!"

"You will fail to access my memory. They are protected by the Asting," Kavi said. "So do not waste your energy."

"You... You can't touch me!" Rocky said incredulously. "No. No! You can't do this!"

"I give you one chance to remove Maya's memories from Ava or you will have no memories left of her or you or anything else," Kavi said.

Chinchin, who was holding the unconscious Ava down, looked up at Kavi. Her eyes were welling up in accepting the reality of the situation. Everyone knew they were at Kavi's mercy now.

"Please. I love Maya. Please," Chinchin begged.

"I will not repeat myself." Kavi was still, Rocky's hand firmly in their grip. Rocky nodded, and Kavi let go. Candland watched from the sidelines as Rocky touched Ava's temples. Rocky was so angry he, too, was in tears. Candland had never seen him cry before. He had never seen Rocky lose. Minutes went by. Berns had stopped his attacks and was now perched on the ground between Proru and Rocky. Rocky retracted his hand.

"It's done. The Asting will come for you, unicorn," Rocky wiped his nose and stood up. He looked up to see

Candland. "Maya will know who you chose today, Cand-land. Chinchin, let's go."

"You will not go. You will stay until I am sure you left Ava alone with her own thoughts. Then, and only then, you may go. Please. Sit." Kavi was not smiling, and it was not a request. Rocky and Chinchin looked at each other and then sat. It was clear that neither had ever felt so defeated since Maya's death.

***

Ava woke up. Kavi was the first face she saw. Her head hurt. Next she saw Candland. He was sitting beside her. He didn't look good. Pale. Sweaty. Drained. And most of all, sad.

"Ava. Are you alright?" Kavi asked.

"I think so. What happened?"

"Rocky has promised me he has completely removed Maya from your head. Can you confirm?"

Ava looked away, touching her head lightly with her fingers. She remembered Chinchin headbutting her...

"Can you confirm?" Kavi asked again.

She closed her eyes. There were only echoes of memo-ries—the memory of a memory.

"I... I think she's gone," Ava said.

"Good, can we go now? It's been hours," Rocky said, standing up. "This albino freak's sneeze might kill us now that they're not actually part of the Asting anymore."

"Wait," Chinchin spoke before Kavi could. "The 100 are still out there."

"Great. Thanks for the warning. I'll keep an eye out for them. I'll see you later then," Rocky walked away.

"No, wait. The 100 tried to kill me in Du. Not even Du is safe anymore. They're going to do terrible things. We could stop them."

Rocky laughed, rubbing the frustration from his eyes. "What in the Lights are you talking about? We?"

"Rocky. Listen. We all want the same thing," Chinchin said, turning to everyone.

"You don't know what we want," Candland said quietly.

"Rocky. The 100 are hunting Nylos in The Cache and Pagra needs more Obsidian V. They could be Matching with a dozen at a time now. Who knows! The Nylos need you and Nevarra's home is at risk too. Are you or aren't you an NG?" Chinchin challenged him.

Rocky didn't look up, but he had stopped trying to walk away.

"Candland, the 100, along with Pagra, are a direct enemy of Questus. With the powers, and now, the uniformity they have, they could become a real threat to your kingdom. You might hate your brother, but what about everyone else in the kingdom? There's a rumor that the Blood Chambers don't exist anymore. That would mean they're defenseless to magic. Is it true?"

Candland said nothing.

"Ava. You're in the most immediate risk and so is your Nylo. You either come for the 100 on your terms, together with us, or they'll come for you eventually. Even if you run. It's only a matter of time before they come looking for your axolotl. They'll take all of them to use or kill them so others can't do what they're doing with the mutation."

Ava looked at Candland. Was he actually considering this?

"Kavi. Well, you just wrote off your entire heritage for this Atrox. I imagine you'll want to stick around to help her."

"What about you? What do you want?" Candland asked.

"To be candid. I don't care for Questus," Chinchin shook her head, "But I created the 100. I didn't mean to, but I did. It's my responsibility. I need to stop them. And I can't do it alone."

"You tried to get rid of me," Ava said.

"What would you do? If it was Candland's memories in someone else's body?" Chinchin asked.

Ava didn't say anything.

"It wasn't personal," Chinchin shook her head.

"It was for me," Ava said.

"Listen. We stick together. We take down the 100. Then we all go our own separate ways."

"Why us?" Candland asked.

"A rogue unicorn is one of the deadliest weapons in The Cache. A prince of Questus could mean resources, maybe even a revolution. Rocky has the NGs. Ava... is our bait."

"Glad I can bring something to the table," Ava said.

"What about you? You're a scientist without a lab or any tech," Rocky said.

"Looks like it's time for me to start casting spells then," Chinchin answered.

"I knew it. I KNEW it!" Rocky shouted. "You're the Gatekeeper's daughter!"

CHAPTER 19

THE BLOOD DRINKER

KEYES

Over the months since Prince Keyes had fallen down the stairs and broken his leg, villages bordering the outside of Questus had become wary—including the Tunnels. There were warning signs hung up of desperate reminders of a new curfew, not letting strangers into one's house, and finally, in the vaguest sense, to beware of the "The Blood Drinker." This divided the townspeople into two groups: the worried who took extra precaution, and those that laughed at those taking extra precaution.

It didn't matter though. The deaths had nothing to do with a curfew or being invited inside a home. All that mattered was that the victim was always Marked with magic. That was the only true pattern in the serial deaths that had speckled the last few months.

The anger Keyes held for his brother never cooled

as he spent his recovery in bed. His foot was bandaged up and would heal, but the Blood Candland had spilled was gone forever. It would take hundreds of years to be as blood-rich as the royal family had once been. And Candland, with the royal blood pumping through his veins, could come in and do it again—though Keyes would never allow it. Again the Blood was making him pay. This time, for his arrogance. He shouldn't have let Candland into the Blood Chambers. Only royal blood could tamper with the vases—the resource was protected from everyone else. No one could drink the blood unless a royal hand poured it. Nothing could break the glass... *Unless a royal hand willed it.*

How stupid he had been to think it right to kill his brother in the Chambers. To make Candland understand by showing him what his sacrifice would mean. He should have killed him when the Blood asked him to at the Pre Ceremony. All he had had to do was utter his brother's name. *Candland.*

Keyes was so livid, he snuck from rest early when the nurses were away. He had been able to walk much sooner than expected thanks to small stores of blood in the infirmary that promoted healing. He rode to one of the locations of the Cages. The warden was surprised but greeted him with respect.

"I want to see them," Keyes said.

"See who, Prince Keyes?"

"The Marked. Show me."

The warden walked him outdoors where people stood on the other side of a heavily guarded fence.

"Tell me their powers."

"This one is invisibility."

"Too weak."

"Uh, this one can control water, but only at night."

"Strange," Keyes said.

"This woman can paralyze others."

"This one. I want this one."

"Sir?"

"I want to meet this one. In person. Alone."

The woman behind the fence stood straight, curious, afraid. She had dusty blonde curls and brushed blue eyes. She looked at Keyes.

"Your brother—," the warden started.

"Is damned! I want to see her in a neutralized room. Immediately."

"Very well."

Keyes walked into a small room with wooden walls. The young woman sat, her wrists locked to the table. Keyes noticed the Mark on her left arm. The guards closed the door behind them, leaving the prisoner and prince alone. Keyes rolled up his sleeves.

"The sacrifices we make for those we love are so great," he said. The woman only stared at her hands. "Do you speak?"

She continued to stare.

"For the better. I doubt you'd understand. You're one of them. Like my brother. How would you understand the measures we take to be worthy of power... of protection. You may think I am evil, but I am the opposite. I'll prove it to you. I'll make it quick."

Keyes stood behind her. He took her chin in one hand and using a silver dagger with the rose emblem on the hilt, he sliced her throat with the other. Her eyes were large, full of panic. He bent over, leaned forward. Drank.

It was a messy job. It had not been long since he had seen Candland bleed so, but he was still surprised by how much life flowed from the woman. And then there was holding her upright so he could continue drinking from her throat. The taste was not pleasant, though the feeling of death in his hands felt powerful. Killing on behalf of the Blood for the good of his kingdom was different. He had done wrong by Candland, and the Blood understood he would do right through this forbidden action.

Keyes learned to improve the blood drinking process over time. After his first, he had tried many different methods to make the experience more efficient—using the power of paralysis helped. On his second hunt, he still had not acquired the taste of fresh blood versus bad blood. He had made the mistake of drinking blood that had gone bad from a body he had not kept well. Being a determined young man, he made the mistake of forcing the foul liquid down anyway when it made an attempt to escape through his mouth. He quickly became ill. His mother stayed by his side for three days while he laid in bed until his fever finally broke.

From there on after he was more careful, more open

to the taste of good blood. He would roll the blood in his mouth with his tongue, tasting iron, tasting minerals, tasting *magic*, tasting what it was to drink fresh, healthy blood and teaching his taste buds to detect foul blood, contaminated blood, cancerous blood. Still he continued looking for the best ways to collect blood in the fastest ways possible. He was, after all, playing catchup thanks to his incredibly stupid little brother. With the spirit of an almost Pagrarian mind, he had tried funnels. He had tried hanging bodies in different positions. Still, he needed practice and education—much blood went to waste and it went bad much sooner than he had first anticipated. No wonder the ceremonial sacrifices happened directly underneath the Blood Chambers and the fresh blood was immediately collected in the cool concaves of its new home. He might have asked for guidance from the Blood Council, but this... this was personal.

The Blood Ceremonies, Keyes realized, were full of traditions yes, but much of the ritual was well-thought out for the most efficient blood-collecting and preserving process. A cool, dark, underground environment that didn't curdle the blood—the only oversight being the Blood magicked glass that only royal blood could manip-ulate or handle. Something only Candland had managed to screw up and expose after these hundreds of years.

But these were all mistakes Keyes would learn from. Opportunities to make strong what was weak or broken in him and his kingdom. The Blood was erudite like that. Everything along his path led to something better. He was learning to harness the power of the Blood earlier than any prince before him now that he had taken matters into his own hands. The chambers were being rebuilt, shedding the magical imperfections Candland had taken advantage of before. There would be no loopholes in the Blood's protection this time. Keyes, and only Keyes would have control.

Yes, sins had been committed. Mistakes had been made. His mother and even the Blood Council showed hesitation in his new methods which only meant to Keyes that he must show more strength—for all of them. While absent from Questus, the Blood had given him a second chance. The Blood had chosen him to lead even though he had stumbled at first. And as the Blood Drinker by night, the next ruler of Questus by day, and the Blood's only truly faithful child...

He would make up for lost blood.

ACKNOWLEDGMENTS

I would like to thank my readers first. For years on end, they have heard I have been working on a fantasy book, and without their encouragement, patience, and support, I would not have made it this far with writing. Thank you for showing up, for reading, liking, sharing, and commenting on posts, and just letting me know there is someone on the other side. It does so much more than you may know, and I can't thank you all enough.

A big thank you to Michael Harrington for being so willing to illustrate a map for a world I had only been able to see in my head. Thank you for making my world real.

My cover artist, Rachel Sierra, for helping me visualize my fantasy world without falling into traditional definitions. Thank you.

I'd like to thank my sisters (Meg, Dia, Rena, Nikki, and Misty) and my mother for always being the first to subscribe to my blog, to share my work, and encourage me to throw reason and logic out the window and aim for the moon.

Thank you to my two Nylos, Weston and Hudson, for

being my shadows in my darkest moments—even when I pushed them away.

A thank you to my son, Candland, for re-igniting my imagination with his wonder. Thank you to my daughter, Ida, for helping me slow down and for reminding me to take care of myself. And finally, to my husband for being everything I needed—equal partner, supportive husband, incredible father, detail-oriented editor, devil's advocate beta reader, brainstorming companion, book interior designer, and shameless adoring fan—to take this story to the finish line.

WHAT DID YOU THINK?

Book reviews allow independent authors to continue sharing their stories with the world. If you enjoyed this book, please leave a review and share your thoughts on *Nylos in the Cache* on your chosen platform.

ABOUT THE AUTHOR

Jade Kim Monsen is a Korean American writer who lives in Salt Lake City, Utah and has a strange love for the color green. When she's not reading, writing, or daydreaming, she's spending time with her family, asking strangers what they're reading, and working her day job in marketing.

Subscribe to the JadeKimWrites newsletter to support her work and to receive personal blog posts, book updates, and more in your inbox.

THE STREET TEAM

You know who you are, but I also want to thank each of you personally for your support.

Anita Lee

Ashley Roosa

Austin Miller

Chris Ashby

Courtney Mitchell

Dani Mortimer

David Candland Monsen

Dia Frampton

Gabriel Silva Mateus

Gian Florendo

Huaning "Wendy" Wang

Jerral Datuin

Justin Moss

Kerri and Mike Fuchs

Kris West

Madi Nichols

Mark and Jessica Hollingshead

Matt Aquino

Maverick & June

Michael F Ballman

Nick Wiles

Rosemary Ajuka-LeCroy

Ryan J. White

Sunhee Kim Frampton

Sunny Beatteay

Taylor Miller

Tiffany Rowe

Zita Ann Flatley

www.ingramcontent.com/pod-product-compliance
Lightning Source LLC
Chambersburg PA
CBHW061040310726
48969CB00004B/1030